A SIMPLE ULTIMATUM...

"I won't do it." Rhalles heard the lack of conviction in his voice.

But Jorgen appeared to accept the statement at face value. "In that case," he said heavily, "I am a dead man. Worse than dead. You will inform certain people in your government. They will seize me when I make my next contact with you. I'll be screaming and praying for death before they finish with me. But—they won't get any *proof* of who I really am or who I work for. . . . And—more important for you—I won't tell them where your wife is or who has her. Because I don't *know*."

Jorgen paused. "It will be terrible for me. . . . If I am not dead from mistreatment, I will be reduced to less than a vegetable. But —long before that, your wife will have been killed. Perhaps, not pleasantly.

"And it will be your fault. No one else's. You are now totally responsible, Mr. Rhalles, for whether your wife lives or dies."

"FINELY WROUGHT . . .
SOLID DIVERSION . . .
A KALEIDOSCOPE OF IMAGINATIVE
SCENES."
—*United Press International*

OTHER DELL BOOKS BY MARVIN H. ALBERT

THE GARGOYLE CONSPIRACY

THE
DARK
GODDESS

Marvin H. Albert

A DELL BOOK

For Jan and David

Published by
DELL PUBLISHING CO., INC.
1 Dag Hammarskjold Plaza
New York, N.Y. 10017

Dell ® TM 681510, Dell Publishing Co., Inc.

ISBN: 0-440-11635-X

Reprinted by arrangement with
Doubleday & Company, Inc.

Printed in the United States of America
First Dell printing—January 1979

THE
DARK
GODDESS

PART ONE

THE TRAP

"Pitcher plants . . . entice insects by bright colors to their traps, and allure them to enter by secreting honey at the top of the pitcher. Hairs point downward inside; these allow the flies to walk on to their fate, bribed as they go by lines of nectar; but if they try to return, ah, then they find their mistake; the hairs prevent them. They walk on and on till they reach the water, when they are swamped and clotted in a decaying mass, from which the treacherous plant draws manure at last for its own purposes. The pitchers are thus at once traps to catch animals, and stomachs to digest them."

—In Nature's Workshop, by G. Allen, 1901

ONE

1

The plane on which Irina Frejenko returned from Paris landed at Moscow's Sheremetyevo Airport late in the evening on the twenty-third of February. She had been out for nine days. One half of the project, conceived by her and now under her complete control, was finally operational. The agents picked for it were making their first moves as she had directed.

Now she was back; tomorrow morning she could activate the second half of the project. The man chosen to direct that part was going to be the most vital factor in the entire plan. Once he reached Washington, he would become virtually autonomous. If he made a mistake, the Politburo would have a diplomatic disaster on its hands. And it would be considered *her* mistake. A heavy and frightening responsibility, even for someone accustomed to succeeding in anything she began.

Irina Frejenko was an extremely good-looking woman of forty-eight. Superb figure, strong Slavic face, hard gray eyes that observed and recorded, missing little within range. A colleague at the Serbsky Institute had called those eyes "the windows of a computer." But he had been envious of her extraordinary rise within the Academy of Medical Sciences' Institute of Psychiatry. Which was largely the result of the increasing amount of work she'd done for the Soviet Union's Committee of State Security: *Komitet Gosudarstvennoye Bezopastnosti.* They had shifted her to working full-time inside the KGB two years ago, and both her upward mobility and the envy of colleagues continued. It was said by some, only half jokingly, that if she kept on this way she'd wind up the first female Chairman of the KGB.

There were other colleagues, who admired rather than envied. Such as the psychiatrist she'd helped through a bad time with his mentally and socially disturbed son. He had called her "the mother of us all." Which was as wide of the truth as calling her a computer. Only Valentin understood what she really was inside. But then, he had known her since she was sixteen. Her first man; and there had never been another. Not that way. Professionally, many. Men she obeyed, men who served.

The man who met her as she came from the plane at Sheremetyevo was one of the latter. A tough, wary KGB plainclothes policeman assigned to getting her past customs and identity control without wasted formalities. This he accomplished respectfully and efficiently. Heads turned to watch her follow him to the luggage pickup and out through the big, modern terminal building. Anyone could tell she was part of the *nomenklatura,* the privileged elite; what the East Germans called, in private, a "super-comrade." It was the combination of the obvious profession of her escort and the way she was dressed: full-length sable coat and baby-seal hat, woolen skirt and cardigan from Scotland, silk blouse from Paris, fur-lined leather gloves and boots from Vienna, crocodile briefcase from Rome. The Soviet Union had long ago changed the last part of its "From each according to his ability, to each according to his need." Now it was: "To each according to his importance to the state." Irina Frejenko's importance was growing. But so was her responsibility if something went wrong.

Outside the terminal, she looked along the line of cars, expecting to see her chauffeur waiting with her Volga sedan. Instead, her escort led her to a gray

10

Mercedes limousine. The hefty young chauffeur standing beside it opened the door for her as they approached. Seated in the back was her chief, Vasily Pokryshkin, head of Subdirectorate T, the scientific and technical division of KGB's First Chief Directorate. In her nine days away, Irina had almost forgotten how worried he was about this project.

"Your driver has been instructed to wait for you outside my apartment," he informed her shortly. No greeting, no preamble. Vasily Pokryshkin was not in a mood for any amount of small talk.

"Of course." She got in back beside him. The chauffeur closed the door and opened the trunk for the plainclothesman to put her luggage in.

Vasily studied Irina anxiously. His eyes were a seared blue in a face the color of old ashes. Full red lips made it a mask. Black suit and black turtleneck shirt created a shock-illusion of neckline amputation. It took getting used to. "Everything went well?" he demanded as his chauffeur got in and started the car.

She nodded. "Everything."

She had the feeling he would have preferred to hear that something had gone wrong, and the whole operation would have to be scrapped. Not that she could blame him. Vasily had not expected it to grow into such a delicate monster, when he had first passed on her target projection study directly to Yuri Andropov, Chairman of the KGB. So delicate that Irina was quite sure only three people within the KGB knew all about it: herself, Vasily, and Andropov. Outside the State Security community, it was probably known only to certain members of the Politburo.

It was there that the decision had finally been made. They had been tempted by the dazzling returns her project promised. But so alarmed by repercussions inherent in a failure that became public knowledge that they had hedged it around with almost crippling precautionary restrictions. All the restrictions had a single, quite sensible aim: whatever happened, the source of the project must never be traceable back to the true country of its origin.

Which was why, although their services were being used for bits and pieces of it, Irina Frejenko's project was not even known to the chiefs of the two KGB sections which would ordinarily have been most involved: Subdirectorate S, which supplied and controlled most of the secret agents permanently resident in foreign countries under false papers; and Department V, in charge of *mokrie dela,* meaning "wet affairs": sabotage, kidnaping, subversion, and killing.

Vasily's Mercedes was out of the complex of airport roads now. On the other side of the thick, soundproof glass partition, Vasily's chauffeur tooled the limousine around the lead-in ramp and onto the great highway leading into the heart of Moscow. A light snow was beginning to fall. On either side of the highway old snow rose up in high banks, where it had been bulldozed by the road clearance teams. There was a lot of traffic, mostly heavy trucks. The loud racket of tire chains chewing into iced cement was constant.

Beside Irina, the tensed Vasily drew a slow breath and finally came out with what she'd been expecting and waiting for: "We've selected the agent who will direct the Washington work for you."

"I hope he fits every one of the qualifications I specified."

"Judge for yourself." Vasily leaned forward and closed the curtains on their side of the glass partition, concealing them from the driver in front. Then he opened the briefcase on the floor between his legs. It was a plain black plastic briefcase, worn and cracked with age; one of Vasily's modest eccentricities. He took out a black cardboard folder and placed it on Irina's lap.

There was a single word printed in white ink on the outside of the folder: "JORGEN." This was the code name that had been predetermined as having nothing remotely Russian about it, for whatever agent was selected for this particular assignment. It was the only name by which he would ever be known to anyone connected with the project.

Irina got out her reading glasses and put them on. She opened the folder, and looked at the photograph: sparse white hair and a tanned, powerful face, deeply lined. Tightly controlled mouth, eyes that gave away nothing. A hard, capable, lonely face.

Vasily became impatient with her silent concentration, though he knew well her reputation for being able to read character from photographs. "As you'll see in his dossier, he is a sixty-six-year-old German. Though he has been ours for years, and is utterly dependable, he also does jobs for the SSD. Under our direction, though they don't know that. And he still owns a house in the DDR. Near Stolberg, in the Harz Mountains."

"I see." The SSD was the German Democratic Republic's State Security Service. Not a nice trick to pull on the East Germans, but it fulfilled one of the restrictions placed on Irina's project. If "Jorgen" were caught, a background trace on him must lead to another country, not to the Soviet Union.

"And he's had two heart attacks," Vasily went on, pleased. "The last four months ago, and he hasn't worked since. He's quite fit now, of course. Unless—he undergoes an unusual amount of heavy emotional stress."

Irina nodded her approval. It meant that the man now known as Jorgen could not, if the worst happened, be forced to divulge anything vital. The amount of drugs, psychologically inflicted disorientation, or physical torture required to extract information from him would kill him before achieving the objective.

She turned the photograph finally, and got her first surprise on the first page of the man's dossier. Jorgen had first begun working for the Soviet Union as a member of the German Communist spy network known as the Red Orchestra, which early in World War II had succeeded in passing an extraordinary amount of vital military information from Berlin to Moscow.

"I didn't know any of the Red Orchestra managed to survive," Irina said slowly. "Except those who saved their lives after they were caught by turning in the others to the Gestapo."

"He is one of the very few who managed it cleanly," Vasily told her. "Escaped from Germany to France and disappeared into the resistance movement. As part of a guerrilla group operating in the Jura Massif. Didn't surface again until after the war."

Irina frowned as she reached the bottom of the first page and was surprised again: "He was a spiritualist?"

"No, no . . . not really. He was a student of comparative religion at the University of Berlin before the war, with a purely scientific interest in mysticism. Which, as you know, was also a craziness with many of the Nazi functionaries. An interest in all sorts of witchcraft and related nonsense, from Hitler on down. It became Jorgen's cover. Much of the information reaching us, before the Gestapo broke the Red Orchestra network, was obtained through his contacts with several high Nazi officials, as their occult adviser."

Irina found the third surprise at the bottom of the second page: Jorgen had come to Moscow immediately after the war ended. Arrested upon identifying himself, he had spent two years in the prison section in Lubyanka.

Vasily watched Irina frown again, pausing in her reading, and had no difficulty guessing where she was. "Yes . . . an unfortunate mistake. When he turned up, alive, we had to assume he'd done it by squealing on other members of his cell to the Gestapo. As others had done, to save their own skins. But he finally managed to prove to our interrogators that he was quite innocent."

"After two years." Irina smiled. He definitely *was* a survivor type. Few had survived the Red Orchestra cleanly. And not many could boast of spending two years in Lubyanka Prison and coming out alive.

"He *could* have gotten out after a year and a half." Vasily reached over, turned to the next page of the dossier, and pointed out the pertinent passage for Irina.

She read it aloud: "Prisoner was informed that he would be released, but must immediately leave the Soviet Union and never return. Prisoner refused release under this condition. He stated that he had entered the Soviet Union a free man, and would only leave it as a free man. Free to come and go as he wished in our country which he had served so well. Six months later, prisoner was declared Not Guilty of charges and released under the conditions that he had demanded."

Irina looked up from the dossier, taking off her glasses. "A good, solid idealist." She said it with genuine admiration, but also with a hint of uncertainty.

Vasily understood her hesitation. "But an extremely *practical*, sensible idealist, as his subsequent work for us has proved every time. Read on and you will see."

Irina closed the folder. "I'll read the rest of it tonight. Reading in a moving car makes me queasy."

"All right," Vasily agreed reluctantly. "But you will see. He is the right man."

"I hope so," Irina told him firmly, "since I'll be stuck with him, whether I agree or not."

"Not necessarily," Vasily corrected primly. "If you disapprove strongly enough . . . but, I don't think you will."

Neither did Irina. Because if she objected strongly enough the entire project would probably be canceled. And that she couldn't tolerate at this stage.

"I'm sure I'll find you've made the right choice," Irina said flatly. She opened her briefcase and slipped the Jorgen dossier into it.

2

She didn't take the dossier out again until she retired to her bedroom that night. After a long, relaxing session in the sauna she'd had installed next to the game room in the basement, and the superb meal cooked for her by Luba, the wife of young Serge, the chauffeur. It was snowing harder outside. Big snowflakes plastered against the frosted outer panes of the sealed double windows. But inside the bedroom it was blissfully warm. Wearing the slightly daring nightgown she'd bought on a trip to Budapest the previous year, Irina Frejenko closed the heavy window drapes and got into bed with the black Jorgen folder.

The bed was wide, low, and very simple: a sponge rubber mattress on a five-inch platform of dark wood. Imported from Denmark, like the rest of her bedroom furnishings. Irina propped herself up against the brightly colored cushions, drew the covers up to her waist, and placed the folder on her lap. She put on her reading glasses, but she did not immediately open the folder. First, she just savored the pleasure of being back in her own home.

It was a big house, with three wings, set in a small wooded estate outside the town of Barvikha, one hour's easy drive west of Moscow. Part of the satisfaction Irina derived from it was in the knowledge that she had *earned* it. By unremitting hard work. And by climbing each step of the political ladder with careful determination.

The first step had come, after some years as a doctor and psychologist in a country that did not regard the medical profession highly, when the Serbsky Institute of Forensic Psychiatry in Moscow had asked her to prepare a report for the KGB. The report was to recommend improved methods in selecting and training agents for special assignments.

It was a touchy business, potentially dangerous. To recommend changes and new methods implied criticism of present KGB practices. And the people responsible for them. Nobody wanted to get stuck with this particular assignment.

Irina had accepted it. But during her preliminary studies, she had made a point of consulting every prominent KGB officer she could inveigle into a meeting. Respectfully soliciting their advice and opinions on specific problems. Letting them see her carefully write down their answers. So that, when the report was finished, they would feel that even the most drastic suggestions merely incorporated their own ideas—rather than being the criticisms of an outsider.

In preparing the report, Irina had meshed what she considered the best of standard KGB methodology with the most interesting studies along the same lines that she could obtain from other countries. Such as the Clinical Analysis Questionnaire and the Dynamic Personality Inventory, devised by psychiatrists of the British Ministry of Defense to help select soldiers for specialized jobs. Especially useful from these had been two tests to discover recruits with what the British labeled Factor D2 and Factor D3—lack of inhibition against suicide; and depression finding release only in strong adventure. These tests had been used by the British to rule out applicants for bomb-disposal work. Irina had revamped them to help the KGB pick men for highly dangerous tasks involving violence and possible death.

Most of the American material she had used came from digging into the files of Moscow's U.S.A. Institute in the three-hundred-year-old mansion near Kalinin Prospekt: the tests for delicate mechanical abilities devised by U. S. Army psychologists during the Vietnam War. Studies, by such CIA-backed private firms as New York's Human Ecology Fund and Washington's Psychological Assessment Associates, on how to judge a person's hidden weaknesses by the way he or she moved and dressed. The research at the U. S. Naval Hospital in San Diego in selecting people with the right amount of "passive aggression" as potential killers; and training them through constant viewings of close-up films of wartime slaughter, bloody industrial accidents involving loss of limbs, tribal circumcisions, and decapitation—until the trainee acquired a matter-of-fact attitude toward any amount of violence.

Irina's report had been received with approval and led to a more important KGB-related assignment: she was made part of a Serbsky medical team devising improved methods of re-educating political dissidents—by psychopharmacological means.

She was not squeamish about the idea of forcibly administering a mixture of haloperidol, insulin, and reserpine with electrical shock treatments to achieve this "re-education." Doctors who were squeamish did not get past medical school. And once you accepted that political dissent was a disease, you could not find fault with any treatment that cured the disease. If some of the "patients" came out of the prison mental hospitals prematurely senile from these treatments, it was for the greater good of the greater number: the welfare of the People and the health of their State.

Irina's success this time was crowned by her being sent to establish these methods in two of the twelve prison mental hospitals scattered throughout the Soviet Union: in Dnepropetrovsk and Poltava. Which had led in turn to her being sent to the World Psychiatric Association's convention to fend off attacks on Russian use of these methods.

Again, success; and her next step up, into the KGB itself. Her first assignment there had been as part of an interrogation group lent to Syria during the 1974 war, to extract Israeli military secrets from captured enemy pilots. The Soviet interrogation team used injections of succinylcholine on the pilots. Succinylcholine caused agonizing muscle spasms and paralysis of the lungs. Unless administered carefully, the victim died from being unable to breathe. Administered with proper skill, the effects did not last long enough to kill. The victim came out of it alive, but psychologically demolished. The pilots were given a breather, and then another injection. Repeated regularly until they talked or became too mentally disoriented to say anything that made sense.

As a beautiful woman, Irina Frejenko had no trouble performing the real reason for being part of this team: getting to know important Arab political and military men. Using her own special talent, reinforced through her constant research, to detect useful flaws in the characters of these men through their mannerisms and speech patterns. When integrated with other operational data from their detailed biographies, Irina's observations formed the basis of target studies that resulted in three of the Arabs subsequently working directly for the KGB.

This had become Irina Frejenko's basic work for the KGB: assessing prominent foreign figures and seeking out flaws that could be used to Soviet advantage. It had earned her this house. It had also led quite logically to a desire—and finally the opportunity—to create a project of her own. This was the project which had taken her out of the country for nine days. The folder she now held on her lap contained its final piece of human machinery.

Tonight she had the house to herself, except for Serge and Luba. Their room was in the wing at the other end of the house, behind the kitchen. Her son, a chemical engineer, was off directing improvements in a plant outside Minsk. Her daughter was in Warsaw, where she'd won a commission to execute the sculpture for the entrance plaza of a new government building.

Irina had phoned her husband's office on reaching home and finding he wasn't there yet. It was always possible he was working late, though that was not his way. An assistant draftsman who *was* working late told her that Valentin had left early, just before the message arrived that she was returning from abroad.

Which meant that, not knowing she was back, Valentin had gone to spend the evening and night with Anna, his latest young girl friend. Irina had considered phoning to tell him that she was back. But she'd finally decided it was better for her to be alone tonight, since she needed to prepare herself thoroughly for the meeting with Jorgen tomorrow.

Irina felt a bit of loneliness, but no resentment toward Valentin. She understood quite well, and sympathized with, the bruised ego-need that caused Valentin to seek out the reassurance of those easily impressed little girls. He was an architect with the city-planning commission of Moscow, and was respected in his field. But though five years older than Irina, and in her opinion more deeply intelligent than she, he had never tasted one tenth of the professional success she had won for herself. And never would. Because he lacked her relentless drive, and the kind of quick cleverness required to rise to the top of any complex organization, socialist or capitalist.

That Valentin was still very fond of her Irina had no doubt. That was her emotional security. He always introduced her to each new girl friend, early in the relationship. If Irina disapproved, Valentin dropped the girl without an argument. She approved of Anna: somewhat stupid but affectionate as a puppy, and properly respectful. She knew her place.

Irina glanced at her wristwatch and sat up straighter against the cushions. Opening the folder, she gave her full concentration to the pages of Jorgen's dossier.

It was one of the most impressive clandestine agent biographies she had ever read. A record of solid accomplishments abroad that began with his work for the Red Orchestra as an idealistic young German Communist. It continued with only two interruptions —his two years under false charges in Lubyanka Prison, and his first heart attack—up to his second heart attack four months ago. Since then Jorgen had been on recuperation leave with full pay, living quietly in his house in East Germany for the first few months. Three weeks ago he had returned to Russia and settled down in the second home he owned, in the country outside Tula, a three-hour drive south from Moscow.

Irina noted with interest that his wife, a native of Leipzig, whom he had married shortly after his release from Lubyanka Prison, had three years ago suffered a nervous breakdown. In spite of extensive treatment at the hospital for elite patients in Kuntsevo, her condition had degenerated into helpless schizophrenia. With no hope of recovery, she was now a patient in a luxurious Black Sea sanatorium established by the Ministry of Health's Fourth Department, for relatives of important Soviet functionaries. Though she no longer recognized her husband, and Jorgen had been for some time living with a young German mistress, he continued to visit his wife once a month when not on assignment abroad.

The last item in the dossier was the latest medical report. It pronounced Jorgen ready, physically and mentally, to resume active duty.

It had taken Irina an hour and a half to absorb the entire dossier. She turned back to page one and began again. This time she dwelled on certain details, paid special attention to Jorgen's performance during missions involving extreme danger, studied his experiences at subverting high-ranking foreign functionaries requiring especially delicate handling.

He had performed well under varied conditions. Some of his operations were classics of successful espionage. He had supervised Operation Brunnhilde, using agents of East Germany's secret service to steal the plans and test-performance reports of the joint British-French Concorde; enabling Russia to come out first with its own SST, the TU-144.

He had also subverted one of the highest officers of SHAPE, Supreme Headquarters Allied Powers Europe, and extracted NATO secrets from him for two years, until the officer killed himself when his activities were finally uncovered through accident by the *Militärischer Abschirmdienst,* West German military counterintelligence.

In England, he had penetrated the highly secretive Defence Operational Analysis Establishment, by subverting one of its computer specialists. In Belgium he'd blackmailed an Air Force general and obtained complete specifications of a new laser range finder, plus the latest development in high-power microwave communications.

In France he'd penetrated an electronics firm specializing in underwater military equipment, through an executive who was still passing on information. In Italy he had uncovered a Soviet embassy secretary who was in secret contact with CIA agents, and spirited her back to Russia, outwitting an American killer squad sent to stop him. All this, without his true identity or his face ever becoming known to Western agents.

Jorgen had also operated successfully in the United States, back in the early sixties. He had cultivated a code expert fired by NSA because of incipient alcoholism, and persuaded him to defect. By the time a routine NSA security checkup chanced on what had happened, both Jorgen and the code expert were gone. Again, Jorgen had managed it so well that the subsequent intensive American investigation failed to turn up the fact that anyone remotely like him had ever been in the country.

It was a few minutes past midnight when Irina closed the black folder and put it down on the bear-skin rug beside her bed. Her nerves were crawling with excitement. Jorgen would do. Vasily and the Chairman had chosen well. Irina had only one slight worry: Jorgen might be getting old for this kind of work.

On the other hand, it *required* age, to acquire the experience needed for Jorgen's assignment. Irina knew that the possibility Jorgen might make a mistake was no greater than the chance of her project going wrong for any of several other reasons. She didn't really think it would go wrong. The project had been planned with care, gone over time and again for weak points. But—failure was always possible, in even the most intelligently planned operation.

If it did fail, she knew what would happen, on a personal level. Because she knew what *she* would do, if she were the Chairman of the KGB. Everyone below his level who understood the project would have to disappear, to ensure against their ever being able to talk about what had been at stake. That meant herself, of course. And Vasily. And probably even poor Valentin, because they couldn't be sure she had never discussed any of it with her husband.

Irina Frejenko got out of bed, went to her bathroom, and took a pill. She must get a good night's sleep, so she would be clearheaded for her first meeting with Jorgen. She wished, as she got back into bed and turned off the light, that she *had* called Valentin, so she would have him with her now. Taking off her reading glasses, she put them down on the rug beside the Jorgen folder. She unstrapped her watch and placed it flat on top of the folder. Then she lay there in the dark, listening to the beating of her heart and waiting for the pill to take effect.

TWO

1

Jorgen's skis hissed over iron-hard snow. On either side tombstones and stark black trees appeared and vanished in the frosted morning mist. He dug in the sticks and propelled himself to the left, following the curving path inside the small cemetery ten miles east of Tula.

The air had a frozen quality that made breathing difficult. Jorgen had a sense of moving through solid cold. It seemed to weigh heavily upon the snow under his long Russian-style skis, and expand upward against the white sky. Air burned in his throat and lungs. His eyes had become a congealed gray. His face was a cold-scorched red, the skin stretched painfully over the strong bones and angry cracks beginning to form in the deep lines.

But he was used to cold, and the exercise was good for him.

"Regular exercise and regular sex," Dr. Brauer had told him. "And at least eight hours sleep each night. These are the three keys to relaxed nerves. And a relaxed nervous system is your key to health and longevity. Plus the simple, sensible diet."

"And I'll live to a ripe old age."

"I guarantee you one thing." Dr. Brauer's smile had been bittersweet. "You'll outlive me."

Dr. Brauer was seventy-five.

Jorgen reached his father's simple grave and paused to look at it. But not for long. Seventeen below zero was not a temperature for remaining stationary out in the open.

The tombstone irritated him, as always. He'd been abroad when his father had died; the local government had buried him and picked the stone. It was low, squat, dark brown; nothing like the man in the ground under it. His father had been tall, thin, and pale.

There was a high cap of translucent ice on top of the stone. Most of the rest was buried inside a cocoon of snowdrift. Including his name. It didn't matter. Jorgen had not come to pay homage, nor to grieve. The grave merely served as a convenient marker: a turning-back point for his early-morning ski.

But it was strange, Jorgen thought. His father had meant a great deal to him for so long. Dead, he left nothing inside Jorgen, except his own isolation.

He was an orphan now—that had been Jorgen's crazy thought when he'd learned his father was dead. Crazy, because he'd already reached fifty by then. But that had been his feeling: Now I'm an orphan; now I've got no one.

His father was in this grave. His mother had died long ago—in Ravensbrück, because of her only son's activities as a spy in Nazi Germany—and was buried in some mass grave. And his wife was a permanent resident in a mental institution whose luxury was pointless because she didn't know where she was at any time. Was he somehow responsible for that, too? He did not think so. But possibly he had contributed. Certainly the strain of living so long with fear had not helped her.

No children, either. The doctors had not been able to tell why. They'd both seemed capable. Perhaps it had been her nerves. That had always been her weak point.

Jorgen turned away from the grave. Skiing easily, the skill and strength still taken for granted, the physical pleasure still gratifying. Outside the cemetery he turned west, returning over his cross-country route in the direction of his house outside Tula.

A stretch of hilly, snow-shrouded farmland, with scattered bare-branched oaks and elm trees. Then into the evergreen woods, skiing over snow crust along a narrow trail between the heavy firs and pines. The tree trunks were beginning to smoke as the morning air warmed.

When he emerged from the trees, he was surprised to see Vilma's black Volga parked there on the road that ran along that edge of the woods. Vilma stood beside the car, smoking a cigarette. Jorgen skied toward her. She tossed away the cigarette and waved when she saw him, the big child-like grin engaging her whole face. She was a cheerful little thing, pretty and plumply rounded, her blond hair almost as pale as his white hair. In bed she had the generous eagerness of youth discovering and reveling in a new world. Exactly what Dr. Brauer had ordered. In or out of bed, she had a fairy-like quality that enchanted him. He would miss her when the time came.

"You had a phone call," she explained as he neared her. "She said I should find you and give you the message."

"She . . . ?"

"I didn't ask her name. I just assumed it was your boss. Sounded like."

Vilma did not know what he really did, but was under the impression he worked for a woman. Because he'd once told her he was a traveling executive for an east-block export firm, and that his boss was named Galina Borisovna. A name she'd never heard before, since she lived in Germany. Between Russians, it was a jittery nickname for the KGB.

She suddenly laughed and hugged him tight. "Your face is so *red!*"

He put his arms around her gently. "What was the message?"

"Just to tell you that somebody named Jorgen was ready, so you should come to the office today. As soon as possible."

Jorgen was the code name that they'd given him five days ago, for the new assignment about which he was still in the dark. So the time had come. He was being activated.

Excitement quickened his blood. He pulled away from Vilma and leaned against the car, beginning to remove his skis. Long ago he had lost the inspiration that had driven him in the Red Orchestra, and for quite some time even after Lubyanka. He could think of no special reason for that loss, no single event. The conscious motivation of pride-in-faith had just left him, over the years.

But this was the life he had made for himself; he could no longer shed it even if he wished to. And he didn't wish to. His profession was what he was, all there was to him now. In place of pride-in-faith: pride in his professionalism. He was, he thought wryly, like an old racehorse, pawing the ground eagerly at the distant sound of a new race starting.

Vilma got his fur-lined boots out of her car and gave him each one as he removed each ski boot. As he straightened after fastening the last one, he caught sight of a small bird flying up out of a pine tree. Automatically, Jorgen watched it go, trying to make out what it was. But it was too small, and its flight too swift. A young crow, perhaps; or a Siberian jay.

Vilma looked up to see what he was watching. Suddenly she pointed higher. "Look!"

A dark speck had materialized out of the mist above the bird Jorgen had been watching. The speck grew swiftly larger as it streaked downward. A gyr falcon.

The bird below it abruptly swerved in flight, hearing the winged death plummeting upon it. But it was too late for evasive action. The falcon struck, hard. Its victim somersaulted in the air, stunned. The falcon swooped, in a curving dive of breathtaking grace and savagery. Talons and beak caught the falling bird, and held fast.

Something small and soft struck Jorgen's left cheek. It didn't hurt, but he instinctively ducked and twisted. Vilma looked at him, her face gone somber.

She reached out and wiped her gloved hand across his cheek. Jorgen looked at the reddish smear on her index finger.

He had been struck by a drop of falling blood.

When he looked up again, the falcon and its victim were a merged speck rising into the white mist, vanishing toward the broken hills to the south.

A bad omen. Whatever they were sending him into this time, it would contain a bitter seed.

2

Shortly after it was finished, Soviet agents had obtained the architectural plans and blueprints of the CIA's mammoth Virginia headquarters—a striking example of recent developments in a long tradition of military architecture reaching back to the fortress complexes of the early Middle Ages. The joke in Western intelligence circles was that the KGB fell in love with the stolen plans—which explained why its own new building in the countryside beyond the Moscow suburbs was in many respects almost an exact copy, inside and out.

But the KGB brain center remained in a solidly constructed, old-fashioned building on Moscow's Dzerzhinsky Square, a few blocks from the Kremlin. An insurance company until the Revolution, it was built around an open inner courtyard with two doors leading into a prison section whose name, Lubyanka, had inspired fear for over four decades. That name had come to be associated with the entire building.

Jorgen did not like this building. But he was quite

sure the reason for his dislike was not the two years he had spent in its prison. In fact, he remembered those two years with some nostalgia; as a tribute to the tough romanticism of his youth. It had been a battle of wills and wits, between him and the NKVD—a forerunner of the KGB. And he had won that battle.

Their methods had been different in those days. They hadn't yet completely adopted the combination of physical and psychological torture learned from the Nazis and psychologists. They hadn't been really harsh with Jorgen; merely persistent. The method then had been to wear down resistance through repetition and boredom.

They had interrogated him twice every day, after breakfast and again before supper. With a German interpreter. They'd never wakened him at night and had given him fair food, but no books, papers, or other reading material. For the first six months he'd shared a small basement cell with a Hungarian named Klar, who'd been in longer. It was the Hungarian who'd taught Jorgen Russian, and how to survive Lubyanka.

"There are three rules," Klar had instructed him. "First, shave every day, so you'll remember you are a man, not an animal.

"Second, do setting-up exercises regularly, several times each day. To keep your body fit and your mind alert.

"Third, never admit *anything* that isn't true. If they ask you to sign a paper which says you ate chicken at a certain meal, when you actually ate fish, refuse to sign the paper. That is their method—to get you used to accepting small, unimportant lies. After that it becomes progressively easier to forget the difference between falsity and truth, and begin accepting the big lies."

After six months, Jorgen had been shifted to a different cell, which he'd shared with three Russians. With them he'd occupied his mind by perfecting his command of Russian. He never learned what happened to the Hungarian, but he continued to survive on his three rules: denying all charges against him; refusing to sign anything in any way false; keeping himself sane by shaving and exercising regularly each day. And by constantly telling himself: "Be calm, be quiet, be patient—one day at a time."

A year after he'd entered Lubyanka, the NKVD people changed as a result of a reorganization—and the interrogation started again from scratch. But now with Jorgen able to contradict and correct his interpreter in Russian, and to strike out any false bits in each statement they asked him to sign. After another six months the new crew had given him permission to leave Russia, if he'd sign the agreement never to return.

It was after Jorgen's refusal to leave under that condition that they'd begun allowing him books to read, and giving him much better food. Sometimes he even ate with his interrogators, who'd come to regard him as one of them. The questions of some of the younger ones became a form of hero-worship, respectfully eliciting his stories of the Red Orchestra's accomplishments in Berlin. Six months of that, and he was out, on his own terms.

So, he'd won. An achievement that was still a source of pride. And pride was probably the only motivation left for the work he did. He did it for himself; his dedication was to the challenge, and to his own competence. It was certainly not to the kind of people who now worked inside Lubyanka.

They were an alien race to Jorgen: bureaucrats—no different from the functionaries of bureaucracies all over the world, under any kind of government. Interchangeable, actually. Jorgen had understood this truth for some years now: the top government officials of the United States and the Soviet Union could exchange places with ease. Including the President and the Premier. There would be no change; no one would notice any difference. Like computers, bureaucracy functioned the same wherever it was placed, in the CIA's Langley or the KGB's Lubyanka.

Irina Frejenko's office was on the second floor of Lubyanka, facing the square; next to an old rococo staircase that led up to the entrance of the Chairman's suite on the next floor. At three o'clock that afternoon the curtains were closed behind the window of Irina's office. The small room was in darkness, except for the flickering light of the 16-mm film she was projecting onto a screen she'd set up between the filing cabinet and the safe. Jorgen leaned forward a bit in the chair beside Irina's desk, to study the young woman the film had just shown emerging from a small museum. The camera zoomed in on her face.

It was an odd, interesting face. Flattish features, but not unattractive, alive with vitality and humor. Wide cheekbones exactly as prominent as the broad forehead. Large, full mouth. Long dark eyes. Straight, pitch-black hair. Jorgen read the intelligence and quiet sureness in that face; and the sexuality.

"Moira Rhalles," Irina Frejenko supplied from behind the projector on her desk. "I thought you should know what she looks like."

Jorgen watched her coming toward the hidden camera, unaware of it photographing her. "She looks like one of ours. A Tartar."

"In a way she is. If you consider that the American continent was first inhabited by migrant hunters crossing a land bridge from Siberia to Alaska."

"So she is an American Indian."

"Half. Her mother was an Indian. From southeastern Canada, near the Great Lakes. A tribe called the Ojibwa."

Moira Rhalles had turned away from the camera's point of view. The camera followed her as she walked toward a parked car. She was small, with a strong, vibrant figure. An archaeologist, Irina Frejenko had told Jorgen; twenty-eight years old, and on her way up in the academic world.

Jorgen read the confidence and controlled power in the way she moved. "What about her father."

"He was of Scottish extraction."

Past tense again. "They're both dead?"

"Long ago. Car accident."

Jorgen had no further questions. Moira Rhalles was not his part of the project. She belonged to the part with which he had no connection at all, run by people he didn't know. His part was her husband.

Moira Rhalles got into the car. As she shut the door the film went dark—then resumed with a return to Jorgen's man: Alexander Rhalles.

In this filmed sequence he was coming out of the narrow brick house in the Georgetown neighborhood of Washington, D.C. He carried a large suitcase in one hand, briefcase in the other. The camera stayed on him as he reached the curb and waited, looking uncertainly to his right. A tall, skinny, good-looking man, forty years old. The mouth generous and sensual, but kept secretively firm, like a locked purse. Behind the horn-rimmed glasses the eyes were those of a man who seldom emerged from his protective shell. A clever, vulnerable man; long accustomed to concealing the fire inside.

That fire would have startled people from time to time, Jorgen imagined, when it showed through the painfully shy exterior. But it would show only in his work—and perhaps with his wife.

Jorgen thought about the young woman he'd just watched on film. Yes, it was there in those dark Mongolian eyes of hers: the habit of searching for what was beneath the surface. She would have realized what was hidden inside this stiff, awkward man. And gone after him. It couldn't have been the other way round. Rhalles would not have gone after her, or any woman. He didn't have that kind of nerve. But other kinds,

Jorgen decided as he stu—
And stubbornness . . .

A taxi pulled up in fron—
driver as in a previous film
Rhalles to the White House. J—
force a wide smile. The driver —
and stuck out a hand, greeting Rh—
familiarity.

There was a barely perceptible —
Rhalles shook the extended hand. Jorg— — the
smile become smaller, less a grimace, — an expression of feeling.

So he didn't dislike people, then. Just afraid of
them. But able to respond like a child, after initial
wariness, to aggressive warmth. Strange, to still be like
that, considering the man's accomplishments and position.

The driver put the suitcase in the trunk of his taxi.
Rhalles kept the briefcase as he climbed into the back
seat. The screen went black for a split second. Then
another film clip. Rhalles walking; university campus.
Jorgen leaned back in the chair to ease the tension
forming at the small of his back. He continued to
study the man on the screen, seeking out telling ges-
tures and expressions.

When the final film clip ended, Jorgen got up and
stretched himself. He went to open the window curtains. His eyes narrowed against the afternoon light
that flooded into the small brown and green office.
Behind him, Irina Frejenko was disconnecting the
projector on her desk. Jorgen remained at the window, gazing down at the square in front of Lubyanka.

Everywhere, little puffs of steam rose in the cold
air: the breaths of walkers moving carefully across the
ice slick. Last night's snow had been bulldozed to one
edge of the square, forming two frozen white hills
rising as high as the second floor of the department
store on the far side.

A small child emerging from the Metropole Hotel

mother, skidded, fell, and rolled
ossible to tell if the child was boy or
fat. Just a round fur ball: fur hat, fur
boots, and under the fur layer on layer of
. The mother, hurrying after, slipped and sat
down hard on the icy stones. People converged with
deliberate movements and legs spread for balance.
Child and mother were helped to their feet, dusted
off . . .

"Well, Jorgen, what do you think?"

He turned from the window. Irina Frejenko was
crossing her office to roll up the screen. A handsome
piece of woman, Jorgen thought. But he would have
as soon slept with a leper.

"I don't know yet," he told her. "It has to simmer
in my head awhile. Even then, I won't *know* until I
actually meet him, talk with him, listen to his responses. Until then, it is all little more than informed
speculation."

"We already know a great deal about him. From his
past history. Enough to make certain assumptions
about how he will respond."

There was an overwhelming force of personality
behind her soft, precise voice. Jorgen resisted it instinctively. "Assuming," he growled, "is not the same
as knowing."

He didn't like *anybody* who worked in Lubyanka.
They were all of them dirty—ingrained with the filth
of the work they did, the methods projected for ac-
complishing the plots they hatched here. Jorgen did
not consider himself dirtied in executing these plots
for them. The difference, as he saw it, was obvious.
He compared it to big-game hunters. The dirty ones
were those who flew low over game areas in helicop-
ters and shot down at their victims from the air, with
no risk at all. Quite different from a hunter entering
a jungle alone, armed only with a bow and arrow
and a knife, to stalk tigers who were also stalking

him. In carrying out the ᴏ_____
yanka, Jorgen ventured alo_____
infested with alert enemies, a_____
each time and every moment _____
and sanity. The danger cleansed _____

Irina Frejenko felt Jorgen's re_____
checked the impulse to contradict h_____
be counterproductive, and become _____
over semantics. Silently, she leaned t_____
and folded stand against her safe, re_____ the
way he'd entered her office two hours ago: the slow
walk, all attentive nerves and alert readiness. The
level regard with which he'd assessed her. A formidable man. She did not underestimate him, though she
knew he underestimated her.

Returning to the leather-padded swivel chair behind
her desk, she studied Jorgen thoughtfully, smiling
with her mouth. He stood there by the window returning her gaze with a small smile of his own, faintly
mocking. He had, she thought, the look of an old,
battered, cunning eagle. Both hunter and hunted,
gnarled and toughened by time and battle.

She could understand his underlying hostility. He
was a field officer. She was a desk-bound supervisor,
and to him her opinions were interference in an operation that was now entirely his to control. But he was
wrong. It was still *her* project. She was the one who'd
first conceived the possibility, selected the target, or-
ganized all the supporting data, planned it down to
the last detail. Basically, Jorgen was just a highly
skilled human tool she was using to execute one half
of the operation. She had to exercise some control
over him, while she still could.

Irina Frejenko placed both hands flat on the edge
of her desk. "With this man," she began in a quiet,
reasoned voice, "the weak point you must constantly
apply pressure on is his responsibility for the welfare
of his wife. That is where he will be vulnerable; and

control over him, you must al-
...m that whether she lives or dies is in

...en advanced from the window. He turned the
...ra chair and sat down on it, facing her across the
desk. His smile was gone. "You seem to me an intelligent person." His tone was mild and his eyes looked
directly into hers. "Your position of authority confirms that. So I assume your judgment of the target's
character will prove correct. But I prefer to make
these judgments for myself. Just give me the solid information you have on him. The pertinent operational data from your target study. His books, lec-
tures, professional papers, copies of any personal cor-
respondence available. And allow me to draw my own
conclusions about how to handle him."

Irina Frejenko showed no irritation. "I am a psychologist by profession. With considerable experience.
And I am good at it."

Jorgen lit a cigarette and dropped the match into
a red glass ashtray on her desk between the brown
plastic memo tray and a small wood-framed clock. The
black hands of the clock were stopped at fourteen
past twelve. She was not the sort of woman to forget
to wind it; so she was the kind who kept things that
no longer worked. He let cigarette smoke drift from
his mouth and looked through it into her eyes again.

"I'm something of a psychologist myself," he told
her, in the same measured tone. "My freedom has
often depended on it. And sometimes my life."

"I know," Irina Frejenko said respectfully. "Beginning a long time ago, when you posed as a psychic
consultant to some highly placed Nazi officers. I do
not underestimate the understanding of human behavior you must have acquired through coping with
those crazy quasi mystics. But . . ."

"Good," Jorgen interrupted. "In that case I'd also
like to see some samples of Rhalles' handwriting, if
you have them. Especially his signature."

36

She frowned uncertainly.

He explained: "Sometimes what a man hides of himself shows up there."

"Character analysis through handwriting?" It was Irina's turn for a faintly mocking smile. "A moment ago you were insisting on nothing but 'solid information,' and ridiculing my use of scientific psychology. Now you want to use something derived from charlatan fortunetellers of the Middle Ages. Akin to cabalism and alchemy. Not very consistent, would you say?"

Jorgen's laugh was soft and deep, as pleasing as his voice. "I admit you make your point. You have your brand of foolishness, and I have mine. On the other hand, mysticism—even as practiced by people who *knew* they were fakes—has had several thousand years of delving into basically the same areas that your profession is just beginning to explore. They probably gained a few insights."

She was almost certain he was baiting her, but she was curious. "Is it possible you believe some of that occult mumbo jumbo? I assumed it was merely once an expedient cover for you."

He shrugged, and smiled. His smile was charming, warm and sure. "Sometimes I believe. Sometimes not. I have moods."

"I'm surprised," she admitted frankly.

"Magic is the science of the jungle—you remember who said that?"

It took her a moment. Then she had it: "Carl Jung. A sadly flawed psychologist, I'm sure you'll agree. Lost in myths and legends."

"Myths can teach us quite a lot about human nature." Jorgen took a deep drag at his cigarette. He let the smoke trickle out between thinned lips as he continued softly: "Do you know that six-six-six is the mark of the beast? Or that there is a tree in Madras where the children leave their messages to God? Or that a sword that has killed one hundred times must be buried deep in the ground because it has acquired its own thirst for human blood?"

He reached out and took hold of the amber pendant hanging from her neck by a slim silver chain. "Or that amber is the congealed tears of lonely women?"

Irina Frejenko felt oddly disturbed. The photograph hadn't prepared her for the peculiar quality of depth in his eyes. She had an uneasy sense of sinking into that depth. And his hand seemed to be holding more of her than her amber pendant. "I'm afraid I don't understand what you are trying to say . . ." Her voice seemed to her to have lost strength.

"Because," he explained blandly, "it is mumbo jumbo. About as valid as the claim that psychology is a science."

She drew a shallow breath. "The material you want about the target is in my safe." She stood up, forcing Jorgen to let go of her pendant. She had a sense of relief as she went around her desk toward the safe. As though she'd broken some alien hold on her mind.

And she began forcing herself to accept, finally, what she'd known was inevitable: the fate of her project was slipping away from her, into the hands of others.

3

"If you fail," Irina Frejenko told him flatly during their final meeting, "we have taken measures to ensure that there is no way for anyone to prove that you are anything but an independent adventurer. With no link left that connects you to us."

She had become accustomed, by then, to the tricks he'd used to assert an almost hypnotic influence over her in their first meeting. And he'd slowly stopped using them—either because he saw they no longer shook her, or because the true gravity of what he was being sent into had sunk in.

Opening her safe, she showed him a taped cardboard box with the code name hand-printed in black on a yellow label: "JORGEN." "In that is every copy of every form ever filled out by you or about you. If anything goes wrong, I'm to burn it. Leaving absolutely nothing to prove that you were ever in, or in any way connected with, the Soviet Union. You've been given a U classification on this one. You understand that."

He understood it. If the operation came apart, for any reason, there'd be no help for him; no chance of being included in some future exchange of arrested agents. He would be—utterly alone.

It wasn't the first time. But it was no less unpleasant a prospect for that.

His smile this time had a bitter edge. "So simple from where you sit. A flare of a match, and you wipe me out. I never existed."

Irina Frejenko thought about what was going to happen to her if it went wrong.

But all she said was: "Yes. That is the way it is."

THREE

1

Through most of 1939, Jorgen's section of the Red Orchestra in Berlin had used a book code, based on a volume of the works of Nietzsche. Using the same book almost every day over the period of a year to encode and decode messages, one got to know most of it by heart. There were phrases that Jorgen could still repeat word for word, even after so many years.

On his last night before starting out, he remembered one of them, especially—on the recklessness of any man who operates on his own, ignoring the rules and conventions of society:

"He ventures into a labyrinth, he multiplies by a thousand the dangers which life as such already brings with it; not the smallest of which is that no one can behold how and where he goes astray, is cut off from others, and is torn to pieces limb from limb by some cave-minotaur of conscience. If such a one is destroyed, it takes place so far from the understanding of men that they neither feel it nor sympathize. And he can no longer go back! He can no longer go back even to the pity of men."

2

Icicles hung from high strands of barbed wire, glistening in the cold moonlight. The night air was spiced with the odor of pine.

The barbed wire topped an endless steel-mesh fence, ten feet high, made of closely woven razor wire. Jorgen stood beside this inner barrier, waiting to cross the Death Strip. He waited patiently, his boots planted ankle deep in the last of the winter snow. His gloved hands were clasped together behind his back. He tilted his head to observe the moon through a thin web of cloud.

There were two rings around the moon. The inner ring was bluish green; the outer ring, pale white. A good omen, to counter the evil portent of the fallen drop of blood.

Jorgen smiled at himself. There was where it all began: with the little superstitions, learned as a child, stimulating his curiosity about the roots of faith. These had led to his studies of comparative religion, with his specialization in the Gnostics. Leading in turn into the perilous contacts with Nazi mystics and into the profession of espionage.

And now all that was left was a perverse relish for indulging in the old superstitions of childhood.

Jorgen squinted through the steel mesh. The searchlight on top of the watchtower had been turned off. So had the headlights of a border patrol van, parked on the narrow concrete roadway running the center of the Death Strip. The dark figures of heavily-armed police moved back and forth between the inner and outer barricades, caging attack dogs and switching off some of the antipersonnel booby traps. Preparing for Jorgen's crossing.

The Death Strip formed a barrier 850 miles long, constructed to keep East Germans from escaping to the West: a complex of electrified fences, machine-gun towers, blockhouses, and antivehicle trenches. Every mile of it a maze of minefields; with clusters of self-triggering grenades and shotguns positioned at varied heights, activated by devices ranging from simple trip wires to sophisticated acoustical sensors.

The point that had been chosen for Jorgen's crossing was a pocket in the hills at the southern end of the Thuringian Forest, below Meiningen. It was beautiful country, a maze of heavily wooded hill ranges rising one above the other under their blankets of snow. Behind Jorgen, the thick, high forest ended abruptly, shorn clean fifteen yards from the East German side of the Death Strip. The forest resumed on the other side, just beyond the frontier warning fence.

In the pale moonlight, Jorgen could see the other side clearly. But there was little likelihood that his crossing would be spotted. The area over there was patrolled infrequently, at known intervals. The West Germans had no need to keep their own people in, and no objection to East Germans escaping to join them.

Jorgen straightened slightly as the figure of a man emerged from the dense timber on the other side. Two border guards opened a gate in the warning fence as the man reached it. One of the guards turned and led the way along a zigzag route in Jorgen's direction. The man followed, sticking close.

Reaching the small gate in the steel-mesh fence beside Jorgen, the guard unlocked it and stood aside, remaining discreetly within the barrier. The man who'd come from the other side stepped through. A tough, middle-aged agent from the KGB's "wet affairs" department.

"What is your name?" he challenged Jorgen in Russian.

"Joachim Frenzel," Jorgen answered.

"You are now. Here are his papers." The agent handed over a thick envelope.

Jorgen examined the contents, then stuck it in his pocket. "I hope you buried him deep?"

"Deep enough. Ten miles out at sea, encased in cement. *After* using acid on his face and fingers."

It had been the real Joachim Frenzel's misfortune to be Jorgen's age, with the same basic physical characteristics. In addition he'd had neither relatives nor friends to start wondering about what had happened to him. He'd lived like a hermit, and his only contacts had been through his business: a small stamp shop in Hamburg. Even these business contacts would have no reason to be curious about his disappearance. Because he had sold his shop and broken the lease on his apartment—to move to the United States and open another stamp shop there.

It had not been difficult to arrange. The agent who had killed him had posed as an investor, interested in expanding into small businesses in America. He'd proved his sincerity with a tempting advance, and Frenzel had applied for permission to enter America and work there. Because of the liberal immigration quota for West Germans with a proven means of earning a living, his application had been quickly approved. Joachim Frenzel had left for the airport, and wound up under the sea.

His immigration and work permits were now in Jorgen's pocket, along with the rest of his identification and the redated airline ticket.

Jorgen took out the keys to the car he'd used to get to this part of the Thüringer Wald.

The other man handed over a set of car keys in exchange. "Have a good trip, whatever it is for."

"You too."

The man smiled for the first time. "Oh, I intend to." He went past Jorgen, toward the car parked at the edge of the forest.

Jorgen doubted that the smile would last long. The wet affairs specialist was undoubtedly looking forward to enjoying himself in Moscow for some time, celebrating his latest success. Instead, what he was going to get was an immediate transfer to some remote place deep in Eastern Russia. Where he was unlikely to ever meet anyone interested in his last assignment outside the Soviet Union.

Irina Frejenko—or someone even higher up the

ladder—was taking no risks at all, no matter how slight, that could be avoided.

The East German border guard relocked the gate after Jorgen stepped inside. "Please stay close behind me," he instructed, with due respect. "Do not stray." He turned and led the way along the erratic safe route.

Jorgen stayed precisely behind him. They went around a low iron and cement bunker, and through the dark shadow under the watchtower. As they approached the patrol driveway there were threatening growls from the attack dogs in their cage somewhere to Jorgen's left. On the other side of the driveway they entered a flat, empty stretch where the guard moved with special attention. Jorgen followed with equal care, hyperaware of unseen land mines and trip wires close on either side.

Suddenly they were at the edge of the escape-vehicle trap: a cement-lined ditch nine feet deep and fifteen feet across. The guard did a precise right turn and walked along the edge for ten yards. Jorgen made exactly the same turn and followed, to an iron ladder leading down. Reaching the bottom, Jorgen was grateful his boots were high and waterproof. He sank to his calves in the slush of melting snow.

They sloshed across to the other side of the ditch, and climbed out by way of a second iron ladder. At the top lay another open stretch planted with SM-70 trip mines. The guard twice changed direction sharply in crossing it.

That brought them up against another high steel-mesh fence of razor wire topped with barbed wire. The guard turned to the left and walked along the fence with his sleeve touching it. Jorgen did the same. After a dozen yards, there was an opening in the fence. The guard led the way through. The second guard was still in position, holding open the gate in the barbed-wire warning fence, waiting for them.

Jorgen's guide stopped there, turning to face him and saluting. "Beyond this point there is no danger."

Jorgen thanked him and went through the gate, into West Germany. He headed for the point where he'd seen the Russian emerge from the forest. Behind him he heard the clang of the gate being shut and locked.

Finding the path, Jorgen followed it into the forest, walking quickly. There was no possibility of straying from the path. It was hemmed in on either side by thick tree trunks and dense underbrush. Four minutes brought him to a narrow road and the waiting car. It was a red Porsche, with a sticker on the rear window bearing the name of a rental agency in Munich.

Tooling the Porsche along a series of similar country roads brought him to Route 279. There was little traffic on the highway this late at night, and he made good time to the interchange outside Nürnberg. There he turned onto the E6 Autobahn and sped south toward Munich.

It was a few minutes before midnight on the nineteenth of March.

In KGB parlance, Jorgen was "beginning to swim" —on his own in enemy territory.

3

He entered Washington, D.C., late in the afternoon on the twenty-seventh of March, Driving a car he'd rented in Florida, using Joachim Frenzel's Diners Club card. He hadn't been able to fly up, because he couldn't risk an examination of what was inside the large steel suitcase he'd acquired down there.

He'd been given four possible night-rendezvous times to be on that empty stretch of Florida beach. It hadn't been until the third night that the small boat had arrived, bringing the steel suitcase. As soon as Jorgen took it, the boat headed back out to sea—

to the Soviet atomic submarine waiting safely just outside the territorial limit. And Jorgen had headed north with the precious cargo it had delivered to him.

It was now buried in a wooded area of Virginia, some sixty miles south of Washington. To wait until Jorgen found an apartment to install it in.

This afternoon it was too late for apartment hunting. Tomorrow morning would be soon enough to start. Which left Jorgen the rest of the day for something in which there was no practical value—but some satisfaction of the excitement building up in him as he reached Washington.

The District of Columbia was experiencing an early spring. Trees and fields were already greening, and warm air rushed through the open windows of the car as Jorgen drove across the Potomac on the Memorial Bridge, into the heart of the capital. Leaving the car in a K Street parking lot, he walked around the corner to a large red-brick hotel on Fourteenth, where he'd once stayed in the past.

He remembered it as expensive and extremely comfortable. It was no longer either. The room he was checked into was cheap and seedy, its dirty windows looking out at a partially demolished office building. Jorgen was tired from the long drive. But this room held no temptation to settle in and put off what he was so eager for: a look at the ultimate objective behind his human target.

Dumping his topcoat and single piece of luggage on the sagging bed, he took the elevator back to the sadly run-down lobby and went out. Next door to the hotel there was now a small, cluttered grocery. Jorgen remembered something. He went in and bought a bag of peanuts. Carrying it, he started down Fourteenth Street.

It had once been the center of the city. But, like the hotel, this street and the neighborhood around it had come a long way down since Jorgen had last been there. The big businesses had obviously moved elsewhere. Their buildings were now either boarded up or given over to shabby stores, bars, topless joints, burlesque houses, cheap cafeterias, and pornography shops. Only three blocks from the White House, Jorgen passed a place advertising itself as "The Nation's Biggest Porno Center."

Jorgen felt a surprising surge of anger against a people who could allow their capital to sink to such depths. It cheapened his objective, and thus the work he was doing. But once he turned to his right into H Street he began to feel better. The big government buildings still rose to his left, as imposing as he'd remembered them. There were some new hotels, office buildings, and shops on his right; all satisfyingly elegant. And straight ahead, Lafayette Square was still there waiting for him, the grass already green.

Entering the small park, Jorgen at first avoided looking in the direction of what he'd come to see. Holding back, deliberately letting the excitement build in him. Instead, he strolled around the curving red-brick paths, renewing old acquaintances: the big, old bald cypress, still with the remembered label on it: "*Taxodium distichum*." The green statue of General Jackson in the middle of the square, mounted with impossible ease on a rearing horse and doffing his hat, surrounded by four green 1812 cannons.

And the statues at the square's four corners, of European officers who'd come to help America win its revolution: Lafayette, rising above a bare-breasted girl offering him a sword. Rochambeau, with his angry green eagle. Baron von Steuben, to whom Jorgen had sometimes fancied he had a certain resemblance. It was the fourth statue that bore the chiseled words which Jorgen had always found somehow moving: "And Freedom Shrieked as Kosciuszko fell."

And the squirrels, looking exactly like the ones who'd flirted with him in the past. Not the same, of course, but at least their descendants. Jorgen hefted the small bag of peanuts. The nearest one, clinging head-down to the trunk of a cypress, regarded him with frightened, attentive eyes. Jorgen tore open the bag and took out a peanut. The squirrel raced down, approached halfway, stopped warily. Jorgen held out the peanut. The squirrel advanced again, almost to his right shoe. Jorgen dropped the nut, and the squirrel caught it on the first bounce, scampering back to its tree before beginning to shell it.

Other squirrels gathered for theirs, flirting and posing on their hind legs, forepaws begging. Jorgen tossed a nut to each, until the pigeons began converging on him. Jorgen didn't like pigeons but was philosophical about it. Dumping the rest of the nuts in his hand, he flung them wide. To the strongest and fastest, as with everything in this world.

He noted that the grass in the square was already badly in need of mowing and some reseeding. But the black park benches had recently been repainted. Jorgen walked to an empty one facing Pennsylvania Avenue and sat down. And finally allowed himself to look.

There it was, directly across the street from him. The White House, behind its low iron fence posts that did not obstruct the view. With a uniformed policeman standing beside one of the white columns set in a graceful half-circle in front of the center section of the building, and the flag fluttering atop the tall pole on the roof. They called it Old Glory, Jorgen remembered.

A fittingly impressive, beautiful structure. Right there in front of him. Seeming so close, he might almost reach out and grasp it. There was no feeling of letdown. Anticipation swelled inside him.

Patience, Jorgen warned himself. Patience . . . His function now, as soon as he settled in and established cover, was to initiate contact with his small apparatus, organize its segregated channels of communication, and make certain its courier line was ready to operate effectively.

And after that, just to wait. Until the other part of the project, with which he had no connection, was successfully executed. The part concerning that young woman with the interesting Tartar face and dark Mongol eyes. The one he'd watched on the screen in Irina Frejenko's office. Moira Rhalles.

Jorgen leaned back on the park bench and thought about her, as he continued to gaze at the building in front of him on the other side of Pennsylvania Avenue.

FOUR

1

The goddess had emerged out of the mists of time, a disturbing glimpse into the dawn of the human mind. If she was authentic, she was at least twenty-thousand years old. A dark, delicately carved Stone Age goddess of sexuality, birth, fertility, and death. It was she who drew Moira Rhalles into the cave. But in a sense it was the conditions under which Moira had been raised that led inevitably to her being there.

Her father and aunt had been the sole inheritors of a respectable family fortune acquired from the lumber business. Her father, a warm-hearted man with an excellent but lazy mind, used his portion of the inheritance to dabble in California politics and pretty girls, and indulge a dilettante's passion for pre-Columbian history. Aunt Clara invested her inheritance in the only real love of her life, art. The estate she bought thirty miles north of San Francisco, in Marin County, had a sprawling, many-roomed Spanish style house. She named it Villa Leonardo, and every year she invited five young artists to live and work in it, at her expense. It was there that Moira's father met her mother.

Aunt Clara met her first, in Montreal, where she was beginning to achieve a name as a young painter who warranted watching. She accepted the prospect of a free year at Villa Leonardo eagerly. Less than a month after she moved in, Aunt Clara's brother turned up one day. After an hour with the Indian girl, twenty years his junior, he was ready to put his career as a playboy behind him. Her interest in *him*, Aunt Clara used to recall with nostalgic humor, was at first concentrated on his car—a souped-up red Lancia.

She was crazy about fast cars. Crazy was her own word for it. She had a mild obsession with the notion that a streak of insanity ran far back through the history of her tribe. The ancient horror stories of the Ojibwa Indians concerned legendary monsters that crept into people's brains and took over.

The worst was called the windigo, which came during the bitter winters of the Canadian forests. People taken over by a windigo acquired an insatiable hunger for human flesh. They had to be hunted down, killed, and burned; because only fire could destroy a windigo. That was the worst of the brain-seizing monsters; but there were others. It was one of these, Moira's mother used to joke, that she sublimated through her passion for racing cars.

"I don't want to die of sickness or old age," she'd once confided to Aunt Clara. "When I go, I don't want it to be anything disgusting like that. My ambition is to go out in a blaze of glory—in one big, screaming tangle of crashing metal."

Her other passion had been to use her art talent to fight her way up out of the poverty of her childhood in a Canadian reservation. After she married, her fear of sinking back into that poverty left her. And she never painted again. But if she had married Moira's father for his money and car, she did come to love him; too much, judging from the way they died.

After they were married, they often went out nights on infrequently traveled highways with the Lancia— and its successors—and took turns racing it, full speed. That suicidal enthusiasm was reined in somewhat after Moira was born. But even then there was the knowledge in the back of their minds that, if something did happen, Aunt Clara could be depended upon to become an excellent substitute parent.

It happened when a doctor told Moira's mother that her husband was dying of cancer. He left it to her to break it to him. Instead, she drove the newest Lancia head-on into a canyon wall, killing them both instantly. The speedometer needle was found to be stuck at the 120-mile-an-hour mark.

Aunt Clara had regarded it as a heartbreakingly romantic death. Moira had believed it the work of something akin to a windigo, and it wasn't until she was in her mid-twenties that she stopped having nightmares about it.

She was seven when they died. After that she lived with Aunt Clara, in the Villa Leonardo. Being constantly among hard-working young artists, getting a crush on a new one almost each year, quite naturally heightened her own interest in an art career. But by the time she was eighteen she'd decided that, though her drawing was quite good, she didn't have the obsessive talent required to be a serious paniter. So she turned, at first, toward making a career as an art historian.

Gradually, she found the art she was most interested in was the art of the ancients. Which led her into archaeology.

And ultimately, to the cave.

2

The entrance to the cave couldn't be seen from above. And there was no visible path. But Gaspard Martinot angled down the steep, uneven slope with the certainty of an experienced hiker who'd used this approach before. Moira Rhalles followed him swiftly —a small, sturdy figure moving with surefooted skill, instinctively planting the ribbed rubber soles of her boots where they'd find secure traction among the broken humps of rock.

Behind her, Christine was having trouble keeping pace. Christine was five years younger than Moira, and she had the look of a tall, slender athlete. But she lacked Moira's experience in fieldwork. Several times Moira heard her slip on loose stones and fight to regain balance. Moira didn't look back. Her attention stayed on the terrain around Martinot's short, heavy legs, as he led the way down.

Her own legs adjusted automatically to what was coming, as she pulled the light padded anorak tightly around her and closed the fastenings. There was warm April sunlight up on the ridge behind them, but the air became sharply colder as they descended into the shadows of the narrow gorge. In the depths below a trapped wind clawed at sparse, stunted trees, and the mountain stream churned into white froth battering through fallen boulders. Out of habit, part of Moira's mind registered the earth history told by the rocks down which she scrambled.

The geology of this part of southern France was notoriously difficult to unravel, and the confused variety of formations inside the gorge was typical. The fold mountains through which the water had cut this gorge had been created by cataclysmic fractures and shifts in the world's crust—wrenching massive areas of that crust one on top of the other, twisting and compressing the result, and then repeating the process over again.

Between times, the sagging surfaces of these crustal overfolds had been attacked by glaciers, grinding and carving their way across enormous distances, and carrying masses of detached rock with them from one area to another. In addition, the retreating seas that had for long periods covered this part of Europe had left behind thick layers of hardening deposits, to be

53

caught between and under the collapsing upthrusts of the next earth spasms.

The side of the gorge Moira was descending exposed this history: folds and overfolds, beds and extrusions, vastly separated in time but forced together in fractured pressure sandwiches of differing color and composition. Dolomitic and coral limestone predominated here, from the 125 million years this area had been the bottom of the sea, before the violent rise of the Alps had hurled the waters away to the south.

It was on one of the limestone ledges that Gaspard Martinot paused in his downward climb. He crouched, braced one hand on the edge, and dropped out of sight below it.

Moira reached the ledge and looked down. Martinot was just below her, standing on a narrow level space where dense bushes grew, easing the straps of his pack from his thick shoulders. Below him, a convoluted cliff of brown-stained rock dropped almost sheer into green water churned with froth. The battering sound of the rapids below was loud here.

She turned and looked up at the crest of the slope. Sunlight glinted off the binoculars with which John Borelli was following their descent. He was still sitting in the jeep they'd parked on the dirt trail up there. Above him, several milky clouds hung in the clear blue sky. Their positions hadn't changed much, but their shapes were in constant change, as though each contained its own slow whirlpool.

Moira turned back to the edge of the limestone ledge, and jumped down beside Martinot. He straightened, no taller than Moira but much wider. Thick peasant muscle with an overlay of fat. A peasant face, too: the small eyes suspicious and clever, the meaty features blurred by too much wine and weather, the expression habitually guarded.

"There it is," he said gruffly, making a small gesture.

Moira looked down at the entrance of the cave. The opening was lower than their hips, but wide. A twisted stone mouth, with gnarled, eroded lips. Inside the mouth was darkness. Moira exerted a grip on her nervous system, in anticipation.

The childish terror of dark, enclosed places had never been fully conquered. But in spite of it she had explored the insides of dozens of underground tombs and grottoes. She could not have continued in her profession if she had not learned how to control the loathing.

Martinot looked upward impatiently. "Where is the other girl?"

As though in answer, several small stones rattled over the lip of the ledge above their heads. Then Christine's lower legs appeared, dangling over the edge. She was sitting on the ledge, easing herself forward. When the rest of her appeared, Moira reached up a hand and helped her down.

Christine nodded her thanks, looked quickly from Moira to the low cave opening. She was breathing hard, her narrow face tensed.

"Take a rest," Moira said, and glanced down at Martinot.

He'd squatted to open his pack, taking out a construction worker's hard-hat with a miner's lamp fastened to it. He put it on. Wires ran from the lamp to a battery pack, which he clipped to the back of his belt. He produced two flat flashlights, each with a looped canvas strap. Moira hung one around her neck, gave the other to Christine. The next item Martinot took from his pack was a nylon climbing rope, about fifty feet of it, tightly coiled. He snap-linked the coil to his belt with a steel clip, then got out a canteen with a ragged canvas cover. It could have been a World War II souvenir, like his jeep.

"You carry this," Martinot said, handing it up to Moira. "Loop it over one shoulder and under the other arm." He sat down on the ground in front of the cave. "Inside it becomes higher very quickly. But always look above before you straighten up. In places the roof becomes lower suddenly. With many sharp edges."

"Let's have a drink first," Moira said, uncapping the canteen. Ignoring Martinot's irritated look, she drank a mouthful, and passed the canteen. Christine took barely a sip and handed it back without looking at Moira. She was staring down at the cave entrance, her face still tight with strain.

Moira frowned a bit. "You can wait out here for us, if you want."

"No." Christine forced the word through stiff lips.

Another claustrophobia victim, Moira decided. That's all I need at this point. "Just stick close to me," she told Christine. "You'll get used to it, once we're inside."

"Let's go," Martinot growled. He bent his head almost to his knees, and pushed himself sideways. The backs of his shoulders barely cleared the top of the cave mouth, and then the darkness inside swallowed him.

His lamp glowed in the gloom. "Come!" his voice growled.

Moira snapped on the flashlight hanging from her neck, lay down on her side, and eased herself into the cave. A moment later Christine crawled in after her. They paused for a moment to allow their eyes to adjust.

The interior of the cave's mouth was not as dark as it had seemed from the outside. Dull daylight entered through the low opening, which framed a section of green forest and rock formations on the other side of the narrow gorge. Even without their artificial lights it would have been possible to see each other and the general shape of the cavity they were in. It was like an inverted cup. The dome was high enough for them to sit up straight, though Christine, a head taller than Moira and Martinot, had to bend her neck slightly. The ground was cushioned with moss and ferns.

Martinot got his knees under him and turned to his left. The beam of his head lamp steadied on a vertical fissure between two rock formations crushed together by the weight of the land mass over them. It was about four feet high, and just wide enough for a person to squeeze through.

"Stay close behind me," Martinot told them. "There are many passages down there. It is confusing, and one could become lost in it. But I will go slowly. Do not be afraid. None of it is dangerous, though some of it is awkward."

He led the way, squeezing through the fissure. Moira crawled in after him, followed by Christine. They entered a low, narrow passage that made one turn, and then another, gradually corkscrewing downward into the subterranean core of the cave system. The descent took them into a total darkness unknown on the surface of the earth. A solid inky black, which their lamps penetrated but could not disperse. The dull yellow beams illuminated what they shone upon directly, but all around them, pressing in close, the blackness remained.

The stones over which they crawled became damp; and then increasingly covered with thickening layers of sticky wet clay, which clung to skin and clothing. Ice-cold moisture dripped from the low roof of the passage. A thick ooze spread down the walls pressing in close on either side. In the utter absence of outside sounds, the dripping of water was intensely magnified, almost painfully sharp in the ears. Far below, the surging of a deep underground river through constrictions of rock created echoing whispers within the dark labyrinth.

Now that she was in it, Moira's fear was gone. Replaced by excitement, eagerness. Her mother had taught her how to work that emotional switch, back in California when she'd been about six, and scared to ride the big horse they'd bought for her.

"The emotions are pretty dumb, baby. All you've got to do is tell them that the strong thing you're feeling isn't fear. It's the thrill of excitement. Just keep telling yourself that. You'll be surprised. It's easy as hell to fool your nervous system like that. I do it all the time."

Especially driving that souped-up Lancia 120 miles an hour.

But she had been right. It had worked; and it still worked. Her mother would have been amused at the way she was using it now. If she'd stuck around, instead of finally using the Lancia deliberately to join Moira's father in a double wipe-out.

Moira doubted that her mother would have had much empathy for the *reason* she was now using her old emotion-switch trick. If she were descending into the guts of this cave system for sport, that her mother would have understood. For her mother, adventure was purely a physical thing. Intellectual curiosity about the past was never of interest to her. "Folklore," she'd called it, with bitter-edged sarcasm. "Playing Injun" for tourist tips as a child on the reservation had left scars that never stopped itching.

It was from her father that Moira had acquired her taste for what he'd called, affectionately, "rummaging among the broken bones of the past." Almost everything else she'd gotten from her mother—her physical appearance, the tart humor, the strength and agility. But it was her father who would have quickened to the lure that now drew Moira down into the depths of these caves under the southeastern jut of the French Alps.

Was the lure Martinot had showed her the genuine article? She thought so, or she wouldn't have come. Had he really found it down in here? On that question Moira's inquisitive eagerness was leavened with scientific skepticism. But the location of the cave system, under the mountains flanking the Ubaye River, made the find a distinct possibility.

Southeast of the Ubaye River area was the Roya Valley. Where it reached the Mediterranean there were caves in which had been found some of the earliest remains of Homo sapiens in Europe: the Grimaldi man. Halfway between those caves and these was the savage and still-uninhabited section of the Provence Alps where Moira had been digging with her group from the archaeological department of the University of Pennsylvania: the Valley of Marvels, containing cliffs and boulders upon which an unknown people, who had left no other traces behind, had chiseled some forty thousand strange designs and figures. For a primitive people on the move north from that area through the Alps of southeast France, one natural route was provided by the Ubaye River.

Also, more discoveries of the earliest known examples of art—the hunting-cult cave paintings of the Upper Paleolithic period—had been made in southern France than anywhere else in the world. True, the main concentration of these primitive religious paintings was west of the Ubaye River area. But others had been found as far to the east as the Caspian Sea area. And the small, stylized Aurignacian cult statuettes, of the goddess of birth and death, had turned up within a broad belt reaching from southwestern Europe to the edge of Mongolia. This network of caverns in which Martinot claimed to have made his find was well within that belt.

Archaeologists called these goddess statuettes "Venus figures." They represented the oldest form of religious worship ever discovered. It was one of these that Martinot had shown Moira.

What Moira sought now was supporting evidence: other remnants of Old Stone Age man, which could be related to the figure of the goddess.

The passage they were negotiating had leveled off. It was widening now, the roof lifting. In the beam of Moira's lamp, Martinot rose from his knees. He moved on in a crouched walk. Moira did the same. The clay underfoot thickened and hardened. A trench deepened down the middle, channeled by an underground stream that ran in the trench when prolonged heavy rains hit the mountain above. It made for awkward walking. Trailing her hands along the side walls to support herself, Moira felt deep horizontal grooves cut into the living rock by the same stream. Which meant that the rain water had been finding this same route over thousands of years, as it surged toward the depths of the phreatic zone, the water table underlying the entire area.

Suddenly they were in a low, wide chamber formed by the intersecting of several passages converging from different directions. Martinot led the way into a passage to the right, followed it around a sharp bend, and stopped at a ragged, vertical slit in the left wall. He looked back to make sure the two women were still close behind him. The flare of his lamp almost blinded Moira, then shifted past her to locate Christine. Reassured, he turned out of the passage they'd been following, entering the break in the wall.

Moira squeezed through after him, hearing Christine right behind her. The narrow side passage angled steeply downward. They dug heels into thick mud mixed with small stones, to keep themselves from sliding. The damp cold increased sharply.

After about sixty feet the passage leveled off. And forked. Moira and Christine followed Martinot into the left fork. It took them under the bottom of a well-like shaft, and past small dark grottoes. Moira shone her lamp into several of these in passing. So far in their descent, she hadn't seen a trace of primitive cave ornamentation.

That did not surprise her; and she continued to

reserve judgment. Whether in Europe, Africa, or the Middle East, when works of prehistoric cave paintings had been discovered, it was not usually in easily accessible parts where primitive people had lived. Nor even where some had buried their dead. In most cases it was in deep, difficult-to-reach recesses of the cavern networks that the images of cult magic, ancient sorcery, or rudimentary religions—whichever you cared to call it—had been found.

Why these paintings and engravings had been fashioned in such dark, inaccessible depths still had not been satisfactorily explained. It remained a puzzle for archaeologists to speculate upon.

But *sculptured* figures of these ritual images were *not* usually found so deep. Which either increased the value of Martinot's find, or meant he was lying about *where* he had made it.

Moira almost walked into Martinot's back as he came to a halt. He bent his head, shining his lamp downward to show what had stopped him. The passage ended there, at the edge of a deep abyss. Martinot's light probed into its darkness, but could not find a bottom to it.

He raised his head, and gestured to the left. There, a narrow, natural stone bridge curved across the abyss, to a downsloping ledge on the other side.

"It is easy to cross," he told them, unclipping the coil of nylon rope from his waist. "But since you are not experienced speleologists, it will be wiser to use a lead rope, and take no chances."

One end of the line he looped over one shoulder and under the other armpit, fastening the loop with a bowline knot across his chest. He played out about seven feet of rope, and showed Moira how to tie into it with a similar chest sling. From her, he played out another length of the rope, and helped Christine tie herself into the end. Moira turned slightly, her light showing Christine's frightened face.

"I'm all right," Christine assured her angrily, through clenched teeth. "Stop worrying about me."

Martinot looked thoughtfully at Christine's expression, and without another word led the way across the natural bridge. Moira and Christine followed him, each allowing just a little slack in the rope between them. The bridge was a bit slippery, but otherwise not difficult. If you didn't look into the bottomless abyss under it.

They reached the other side in seconds. Moira drew a slow, deep breath as Martinot untied them from his lead rope. He coiled and hung it back at his waist, and led them down the sloping ledge.

Part way down, with the bottom of the pit still hidden in the murk below, he turned into a wide crack in the wall. It widened into a high side gallery that curved to the right. But Martinot did not continue in that direction. Instead, he went down on his hands and knees, and crawled out of sight into a low dark space, under a thrusting shoulder of rock covered with a flowstone film that glistened orange where lamplight touched it. Moira and Christine crawled under the rock shoulder after Martinot, into a low, short tunnel that led them downward again.

At the bottom Martinot was waiting, standing up. They got to their feet beside him, in the entrance of a huge chamber. Its dark walls curved upward toward an unseen dome. The lower part of the chamber was choked with massive fallen boulders, piled haphazardly on top of each other.

"After this," Martinot said, "the difficult part is behind us. It will become quite easy."

There were large open spaces between and under boulders, in every direction. Martinot climbed in through one of these spaces, with the women behind him. They began working their way through the heart of the boulder pile. Every few feet there were more openings to choose among, above, below, to either side. But Martinot threaded the maze slowly enough for them to stick with him.

When they finally emerged from under the pile of boulders, the route became as easy as he'd promised: a series of galleries through which they could walk upright, with solid footing all the way. The thundering of rushing water became steadily louder. The cool air of the cave became extremely moist as they neared its source.

They entered another large chamber—and Moira stopped for a moment, staring about her with delight. The place was a maze of calcite formations that seemed equally derived from fairy-tale illustrations and nightmares. Moira had seldom seen such a variety of them in one place before, such a confusion of monstrous shapes and vivid colors. The creations of aeons of water, permeated with carbonic acid, dripping and oozing through limestone. Bringing along in places the reds and greens of iron and copper oxides. The whole of it studded with huge rock crystallizations.

As they moved through this alien subterranean maze, the lamps of the three from the world above flashed across one dazzling array after another: what looked like massive bunches of yellow grapes and snow-white bananas and red cauliflowers sprouted from walls between frozen green waterfalls. Grotesque shapes bulged from the uneven floor, some the size of men and others as big as houses: twisted spires, decaying mushrooms, swollen domes. Some rose to join giant stalactites hanging from the darkness above, forming misshapen columns.

Moira's boots sank in soft layers of ocher-colored clay-dust. She trailed Martinot through the formations and around large stone hollows filled with mixtures of drip water and chemicals, forming blood-red and emerald-green pools of liquid mud. Her ears were stuffed with the crashing echoes of pounding water, seeming to come from all directions.

It wasn't until they reached the other side of the cavern that Moira saw where the sound was coming from. It issued out of a ragged opening in the wall, together with a steady spray of blown mist that soaked their faces and clothing. Martinot headed into this opening without a pause. Moira started in after him.

The thunder of water was too loud for her to hear Christine fall behind her. But she did hear, faintly, the scream of pain.

She turned around, quickly. Christine was on the ground, her face contorted, both hands clutching the ankle of her doubled right leg. Moira reached her swiftly, crouched down and forced the hands away, to probe the ankle with her fingers.

Christine's lips thinned back over teeth gritted against the pain. "I slipped!" She had to yell to be heard through the thundering of water. "Damn it! Oh damn it!"

"I can't feel any break," Moira shouted back. "It could be sprained or hemorrhaged. Wait here. I'll get Martinot."

Motioning Christine to stay put the way she was, Moira straightened and hurried into the wall opening after Martinot. He was out of sight around a tight bend of the narrow passage inside. With flying mist blowing against her, Moira turned the bend, pushed on—and came to a jolting stop.

She was out of the passage, on a ledge that hung over emptiness, in an almost sheer-walled cavern. One of these walls rose straight up high above Moira; beneath the ledge it dropped just as far straight down.

Fighting dizziness, Moira spread her feet further apart and leaned back slightly, her hands gripping at the wall edges of the passage opening behind her. On the other side of the cavern, a bit higher than her perch, a waterfall gushed out of a hole in the rock, and poured into the pit below. Spray from the waterfall had congealed on surrounding walls, forming patterned calcite draperies flowing downward in petrified imitation of the cascade. Of Gaspard Martinot, there was no sign.

He was not on the ledge, which led to her left, into another passage opening. And she was quite sure he would not have disappeared into the other opening, without first checking to make sure that the two following him were still there.

Moira forced her hands to let go of the wall edges behind her. Forced herself to take two short steps forward, to the brink of the ledge. She brought one hand around in front of her, took hold of the lamp hanging from the strap around her neck, and aimed it downward.

There was the underground river at the bottom; surging out of one tunnel and into another, filling a small black lake. The surface was smashed by the force of the waterfall, which had torn great sections of stone from the wall it issued out of. The jagged peaks of these fallen rocks stuck up out of the black turbulence.

Gaspard Martinot's broken figure lay twisted between two of these jagged protrusions; caught fast by them in spite of the water battering at him. There was no possibility he was still alive. His head had been smashed in, apparently from striking a rock when he fell.

But, why had he fallen? The thunder of river and waterfall filled Moira's brain, making it impossible to think clearly. Sick chill drained through her veins.

She glimpsed—or half-sensed—the movement to her left. And turned her head in that direction.

A man she had never seen before stepped out of the other passage opening. He was very tall, and most of him was lean. But the shoulders and chest were massive. He was almost entirely bald, and his hawkish face was creased with the deep lines of an old man. But he came along the ledge toward her with the careless grace of a cat.

Moira turned to dart back into the passage behind

her. And saw a figure coming through its shadows. For a second she thought it was Christine.

But it was not. It was another man she'd never seen before. This one was younger, in his thirties, with a powerful, stocky build. He wore a black wet-suit, and a scuba mask hung around his thick neck. His broad, strong-boned face was deeply tanned, except for a patch of gray staining his left cheek.

Some kind of birthmark, perhaps . . .

He came toward her. There was something in his hand. It had a vaguely familiar, disturbing smell.

In the world above, it was a few minutes before eleven o'clock in the morning.

In Washington, D.C., it was a few minutes before 5 A.M.

FIVE

1

Confined on the south by the Potomac River, and on the north by a cemetery and park, Georgetown was one of the smallest residential neighborhoods in Washington. It was also the prettiest. With the university forming its western side, and the government buildings of downtown Washington beginning just to the east of it, on the other side of Rock Creek, it had a reputation, sometimes justified, of harboring the intellectuals of the nation's capital.

The area of its main artery, Wisconsin Avenue, was packed with small boutiques, restaurants, bookshops, antique shops, and glossy bars—and usually jammed with college kids. But the rest had a remarkable atmosphere of old-fashioned, genteel tranquility: Quiet, cobbled streets with brick-patterned sidewalks, lined by large old shade trees and smallish, well-kept homes from a bygone era.

Folklore ran through every street. It was added to as people of interesting potential moved in upon election or appointment to office, and out after having contributed their share to the legends of hard-won victories, shattering failures, and exposed scandals. Jack Kennedy's family had lived on N Street before moving into the White House. The house Alexander and Moira Rhalles had rented, when he became the President's adviser on foreign affairs, was on O Street.

Halfway between Wisconsin Avenue and the university, it was a narrow, three-floor row house with two beech trees out front. Built in the late eighteenth century, redone in the Victorian style of the late nineteenth century, restored to mint condition in the 1930s, and kept that way with a fresh paint job every year. The walls were whitewashed bricks, the front door and shutters were painted dark red, and the trims below the steep pitched roof were bright black.

On that warm, heavy-aired April morning, it was the first house on the block to show signs of activity.

Alexander Rhalles hadn't slept well. It was just past six-thirty when he came fully awake in the bedroom on the top floor. His arm lay across Moira's pillow. He decided that the restless night could be blamed on the fact that he was already missing her too much.

When they were separated, the first week usually wasn't bad. It gave him a chance to sink totally into his work. His real work, as differentiated from his role as presidential adviser, which he still insisted on regarding as a short-term hobby.

Which had, on occasion, provoked Moira to irritating amusement: "Don't kid yourself, Alex—you *love* it. And I don't blame you. The taste of power. The most important political figure in the world needing your advice."

"The President," he'd corrected her flatly, "doesn't *need* me. Not one bit. Don't kid *your*self. Nothing I say is going to change any world-shaking decisions. The President will do . . . whatever his basic White House team tells him . . . that the latest polls report . . . will be most popular with the majority of the voting public."

"Come on, he's not *that* weak."

"He's a politician. That says it."

"But you like him, anyway."

"Or I like the implied flattery."

"Because he does need you—at least psychologically. And you do love it, like a kid with a shiny new toy."

He'd smiled, a bit ruefully. "Well, you have to remember—I haven't *had* many toys to play with."

"You've got me."

God, he missed her.

By 7 A.M. he'd showered, shaved, had some instant coffee with a jellied roll, and was at work. His study, and Moira's adjoining it, took up all of the second floor. With his wife away he paced restlessly through both rooms as he talked into the portable recorder hung from his shoulder. Stopping occasionally to check notes arranged neatly all over the top of his big desk, or one of the reference books open to pertinent pages on his table, the mantelpiece, the two chairs, and the green leather hassock. And beginning to chain-smoke his way through a pack of cigarettes.

A tall, thin, intense man; his eyes dreamy now behind the thick lenses of his glasses; deeply immersed in the subject of his new study:

Changes in the tactics of guerrilla warfare in small countries, caused by the contending world-strategies of the big-power nations.

"Judging by the subjects you choose to research, you've got to have an awful lot of violence in you." She'd said that the second time he'd been with her. "Where do you *hide* it? Let me *see* some of that violence."

He *had,* shocking the hell out of himself.

She'd been right about his subjects, of course. Wars, revolutions, the techniques of the *coup d'état* down the ages; political assassinations as acts of faith; the price ordinary people had paid in mass struggles for liberty, and the reasons they had usually lost even when their leaders had won. Work which had made his reputation far too young for the comfort of competing historians. And which had been his only emotional outlet, until Moira.

The big one had come after Moira: his study of the contending philosophies and personalities of Luther and Erasmus, as applied to *The New Wars of Religion*—in Cyprus, Lebanon, Uganda, Israel, Ulster, and the Philippines. That one had gained him the Nobel Prize for History, at the age of thirty-eight —two years ago. Which had, in turn, gotten him invited to a White House dinner for personal congratulations from the President.

It was at that dinner that the President had become intrigued with Rhalles' somewhat sardonic comments about contemporary international problems, from his historical perspective. Since then Rhalles had become, without fanfare, the President's closest adviser and confidant on international affairs.

While it was not a secret, neither was it quite official. It was more in the nature of a personal, private relationship that had grown between Rhalles and the President. Officially, the chief presidential advisers on foreign policy remained Secretary of State Lobsenz, Secretary of Defense Hall, and Admiral Kane, director of the National Security Council. Alexander Rhalles had no open voice in the corridors of power. But he got to know pretty much everything that was going on in those corridors. Frequently, at the President's request, he sat in silently, just listening, at high-level White House conferences in the Oval Office and the Cabinet Room. At the end of most working days he sat alone with the President for up to an hour, discussing the problems that had come up in the day-by-day working out of world affairs.

The President was using him, of course. First as a sounding board, for his own thoughts on subjects that troubled him. Secondly, to milk Rhalles for sharp—sometimes acidly critical—viewpoints on these problems. Which the President could then use to impress congressional contacts and newsmen, and to test the opinions of his cabinet heads and foreign policy officials.

In the old days Rhalles would have resented having his mind used as another man's tool in this manner. But Moira was right, he did enjoy it. The temptation to be, for a time, part of the history he studied was too strong to resist. So was the flattery in the fact that the President of the United States needed him and found him interesting to spend time with.

It was extremely doubtful that the President would have found him of any interest at all, in person, if their meeting had occurred a year before he'd won the Nobel. Very early in life, Alexander Rhalles had discovered in himself a total lack of ability to deal with others on a give-and-take basis. From a withdrawn, uncommunicative child, he had grown into a stiff, secretive, self-protective adult. "The iceberg" they'd called him, in academic circles, showing only a forbidding tip of himself to those around him.

Resigned to a monk's life, he'd compensated by complete devotion to his historical research and writing, emerging only to teach; and that only because it was obligatory. As a teacher he was not bad, lecturing on his only interest. Though even there he could not or would not engage in extraneous conversation. The lack of ability to relate extended, as it was bound to, into his sexual life—or lack of it.

Until the year before the Nobel. That was when Moira had entered his life. And that had changed his world.

2

By 10 A.M. his brain was getting fuzzy, and he was out of cigarettes. Leaving the tape recorder on his desk, Rhalles went back up to the bedroom and changed into dungarees, tennis shoes, and a polo shirt. Outside, soggy clouds were beginning to lower over Washington. But there was a hazy glare to the sunlight streaming in the windows. Rhalles changed to his dark prescription sunglasses before going out.

During much of his life, those were the kind of glasses he'd worn day and night, inside and out. Supposedly because his eyes were hypensensitive to light.

Actually because he wanted something to hide behind while he observed the outer world.

There was a description by Bacon of Henry VII that had appealed to Rhalles in his youth: "The King always stood so that others were in the light to him, while he was in shadow to them."

Rhalles seldom wore the sunglasses anymore.

Chalk up another one for Moira.

It amused him, letting her handle him so easily. Most of the people in his life had found him difficult to deal with, impossible to influence.

He still wasn't easy. But easier.

"I will never again," he'd told her, "underestimate the power of a bad woman."

Her technique was quite simple, once you caught on to what she was doing. She believed in the basic carrot-and-stick approach to human relationships. When people pleased her, she was absolutely delicious to be around; displeased, she could be a growling pain in the ass. It could be damned annoying at times. But he had to admit it usually worked; and he knew himself to be a tougher subject than most. She'd had a lot of practice before she'd tackled him.

By 11 A.M., Alexander Rhalles was approaching the finish point of his almost daily half-mile jog around the outdoor track on the university campus. It wasn't as hard as it had been when he'd first made the jump from the quarter-mile. But it was still no picnic for him. He was dripping with sweat. The wind hissed between his bared teeth and burned his lungs. And his long legs were getting heavy and shaky, reduced from pumping to plodding.

Well, Moira, he thought with sour humor, I hope you're satisfied.

"If you won't give up smoking then you've got to take regular exercise to clean out your lungs," she'd decreed flatly. "You're a lot older than me, don't forget. I don't want you dying on me before I'm tired of you."

It was a lot easier when she was there to run with him. Doing anything with Moira was fun. But he did it, dutifully, even without her presence. Because he knew it would please her.

There was nothing altruistic about that, he knew. Her pleasure in him had made him young; for the first time in his life.

He walked fast as he left the track, giving his heart and lungs a chance to adjust. His legs were tired from the run as he went out through the campus gate at thirty-seventh and headed back along O Street to the house three blocks away. But his head was clear again. And all of him would soon feel light and vital, ready for a full afternoon of work, after a shower and a small, nourishing lunch. The kind Moira had introduced him to.

It was amazing, how much of his life revolved around her, even when she wasn't there. That stirred no trace of resentment in Rhalles. What it did evoke was remembered and anticipated pleasure.

Moira was his wife, his lover, and the only real friend he had ever had.

It was shortly after one in the afternoon that the man Rhalles had noticed before came over and spoke to him.

Rhalles had taken his lunch at a health food diner on Wisconsin, near the Georgetown Movie House. There were two new posters pasted across the others above his booth: one announcing "Big Waterbed Sale!" the other advertising "The True Decadence Discotheque." The big headline in that day's Washington Post said: "D.C. HEROIN ADDICTS UP 41 Pct. IN YEAR."

He took the newspaper with him when he left the diner. Since becoming a presidential adviser he'd gotten into the habit of keeping up with current events. There'd be no private conference with the President that evening, because of the reception at Anderson House. He'd be seeing the President there, though probably only briefly. It wasn't the sort of affair Rhalles ordinarily cared to attend. But with Moira in France there wasn't much else to do. And there'd be a couple of men there who might be interesting to talk with. It was scheduled to end early, leaving him time to take in a movie before going to bed.

He felt the eagerness to get back to work building in him as he crossed Wisconsin and re-entered O Street. But first he stopped into the Sorbet ice-cream parlor, for a small cup of strong Italian coffee. Carrying it out to one of the brown, wrought-iron sidewalk tables, he settled down under the shade of a yellow and white umbrella.

There was a young university couple arguing passionately in whispers at a table at his left. Observing other people, instead of always remaining sunk inside himself, was something still quite new for Rhalles, and he felt a certain delicious perversity in doing it. The boy, in a brown and white track suit with blue sneakers, had Latin features and a small, neat mustache. The girl wore a blue striped blouse, dungarees, and sandals. She had long straight blond hair and a plumply rounded body. Judging by the way they leaned toward each other as they whispered, Rhalles concluded, their argument was the traditional one of very young couples: love versus lust.

The man he had noticed before was seated at a table to his right. A strongly built man in his sixties. The face was strong too; with deep tight creases and a harsh-looking mouth. Sparse white hair contrasted with a light suntan.

Rhalles had seen him several times in the last week; always here, having a leisurely coffee.

This time, as he looked at him, the man looked back. Rhalles hastily looked down, taking a sip of his coffee, fighting embarrassment at having been caught staring. But the man was standing up, coming over to Rhalles' table.

"Excuse me, sir. May I borrow your sugar? They forgot to leave some on my table." The man's voice was surprisingly warm and pleasant. With some kind of European accent. In spite of the harsh mouth, his smile was charming.

Rhalles hesitated, but only for the barest fraction of a second. Then he broke through his stiffness: "Of course." He held out the jar of brown sugar lumps.

The stranger selected two lumps, taking his time. "Thank you. Very much." He looked at the thickening clouds, then back to Rhalles' face. "Do you think we will have rain?"

"Probably. By tonight." Rhalles had the man's accent now. "Are you visiting from Germany?"

The smile broadened. "My English is still so bad? Yes—from Germany. But not as a visitor. I have come to stay."

Rhalles felt his own smile in place. "Well, I hope we meet with your expectations."

"I am sure you will."

Rhalles finished his coffee and got to his feet. "Nice talking to you."

"It was my pleasure, I assure you."

Jorgen stood there and watched Alexander Rhalles walk away, down O Street. No matter how much you knew about your man, you never really knew him until you had talked with him. It did not necessarily give you anything new in the way of concrete information. But it gave you what you needed more: a *feel* of the man.

Jorgen wrapped his attuned senses around that feel as he watched the figure of Rhalles grow smaller nearing the white-washed brick house. Two hours ago he had received a phone call from the Baltimore contact.

The operation had finally begun.

Jorgen wondered how much longer it would be before Alexander Rhalles found out.

3

It began to come down at four in the afternoon: a hard, steady tropical-swamp rain. But in the tropics you could expect such a rain to spend its force and clear the sky. Here it just kept coming, straight down. The biblical forty days and forty nights, it occurred to Washingtonians, must have begun like this.

The spaces between the clouds continued to fill up. By five they had merged with each other. A single dark gray roof of cloud hung on the city, low and solid. The rain continued to pour out of it.

It brought night to Washington a full hour ahead of schedule. And still showed no hint of letting up at 8:30 P.M., when Beth Wagner drove her old Fiat 850 out of the parking driveway between the White House's West Wing and the E.O.B.—the Executive Office Building. Street lamps and headlights reflected dripping, shattered gems across the drenched windshield as she grimly headed through the downpour toward the reception the President was attending.

She was a dark messenger of death; and she didn't like it. But she didn't flinch from it. Beth Wagner had never flinched from anything in the thirty years she had lived so far. Including the two things she *should* have flinched from: marriage to the handsomest dentist in Washington—and that window overlooking a street fight between Beirut Muslims and Christians on Boulevard Saeb Salam.

"Blue Eye" was her nickname now. Singular. A narrow black patch covered the eye that had been destroyed. She rather liked it, except for the throbbing headache that too often radiated from what was under it. The patch made her look interesting, and made people take her seriously. Which no one had done before it; she'd always been too young-looking and picture-pretty.

That was what had hampered her every attempt to get serious assignments as a newspaperwoman. It had driven her finally, in desperation, to wangle herself to Lebanon to cover the civil war for a string of small Midwestern weeklies, for a price so low they just couldn't resist. Everybody took war correspondents seriously, no matter what they looked like.

She'd been in Beirut less than a week when she'd snuck into the ruined office building on Boulevard Saeb Salam, and made the mistake of showing herself inside that window. Someone among the gangs exchanging submachine-gun fire in the street outside had lobbed a grenade. It had exploded against the wall just above the window. She'd flinched back then, much too late. The upper windowpane had shattered, and a sliver of flying glass had gone deep into her right eye.

It had been during her recuperation period back in Washington that Beth Wagner had begun doing political public relations work. Which had led to her present job: assistant deputy to the White House press secretary. She'd been clearing the last of the day's releases in her superior's ground floor office in the West Wing when the phone call had come in.

It had been from a night duty officer at the State Department, passing on the message just received from the U.S. Embassy in Paris, which had gotten it from the American Consulate in Nice. Beth had sat there quietly for a while after hanging up. She didn't really know Alexander Rhalles; she doubted that anyone did, except perhaps the President, who for some reason doted on him. But she had met his wife several times, and had found her a woman easy to like and impossible not to admire.

Getting her plastic rain hat, coat, and overshoes from her own office in the E.O.B., Beth had headed for the reception. It was buck-passing time. The President would be there. So would his alter ego, behind-the-scenes manipulator and official bastard: Harvey Ross, chief of the White House staff. It was not up to her, after all, to decide who was going to have to give Rhalles the bad news.

The reception was being given by the visiting President of Algeria. His American ambassador had advised him well. If you were going to throw a really big Washington party, Anderson House was the prestige address to do it in. If you could. It required both a lot of money and considerable political weight.

Anderson House was a large, elegant mansion on Massachusetts Avenue in the heart of Embassy Row. Almost every evening the area around it was snarled by embassy functions. Rain made it that much more difficult to get near by car. The fact that the President of the United States was going to be there made it impossible. Screening roadblocks set up by the metropolitan police had traffic backed up in the downpour for several blocks in every direction.

Beth Wagner parked five blocks away and sprinted through the rain, jumping huge puddles with an easy agility.

Anderson House was aglow with festive lights that fought a courageous battle against the night rain. There were patrol cars, police motorcycles, and red-lamped barriers at every intersection around the block. The street out front and the semicircle driveway were jammed with black limousines. The wall under the entrance portico, on both sides of the open doorway, was lined with security men—U.S. and Arab. Incredibly, some of them were still wearing their ritual sunglasses, in spite of night and rain.

Beth joined the tangle of umbrellas under which people were crowding their way under the shelter of the entrance portico. Once out of the rain, everyone became less frantic about it. Umbrellas came down and closed, and men stood politely aside to let women and elder statesmen go in first. Beth stripped off her rain hat and let the water pour from it onto the marble flooring as she entered the wide foyer.

It was crowded with power, and the wives of the powerful. Top foreign diplomats, high-level U.S. government figures. A very exclusive affair; not even the press had been invited. They'd have to be satisfied with a release from Beth's boss, and coverage by White House cameramen. Beth had to admit she still got an involuntary thrill out of this kind of atmosphere. Women, she reflected ruefully, are such suckers for power. No wonder senators and congressmen fought so damn hard to get re-elected. Back home no girl would look at most of them. Washington was the easiest place in the world to get laid—if you had political clout.

There were high arched doorways to the left and right of the foyer. The one to the left led into a mirrored alcove that had been converted into a checkroom. Beth got out of her raincoat as she joined the line entering it. Easing forward with the line, she took off her plastic overshoes by balancing first on one foot, then on the other. Pleased with how well she'd learned to do it. Losing an eye disturbed your sense of balance.

A Secret Service man leaned against the wall on one side of the checkroom entrance; and an Arab bodyguard type leaned against the other side. Both had hearing-aid buttons in one ear and miniature microphone buttons in their lapels. They scanned her briefly as she went in. Then their eyes switched to people in line behind her.

"Keep them handy," Beth told the white-jacketed man behind the checking counter as she left her things. "I won't be staying long." She recrossed the entrance foyer, to the other arched doorway. There was a poem beautifully painted on the wall over the arch:

> Through this Door
> Come and Welcome Be—
> Our friends and guests
> Most cordially

Flanking this archway were *two* men from the Secret Service, and *two* of their Algerian counterparts. Between them a plump young Washington matron sat at a desk holding her pen poised over the list of invited guests. She wore a black chiffon evening gown, a big red corsage, and an expression that showed she was fully aware of the tremendous position of responsbility that had been bestowed upon her.

. "Your invitation, please?"

"I don't have one," Beth told her. "I'm from the White House press office. I have an important message for the President. Urgent."

"I'm afraid you can't . . ."

"That's all right, Marge." It was one of the Secret Service pair who'd spoken up; the shorten one, with the ugly-cheerful pockmarked face. "Blue Eye does look like a lady pirate, but she's on our side."

Beth remembered seeing him around the White House, though she didn't know his name. She gave him a caustic grin. "Thanks, Scarface."

He grinned back.

The woman on the reception desk forced a bright smile. "Well, I suppose if *you* are vouching for her . . ."

"I am. Go on in, Mrs. Wagner."

She entered a huge room with a mob of people standing seven deep to get at a long table loaded with food and liquor. Everybody in Washington loved Arab parties; the food was always sensational and the liquor never ran out. There were probably at least five other tables like this one, at strategic locations all over the house.

The far end of the room opened into another foyer, where Beth saw the end of a two-by-two line of guests waiting with drinks in their hands and expressions of long-suffering patience on the faces. The reception line. It went up the wide stairway, turned where the stairs turned, and vanished into the rooms of the floor above. Somewhere, at the other end of that line, would be the two heads of state and their wives, dutifully performing the heavy labor of shaking hands with every single invited guest. It would take a couple hours.

Beth angled for a door on the other side of the room, heading for a back stairway that would get her to the second floor without having to battle the line. Her path was suddenly blocked by a tall man, extravagantly handsome and beautifully tailored. The Iranian Ambassador.

"Beth, my dear!" His English had just the right touch of accent to add an exotic flavoring. His smile knew it killed women dead. "I sent you an invitation to my last party. *Why* didn't you come?"

"Because you forgot to invite my husband, too."

His parties, of the sort he'd invited her to, were notorious: two women for each man, so the women would be eagerly competing and the men could be choosy. A lot of alcohol and porno films with spiced foods, to loosen everybody up—then into his sauna.

"Why should I invite your husband? I don't have a toothache." His smile widened to show a perfect set of gleaming predatory teeth.

"I think you're *going* to, though," she told him. "That looks like a cavity starting, on the right molar."

He turned automatically to look for a wall mirror. Beth went around him into the next room. Past another pair of security men on the doorway. With the same ear and lapel buttons, and the miniature walkie-talkies and revolvers hidden under their jackets.

The next large room was two stories high, with another crowd around a serving table on the near side of it. On the far side half a dozen couples were dancing to the music of a five-piece orchestra playing on a wide interior balcony. Saxophone, two violins, accordion, and cello. Beth crossed to the open stairway that led up to the balcony. There was another security pair at the foot of the stairs. This time she knew the name of the one from Secret Service.

"Hello, Cherney. I've got to get up there to the President."

"Well, good luck to you, Mrs. Wagner. It's a real mob scene. Take the left door." He nodded to his Arab partner, and she went up the steps between them.

At the top, to the left of the musicians, three closed doors led off the balcony into second-floor rooms. She opened the last one to the left, eased in, and shut the door quietly behind her.

It was a small room, utterly quiet though it was jammed with men, most of them Secret Service and White House staff. Through an open door on the other side of the room she could see the back of the President's wife, with her husband's shoulder visible on one side of her, and a slice of the back of the Algerian president on her other side. They were facing the reception line, which shuffled forward two at a time, paused to murmur and touch hands, and moved on out of sight, regular as a human assembly belt.

Beth focused on the bald head and huge shoulders of the man she wanted now. He was standing just inside the open doorway, back to her, critically observing the progress of the reception line. Harvey Ross, the White House chief of staff, absolute ruler of what went on around the President; who got to him, and who got blessed, stuck, or struck by what came from him. A hard son of a bitch, with a formidable mind and a willpower of steel. He'd earned the dough for law school as a pro football running

who'd found some little statue from caveman times down inside there.

"Another archaeologist was supposed to go in with them. Dr. Borelli. University of Pennsylvania, same as Moira Rhalles. She was part of a team dig in the area, but this cave was something else. Anyway, Professor Borelli got sick at breakfast and wasn't up to it. So he waited outside while they went in. The wait got too long and he began to worry. By then he was feeling better so he went in for a look, but couldn't find them so he went for help. A couple of experienced local spelunkers went in—cave explorers . . ."

"I know what a spelunker is," Ross snapped.

"They found the guide caught in some rocks at the bottom of an underground waterfall. Dead. The way the spelunkers work it out, the three of them must have been roped together, because the guide still had one end of it tied around him and the other end was shredded off. Looks like they were on a narrow ledge and one of them slipped off, dragging the others along by the rope. The guide split his head open in the fall."

"And Moira Rhalles?"

"They couldn't find her. Or the other woman. There's a strong river down there at that point. Dragged them both away, deeper underground. The spelunkers got in a special rescue unit from the French alpine troops to help. With ropes and scuba gear. They explored further along the river, as far as they could go. They found one of Moira Rhalles' boots, stuck between some rocks. And the other woman's smashed camera, further on. But that's all."

"No question they're dead?"

"None at all. Even if getting slammed on the rocks didn't kill them, the river's completely submerged beyond the waterfall. They couldn't have lasted without air as far as the rescue unit got using scuba gear. And beyond that the river goes on for miles underground."

Beth stopped talking. She felt weary, drained. Ross

continued to sit on the edge of the bathtub, an unusual faraway look in his eyes. "I read about a case like that once. A man got caught by an underground river in the north of Spain. Parts of him came out the other end, four months later. But that's unusual. More likely, nothing of Mrs. Rhalles or the other girl'll ever be found."

"What does it matter?" Beth snarled. "The fact is, they're dead."

"Yeah." After another pause, Ross stood up. "Okay."

"What about Rhalles?"

"Like you said, somebody's got to tell him. So I'm elected."

"Thank God. I was scared for a minute I'd be the one stuck with it."

Ross looked at her in surprise. "I'd never load something like this on a woman."

Beth Wagner straightened away from the sink, flaring. "You figure you're the only one in the world with guts, you son of a bitch! Well, you're wrong. Other people can be just as tough as you, when there's a need to be."

"I've heard that before. It never turns out to be true." He opened the bathroom door.

"I'll go with you."

"I don't need anybody to hold my hand."

"Maybe *he* will."

Ross nodded slightly. "There is that."

They went out to the balcony and down the stairs, searching.

SIX

1

There was a large garden area behind Anderson House. The Algerians had covered it with a high, candy-striped tent. Rain drummed steadily on the tenting, making a soothing background noise. Under it the garden remained dry and cozy, warmly lighted by gaily painted oil lanterns and several blazing torches that were regularly renewed by members of the catering staff. Guests radiated from two big groups centering around the serving tables on either side. They mingled in smaller, shifting groups, carrying refilled drinks and plates of food.

Alexander Rhalles was at the moment stuck in a three-man group in one of the far corners. He stood with a half-finished glass in his hand and a growing expression of sardonic resistance on his narrow face. The other two men were the Defense Secretary and the man he had introduced to Rhalles; one of the capital's most powerful influence peddlers, William Valentine, a lobbyist for the military-electronics industry.

"As it stands now," Valentine was saying in his precise, concerned voice, "the armies of Russia and its Warsaw Pact puppets are more than twice as big as ours and our NATO allies. They've got five times more tanks and artillery, double our number of strategic missiles, combat ships and megatonnage . . ."

"And we've got an overwhelming superiority in military aircraft," Rhalles countered. "Both tactical and strategic."

"Yes," Valentine agreed soberly. "That, and our more sophisticated military technology, are our only balancing advantages. If the latter winds up crippled because of this OMB investigation of expenditures for technological experimentation . . ."

"You're wasting your time," Rhalles cut in. "If you want to pressure the President you can do it yourself. I understand you play golf with him often enough. You don't need me to whisper in his ear for you."

Valentine grinned. "Every little extra helps."

"You won't get it from me. I'm not on your side."

The Secretary of Defense was scowling at him. "Does that mean you're *against* American preparedness?"

Rhalles gave him a thin smile. "I'm against people who yell 'preparedness' as an excuse every time they want to siphon more of the people's tax dollars into the pockets of our military-industrial complex. Too much of the country's income is already pouring into pure waste. Your department is as responsible as any for the almost fifty billion dollars spent just for producing and storing federal forms and interoffice memoes. Try cutting down on that paper work, and use what you save for your military toys."

"There is justice in what you say," Valentine acknowledged smoothly. "But there is wasteful paper work in any form of government. That doesn't alter . . ."

"Forget it," Rhalles snapped. "I'm not your man, Mr. Valentine."

"Please—call me Bill. And I'll call you Alex, **if** I may."

"No."

The Defense Secretary gave him a look of disgust. "Aw, come on, don't be such a hard-nosed bastard."

"That's okay," Valentine said blandly. "He thinks I'm too pushy. And I guess I was. Sorry." He started to turn away, suddenly turned back to Rhalles. "By the way, how is the group Mrs. Rhalles is with doing over there with their dig in the Valleé des Merveilles?"

"Suddenly you're interested in archaeology?" Rhalles demanded sarcastically.

"Nothing sudden about it. I took my Master's in archaeology. Did two Mideast digs, spent three months in Yucatan. A long time ago, I'll admit. But I've kept up my interest."

Rhalles was surprised. "I'd have thought you'd have studied economics, or . . ."

"No. Archaeology. Someday perhaps I'll tell you how *that* led to my present criminal activities." Valentine smiled. "You'll find it a strange story. I do, myself." There was the slightest pause. "You know, I'm on the board of the Marsden Foundation. As part of my special interest, I've been responsible for the foundation contributing considerable sums for digs, in Crete and the Persian Gulf area. If your wife has a project of her own she would like to develop and lead, I could check into the possibility of a Marsden grant for it."

Rhalles almost laughed. "You never quit, do you? If you can't get in one door, you try another. The answer stays the same, Mr. Valentine, forget it."

"Perhaps that is a decision your wife would prefer to make for herself?"

"This one I'll make for her, since she's not here. If she has anything going that deserves a grant, she's quite capable of getting it for herself. On merit. Without political strings attached."

"There would be no strings . . ."

"Goodbye, Mr. Valentine." Rhalles drained the rest of his drink, turned on his heel, and stalked toward one of the garden tables for a refill.

Harvey Ross waited until Rhalles had the refill in his hand, then tapped his shoulder.

"I have to talk to you, Alex."

Rhalles turned and looked at him. Ross always used first names; it didn't mean anything. There was a certain grudging mutual respect between them, but they were not fond of each other. Ross was extremely possessive about *his* President. He didn't like anyone having access without going through him. Rhalles had felt his resentment from the start, and responded with a cool, polite reserve.

He gave Ross a bare nod of acknowledgement, and looked at Beth hovering close, looking frightened. "Hello, Mrs. Wagner. What's the matter?"

"We need some privacy first," Ross told him. "Let's go find some." Without waiting for an answer, he turned and headed for the interior of the house.

Rhalles looked questioningly at Beth. She looked away quickly, and went after Ross. Rhalles took a swig from his glass and followed them in, curious.

Ross led the way into a plush, paneled library where several younger couples were sitting it out on the sofas under the built-in bookcases. There was a side door leading to a narrow flight of steps. At the top, Ross led them into a very small, bare room, with a tiny window looking down on the room where the musicians were playing on the balcony. The rumor was that the original Mr. Anderson had used this room as a secret place from which to peek down on his guests.

Ross leaned against one wall and shot Beth a look. She closed the door and put her back to it, both hands locked behind her.

"What *is* it?" Rhalles asked, worried now. The first wild thought was that the President had had a heart attack.

Ross told him. He told it simply and straight, almost word for word as Beth had told him. Without any double-talk or softening phrases. At one point he reached and took the glass out of Rhalles' hand. Rhalles didn't notice.

He heard Ross out without a word. When it was finished, there was a moment's silence. Then Rhalles said quietly: "I've got to get over there. She's not dead."

Beth Wagner's single eye filled with tears.

Ross said harshly: "Yes she is, Alex. You've got to accept that. They'll probably never find her body. But there's absolutely no possibility of her surviving down there. Do you understand what I'm telling you?"

There was another short silence. Rhalles looked at his hands, as if searching for something, then lowered them. "Yes, of course I understand." His voice was steady. "And thank you for telling me. I imagine it was difficult for you."

Ross stared at him, startled by the lack of emotional response. "I'll get someone to drive you home," he said slowly. "And some sleeping pills. You'll need them tonight."

"No. I don't need anything." Rhalles turned his frozen face toward Beth. "I have to go now."

She moved out of his path. He opened the door and went through it. She looked at Ross. "That was even worse than if he'd broken down and started crying . . ."

Ross was frowning to himself. "Yeah. Delayed reaction, I guess."

He still didn't get it. But those who had known Rhalles before Moira would have understood; he was once more "the iceberg."

With a difference. Far below the surface, out of sight and out of contact with any other human being, now that Moira was dead, that complex submerged part of him was breaking apart.

Beth Wagner didn't know anything about that. But she sensed something that made her turn suddenly and hurry out after Rhalles.

She caught up with him down in the entrance foyer, grabbing his arm to stop him. "Wait a second till I get my things."

He stared at her, his eyes blind behind the thick lenses. "What?"

"I'm going home with you. You can't be alone tonight."

Rhalles shook her hand from his arm. "Leave me alone." Each word struck her like a hard, cold whiplash. She fell back a step, involuntarily, shocked.

He walked out into the night rain.

His car was three blocks from Anderson House. He got in and drove to Georgetown. Stopping at the house only long enough to get his passport. He didn't have much cash. The credit cards would have to carry him. He called a taxi, had it take him out to Dulles International, and used a credit card to book a seat on the next plane to France. Boarding was in half an hour. The man at the Air France counter told him he was lucky there was a place free.

A tall man with broad shoulders and bleak eyes came in while Rhalles' ticket was still being filled out. He listened a moment, then went to a payphone and made a call. When he came back, Rhalles was leaving the Air France counter.

"Mr. Rhalles, just a minute. Harvey Ross sent me after you, to make sure you were all right. Your taxi was pulling away just as I reached your house . . ."

Rhalles stared at him though he didn't quite hear or understand.

"I'm sorry, about your wife. I know what it's like. Lost my kid brother in Nam. Saw my buddies killed in Korea. Nothing anybody can say, I know that."

Still Rhalles did not speak.

"I just made a call," the man said slowly, hoping some of it was sinking in. "State'll get on the horn to Paris. There'll be somebody to meet you when you get off the plane. I'm to tell you: anything you need, you just ask."

"Thank you." Rhalles turned away stiffly and walked in the direction of the departure gates.

The man watching him go remembered others he'd seen look and move like that. In Korea, during the long, bloody retreat from the shock waves of the Chinese assault. He'd probably been walking like that himself, at the end, because he had no conscious memories at all of the last few days of it.

2

Alexander Rhalles came back six days later. But not to Washington. He took the Nice-Paris-New York flight. By then he had absorbed and understood it. She was dead.

He sat rigidly in a window seat on the right side of the 747, looking down at a vast white sea of clouds that covered southeastern France as the plane winged north from Nice. Suddenly, the fantastic grandeur of the Alps reared upward out of the cloud blanket ahead to the right, with pale silvery-blue mists filling the long high valleys between the white-peaked ridges.

Moira was down there under those mountains, somewhere deep in the bowels of the earth. There hadn't even been a grave to look at. And her epitaph had been written by Coleridge out of a drugged dream, long ago: In caverns measureless to man, where a river runs down to a sunless sea. He couldn't get rid of the image.

The Alps were gone, left behind by the speed of the plane's flight. The cloud cover below gave way to flocks of individual clouds, each round and puffy, revealing glimpses of the land under them: farms, highways, gently wooded hills, clusters of houses. Dazzling golden flashes appeared and vanished in the light ground mists as the moving plane caught and lost reflections of sun off river surfaces.

His rage was enormous. Thank God it was not his thumb on the doomsday button. He would have killed the world, for Moira.

Let it die with her.

After Paris the cloud flocks vanished, absorbed into long, solid banks of high mist that sucked much of the blue out of the sky, leaving it pale, anemic. Once into the mist, it proved thinner than it had appeared at a distance. The browns and greens of the land below could be seen, cut by winding black rivers, with tiny tiled roofs grouped around the points where long roads crossed each other at precise right angles.

Just a stupid accident—and it was all over. A pointless, reasonless, meaningless thing. Just like that. He thought of her body, being torn and battered forever by the waters and rocks down inside those dark depths.

The mist thinned away after the coast of Ireland was left behind. From the height of the jet the surface of the Atlantic Ocean looked like hammered pewter under the strong postnoon sun. There were tiny balls of cloud that seemed pasted to that pewter surface, except for the shadow almost hidden under each one. As the afternoon wore on, each cloud moved steadily away from its shadow. Finally it required some thought to recognize a cause-and-effect relationship between the two.

He'd relished the power she'd given him over her.

"You smell like my father," she told him once.

"That's one lousy reason to fall in love with a man."

"And probably not true. How do I know why you turn me on like this? It's a matter of *skin;* of feel. You excite me because you're dangerously weird. And at the same time you make me feel emotionally secure. A woman doesn't have real orgasms unless she gets that rare combination. It's as simple as that— maybe."

"And maybe you are even weirder than you claim I am. Dangerously exciting security—that's a combination for you."

"Just put that hand back where it belongs, baby, and don't talk so much. Or you might talk it out of existence. And that really scares me."

"And this—does this scare you?"

"Oh, yes it does. Please, sir, may I have more?"

The plane was angling down over Massachusetts Bay toward New York. The surface of the Atlantic had changed dramatically. It was wind-churned into big patches of dark greens and blacks, with wide slashes of white froth. Low clouds were being torn to shreds by the same winds. The plane bucked its way through on the downward flight path to Kennedy Airport, Long Island.

The connecting flight to Philadelphia went through a dull gray overcast that dirtied the colors of the land beneath. Alexander Rhalles stared from the window feeling disconnected. From the world, from life, from people. And most of all, from himself.

It had taken her a while to establish links inside him, from one compartment to another. Now they were severed beyond repair. It was worse than before Moira. Because now he knew what he had lost.

3

The farm was west of Philadelphia; twenty acres of the rich soil of Pennsylvania Dutch country. Chickens, rabbits, a milk cow, and four goats, a basic vegetable patch, a cornfield, and plenty of fruit trees. Not too much for Rhalles' brother, Nick, to manage; more than enough for him to live on.

For the two of them, from now on. Alexander Rhalles could not envision leaving it again. There was nothing out there he wanted anymore.

Nick was two years younger than Rhalles and physically much like him: tall, skinny, much stronger than he looked. He was retarded. Different specialists had pinpointed his mental age at differing figures; pick a number between eight and ten. But he was kindhearted and a good worker. He didn't talk much, but listened well. All that had been necessary was patience in teaching him how to get along in a basic life this close to nature. He'd learned well enough to keep the farm in good shape, and earn his own way.

Alexander Rhalles had brought Moira there, two weeks after they'd begun seeing each other. The farm, with its memories, was a key to what he was. And he'd known that she and Nick would like each other.

He told Nick what had happened to her, when he reached the farm from the airport that evening. There was no one else he *could* have talked to about it. Nick wept for a long time, as they sat there in the big kitchen holding each other. Later, that night, he heard Nick crying again, in the next bedroom.

But Alexander Rhalles did not cry. Hadn't, since he had been told what had happened. Couldn't. There was something crouched tight inside him, waiting. He didn't know what it was waiting for: to cry, or break.

In the morning, Nick's eyes were red and swollen. He watched silently as his older brother took the first turn at making breakfast for them; the kind of big breakfast he never ate in the city. After breakfast Nick stood up and gripped his shoulders, looking into his eyes. Then he went outside to begin the day's work.

Alexander Rhalles washed the dishes, and then strolled to the far end of the farm. He climbed a low hill and stretched out on his back in the high grass under the shade of a cherry tree. Linking his hands under his head, he gazed up at the branches and leaves, with the sky beyond. Smelling the old smells of earth, vegetation and distant animals. Aware of his brother at work unseen back near the small barn. Just as he was sure Nick was aware of him, and where he was.

They'd been close since the three years when Rhalles had spent all his time here, not going to school. From the time he'd been twelve until he was fifteen.

He'd skipped three grades before that, and had

been in a class of students three years older than he, when the hygiene teacher had shown those colored slides of what venereal disease could do to a person. As an object lesson about the fruits of sex before marriage. Rhalles had hit the floor in a dead faint. And been sick for a month afterwards. The doctor had insisted he be kept from school until he could rejoin with his own age group, and forget about his being a genius.

That was one of the memories that had always shamed him, until he'd shared it with Moira. Now it was just something that had happened to him.

Another was when he'd been nineteen, and suddenly realized his full strength. His father had been at it again: drunk and slapping Nick around. Rhalles had knocked his father down the basement steps. Followed him down and stamped him. Breaking his arm and two ribs and some teeth.

His father didn't hit anybody again from then until he died ten years later, of mean old age. Nick had watched, not saying anything. Whatever he'd felt or thought stayed inside him. Their mother hadn't been around when it happened. As usual, she'd been in her apartment in the city, where she paid a succession of young boy friends to live with her for varying periods.

She'd been thirty-three years younger than her husband. Rhalles had seen a photograph of her taken at the time her brother had imported her from Greece, as a bride for the owner of the restaurant he worked in. She'd been sixteen and exotically beautiful. And she had hated her enforced husband on first sight. In response to which, once he got over the delight of having a gorgeous young thing in his bed, he quickly learned to hate her back.

He'd bought the farm as a place to stick her, with the kids. So he could run his restaurant in peace, without having to face her every day. But he was the one who wound up living there most of the time, after he'd retired. While she moved back to the city. To die young, of liquor and pills and a rheumatic heart.

It was all part of him. So he had shared it with Moira, along with the rest of him. Just as she had shared all of herself with him.

Now only Nick was left.

He heard, without curiosity, the sound of a car coming along the dirt road that curved past that end of the farm.

It stopped close to the bottom of the hill where he lay. Rhalles raised up on one elbow and turned slightly to look down. A strongly built man with sparse white hair was climbing over the split-rail fence. Behind him was the parked car. Rhalles sat up and pushed his glasses higher on the bridge of his nose, squinting through them as the man jumped down on his side of the fence, inside the farm.

Jorgen looked up the hill, and saw Rhalles in the shade of the tree. He started up the hill toward him.

Rhalles realized then why the man looked familiar. He slowly stood up. Suddenly understanding, with absolute clarity, what the crouched thing inside him had been waiting for.

Jorgen came to a stop a few feet away from him. There was a cassette player hanging from one shoulder on a strap. His hands hung at his sides, tensed fingers slightly curled. "Your brother told me where to find you." His eyes watched Rhalles' face carefully. He spread his legs a bit more, automatically, ready to move quickly if it became necessary. "I think you recognize me."

"Yes." Rhalles took a quick breath. The smell of crushed grass was strong on his clothes.

"I bring you very good news, Mr. Rhalles. But it will also be a great shock. Please sit down."

Rhalles did not move. He was squinting at Jorgen.

His face was pale, the skin stretched taut over the sharp bones.

Jorgen made a small sound that could have been a sigh or merely an indrawn breath. "Your wife is alive, Mr. Rhalles. And quite well. This is the truth. I have brought proof for you."

Rhalles almost lost his balance. With one hand he groped just above his head and seized hold of a branch of the cherry tree. He hung onto it, waiting for the dizziness to subside. His eyes remained fastened on Jorgen's face.

"Your wife has not been harmed in any way," Jorgen continued. "Nor will she be. *If* you do exactly as I tell you. Starting now. Please sit down."

Rhalles let go of the branch and put his hand against the trunk of the tree. Slowly, he lowered himself to the grass, still watching the other man.

Jorgen remained standing. He unslung the cassette player from his shoulder and swung it down to Rhalles. "Press the button marked Play. Firmly."

Rhalles braced the machine on one knee. He was surprised to see that his hands were not trembling. With his thumb, he depressed the button, starting the tape.

There was a sound like distant static. Then the voice of Moira: "Hello, Alex . . . Don't worry, I'm okay . . . I know it's hard to believe, but I *am* . . . These people want me to tell you . . . Nothing will happen to me, if you do what you are told."

Moira's voice ended and the faint sound of static took over again. Rhalles continued to hold the machine, listening, waiting.

"There is no more," Jorgen told him. "The rest of the cassette contains nothing further. Stop it and listen to me now."

Rhalles depressed the Stop button. He raised his head and looked up at Jorgen. His mouth was partially open, his breathing shallow.

Jorgen read his expression. "Should you be tempted to do something foolish," he said quickly and firmly, "I will tell you immediately that *I* do not know where your wife is. Nor do I have any direct contact with the people who are holding her. I do not even know who they are. So no foolishness; no tricks—if you ever want to see your wife again, alive. She is a hostage, to ensure that you will co-operate with me. For *her* sake, your co-operation must begin at once. Now. You must do what I tell you, please understand that."

The two men looked at each other, Jorgen giving Rhalles time to absorb what was happening, and adjust his thinking to it.

Rhalles cradled the cassette player gently in both hands, raising it slightly from his knee. He looked at it, then back up at Jorgen. Behind the thick lenses, his eyes had a peculiar shine. "It could have been faked."

Jorgen shook his head. "You know her voice."

"It could have been taped before they killed her," Rhalles pointed out softly. "She could still be dead."

But he knew it wasn't so. She was alive.

"It was anticipated that you would want further proof," Jorgen told him. "I will have this proof, when we meet again, in a few days. Another cassette, on which your wife will tell a bit of the news of the day. Proving that she is recording it *now*. Such proof will continue to be delivered to you after that. Once each week. Proof that she remains alive and unhurt, as long as you co-operate with me."

Rhalles looked again at the cassette machine he was holding. Joy swept him like a cooling wind. He laughed softly. There was no hysteria in it; only pleasure. Jorgen, watching him closely, finally allowed his nerves to relax a bit. He lowered himself to the grass near Rhalles, in the shade of the tree.

"I am glad to be the bringer of such happiness," he said, quite sincerely. "It hasn't happened often in my life."

Rhalles leaned his shoulders against the trunk of the tree. His smile was brittle, but it was there. "I'll bet it hasn't. Who are you working for? East Germany, or the Soviet Union directly?"

"Neither. This is strictly a private enterprise. For profit. The people who engineered it naturally expect to sell the results. To whom, I do not know. Perhaps to whoever bids the most for it. All I know is my own part, with you. As I've said, I don't even have any connection with the people whose part concerns your wife. Except emotionally, of course. My life, as well as your wife's, is now in your hands."

"A private enterprise? I don't believe that, you know."

Jorgen shrugged. "It will hold up, if I am arrested. It doesn't matter if you believe it. You do believe your wife is alive. She will stay alive . . . it is up to you."

Rhalles gestured with the cassette player. "It'll take more than hearing her voice occasionally to make me co-operate. I have to see her—*see* that she's all right."

"Quite impossible."

"It'll have to be arranged," Rhalles said firmly. "Or I won't co-operate."

"Yes you will," Jorgen replied just as firmly. 'You will know she is well, because she will tell you so. Once each week, on cassettes. And you *will* co-operate, because that way you know that eventually she will be returned to you. Alive and unhurt."

"When?"

"In less than two years. When the present President ends his term in office. And you consequently cease being in a position to acquire the kind of information my employers want."

"Exactly what do they want?"

"A regular report, at least several a week—day by day when possible—detailing *everything* the President of your country is planning, considering, or even just idly thinking about foreign affairs."

101

"I won't do it." Rhalles heard the lack of conviction in his voice.

But Jorgen appeared to accept the statement at face value, for the moment. "In that case," he said heavily, "I am a dead man. Worse than dead. You will inform certain people in your government. They will seize me when I make my next contact with you. I'll be screaming and praying for death before they finish with me. But, they won't get any *proof* of who I really am or who I work for, to back up what I'll undoubtedly babble before they kill me. And—more important for you—I won't tell them where your wife is or who has her. Because I don't *know*."

Jorgen paused, with perspiration gleaming on his face. He took out a fold-pressed white handkerchief and dabbed at it. He looked into Rhalles' eyes, and there was no doubting his sincerity. "It will be terrible for me," he resumed softly. "I know the techniques used for extracting desperately needed information. By your people and mine. In the end, if I am not dead from mistreatment, I will be reduced to less than a vegetable. But, long before that, your wife will have been killed. Perhaps, not pleasantly."

He paused again, and this time when he resumed his voice was harsh: "And it will be your fault. No one else's. You are now totally responsible, Mr. Rhalles, for whether your wife lives or dies."

The silence lasted perhaps half a minute. Jorgen waited, tensely. Finally, Rhalles nodded. "All right. I've got the picture."

Jorgen could detect no trace of bitterness in the way he said it. Only matter-of-fact acknowledgment. For some reason, that worried Jorgen. But he didn't show it. "Good. After all, loved ones have been separated for much longer periods by wars, jobs . . . Your President has already served half of his final term in office. Two years is not long to wait, when you know you will then be reunited with your wife."

"You're quite certain of that." Again it sounded matter-of-fact.

"Why not? No one will ever be able to prove who the people were who kept her. And it will be in your interest never to speak of it. To embrace a pretext, perhaps: she was washed out of the underground river, found by someone, but suffering from amnesia. A hospital record can easily be faked to back that up. Or you may prefer to rejoin your wife secretly in another country. In any case, you *will* be together again —in less than two years."

"But suppose I can't keep it up that long, even if I try?" Rhalles realized he was only going through the motions. He already knew what he was going to have to do. "Suppose, for example, I have a nervous breakdown under the pressure."

"If that should happen," Jorgen told him somberly, "your wife would be killed immediately. My employers want me to make certain you understand this: If you get sick . . . If you are hit by an automobile . . . If the President of the United States becomes dissatisfied with you and dismisses you . . . No matter what the reason, if you cease being his adviser before he ends his term in office, you will have killed your wife. You will also kill her if you fake information you pass on to me, or leave anything out. You are not my employers' only source. They would be certain to find out, eventually."

"There's another possibility," Rhalles pointed out. "Some branch of our intelligence community may get onto it eventually, through some error by *your* people. Or by accident, through no fault of mine."

Jorgen said flatly: "We would have to assume it was the result of a tip from you. Please, accept what I have said. If I am seized, or if you die—no matter *what* the reason—the day information stops flowing from you through me, the life of Mrs. Rhalles will come to an end."

In spite of himself, Rhalles felt rage building inside him. Jorgen saw it, and moved quickly to soothe it: he leaned forward slightly, both hands spreading, palms turned toward Rhalles in an oddly supplicating gesture.

"*Please* . . ." Jorgen's voice was low, persuasive, and troubled. ". . . Don't think of me as your enemy. I am not. We are *together* in this—you, I, your wife. Our interests are the same. I am not the originator of this. I am as much its victim as you or your wife. The three of us will suffer if something goes wrong. We must work together, to ensure that nothing does."

Rhalles remained silent for a few moments, getting himself under control. Then he nodded slightly. "All right." His voice had no shade of meaning in it at all.

Jorgen rose to his feet. "You need time to think about it. I will contact you again, in a few days. With a new cassette from your wife." He gestured at the cassette player. "Keep it. You will need it, if you decide to help. If you decide otherwise, none of us will have any further use for it."

He walked back down the low hill. Rhalles sat against the tree watching him climb the fence and get back into the car. He continued watching as the car backed, turned, and headed away along the dirt road, churning dust behind it.

Then he pressed the rewind switch of the machine he was holding. When the rewind clicked to a stop, he depressed the Play button.

Moira's voice came through again: "Hello, Alex . . . Don't worry, I'm okay . . . I know it's hard to believe, but I *am* . . . These people want me to tell you . . . Nothing will happen to me, if you do what you are told."

Rhalles snapped off the machine. He already knew what he was going to do. Between committing treason to his country and keeping Moira alive, there was no contest. None at all. A nation was an abstract concept for which individual human beings were asked to sacrifice their lives. Not this time. Not Moira.

Two thousand years had passed since the gods decreed that the war fleet of Greece could not sail against Troy unless Agamemnon sacrificed his daughter. Patriotism had dictated his choice. He had killed his daughter so that his nation could win its war against its enemy. And nothing was left of that victory, except the horror of Agamemnon's decision, shrieking unforgotten through the corridors of history.

Rhalles would do what they wanted of him. Playing it tame and obedient. Holding back the rage, waiting. But not forever. Not for two years.

The chance for a countermove would come, of that he was quite certain. But first he must wait. For a signal—a sign of some kind.

And it could only come from Moira.

SEVEN

1

Something jolted her out of sleep. Dream or reality, it was gone before she was fully awake and could identify it. She lay there and concentrated, searching her mind, trying to find what it had been. For some reason it was important that she remember.

The thick walls of the room in which they kept her were of stone. Hand-chiseled blocks of varying sizes and uneven shapes, set one into the other with remarkable craftsmanship. After so many centuries there were still no cracks large enough to let light through. The sides of the stone blocks facing into the room had been left rough-hacked, the way they'd come from the quarry.

The stone flooring was likewise rough, pitted with age and shined in places by the pacing of prisoners over hundreds of years. Moira already knew the room intimately enough to pace it back and forth with her eyes shut: five steps in one direction, four in the other.

The ceiling was of similar stones, cut in wedge shapes to form a barrel vault. The pull of gravity and the angles of the wedging had held the vault solidly in position for some eight hundred years. So far Moira had been unable to come up with any method of burrowing through that solidity to freedom.

She had been unconscious when they had brought her here. Since regaining consciousness, she had seen nothing else of the building in which she was held prisoner. Only this room. It seemed to be a part of a square tower. Judging by the erosion of the stones, it was very old. The basic construction techniques narrowed down to somewhere between the tenth and twelfth centuries.

The heavy oak door, locked from the outside by slide bolts and reinforced by thick iron bands, was more recent: sixteenth or seventeenth century, Moira had decided.

The single window, which pierced the four-foot thickness of the outer wall, was narrow, with a Saracen arch. The iron bars across it were rusted but immovable; she had tested them the first night. The window gave a view, across an open space of about two hundred yards, of a steep, densely wooded hillslope. The thickness of the wall around the window opening made it impossible for her to get a sufficient angle of vision to see above that slope, or to either side of it.

Early on her second morning in this cell, she had stood the bed on end against the wall next to the window. She had used it as a ladder, to get as high as possible and look sharply downward through the window, trying to see what lay below, between the tower and the slope. That had gained her a view of only one thing: the corner of another old stone building, a bit below and to the left of her tower window.

Set into that corner was a thick, badly eroded stone column. A tall figure had been carved out of much of the column. The head and arms had been lost long ago. All that remained were the long, flowing stone draperies of the figure's gown. These had been chiseled simply but with great delicacy. One fold was edged with a remnant of what looked like a Westernized adaptation of Byzantine decoration.

Moira's educated guess was that she was in part of a fortress-castle dating back to the eleventh century. But relatively modern touches had been added inside her room. In one corner a circa 1920s flush toilet and sink with cold running water had been installed; the pipes imbedded in the stone wall behind them. There was a heavy old-fashioned bureau with three drawers, topped by a wood-framed mirror. And the mattress on which she lay was fairly new, resting on a steel-spring web fastened to a simple iron frame.

There was also a single shielded electric light, sunk in the ceiling vault and protected by a small basket of thick iron wires. It was controlled from outside the room; and it was out now.

Moira lay in darkness, waiting for dawn to show at the barred window, trying to remember what it was that had wakened her. Something real—or a dream? Or a combination of the two? Moira remembered something from her childhood that had been like that: part real, part dream. She was still uncertain where one ended and the other began.

She was ten or eleven. Next to Aunt Clara's place was a boarded-up house inside a small, overgrown walled estate. Late one afternoon she climbed over the wall to sneak a look inside. Lying almost hidden among the tall weeds lay an armless statue of a nude man.

The discovery especially excited her because she'd just read an old biography of Heinrich Heine. As a young boy, Heine had found a fallen statue of a female nude in almost exactly the same circumstances. In the moonlight, he'd lain with his arms around the statue, his face pressed against its stone breasts.

That night Moira slipped out of her bedroom and made her way to *her* statue. She stretched out on the ground under the moonlight and put her arms around it. After a time, the statue grew arms which wrapped themselves around her.

That part, of course, was a dream. But the rest of it? She had found the statue, of that Moira was certain. But had she really gone to it in the night, or was that only a transposition from Heine's story? It was never quite clear.

Much later in life she told the story to one of her lovers, because his name reminded her of it. Everyone in Chicago, where she'd gone for her first four years of college, knew him as Peter. Some called him Pete; though not many, because he was choosy about letting anyone get that close to him. But his mother was French and had actually named him Pierre-Ange.

That could be translated as Stone Angel. It fitted, so she called him that, as long as their affair lasted. Which wasn't long. He was part of her period of getting involved with lovers that didn't last. Not their fault; probably hers. She went after them for the wrong reasons: the thrill of chase and conquest, and the attendant sexual excitement. Which regrettably diminished with repetition.

Until Alex.

She'd gone after Alex for the same reasons, while she'd been a graduate student in his ancient history class at the University of Pennsyslvania. Most of the students called him the iceberg, or the monk. Other girls had tried, and failed. The challenge was too tempting to resist.

He hadn't been easy. But she'd won—and gotten more than she'd bargained for: the unleashed passions of a man who'd kept his fantasies locked inside him for far too long. With Alex, it kept getting better with time.

Of course there were periods in which their love-making became more pleasantly relaxed than excitingly imaginative. But then, suddenly, there'd be a wild surge of rediscovery, and it would all start over again, like in the beginning. Incredible, after so long with him. And nobody else. Because she no longer needed anybody else.

Lovely Alex . . .

But damn him, for getting her into this mess.

Her captors refused to say anything about why she was being held here—wherever *here* was. But Moira didn't need to be told to know that it had to be somehow the result of Alex taking on the position of presidential adviser.

What had wakened her? Her mind kept returning to that as she lay there in the dark, waiting for dawn. The two blankets covering her were enough to keep out the dry cold of night. She even had clean sheets and a comfortable pillow. So far, her captors had treated her well.

There were the two of them that she knew of, though she had a feeling there might be others who didn't show themselves. The two she knew were the men from the cave. The younger one said his name was Bruno. The older one was called Lorenz. They obviously regarded her as a valuable object, to be preserved in the best possible physical condition and spirits, under the circumstances. So far she had been careful to do nothing that would provoke them into a change of attitude.

But she was going to have to, soon. It wouldn't be pleasant, but it had to be tried. Afterwards, if she came through it intact, she could return to acting docile.

With one hand, Moira idly caressed the rough stones of the wall beside her bed. Her mind drifted, to Alex. Deep longing for him surged in her, bringing with it anxiety and the knowledge of what he must be suffering.

Sternly, she forced these feelings away from her. She couldn't afford to think of anything that would soften or muddle her judgment. She wanted to survive. For that she had to stay tough, alert, clever. Working out everything she said or did with cool forethought.

When very young, Moira had been fascinated by one of the books she'd found in her Aunt Clara's library. It was about salt-water fish. One in particular had excited her imagination: the blowfish. A relatively peaceful, harmless sea creature, except when attacked. Then it blew itself up into a round ball, from which it protruded dozens of sharply pointed spines.

Even sharks were afraid to attack an inflated blowfish. They ate only those they managed to catch asleep. Even then, unless they killed the blowfish first, they regretted their meal. For, once swallowed, the blowfish woke up and inflated themselves. The projecting spines made it impossible for the shark to digest them. Fishermen cutting open sharks they'd caught had occasionally found inflated blowfish still floating alive inside the sharks' sorely lacerated stomachs. There were even instances of swallowed blowfish patiently eating their way out through the belly of a shark. Escaping, and in the process killing the enemy that had eaten them.

Be a blowfish, Moira told herself viciously.

And suddenly it came to her—what had wakened her.

It had been a distant sound: a police or ambulance siren. But of a specific kind, an urgent up-and-down "pan-pon" wailing. And there was only one country in which she had ever heard that particular kind of siren: in France.

Moira lay rigid on the bed in the darkness, considering it carefully, anxiously. Yes, she was sure of it. That was what had wakened her, entering a compartment of her mind that had been waiting for some confirming sign. But—had it really come from the distance *outside?* Or from inside; from a dream born of trying so constantly to find out exactly where she was?

She continued to lie there in the dark, all of her concentrated. Only her hand moved, feeling the shallow mason's mark cut in one of the blocks of stone above her bed. Her fingers traced its outline as she put together the bits of information she'd been hoarding since she'd first regained consciousness in this cell.

Her watch had been taken, and neither Bruno nor

Lorenz would respond when she'd asked what day it was. Just as they didn't answer when she asked if they'd killed Christine, as they'd killed Gaspard Martinot. So there'd been no way to know how much time had elapsed since she'd been chloroformed inside the cave. It could have been several days, if they'd continued to administer further doses of sedative. In that amount of time, they could have moved her to any part of the world.

But she was not in *any* part of the world. She was in one definite place. While part of her mind had been occupied in seeking some method of eventual escape, the rest had been working steadily on the problem of narrowing down *where* they had brought her.

The architecture of the tower, together with the sculpture of the column figure she'd glimpsed outside, meant to Moira that she was still somewhere in Western Europe. The days were too warm for it to be far north; and the nights too cool for the far south. Somewhere in between, then. The north of Italy, Yugoslavia, or Spain. Parts of Austria, southern Switzerland, or southern Germany. Or the lower half of France.

Bruno and Lorenz always spoke German between themselves. But Moira was quite sure she was not in any part of Germany. Lorenz knew a little French, in addition to German. Bruno pretended to know no French at all; and when Moira could not understand his German he shifted to English. But he had a slight accent in the first, and a heavy one in the latter. The accent, Moira was fairly certain, was French.

There were two other indications that she was not in Germany: fireflies and singing frogs.

Every night thousands of frogs had endlessly croaked their chorus in the countryside beyond her tower. And each night she had watched the glowing of innumerable fireflies blinking on and off outside her window.

Fireflies had practically become extinct in Germany for years; and so had the "singing" variety of frogs.

Both for the same reason: continuing overuse of DDT and related insecticides. The same was true of the farm areas of much of Europe. She wasn't sure about Austria or Spain. But in France that variety of frog had never died out; and fireflies had returned some years after the use of DDT was curbed.

So—she had narrowed where she was down to France, northern Spain, or Austria.

The "pan-pon" siren that had wakened her eliminated Spain and Austria. Unless the sound had been part of a dream. She could still not be certain, no matter how much she thought about it. All she could do now was to pray for some new piece of evidence to come along to confirm that she was in France, before she had to use it.

Because whether it was confirmed or not, she was soon going to be forced to wager her life on the assumption that it was correct.

2

About an hour after dawn Moira heard a car approaching outside. It stopped somewhere not far from the bottom of her tower. By then Moira had done her first half hour of exercises for the day, something she was careful not to let her captors know about. She had washed thoroughly, and dressed, in the clothes she'd been given, to alternate with the ones she'd worn when she'd entered the cave. While she wore one set of clothing, the other was taken away to be laundered. There was a German label in the blouse they'd had ready for her. The rest—slacks, socks, underwear, pullover—had nothing to indicate where they came from.

As she waited for her breakfast, she stood at the window. The bottom was exactly the height of her chin. She looked across at the slope, trying to read something useful there. But she had tried that before, without result. The trees over there were the kinds found in many parts of Europe; there was nothing special.

The slide bolts on the outside of her door clanked open. Moira turned from the window. Her stomach knotted when Bruno stepped inside. He was carrying her breakfast on a tray; but he also had a small cassette machine.

The time had come.

She forced herself not to look at the machine as she took the tray from him. Sitting down on the edge of the bed, she balanced the tray on her lap. "I could use a table and chair in here," she grumbled.

Bruno nodded but did not speak. He stood there by the door, his stocky figure planted securely on short, slightly spread legs. His wide-boned face had an ingrained bitterness. The pale gray eyes watched her with a certain superficial interest, as they might have watched a fly on the wall. There was a peculiar lack of depth in his eyes, and no trace of humor. But that did not delude Moira into underestimating the intelligence behind them. A hard, practical breed of intelligence, she judged; well co-ordinated with the rest of him.

There was a quiet, deadly self-assurance about everything he did: the way he moved, the way he spoke. A man used to dealing in violence and intrigue, with a lethal capability waiting inside the abnormal self-control.

Moira had to force herself to eat, though it was all good: eggs, ham, homemade bread, coffee with milk. Usually he left her to eat alone. This time he stayed there, waiting. She remained intensely aware of the cassette machine.

Be a blowfish, she reminded herself fiercely.

One thing in her favor: they couldn't kill her as long as they needed her. That was her equivalent of the sharp spines of the blowfish. These human sharks had swallowed her, but they couldn't digest her, not yet.

Stay alive and stay afloat, she told herself desperately.

Eat your way out.

"Another thing I need," she told him, "is to be allowed outside for some exercise. I'll get sick if you keep me shut up in here all the time."

"You should do setting-up exercises in here," Bruno pointed out, in German. He had a deep, rasping voice.

Moira made an impatient gesture. "Please, talk English. It's too early in the morning for me to figure out your German."

Bruno repeated himself, slowly and awkwardly, in English. The accent *was* French. She was sure of it.

Almost sure.

"I need some sun on me," she said, trying to draw him out. "And books—I'll go crazy with nothing to do all day."

"The books—I will try."

It wasn't enough. She needed to hear more. "That odd patch on your cheek, is it a birthmark?"

He didn't answer. Instead he told her, in German: "Finish your breakfast."

"What?"

"You understand me. Your German is good enough, I know that."

"I don't understand you," Moira insisted irritably.

"Finish your breakfast," he repeated in German.

Moira gave it up, letting the deliberately induced anger well up in her to counteract the growing fear. She slammed the tray down on the floor, upsetting the cup and spilling coffee. "I can't eat with you standing there staring at me all the time, dammit!"

Unperturbed, Bruno placed the cassette machine on the bureau and took a piece of paper from his pocket. "You have to speak to your husband now. Just read aloud what is written here. Word for word, the way you did before."

It required an effort of willpower for Moira to stand up. Her legs were shaky. She took the paper from his hand.

On it was printed: "Hello, Alex. That was a terrible plane crash in Florida yesterday. Eleven people dead. Remember, I'll be all right if you just do what they tell you to."

Moira slowly crumpled the paper in her fist, then spread her fingers and let it fall to the floor. Her dark eyes had acquired a hard shine that made them difficult to read.

"I won't do it." Her voice was quiet, but as hard as her eyes.

Bruno was surprised. There'd been nothing to prepare him for this. She had obediently taped the first cassette, with no trouble at all. Clearly wanting to survive, and understanding that her fate was in their hands. He'd come to regard her as an unusually sensible woman, until this moment.

"Don't be foolish," he told her, the German words slow and calm. "You have no choice."

Moira stuck to English: "I've just *made* a choice. You're not going to use me to destroy my husband."

"I am not doing *anything* to your husband. I do not even know who he is. All I know are my orders, which concern you alone." He gestured at the cassette machine.

She had the feeling he was telling the truth. But that altered nothing. She shook her head. "No." Total defiance was concentrated in the single word. He was right, she knew: what she was doing *was* foolish. Unless it achieved its purpose. If not, it was worse than foolish.

He was scowling at her, but there was no threat in it, only irritation. "I thought you were different." He was genuinely disappointed in her. "But you are like all women, after all. Everything must be explained to you, in words. Very well: if you do not obey, we

116

will have to hurt you. As much as is necessary to force obedience from you."

"But you have to be careful about that." She didn't like the way her voice trembled. "Hurt me too much and I could have a heart attack. Dead I'm no use to you."

"I know how to hurt people without killing them," he told her impatiently. "I will not like having to use that experience on you. But that will not make your suffering any easier." He indicated the cassette machine again. "We have no time to waste. Make the recording. I won't ask again."

Her mouth was dry, and her throat too tight to speak. Her answer was to reach out and sweep the machine off the bureau.

The speed of Bruno's reaction, and the economy of swift movement that followed it, was startling. His body bent and one hand caught the falling cassette machine, a scant inch from the floor. He straightened, put it back on the bureau, and with the same hand seized her left wrist.

"You are an idiot," he said angrily, and dragged her after him through the open doorway.

Moira drew back her free arm and struck him across the ear. It wasn't a slap. She hit him with her fist, as hard as she could. It caught him off balance and staggered him sideways, knocking his head against the edge of the doorway. His grip weakened. Moira tore herself free and ran past him.

There were deeply worn stone steps in a narrow spiral passage that came down from the top of the tower and continued toward the bottom. She went down them as fast as she could, her hands brushing the rough walls on either side to keep her from falling.

Behind her Bruno shouted: "Lorenz!"

Moira passed an open door, glimpsed a simple bedroom inside it. Further below, daylight showed from the bottom of the spiral passage. She raced down toward it. The daylight filled a narrow door, leading out into the open. She was almost to it when the opening was blocked by the tall figure of Lorenz.

He looked at her in surprise. Then he grinned, and his right hand moved to his side. "No, you don't, little bird."

Moira bent to drive headfirst into him. But then his hand came up, in a fist, with the gleam of a long knife blade protruding from it. Moira stopped herself, her heart pounding. She straightened, studying him, ready to kick at his right arm. But he was balanced too well, and held the knife too expertly. And a sick sadism had crept into his weathered, deep-lined face. She couldn't get past him. He wouldn't kill her with that knife. But he would cut her, badly, and enjoy doing it.

There were footsteps behind her. Moira turned and looked back. Bruno was coming down the stone steps, not hurrying. There was no anger in his expression as he reached her. There was even a hint of admiration. He seized her wrist again, this time twisting it behind her back in a hammerlock that brought her up on her toes with a gasp of pain. Bruno eased the hold a fraction, just enough to allow both her feet to rest firmly on the ground again.

Lorenz lowered the knife, sliding it back in the sheath attached to his belt. "What happened?"

"She refuses to make the recording," was all Bruno told him.

"So?" Lorenz grinned again. "And what do we do about that?" He reached out a hand and petted Moira's cheek.

It was worse than a slap. Moira twisted her face away.

Bruno snarled softly: "You do not touch her."

Anger flamed in the older man's eyes. But whatever he saw in Bruno's face instantly quenched it. Lorenz looked at the hand that had caressed her, shrugged his shoulders, and used the hand to scratch his massive chest. Bruno pushed Moira past him, out into a small sunlit courtyard.

She looked around her quickly. The license plate of the car she'd heard could support her belief that she was in France, or contradict it. But there was no car. The courtyard they were crossing was not at ground level. It was an upper-level interior terrace.

The stones of its paving, which also roofed the chambers underneath the terrace, were larger than the ones in the tower—probably Roman workmanship. There were some similar stones, stuck in among others of several different cuts, and sections of thin Roman bricks, in the partially collapsed curtain wall on one side of the terrace. Gaps in the wall showed the same hillslope that could be seen from her tower window.

Rising over two sides of the terrace was a jumble of ruins. There was part of a Saracen-style postern-gate guardhouse, almost entirely strangled by thick vines. A Romanesque chapel with a tree growing through the missing roof. Shattered wall sections of a long building that might have been a barracks, and what looked like the lower half of an armory—both with Gothic buttressing, festooned with wild flowering bushes growing out of masonry crumbling to dust. Beyond these ruins all that could be seen was sky.

The view on the fourth side of the terrace was blocked by the square tower in which Moira had been kept; and behind that a larger round tower with slit windows and a pointed turret with most of its slate tiles missing, showing burned timber remnants.

All she knew now, that she hadn't before, was that she was inside a hilltop fortress complex that had been built and rebuilt over many different periods. Most of it too ruined to be habitable. Her square tower appeared to be the best preserved part of it.

The center of the terrace paving had fallen in.

Bruno marched her around the wide hole. Moira glanced down in passing, into the shadowed wreckage of what had probably once been the fortress stables. They reached a pointed-arch gateway in the main wall. Inside, another tight-spiral stairway led further down. Lorenz took a battery lantern from a nail, snapped it on, and went down first.

They needed the artificial light. The walls of the corkscrew passage contained occasional slit windows, but these were filled with dirt, weeds, and vines. The steps were badly weathered, with large open cracks. At the bottom were two rusty iron doors. Lorenz forced one open on squealing hinges, and they stepped into sudden sunlight.

They were in a series of three roofless storage chambers. Passage through them was made difficult by trees and brush sprouting out of piles of stone rubble, brick dust, and scorched timbers. At the far end was another set of narrow stone steps, these leading straight down without a turn. They descended into a windowless vault dominated by the broken brick upper structure of a large well.

On the other side was the beginning of a low underground tunnel, dirt-floored. It ran straight, then made a sharp-angled bend, passing regularly spaced dark stairwells leading upward. Moira guessed they were in an underground corridor once used to shift defending troops from one point of the main curtain wall to another without exposing them to enemy fire. Sections of the lower part of the retaining wall on one side were of solid Roman construction. The rest of the masonry added to complete the subterranean corridor was from a much later time.

Moira struggled against rising terror as they went down another flight of narrow steps, deeper under the fortress. They passed several very low iron doors, rusted shut. The steps came to a dead end. In the smallish space at the bottom a round iron plate, resembling a manhole cover, was set into the solid rock floor. There were several small holes in it, and slide bolts locked it in place.

Lorenz squatted, put the lantern down, and yanked the bolts open. Using a lot of strength, he raised the round iron cover and shoved it to one side. Beneath was a black hole whose dimensions Moira could not determine. Her nerve ends crawled.

"Down there," Bruno told her quietly, "is what they used to call a bottle cell. Because it entirely encloses you in rock, just as if you were stuffed inside a bottle. Impossible to move at all, though the air holes allow breathing. It was a favorite of the Middle Ages. Men known for their courage went insane in these, in a surprisingly short time."

He waited, letting her digest it. Then he said: "One last chance, Mrs. Rhalles. Will you record the message for us?"

It took her time, and it came in a harsh whisper, but she did finally manage to say it, with strained finality: "No."

Bruno made an angry sound and held her in position with both her arms against her sides. Moira struggled and kicked back against his shin. She knew her strength, but he was much stronger. He kept her clamped against him and took what she was doing to his shin without a sound. Lorenz knelt to untie her shoelaces. Moira almost succeeded in kicking him in the face. But he stopped that by wrapping one arm around her knees. Without removing her shoes, he retied the laces one to the other, so her feet were fastened together.

Rising, Lorenz unbuckled her belt and pulled it free. Looping it around her waist and forearms, he rebuckled it tightly. Then the two men began forcing her down into the narrow opening. Struggling against them would only weaken her and achieve nothing. They would stuff her inside that hole anyway. Fighting them would only delay the inevitable, from seconds to minutes. And she was going to need all the strength she had left.

When her feet touched bottom, she found that she could shift herself to either side less than two inches, and hardly at all backward or forward. Rock pressed against her back, trapped her legs and shoulders, flattened her nipples. The light from above showed her the rock an inch from her eyes. She tried to move her head, and found she could turn it only a bit before rock stopped the movement.

The heavy iron cover clanged down in place, inches above her head. Now there was timeless darkness, and no sound but her quickened breathing. She bent her head forward slightly, and her nose and forehead touched rock. She flinched from the contact, and rock pressed the back of her skull. Her stomach convulsed, and she clamped her teeth together against the urge to vomit. Kept them clamped, until tiny needles of pain radiated in her ears and the hinges of her jaws.

Desperately, Moira fought the rising hysteria. She tried to counteract it with memories of love play with Alex. But the remembered images and emotions kept dissolving, soaked up by the rock that entombed her. She tried concentrating on whether she had really heard that French siren, but she couldn't hold onto that, either. Every thought she began fragmented before the only reality:

She was a kernel of living flesh imbedded inside a limitless mass of solid rock.

The rock was coming to life, beginning to move, crushing in on her. Ridiculous. She started to laugh, and was horrified at the sound that came out. The struggle to stop herself from making those sounds left her drained.

How long had she been buried alive like this?

In the silent, pressuring darkness of the rock Moira fought her doomed battle against the claustrophobia remorselessly squeezing reason out of her brain, and overwhelming her entire nervous system.

3

When they took her out she was shrieking mindlessly. Her forehead was lacerated and her nose bleeding, from attempting to knock herself unconscious against the rock in front of her face. It was difficult for them to handle her. She was wracked with spasms, utterly unco-ordinated. And her skin was slippery with sweat that had drenched her clothing. Even her shoes were soaked with it.

When they put her down on the ground she instantly curled herself into a tight fetal ball. Her screaming weakened, and changed into incoherent babbling. The spasms subsided into small shudders. Her eyes, adjusting to the light, stared at them without seeming to see who they were.

"She's no good to us this way," Lorenz said disgustedly.

"Hold her arm," Bruno told him, and dripped alcohol from a half-pint bottle into a pad of cotton.

Lorenz held Moira in position with one knee and took her arm with both hands. He forced it open, bracing it across his thigh. Bruno swabbed the inside of her upper forearm. Then he opened an aluminum box the size and shape of a cigar box. He took out a disposable hypodermic needle in a plastic sterilization sheath. Without haste, but with that economy of movement that got things done without wasting time, he ripped the sheath open. The hypo was preloaded with sedative. He inserted the needle expertly, finding the vein and slowly pressing the plunger home. The needle was withdrawn with the same smooth skill.

The sedative raced through her veins, spreading swiftly.

"You can let her go now," Bruno said. He sat back on his heels, observing Moira.

Gradually, her shudders and babbling dwindled and ceased. Moaning softly, she uncurled a bit from the fetal position, arms and legs going limp. Her eyes closed.

Bruno slapped her sharply. Her eyes snapped open, staring up at him.

"Do you know who I am?" he demanded. "You remember me?"

Her mouth twitched. Words came out that made no sense. Finally she managed to shape the word she wanted: "Yes . . ." It was a whisper. She began to sob convulsively.

Lorenz shot an anxious frown at Bruno, who kept his attention on Moira.

"Listen to me," he told her loudly. "You will make the recording for us now. Then we will take you back to your bed, and you can sleep comfortably. No more suffering."

She continued to sob, and her heavy eyelids began to droop.

Bruno said harshly: "Do you want us to put you back down inside that hole?"

Her eyes snapped open again, wild with horror. "No!" It was an animal scream. Bruno watched her fight for control. "Don't . . ." she begged. "I . . . I'll do it."

"Good." Bruno nodded to Lorenz, and placed the cassette machine close beside Moira's head.

Lorenz opened the wrinkled paper she'd crumpled in her tower room. He held it before her face, spread tight between his hands.

Bruno moved the miniature microphone close to her mouth. "Just read it. That's all you have to do now." He depressed the button to Record.

Moira moaned, her head rolling.

"Read!" Bruno repeated sternly.

She looked at the paper. Her eyes appeared to be having difficulty with the words printed on it. Her face got taut with effort.

"Alex . . ." Her voice was weak, slightly slurred. "Hello, Alex . . . That crash . . . terrible plane crash . . . In Florida. Y-Yesterday—eleven dead . . . Remember, Alex . . . it goes all right with me . . . if you do . . . what they want . . . tell you to do . . ."

The last few words were barely audible whispers. Her eyes closed again as her head sagged limply to one side. Her breathing became deep and steady.

"Not exactly word for word," Lorenz growled, then gave a grudging shrug. "But I suppose it will have to do. We're late with this already. We can't wait for her to sleep it off and do it again."

Bruno nodded slowly, looking down at Moira. "It's close enough. It will do."

It worked, Moira exulted as the waves of welcome darkness swept over her. *My God I did it . . .*

It had cost her, slipping that message in. Now she could only hope that Alex would understand it.

But Moira was not deeply worried about that part. She had met men who were considered geniuses in their professions. Alex had a mind that was sharper than any of them. Of than, she was certain. If anybody would get what she'd slipped into that cassette, it was Alex.

4

Vasily Pokryshkin's office in Lubyanka was larger than Irina Frejenko's, the size commensurate with his position as chief of Sub-directorate T. It was on the same floor, on the other side of the main corridor, its two windows overlooking the courtyard. The floor was covered with an excellent Persian carpet that did not quite reach from wall to wall. There were three modestly framed paintings of Russian country scenes on one wall. The work of Vasily himself; and not bad at all. In addition to his desk, and the usual file cabinets and corner safe, there was a coffee table, a plastic-covered couch on which he slept when nightwork kept him there, and two comfortable old leather armchairs.

Irina Frejenko sat in one of the armchairs, facing Vasily across the desk.

"The Chairman is extremely pleased with the success of the first stage of your project," he told her. "He specifically asked me to congratulate you on it."

That wasn't what she'd come to hear. "It *is* successful. Now I want her brought inside. Within the Soviet Union, where we can be secure in the knowledge that she is safe from outsiders."

"The operation has *begun* successfully," Vasily corrected her. "It is much too soon to be absolutely certain it will continue to be. You must be patient, Irina. In time, if all goes as expected—then we can bring up the matter again."

"We? You and I? Or you and the Chairman?"

"Both."

"It is too dangerous leaving her out there. Where someone might find her—or chance upon her."

"There is a certain minimal danger in that," Vasily agreed. "A danger for you, and me. But there is a greater danger, for the Soviet Union, if she is discovered in the process of being transported here."

"That would not happen. I've explained exactly how it could be done."

"There is always chance, Irina. Now—we must compare the chance of danger to us, personally, as against the chance of something dangerous to the State. Which must we choose?"

There was nothing she could say to that one, Irina knew. She got out of the armchair and stood before him. "It is a mistake," she told him flatly. "I want it on record that I have said so."

"As you wish."

She left his office and crossed the corridor to her own. For a time she stood at her window, gazing down at the public square. Remembering Jorgen doing the same.

"No plan is perfect," Jorgen had warned during one of their meetings here. "You have to prepare it with that in mind. The people carrying it out for you have individual human faults. They get tired one evening and their attention is on the wrong thing at the wrong time. Or the mechanics of the operation develop accidental faults. A courier gets sick. A telephone goes out of order. A contact is voided by a chance rainstorm. Even computers acquire faults, you know."

Irina Frejenko did know. She had done all she could to ensure that the project would continue to operate effectively even when cracks developed in it. She considered the failure to immediately bring Moira Rhalles inside the Soviet Union to be the first such crack—though she did not honestly believe it need be a serious one.

But there were two other cracks she did not know about.

The first was the human failure of Moira's captors to hold her to the exact text planned for her cassette recording.

The other had occurred long before, in the preliminary research for the project. It was a small mistake of omission; the sort that was almost inevitable, and ordinarily of no consequence. The researchers were the best available, and had worked hard at their assignment to provide complete backgrounds on Alexander Rhalles and his wife. But of course it was impossible to discover every single moment of a person's life; even with the subject's co-operation, certain things would be forgotten.

So the researchers had failed to turn up the information that, at one point in her life, Moira Rhalles had had a very brief affair with a man named Sawyer. Whom she had sometimes called, during that short period, "the Stone Angel."

EIGHT

1

On Thursday afternoon Alexander Rhalles sat in the Oval Office trying to register the main points of what was being said about Western European defense capabilities. The Secretary of Defense and the Director of the CIA sat in one of the sofas flanking the long coffee table. The Secretary of State and the President's Assistant for National Security Affairs were in the other. The President was at one end of the coffee table, in the beat-up brown leather wing chair that had been with him since his days as junior senator.

Rhalles sat in a cane-back chair facing in the direction of the President's desk, and the three tall windows behind it. Through them he could see the elm trees on the south lawn of the White House being moved gently by an afternoon breeze. The air-conditioning was on and the windows were closed, but through them came a faint sound of the lawn mower in action somewhere near the rose garden. Rhalles stole a look at his watch. It was a few minutes past four o'clock.

He still had eighteen hours of waiting ahead of him before he would know if the man he had sent for would come.

Rhalles had never met the man, and could not be sure what would motivate him. From what Moira had said, he was not a man moved by pity. But *curiosity* might bring him. The letter Rhalles had sent was unsigned. There was not even an address to which the money Rhalles had enclosed could be returned, if he decided not to come.

128

Rhalles had written him: "This money will cover your first-class round-trip plane fare and accommodations, from Paris to Philadelphia and back. I will phone the Philadelphia Hilton at the end of this week, on Friday morning at exactly 10 o'clock. Please be there. I guarantee that what I have to talk to you about will be financially rewarding for your firm. There is also a special reason why it will interest you, personally. Please do not send someone else. You are the only person, anywhere, whom I can trust in this matter."

Was it enough? Would he come? The suspense of waiting to find out was putting an increasing strain on Rhalles. He schooled himself not to show it.

But the President had not lost that special sensitivity that astute politicians acquire toward the moods of people around him: "How're you doing, Alex?"

Rhalles raised his eyes from one of the gold flowers in the green of the carpet and forced a smile. "Just fine, Mr. President."

"You had a look like you weren't quite with us."

The Secretary of State said: "Maybe I was boring him." He sugared it with a laugh that was meant to be hearty and understanding.

The President didn't laugh. He studied Rhalles with momentary concern. Not normally overly warm with the people who worked for him, he had nevertheless been touched by the news of Moira's death. He had tried to persuade Rhalles to take more time to recover from the shock, before returning to his advisory duties. But he had given in when Rhalles had insisted that only work could keep him from brooding on it.

The wife of the President was more deeply affected by Rhalles' tragedy. Last weekend Rhalles had been invited to the Virginia farm they frequently used for a short change of scene. Since then everyone around the White House had been treating Rhalles with the extra respect due a star on the rise.

The president looked from Rhalles to his Secretary

of State. "Maybe he just doesn't agree with you. Alex is an expert on the history of guerrilla warfare, you know."

"My department's got some heavy experts of its own. I haven't said anything that doesn't have solid support from their studies."

"I think," Rhalles said edgily, "that they're overestimating what even well-armed guerrillas could accomplish, if the Soviet Union really were to shove their armed forces into Western Europe. Historically, guerrillas have not been successful against a strongly motivated totalitarian government with a large and loyal army. Unless they've gotten massive support, in material and-or manpower, from another major power."

"I agree with Rhalles completely," the Director of Central Intelligence drawled. He looked a bit bored with the discussion.

"I do too," the Defense Secretary climbed in. He prepared to ride his favorite hobbyhorse: "I keep saying it—we can't depend on conventional weapons or forces to . . ."

Major General Masursky, the President's Assistant for National Security Affairs, interrupted caustically: "Guerrillas aren't what I'd call *conventional* forces. Anyway, what Alex just said about massive support from another strong power—*that's* where it's at. How much *would* we be ready to deliver, if the shit hits the fan?"

"After the fact?" the Secretary of State demanded. "Be way too late by then. The ball game'll be over. We'll have lost. No replays. Now, judging by that speech in the Politburo this morning, the Soviet Union's increasingly tempted by the notion they could overrun Europe with their conventional forces so fast we wouldn't be able to use our battlefield nuclear capability without hitting our own allies. And they're right. So we've *got* to consider the organizing, ahead of time, of native underground units to . . ."

"That," the President cut in, "would get us accused

of trying to subvert the governments of our allies." He glanced at the oak grandfather's clock against the east wall. "I have exactly thirteen minutes before my next appointment. Let's deal with the reality: how to bring NATO's conventional defense capability up to a combat readiness that'll *discourage* the Soviet temptation to consider a surprise assault."

The conference went on for another ten minutes. Rhalles gave it surface attention, not joining in. He felt a vague distaste as he watched and listened to each man in turn. They brought out the worst in him: the old Alexander Rhalles with his distrust of people's motives.

Of the people around the President, Masursky was one of the few Rhalles respected. He had a clean, flexible mind, he thought deeply about everything he learned and heard, and he talked straight. When anyone said anything with a tinge of common sense, he did not immediately strike to protect his own entrenched position; he thought about it before giving his opinion.

Many of the men who ran the Government had had fine minds, originally, as Rhalles saw it. But those minds had become paralyzed, freezing around a single objective: achieving a position of prestige, and clinging to it or increasing it. They had no other motivation for being what they were.

It had probably always been so, in all governments, at all times. The trouble with history, Rhalles had decided, was that your attention was naturally drawn to the exceptional men. But nations were run for much longer periods by men like these. Termites. It was in the nature of any government structure, which Rhalles likened to expanding wood pulp. No bird could fly in it. Only termites could move around within, boring their little power tunnels with never-appeased appetites.

Take the CIA Director, for example; a man of whom Rhalles should have been terrified at this moment, considering what he was doing. But he was not. He knew he had a great deal to fear from some of the CIA Director's hired help. But not the Director himself. Rhalles could look in the man's eyes without a tremor; confident that the man could not read him. The Director couldn't read anything accurately except material on business law. That was his sole expertise. His position had been earned by the money he'd gotten for Party funds, from individuals and corporations to whom he'd explained how it could all come out of taxes, anyway.

The only thing that saved the nation, Rhalles now believed, was the basic motivation of all the various government agencies and departments. Whatever their official functions, the basic drive of each was to grow bigger and stronger. In the process, without intending it, they inevitably collided and tangled with each other like blind airships in a fog, strewing inefficiency in all directions. Thank God for that inefficiency—it was the only thing that saved the people from being totally conquered by the machine of government.

Yet Rhalles had not regretted, until the kidnapping of Moira, the time he had spent inside this machine. It had taught him much. But now it had engulfed him, dragging Moira's life to the brink, and turning him into a desperate traitor.

2

When the others filed out at the end of the conference, the President motioned for Rhalles to stay. Stretching himself, the President walked to the desk that had been a present from Queen Victoria to a previous American chief of state. He selected a cigar from a box next to his appointments calender. In the middle of his desk, under a bronze bulldog paperweight, was a folder marked "TOP SECRET." It was also marked with yesterday's date and "NSSM-3A."

The President had given it to Rhalles to read at lunch. Rhalles wished fervently that he hadn't. It was a National Security Study Memorandum on progress by the United States, and estimated progress in the Soviet Union, in the research and development of three types of laser weapons. The United States was considered to be ahead in the use of high-energy lasers in targeting conventional artillery and rockets. The Soviet Union was believed to be overcoming the atmospheric problems inherent in naval use against antiship missiles. The two countries were estimated to be fairly close in the most ambitious application of lasers: to destroy enemy early-warning satellites and warheads in outer space.

It was another folder that the President picked up. "Did you hear about the hard-line speech Mikhail Krenekov made in Moscow this morning?"

Rhalles nodded.

"I've asked the CIA and our embassy in Moscow to size up Krenekov's chances of winding up as Russia's next General Secretary. Here's the full text of his speech. I'd like you to read and think about it. How long're you planning to stay up there on your farm?"

"I'm only going up for the night, to see my brother. I'll be back in Washington by five or six tomorrow evening."

"Time enough. Call Morton when you get in. We'll set up an appointment to discuss it." He gave Rhalles the folder and watched him put it in his briefcase. "You know, Alex, if the party retains power after the next election, you could wind up with a line job. I'm not saying Secretary of State—but something close."

Rhalles shut his briefcase. "I wouldn't be interested in anything like that, sir."

"You might find you are, when the time comes. You could have quite a career ahead of you, here in Washington."

"I have a career, as a historian. My participation in

133

practical politics ends the day you finish your term in office, Mr. President."

The President could not quite hide a small smile of pleasure, interpreting it as a statement of personal loyalty. "Well, think about it . . ." He looked at the clock. "My next appointment's with Carl Sandermun. You know him?"

"Not personally. I know who he is, and what he does." Sandermun was the head of a group of economists, sociologists, and political scientists who had set themselves up in business as "futurologists"—making long-range predictions about the destiny of the world.

The President read Rhalles' expression. "What d'you think?"

"I think he's a charlatan."

"That's for sure. Nothing but a fortuneteller, posing as a scientist. Hell, nowadays even real scientists are finally admitting they don't know much. Not even why the sun shines; or whether we're still coming out of the last ice age, or heading into the next one. But this Sandermun, he's got an H. G. Wells complex."

"Then why bother to see him?"

"His predictions make headlines. I don't want him predicting disaster for my administration." The hand on Rhalles' shoulder propelled him gently toward the door to the West Wing corridor. "Don't forget about Saturday. My wife's looking forward to your joining us at dinner."

"I'll be there." As Rhalles went out, the door from the Appointments Secretary's office opened and Sandermun was ushered into the Oval Office.

Outside, Rhalles nodded at the White House cop in a chair on one side of the corridor, and the two Secret Service men on the other side. As he turned in the direction of West Executive Avenue, Major General Masursky was coming out of Harvey Ross's office. He stopped when he saw Rhalles, half-raising a hand in a mock peace sign.

"Could you come down to the Situation Room with me for a few minutes?" Masursky asked. "I want to talk a little about that conference we just had."

The Situation Room was one place Rhalles did not want to go. When outsiders entered they were supposed to cover the wall maps that showed the exact disposition of American forces all over the world. But Masursky would not consider him an outsider. "I can't now," Rhalles told him. "I'm on my way to Pennsylvania. Call you when I get back tomorrow. You can drop into my office."

"Good enough." Masursky turned and went down the steps to the basement area. Rhalles felt a stab of anxiety. Suppose Masursky was also in *their* power? Then the man he knew as Jorgen would find out he'd avoided going into the Situation Room, and Moira . . .

Stop it, Rhalles told himself. *Even justifiable paranoia has its limits.*

He went past the chief of staff's open door, down the corridor. Behind him Ross's voice called: "Alex. Hold it a second."

Rhalles stopped and turned. Ross came from his office carrying an eight-by-ten manila envelope. "This is a preliminary draft of the foreign policy speech Halstead, Ryan, and Cotton are putting together for the President. I'd like you to give it a read, see what you think."

"I won't be back until late tomorrow."

"Plenty of time. We've got two weeks to whip this one in shape."

Rhalles slipped the envelope into his briefcase. Ross watched him walk away. Like a man carrying a heavy burden. Ross was grateful that Rhalles never talked about his dead wife around here. But he hoped there was *somebody* he could spill his guts to.

Leaving the West Wing, Rhalles crossed to the Executive Office Building. There were painful cramps in his chest. Ten laps in the E.O.B. swimming pool eased his physical tension somewhat, but did little for the torment in his mind. Dressing, he carried the briefcase down to the E.O.B.'s inner courtyard, and out to his assigned parking spot, marked 48 in yellow paint.

There was a swing barrier across the gate facing State Place. A sign on it announced: "White House Parking—Special Permit Holders Only." Rhalles stopped his car and waved to the uniformed guards in the window-walled booths flanking it. They nodded, smiling as they recognized him, and the barrier swung out of the way. Rhalles drove through and headed for Georgetown to do what he had to do before leaving. Entering his study, he got to it immediately, opening the briefcase on his desk and getting the cassette machine from the lower drawer.

The first thing he read into it was the draft for the President's upcoming foreign policy speech, word for word. Next he told what he recalled from the memorandum on laser development, but leaving out a few important items that could be blamed, if needed, on faulty memory. Then he told about everything he had heard while in the White House that day. Again, leaving out certain things—but always conscious that it would be Moira who would suffer if he was caught at it.

When it was all on the cassette, Rhalles slipped it in his pocket and got down a paper hidden behind books on the topmost shelf. On it was a long list of dates and locations. He noted the location for this day, and went back down to his car.

Driving away from the house, Rhalles checked the rear-view mirror several times. He didn't believe Jorgen could possibly have enough people to watch him all the time. But they might be spot-checking him at odd moments, and the danger was that he didn't know when or how. It was the same with American security.

They had done a thorough security check on Rhalles when he began working for the President. But they were known to do random rechecks on sensitive personnel as a matter of policy.

No one seemed to be following him. He stopped at a public phone booth on Canal Road, and dialed a number. When the phone was picked up at the other end, Rhalles said: "I have a delivery for you." Hanging up, he went back to his car, drove to the location indicated on the list, and planted the cassette. Then he drove back through Washington, and out to National Airport. It was 10 P.M. when the flight to Philadelphia took off.

Twelve hours to go.

3

At nine in the morning, Rhalles climbed the rear fence of the farm and hiked across the neighboring fields in a westerly direction. Half a mile away rose the highest hill in the area. When he reached the top he looked back down the way he had come. There was an uninterrupted view of everything that lay between the hill and the farm. He could even make out the small figure of Nick, moving around near the rabbit hutch. There were no other figures in sight in that direction. No one was trying to follow him.

Rhalles walked down the other side of the hill. When he reached the bottom he changed direction, going north through a cornfield and a patch of woods. A mile brought him to the highway. On the other side was a diner called Sergeant's Tavern, with two trailer-trucks parked alongside. Rhalles crossed the highway and went in.

The booths were empty. The two truck drivers were having breakfast at the counter. The owner, a black-bearded local ex-Marine named Horace, was behind it. He grinned and waved, "Hey, there, Alex, good to see you back. How's the state of the nation these days?"

"Not too bad, Horace. And not too good, as usual. All I want is coffee."

"Coming up. How's Nick doing?"

"Just fine." Rhalles took the last booth in the rear, which put him as far as possible from the counter, and gave him a view through the window of the parking area. He looked at his watch and lit his first cigarette of the day.

At ten o'clock the truck drivers had left and there was a couple with a child in the front booth. Rhalles got up and went through the rear door to the washrooms. In the corridor between a door marked "Guys" and another marked "Dames" was a phone booth. He dialed the Hilton in Philadelphia. and asked for Peter Sawyer.

The operator had difficulty understanding the name. Rhalles repeated it. "He'll have checked in last night. Or early this morning." His hand was squeezed too tight around the phone's earpiece. He waited to be told there was no such person registered.

Instead he heard a room phone being buzzed. It was picked up and a man's voice said: "Yes?"

"Mr. Sawyer?"

"That's right. Who're you?"

"The one who sent you the letter. I'm at a place called Sergeant's Tavern." Rhalles explained how to get there. "If you rent a car, you can be here in . . ."

"I'm not coming any further unless you tell me who you are." The tone was polite but definite.

"My name is Alexander Rhalles. I don't know if that means anything special to you."

There was a second of silence at the other end. "I know who you are, Mr. Rhalles." The tone had changed, but what was in it now was difficult to analyze. "I'll be there."

138

4

An hour later a new two-door Ford pulled into the parking area beside the diner. From the rear booth, Rhalles watched the driver get out: a lean, dark-haired man in his thirties, wearing a black corduroy suit with a longish, loose-fitting jacket. He looked the diner over before coming toward it. There was relaxed strength in the way he moved. When he entered the diner he stopped again, taking in the interior. There was nobody in the place now but Rhalles and Horace.

He nodded to Horace. "Do you have cheeseburgers?"

"Sure. How do you want it?"

"Medium rare. And some coffee, please." He walked to the rear booth and paused again, looking down at Rhalles thoughtfully. His dark face was thin and bony, with harsh lines that made him look older than Rhalles knew him to be. There was hard patience in the set of his wide mouth. The eyes were moody, and calculating.

"Rhalles? I'm Sawyer."

"Thank you for coming."

Sawyer made a careless gesture. "I was curious—and it's a free trip. I can visit my grandparents in Chicago while I'm at it, and still wind up with a profit." A slight smile softened his expression as he explained: "Our company does work for Pan Am. I get the reduced fare for employees."

He sat down facing Rhalles, glanced at the ashtray filled with cigarette butts and ash, then picked it up and put it to one side. The neat, almost delicate way he used his hand made Rhalles think of a precision-tool worker.

Rhalles studied him anxiously, trying to mesh what he saw with what Moira had told him.

Sawyer endured his scrutiny without irritation. Finally he said: "All right, Mr. Rhalles. I know quite a bit about you. What do you know about me?"

"I know your name is Pierre-Ange," Rhalles told him. "Stone Angel."

Sawyer leaned his shoulders against the back of the booth. "She give you a rundown on *all* her former boy friends?"

"She discussed you—that time you were charged with betraying your assignment in Europe as a fact-finder for the Senate Foreign Relations Committee. When they claimed you destroyed evidence against a French business go-between and influence peddler believed to have criminal connections."

"That's putting it mildly," Sawyer said. "He's one of the richest gangsters in Marseilles. Everything from prostitution to smuggling." There was an edge of curiosity in his expression now. "Did Moira think I was guilty?"

Rhalles put it carefully: "She thought—that it was *possible*. She said you liked money. And that you were extremely contradictory—an odd mixture of viciousness and decency."

"A diamond in a dung heap." Sawyer's tone was dry. "And you—what did you think about it?"

"The Government dropped the charges against you."

"Because I threatened to air some dirty linen belonging to the committee chairman. It was a deal. I was guilty."

Rhalles studied him. "Do you mind telling me why?"

"Money," Sawyer told him. Then he added, somewhat grudgingly: "And—this influence-peddling gangster in Marseilles, one of his smaller sidelines is people-smuggling. During World War II he sometimes did it for the hell of it—in addition to the times he

140

got paid. He saved the lives of some people I care about."

"I see."

"I doubt it. My motives were more complicated than that makes it sound."

Horace brought over the cheeseburger and coffee. "You want a refill, Alex?"

"No thanks, Horace." Rhalles lit a cigarette and watched Sawyer eat, slowly and with obvious enjoyment. "I see you haven't lost your taste for American food."

Sawyer's grin was surprisingly boyish. "I'm an odd mixture of France and Chicago, too." He glanced toward Horace returning behind the counter. "You're pretty friendly around here."

"I went to the local grade school. So did Horace. In the last few years we were in the same class." Rhalles stabbed out his cigarette. He was still hesitant about this man to whom he was considering entrusting his life and Moira's. "You've done quite well for yourself since . . . since you stopped being a Senate investigator. This company of yours—Audubon Research—I hear it's one of the best business-security firms in Europe."

"It's not my firm. It belongs to Alain Gassin."

"Yes, but I believe Mr. Gassin confines himself to management and procuring business; while you actually direct all the investigations."

"Investigations account for less than one quarter of the company's activities, Mr. Rhalles. That's *all* I direct. I have nothing whatever to do with the rest of it." There was an undertone in Sawyer's statement; for some reason the point he was making was important to him. "Audubon Research has three distinct departments. The first department is Special Projects. That means doing whatever one company will pay to have done to wreck an enterprise of a rival company: blackmail, spreading false rumors, character assassination, and so forth . . ."

An edge of disgust had crept unnoticed into Sawyer's tone. "The second department is Research. That's the mainstay of Audubon Research. It means industrial espionage, economic intelligence—in plain language, stealing secrets from one business for another business.

"Our third department is Security, which means providing a client with protection against espionage efforts by its rivals. Security has two different sections. One is concerned with before-the-fact: everything from providing guard dogs to giving lie-detector tests to prospective employees. The other section operates mostly *after* there is a suspicion security has been breached—and *that's* my area: Investigating possible leaks, tracing where they come from and where they're going. Plugging the leakage. And fending off special projects launched by business enemies against our clients."

Rhalles nodded. "I understand." His nerves were too tight, and he still couldn't break through his hesitation. He started to light another cigarette.

Sawyer said: "You smoke too much."

Rhalles looked at his cigarette. "Moira always says that."

"Does she?"

"Yes . . ."

Sawyer sighed, washed down the last of his lunch with a swallow of coffee, and pushed cup and plate aside. "I've been trying to make it easier for you," he said gently, "but you won't bite. So let's get down to it. Who has your wife?"

Rhalles stared at him. Then, slowly, he gave a satisfied nod. "Yes. Moira said you were very clever."

"It doesn't require much in the way of cleverness. I read the papers. Moira is presumed dead, but her body wasn't found. Then you go through elaborate maneuvers to meet me in secret." Sawyer paused. "Is that what it's about—government secrets?"

Rhalles placed both hands flat on the table between

them and his eyes searched Sawyer's. "I'm putting Moira's life in your care, when I tell you."

"That's your decision. You can still change it."

Rhalles looked the length of the diner, then through the window beside them.

"Nobody is close enough to hear," Sawyer told him flatly. "Or I'd've told you."

"I have to be sure . . ." Rhalles drew a slow breath, and then told him—about Jorgen, and the rest. All of it.

Sawyer did not interrupt once. He sat and listened, and when it was finished he continued to sit silently for a time, thinking it through. Finally he grimaced angrily, and made a nervous gesture with one hand.

"I don't see anything to do. It's too late. She's somewhere behind the Iron Curtain by now. I know people who can get in and out of those countries. But finding somebody they want to hide in there . . ." Sawyer shook his head.

"I don't think Moira is behind the Iron Curtain." Rhalles said it firmly. He took a small square of paper from a pocket. "There was something strange in her last cassette message to me. I've copied it down, exactly as she said it." He put the square of paper down in front of Sawyer. "The dots indicate her speech pauses."

Sawyer read the typed words quickly the first time. Then again, slowly: "Alex . . . Hello, Alex . . . That crash . . . terrible plane crash . . . In Florida. Yesterday . . . Eleven dead . . . Remember, Alex . . . it goes all right with me . . . if you do . . . what they want . . . tell you to do."

He studied it a third time and then looked up, frankly puzzled. "Maybe it was in the way she said it—the intonation."

"No. It's in the words. After 'Remember, Alex.' That phrase: 'it goes all right with me . . .' Did you ever hear an American put it that way?"

Sawyer looked at Rhalles with new interest. "I do—when I'm speaking French. *Ça va bien.*" He hesitated, scowling at the paper. "You think she's telling you she's still somewhere in France."

"That's my interpretation." Rhalles' face was gaunt with strain.

"France isn't the only country where they use that phrase," Sawyer pointed out carefully. "They have the same way of putting it in Italy and Spain. Germany, too: 'It goes well.' "

"Moira is in France," Rhalles told him firmly. "She always liked the way it sounded in French . . ." He hesitated, suddenly embarrassed. Angrily, he cut through the embarrassment. This was no time for private delicacy; he needed this man too much. "It's a phrase she often used when we were making love: '*Ça va,* baby . . . ?' Always in *French.*" Rhalles repeated flatly: "She's in France."

Sawyer studied Rhalles, and remembered Moira. Sensing what the two had together; and thinking of his own life. He was startled by the strength of the envy that struck him. And the feeling of loneliness that followed.

But none of this showed, in his expression or tone: "All right—she's in France." He frowned, considering it.

Rhalles nodded. His tone was quite definite: "Yes. Will you find her for me?"

"It's an easy country to hide somebody. There are people who managed to stay hidden all through World War II, with hundreds of Nazi police and French informers hunting for them."

"But you *will* try? Without letting *anyone* know what you're doing? It's not only Jorgen's people I mean. If American intelligence gets a hint of what you're doing, the result will be the same. I suppose you consider me a traitor to my country but . . ."

Sawyer cut him short: "You know I don't give a damn. That's one reason you picked me." He rubbed his fingertips together, looking at them absently, thinking aloud: "Starting with Jorgen is one way—but it could be the wrong way. Surveillance on him might not bring anything worth the risk of his finding out."

"Please *don't*," Rhalles said hurriedly. "It's too dangerous. And, I'm inclined to believe what he told me. That he doesn't know where Moira is."

"So am I. It fits this kind of operation. One hand is never supposed to know what the others are doing. There's probably not even a direct line of contacts that can be traced between him and Moira." Sawyer got out a cigarette of his own, looked at it, stuck it back in the pack. "We'll just have to start scrounging around, here and there."

"She's in France," Rhalles reminded him needlessly. "Your company must have connections all over France."

"All over Europe. It'll cost you. A lot."

"Moira's father left her a considerable inheritance. Since she's believed to be dead, it now comes to me. Name your price."

"It's not my price," Sawyer snapped. "I'm going to need help. From professional people who will expect to get paid well and have their expenses covered."

Rhalles looked at him in sudden alarm. "You can't tell anybody else about this. There's too much risk of it leaking out. If the people who have Moira find out what we're doing, she's dead."

"I can't do it alone."

"I realize that. You will need help. But you can tell them what to do without telling them *why*. You can't tell that to *anybody*."

Sawyer considered the man on the other side of the table from him. He decided that Rhalles was in no state to understand that there were certain people who would catch on, whether he explained the whole picture to them or not. People like Annique. And perhaps Gassin, eventually . . .

"Don't worry," he lied blandly, "that part stops with me. Nobody else will know."

Rhalles nodded, relieved. He leaned toward Sawyer, his long, slender hands squeezing into tight fists on the table between them. His voice was low, torn with passion: "Please . . . *find her*."

5

Ten days earlier, the Vienna desk of the CIA had received the first of a series of long, puzzling code messages that had been picked up by an informant in Budapest. The CIA had no way of knowing that it had lucked into the middle of a new, single-purpose communications line—with Alexander Rhalles at one end and Moscow at the other. But they did know that they'd chanced on *something* of interest.

That first message, and those that followed, were passed on for analysis to the code specialists of the NSA, at Fort Meade, Maryland.

NINE

1

Shortly after two on Friday afternoon a steady spring rain began to fall across the central portion of Maryland, beating at the trees that screened the eighty-two acres of Fort Meade from the Baltimore-Washington Expressway. Within the fort's highest-security area the rain hammered against the Marine barracks, turned the asphalt surfaces of vast parking spaces shiny black, and dripped from the pines surrounding two huge, strictly functional modern buildings: the National Security Agency's Operations Building, and its Annex. On the flat roofs of these two buildings the rain formed deepening pools. The water ran down the steel-and-concrete walls, cascading past windows sealed to hold in the air-conditioning.

Coming up out of the basement area of the Main Operations Building, Benjamin Scovil paused at a south window looking toward the electrified fence along Savage Road. He grinned at the downpour. It wouldn't be necessary to water his garden when he got home to Baltimore that evening.

Scovil turned from the window and started down what the NSA boasted was the longest unobstructed corridor in the United States. Accompanying him as a convoy-guard was a ramrod-straight Marine corporal with fingertip-short yellow hair. His regulation summer uniform was freshly laundered and perfectly pressed. Scovil looked scruffy beside him: dirty sneakers, baggy dungarees, orange-and-green sports shirt, long gray-streaked hair curled thickly at the back of his neck. It was his way of thumbing his nose at the military who ran the place, and the stuffy government workers who formed the bulk of its employees.

But nobody turned to stare at him. They got used to people like Scovil when they worked in the Puzzle Palace. He was part of a small oddball group necessary for part of the main function of the Defense Department's NSA: monitoring the electronic communications of the world, searching for anything that might interest the Pentagon.

Without the Scovils, the monstrously expensive ears of the NSA were close to useless: the SAMOS satellites orbiting outer space; the nuclear-powered submarines of the Holystone program cruising the edges of territorial waters in the Baltic and Western Pacific; the buildings rigged as immense radio eavesdroppers in Berlin and Vienna; the entire mountaintops along the Iron Curtain webbed with hypersensitive antennas.

For the massages picked up by the NSA and other U.S. intelligence agencies often meant nothing unless they could be decoded. It was because of its function as a maker and breaker of codes that the NSA's Fort Meade headquarters was known as the Puzzle Palace. To serve that function the basement area under its two buildings contained probably the largest sophisticated assemblage of computers ever designed for cryptanalysis work. Some bigger than a normal house. All densely packed with fingernail-sized chips, each with over a million miniaturized components.

But even the most advanced computers were only tools—unable to perform their functions except when used by people talented and experienced in their specialty. In this case the specialty was code-breaking; and the talent came in an odd assortment of men and women who were eccentric to downright weird: Crossword-puzzle hounds, mathematicians, chess players, amateur astronomers, housewives, former taxi drivers, dropout hippies.

148

There was only one thing all of them had in common: they were people who liked to play around with codes, and had freak talents for doing so. People like Benjamin Scovil, who headed one of the best teams.

He turned into a short, narrow side hall with his Marine escort. There was a Marine seated behind a small gray steel desk, and another standing between the desk and the wall, barring the way. Yellow and black signs announced that the hall was a yellow security zone. The plastic I.D. card clipped to Scovil's belt was blue. His escort snapped to a halt and said briskly: "Mr. Scovil to see Captain Morgenstern. He has an appointment."

The Marine behind the desk picked up his inter-office phone, jabbed a button, and spoke into it: "Civilian blue-card holder to see the Captain, sir." He read from Scovil's belt card: "Name: Scovil, Benjamin H. Classification: J. I.D. number: 5-732-140 . . . Yes, sir." He hung up the phone, got a yellow plastic authorized-visitor card from a drawer, and gave it to Scovil to clip next to the blue card.

His partner told Scovil: "Will you come with me, sir." Scovil's original escort stayed at the desk. The other Marine led the way to a door, knocked, and opened it. He remained on guard outside it as Scovil went in. Flipping a wave at the sergeant who worked as the Captain's secretary, Scovil entered the inner office. He shut the door, settled in a padded metal chair, and grinned at the man behind the wide gray desk: a tall, lanky officer with steel-rimmed glasses and a tired face.

"Cheer up, Morgy, it's raining."

"That I know. How're you coming with the Budapest tapes?"

"That's the thing. We're not."

The Captain's face got a bit more tired. The Foreign Intelligence Staff of the CIA had sent over the tapes, and were still sending them. They had an occasional local informant in Budapest, who got paid on an if-come basis for any interesting information he delivered. Until recently his reports had been of minimal interest, and he'd gotten small change for it. Then he'd chanced on something: a Pole had taken a small office in Budapest as the representative for a Warsaw export firm—which didn't exist. The Hungarian had been paid to rent a nearby room, and given the latest piece of medium-range remote listening equipment.

What he picked up with this was a two-hour tape of a phone call from the spurious Budapest office to a phone number that could not be identified in Warsaw. The two hours consisted entirely of dots and dashes. Why was such a message not sent by radio? Obviously to avoid being picked up by the SAMOS satellite receivers of the NSA. The dots and dashes were not Morse. They could not be broken down into words that made sense in any known language.

In the eleven days since, seven more tapes like it had come through. The shortest was half an hour; the longest almost three hours. All had been sent to the NSA for decoding, and Captain Morgenstern had chosen Scovil and his team to work on it. Now Scovil was telling him they'd made no progress at all.

"Have you tried using the Bump?"

Scovil nodded cheerfully. "Yep."

The biggest and best unit in the NSA cryptanalysis-computer complex—perhaps the most advanced of its type in the world—was an ultrahigh-speed Univac built to NSA specifications a year before. Since it had been installed downstairs, the NSA's own computer engineers had been adding units to "bump" its memory capacity and data-processing time. By now these combined bumps were larger than the original Univac, so it was normally referred to as "the Bump."

"We might as well have fed it into a washing machine," Scovil told Captain Morgenstern. "Looks to me like the messages on those tapes are being turned out by a brand-new electronic cipher machine development. Using a key and the principle of the one-time pad. Changing the code for each letter each time it's used. Never repeating the same code for the same letter. So it can only be decoded by a machine preset to the same random sequence of limitless changes. Something like our KW-9, but *much* more sophisticated. We're stymied, and so is your Bump."

The Captain sighed and leaned back in his swivel chair. "Well, keep working on it." He knew he didn't have to say that. The more difficult the puzzle, the more hooked on it people like Scovil got. They couldn't help thinking about it, around the clock. Probably even making love or asleep, part of their minds went right on playing with possible keys to a solution.

There was a story about a general in the early days of the NSA, who'd been incensed by the code people's disregard for regulation office hours. To make an example, during a conference he'd reamed out a woman notorious for arriving at work two to three hours late every day. She'd explained that she had trouble getting up in the mornings, and pointed out that she frequently stayed late in her office, sometimes to midnight if her work required it.

"I don't give a damn about any work you claim you're doing outside office hours," the General had thundered at her. "You've got a nine-to-five job. Confine yourself to those hours—but give me *all* of those hours. Understand?"

"Yes, sir."

The next morning she had arrived punctually at 9 A.M. In time for an urgent conference on a Red Chinese code that had defied all attempts at solution. She announced that she had discovered how to break it.

"Great," snapped the General. "What is it?"

"I can't tell you," she replied firmly. "I thought of it this morning while taking my shower. At 8 A.M. Outside office hours."

And she'd refused to give her solution until the

General rescinded his nine-to-five order. He had gotten the point. So had all of his successors.

After Ben Scovil left, Captain Morgenstern scowled at a corner of his office ceiling for a time. If the enemy had a breakthrough cipher machine such as Scovil had described, it would be used only to pass secret information of the very highest importance. It was unlikely that either Hungary or Poland had developed such a machine; none of the east-block countries were very advanced in cipher-machine technology, with the exception of the Soviet Union. So it was the Soviets using this new Budapest code. But passing it by a roundabout route, through Hungary and Poland, as if they were nervous about being identified with it.

That made another reason for assuming the information on those tapes was of highest importance. The frequency and length of the tapes meant there was an awful lot of it. Something dicey was going on.

Captain Morgenstern picked up his interoffice phone and asked for an immediate appointment with Major Wren, to give his opinion that this hot potato should be tossed back in the laps of the CIA's Foreign Intelligence Staff, and quickly.

2

In addition to the CIA's highly publicized Langley headquarters, many of its activities were conducted in office buildings scattered around Washington, using the names of cover businesses. The greatest concentration was among the genuine civilian companies on K Street, between Fourteenth and Twenty-first. Washington's in-people called this stretch of seven short blocks Spook Row.

The sign on the outer door of the seventh-floor office at the corner of Nineteenth and K read: *"Duncan*

Textiles." But Fred Duncan was in charge of person-nel research for the regional and country desks of the CIA's Soviet Bloc Division. At a few minutes before five that rainy afternoon, he had a visitor: Christo-pher Budge, from the Langley office of the Deputy of Operations, which dealt in clandestine services.

"We need a highly reliable operator for a tricky collection assignment in Budapest," Budge told Dun-can. He explained about the code tapes. "NSA hasn't been able to solve the code. So it's our ball game. We've got to find the people doing the sending; and the encoding machine they're using. This has a vital-to-national-security tag, Fred. The man we send in there has to be experienced enough to do the job without detection. If the Reds find out we're onto this one they'll change its communications line, be-fore we can track it backward to the source."

"Difficult," Duncan said. "Since our last Budapest station officer was blown we haven't had any of our own people in there. They know all our Hungarian specialists by now. And probably most our division staff over in Vienna."

"That's why I'm here. We need a hotshot the Hun-garians *don't* know on sight. But he has to know the language and Budapest, at least well enough to move around there without too much trouble. Right, it's difficult. Can you come up with somebody?"

"Don't worry," Duncan told him confidently. "I'll do a skills filecheck. We'll find your man."

3

Charles Lang sat in a cube of refrigerated air and gazed across the barren, sun-scorched desert. He was watching the color change from violet to pinkish-gold on Funeral Peak, jutting up out of the arid convolu-tions of the Black Mountains. Outside his air-conditioned station wagon the temperature was 109 degrees in the shade, and there wasn't much shade. Death Valley was the lowest and hottest place on the American continent.

Lang was parked along its southeastern edge, beside the ruins of his father's old gas station and diner on California's State Highway 127, between Shoshone and Death Valley Junction. He held a ball-point pen and a spiral notebook on his lap. On the front seat beside him was an open copy of Julius Hay's *Bridge of Life*. Lang was supposed to be translating it into English from the original Hungarian.

He'd come all the way out here hoping that the isolation, and memories of the old days, would help him to concentrate on the work. Instead he kept staring at the heat-shattered, wind-blasted emptiness around him, drifting into daydreams. Sometimes Lang had the uneasy thought that he was just playing games with himself, continuing to work toward his doctorate in Eastern European languages whenever he was back in California between assignments. He had been away from academic disciplines too long. His guts craved the more vicious disciplines they'd gotten used to. That craving had not been satisfied for over a month now, and his nervous system was getting edgy.

Lang put the pad and pen aside on the open book, giving up. He opened the windows but left the air-conditioning on to help his body adjust to the sudden inrush of dry heat. It poured in on him with enormous, malevolent weight. He began to perspire profusely, but his skin and clothing remained bone dry. The desert heat sucked away every drop of moisture the instant it emerged.

Opening one of the thermos bottles, Lang took a long drink of cool tea to counteract the dehydration. You could survive a couple weeks without food. He knew that from the time he'd spent in a Cambodian cave hiding from Khmer Rouge patrols hunting him two years ago. But you couldn't last a day in this desert without sufficient water, taken regularly. He'd learned that as a kid, over there behind the Black Mountains, in a sand canyon between Suicide Pass and Shoreline Butte. That was where he'd seen his first human corpse. The fool had gone in without adequate spare drinking water, gotten his jeep stuck in a dune, and tried to walk out. The corpse was less than two miles from the jeep.

Lang turned off the motor and air-conditioning and got out of the station wagon. The sun glare stung his eyes in spite of the dark sunglasses he wore. He was of average height, with the body of a fast middleweight boxer. His hair was red, but his skin was deeply tanned without the burn most redheads get. He had a blunt-featured face that was attractive when he smiled. When he wasn't smiling he was not someone other men would pick arguments with in a bar. Behind the sunglasses the hazel eyes had a restless, pensive quality.

Wrapping a bandana around his hand before touching the red-hot handle of the rear door, he opened it and took out a wide-brimmed straw hat. His brain was already beginning to fry under the force of the sun. Lang put on the hat and picked up two boxes of cartridges, wedging them inside his belt. Then he reached inside for the two weapons: a lever-action .30 caliber rifle, and a .22 target pistol.

Dust spurted in small clouds from under his boots as he went through the sand-shredded remains of the gas station. Lang put the cartridges and weapons down in a narrow wedge of shade behind the half-collapsed wall of what had been their small living quarters. Inside the roofless, windowless diner, he found an old coffeepot, two intact cups, and a fruit-juice bottle. He carried them a hundred yards from the wall, and put them down against a low clay slope. A rusted oil drum was already there, painted with flaking red circles and riddled with bullet holes. Mementoes of childhood.

Lang was breathing openmouthed when he returned to the station wagon, his lungs fighting the open heat. He took three more big gulps of the cool tea, and went back to the wedge of shade. Sitting on the ground and leaning his shoulders against the broken wall, he loaded both weapons.

He'd been born on the other side of this wall. And his mother had died in there, bearing him. They'd planned for her to deliver him in a hospital down in Baker, but he'd come three weeks prematurely. His father had handled the delivery, and his mother hadn't recovered.

He was bad luck for women, Lang thought. First his mother; then Duyen, his wife. Since Duyen he'd been careful: no more real attachments. And he couldn't stand whores. But celibacy was better than carrying the guilt.

Lang started with the rifle. The first shot smashed the bottle, the next two disintegrated the cups. Then he took aim at the coffeepot, gently squeezed the trigger. The slug slammed through the pot and bounced it off the clay slope. Lang popped it again while it was still in the air, kept hitting it while it was skittering around.

When the rifle was empty he put it down and picked up the pistol, and slammed all six loads into the oil drum. It made a satisfying amount of noise. Reloading both weapons, he used the rifle again on the mangled coffeepot, then resumed pegging one shot after another into the oil drum with his pistol. He might as well have been hammering nails. It was another way of letting off steam.

When the ammunition was finished he was partially deaf from the gunfire and his nostrils and mouth were acrid from the gunpowder fumes. His chest was heaving and his tongue was swelling with thirst. Getting up, he went back to the station wagon, put the weapons in the rear, and finished off the thermos. He opened another and gulped down some more. As he was recapping it, a Lincoln Continental sedan coming from the south pulled in and skidded to a halt with squealing tires on the other side of the leaning fuel pump.

The man at the wheel was huge even sitting down; and except for the beer-belly, none of it was fat. Beside him was a very elegant brunette. As Lang walked over he saw that she wore a skimpy halter and shorts that couldn't have gotten any shorter. The big man reached across her and opened the door with a wide grin. He had a battered, stupid face and shrewd little eyes. "Surprise, surprise, Langy-poo!" He was a little drunk.

He patted the brunette's thigh and told her: "A little privacy, kid. Won't be long. Take a walk."

"In that sun?"

Lang gestured at his station wagon. "The keys're in the ignition. Shut the windows and turn on the air-conditioning."

She gave Moran a dirty look, then climbed out. As she headed for the wagon, Lang slid in beside Moran and shut the door. The freezing air inside the Continental engulfed him. He opened his mouth wide and drank it.

"Hot as a bitch out there, eh?" Moran pointed toward the station wagon. "And speaking of bitches, what do you think of that one? Nice, eh? Taking her along to Vegas for a couple days."

"How'd you know I was here?"

"From your sister. You know what? She wouldn't let me in the house. Not even for a minute."

"She doesn't like you," Lang told him. As a matter of fact, his older sister didn't like anybody connected with the Company. But he didn't add that.

Moran eyed him good-naturedly. "And you don't either, right?"

Lang didn't bother to answer because Moran already knew it. Moran had led deep-penetration killer squads in both the Orient and Africa. That was all

157

right; people got killed in wartime, including the so-called Cold War. But Moran got pleasure out of killing, and had been known to kill *just* for that pleasure. That turned Lang's stomach.

Moran laughed and patted Lang's knee. "That's okay, I still love *you*."

The strange thing was, he probably did in a way. Most men were intimidated by Moran. He knew Lang wasn't, and he admired that. The scar on his forehead was the badge of his one-sided friendship.

It had started in Saigon, when a street kid had snatched the thick wallet Moran kept in a hip pocket as a symbol of his machismo, sure nobody'd have the nerve to try for it. The kid was about ten, one of the thousands you saw living on the streets of Saigon in those days. Homes gone, parents gone, no adult left to take care of them. So they took care of themselves. *"Bui doi,"* the Vietnamese called them: life's dust. By night they slept in alleys and doorways. By day they begged, shined shoes, scrounged military garbage, extorted meager piasters for not breaking windows, and stole.

The one who'd lifted Moran's wallet had taken off like a rabbit, too fast and agile to be caught. Moran had brought out a .45 Government Colt and taken aim at the kid's fleeing back. Lang had chopped a fist across the side of Moran's neck, dumping him in the gutter.

Moran had gotten up slowly, putting the .45 away. He'd never shoot a fellow American; probably not even if ordered to. But he'd beat the hell out of him. Lang had run, purposefully, into the nearest bar. By the time Moran came in after him, Lang had a full bottle of J & B in one fist. While Moran was still getting his eyes used to the gloom inside, Lang had kicked him in the stomach. Moran had sagged to his knees, and Lang had smashed the bottle across the front of his head.

When Moran had come to, he'd told the doctor stitching his forehead: "That Lang, he's a *mean* sonuvabitch . . ." He'd said it admiringly.

Lang neither returned nor appreciated that admiration. "Who's looking for me?"

"Me. Wanna come along to Vegas? That hunk of white meat over there's got friends just as nice staying at . . ."

"Cut it out, Moran."

"Okay. I'm supposed to ask you two questions, first. Number one: You remember Budapest, well enough to move around there a little?"

Lang felt a quickening excitement. "I only visited it once. College vacation. That's a while ago, but it probably hasn't changed much."

"Good enough. Second question: Your Hungarian still good?"

"Reading and writing, it's excellent. Conversation I can understand, if nobody talks too fast. And I can speak it pretty well. But not well enough to pass as a Hungarian, if that's what they want."

"It's not." Moran nodded. "I think what you've got'll suit them."

"What's up?"

"Search me, except obviously they want you to go to Budapest for something. They said if your answers to both questions were affirmative, they want you to report to Washington. Tomorrow morning. Early. Not later."

"Who do I report to?"

"George Rudofsky."

It was big. Lang opened the door and got out. "Have a good time in Vegas."

"How can I have a bad time? Just send over the meat."

Lang walked back to the station wagon. The brunette ran through the heat to the Lincoln Continental. It took off in a cloud of sand and alkali dust. Lang got into the station wagon and headed south through the desert on Route 127. He switched to the express-way to Los Angeles when he reached Baker.

4

Baker was where Lang and his sister had gone to school. It was there he'd discovered his knack with languages. By the end of junior high his Spanish was better than the teacher's. By the time he left high school his French and German were just as good, winning him a full scholarship at U.C.L.A. A career in government or international business, as a translator or interpreter, was obviously the route for him to go. He switched to Eastern European languages where the field was less crowded and there would be more need for him. Czech came first, then Hungarian, Rumanian, and Bulgarian. His special talent seemed to grow with the more he loaded on it.

Throughout undergraduate school Lang worked weekends and summers as a messenger, and three nights a week as a clerk in a university faculty club. Before starting to work for his Master's degree he had enough saved up for a four-month trip abroad, to get practice using his languages in their own countries. He fell in love with two cities: Budapest, for the easy-going warmth of its people; and Prague, for its exquisite beauty. Lang spent so much time in these that Bulgaria and Rumania were left with only two weeks each.

Budapest had already been overrun with Russian tanks and troops, which had come to teach the Hungarians that they could not play around with a "different," more relaxed brand of communism that did not adhere to the dictates of the Soviet Union. The lesson was still fresh in the minds of Hungarians when Lang was there. He'd gotten his first taste of what it meant to live inside a total police state. It also made him understand that the Soviet Union intended to impose similar police states wherever it could: behind the Iron Curtain now; beyond it later. This was reinforced for Lang later, when Russia taught Prague the same bloody lesson it had given Budapest—and for the same reason: the heresy of trying to introduce some personal liberty into the practice of communism.

Lang had been ready by the time the CIA recruiter had asked him to join the fight against international communism. To him that threat meant something real: the spread of a poison from the Soviet Union that murdered the very idea of individual freedom wherever it entered.

He had not anticipated remaining in covert intelligence work for very long. It was to have been a steppingstone to a foreign service career with the State Department. It didn't turn out that way; and neither did the CIA's original assumption: that he'd do work his Eastern European languages fitted him for, at its Soviet block desks or their networks along the Iron Curtain.

During training another Lang talent showed itself: his knack with weapons. A Langley computer put this together with his knowledge of Spanish, his quick mind, and his athletic body. He was forwarded for further training at the counterinsurgency school in Panama. Then they'd sent him to Bolivia to find out how much he'd absorbed of what he'd been taught—in espionage, countersubversion, and antiguerrilla work.

Lang's performance exceeded their expectations, from the start. He'd turned out to be that most coveted of agents: a dedicated, intelligent "natural." Ecuador had been his next assignment, followed by Laos, Thailand, Singapore, and Japan. Then they'd sent him to Vietnam.

He'd met Duyen in a Saigon bar. She was a hostess there, but not a hooker. And she was the most beautiful creature Lang had ever seen. At first she'd refused to go out with him, embarrassed to be seen with an American. Lang had persisted for weeks, politely, gently.

They'd been married first by an army chaplain, then by a Buddhist priest. Fulfilled love, and marriage, were a heady experience for Lang. But his work required him to move around a great deal, and he'd had to leave Duyen alone in Saigon much of the time. When she'd become pregnant, she insisted on returning to Da Nang to be with her parents. Lang had finally given in. He'd rented a house there large enough for Duyen and himself to live in comfortably together with her parents—and their son, when he was born.

Lang had been away again, in Thailand, when the North Vietnamese forces had closed in on Da Nang with unexpected speed. Lang was one of the intelligence agents who'd warned repeatedly that the Vietcong were much stronger than supposed, and preparing a major strike. His warnings had been ignored and concealed by higher-ups in the intelligence community and military—as they had with similar reports from other sources—because the warnings were considered to be injurious to American policy.

Even Lang had been shocked by the suddenness with which the Vietcong made their final pounce. He'd frantically tried to reach Da Nang before it was too late, knowing what could happen to the wife of an American agent once the Communists took over the city. It had taken three different planes to get him there: a Thai jet from Bangkok to Hong Kong, then an Air Vietnam flight to Saigon, and finally an army helicopter into Da Nang.

The chopper had crash-landed, hit as it descended by the enemy antiaircraft guns moving ever closer to the airport. The airport and city were by then a madhouse of people frantically scrambling to get out before the final fall of Da Nang, with most of the evacuation aircraft that landed too badly hit to take off again. Lang had had to fight against mobs rushing in the opposite direction to reach the house.

The North Vietnamese were not inside the city yet, but gangs of hoodlums eager to curry favor with them were. The bodies of Duyen's parents had been left sprawled on the porch. Inside, Duyen lay in a pool of blood. She'd been repeatedly raped before the slitting of her throat. But they hadn't touched the baby. He was squalling with hunger in his crib.

Lang had rushed his child back to the airport, which was by then being bombarded by enemy artillery and rockets. The last few rescue planes that would ever get out were besieged by South Viet troops clubbing civilians out of the way in their own efforts to escape the city. Lang had shot one soldier and yanked his body out of a helicopter to make room for himself and the baby.

Shortly after they'd landed on the aircraft carrier that would carry the masses of refugees to Guam, a South Viet general landed with his own personal chopper, having left his troops behind in the field to get out with some of his accumulated wealth. His chopper was a big one, but it landed carrying only the General and his pilot. The rest of the space in it had been crammed with the General's loot, including three motorbikes and some furniture. Lang had gone berserk and beaten the General almost unconscious before being subdued by the M.P.s.

The Government had smoothed over the incident. They'd decided he'd had a nervous breakdown, which was probably not far from the truth. Lang had been put on the shelf temporarily, too valuable an operator to be dropped completely.

Three months later they'd need him, in Argentina. That had been followed by Brazil, and then Chile. Lang watched his government shoring up police states as unpleasant as anything the Soviet Union could conjure up. He no longer thought of the United States as a knight fighting to help the peoples of the world achieve individual freedom of choice. Now it was only his hatred of Communists that kept him going.

5

It was getting dark when Lang reached Los Angeles. But he knew the L.A.-Washington flight schedules by heart, and there was still a lot of time before the last one out tonight. He drove first to see his father in Santa Monica.

His father had been pretty old when Lang was born. Now he was very old. For some years he'd lived in one of those suburban communities for retired people, where they didn't let in couples with children or likely to have children. But then he'd become senile, unable to care for himself. Lang and his sister had moved him into a nursing home.

It was a Victorian-style house six blocks in from the beach. Lang found his father watching television in his private room. It took time for the old man to respond to his son's voice. He looked up slowly, then returned his stare to the TV screen without a word or gesture of recognition.

It wasn't always like that. Sometimes he knew who Lang was, even talked with him. This time he didn't. But because Lang didn't know how long he'd be gone, he stayed, sitting there with his father staring at the television set for two hours before leaving.

Lang's beach house was some miles past Malibu, just off the Pacific Coast Highway. The back of the house was built firmly into the ground sloping down to the sand, the front end rested on stilts facing the ocean. His sister put a warning finger to her lips when Lang came in. "Hank's already asleep," she told him softly. "He wanted to talk you into taking him out to Marineland again tomorrow."

164

Duyen had named their son Hoang. In America that had been translated into Hank.

"I can't, Pat," Lang told his sister. "I've got to go to Washington, tonight. And I don't know when I'll be back." He went into his room, locking the pistol and rifle in his closet and pocketing the key so his son wouldn't get at them. He put the bag containing his doctorate work on the desk, which was piled with Julius Hay's plays and articles. Most of them had not yet been translated into English. That would have to wait, a little longer.

Hay was for Lang a healthy reminder of what he was fighting for, and against. Hungary's best modern playwright, he had been imprisoned in the Thirties charged with being a dangerous Communist, and in 1958 he'd been imprisoned again—charged with being a dangerous anti-Communist. Both charges, Hay said in his autobiography, were true.

Above his desk Lang had taped a file card on which he'd typed a quotation from a Frenchman a century before Hay's time: "What terrible masters the Russians would be if they should ever spread the weight of their rule . . . They would bring us a polar despotism such as the world has never known, silent as darkness, rigid as ice, insensible as bronze. Slavery without compensation or relief . . . Henri-Frédéric Amiel, 1856."

Lang's sister came into the room and watched him putting some clothes in a small suitcase. "He'll be disappointed, that you didn't even get a chance to say goodbye to him."

Lang knew it, and felt badly about it. "I'm disappointed too. Can't be helped. You'll have to explain it to him."

"Explain what? That you had to rush off to—I don't know what? To run over your grandmother for the President."

Lang laughed quietly. "Only I don't have a grandmother." He folded a pair of slacks neatly in the bag. "And you know, the guy who said that, he wasn't *completely* crazy. It was just his way of saying that sometimes personal considerations have to be put aside, if the welfare of the country depends on it. Without that, soldiers would never risk their lives to defend their country against invasion."

"The greatest good for the greatest number." Pat's tone was scornful. "That's Communist talk, isn't it?"

Lang looked at her soberly. "Not in my book. Pat, there's too many people who only care about themselves these days. The screw-everybody-else-I'm-all-right people. Don't give a damn about anything bigger than themselves. And, Pat, what distinguishes man from animals *is* caring about something bigger; whether it's art, religion, or country."

"Well, it seems to me to boil down to who you like best: your grandmother or the President. For me, family comes first. Then me. Then my country, I guess. The people who run my country, they're a long way down my list. Personally, I'd run over my President, any day, for my grandmother."

Lang grinned. "Only you don't have a grandmother, either."

He closed the suitcase, put it out in the living-dining room, and then quietly entered his son's room. He knelt by the bed, looking at Hoang in the moonlight coming through the open window, listening to him breathe. The boy was seven now, and beautiful. To Lang, he looked like Duyen.

He leaned down and kissed the round, smooth cheek. His son moved, rolled over without waking. Lang pulled the sheet over him again, kissed his forehead. He got up, and stood for a time looking through the window at the moonlit Pacific, listening to the crash of waves on the beach. Da Nang was a long way.

His sister drove Lang to the airport, and drove the car back home without waiting to see him off. He slept through the flight to Washington, and was at

Langley early the next morning for his appointment. The briefings that followed were thorough and included three hours of meetings at the NSA headquarters in Fort Meade.

Two days later Lang left for Europe, supplied with deep cover and advance authorization. To begin a search which, if he succeeded, would lead him eventually to Jorgen and Alexander Rhalles. And result in the death of Moira Rhalles.

Unless Sawyer found her first.

PART TWO

THE
SEARCHERS

"*There is a profound analogy between that natural passion, envy, and that social function, espionage. The spy hunts on others' account, like the dog. The envious man hunts on his own, like the cat.*"
—Victor Hugo: The Man Who Laughs

Bruno ... the lamp

TEN

1

Bruno had a dream late last night. A girl's face was staring up at him, out of swirling depths. Gradually, he saw that it was the face of his prisoner, Moira Rhalles. But much younger; her face as a child, frightened and appealing.

The young face remained the same, but the body was that of a bird, fluttering wildly inside a dark forest beneath a lake. Slim black branches, whipped by wind, struck at the bird, caught her, held her fast. The branches were strong wires, tightening inexorably as the bird struggled.

The face was the same: staring at him, childishly appealing. And dead.

Bruno woke in darkness with his heart pounding. He sat up on his narrow bed and reached for the battery lamp on the table beside him, switching it on. Squinting against the sudden light in his small tower room, he picked up his wristwatch. It was almost one o'clock in the morning.

He put down the watch and got out of bed, putting on dungarees and slipping his feet into felt slippers. Savagely, he told himself not to be ridiculous. It had been a dream. He was used to bad dreams. They'd been part of his life, as far back as he could remember. But this one was still disturbing him. Picking up the lamp, Bruno went out his open door and up the stone spiral stairway of the old tower.

The locked door to Moira Rhalles' cell was on the next landing. Bruno shone the lamp on it, and told himself again not to be foolish: she hadn't escaped, and she wasn't dead. He knew it—but he found himself drawing the two slide bolts, delicately, to make as little sound as possible.

The hinges were well oiled. The door opened noiselessly. Bruno shone the lamp down at the rough stones of the floor beside the cell, not wanting to wake her with the direct glare. That gave enough reflected light to make out her figure, curled on its side under the blanket. Bruno stood there motionless, listening. Finally he heard it: her quiet, steady breathing.

He backed out, softly, and relocked her cell door with the same care he'd used on opening it.

Inside the cell, Moira opened her eyes all the way, staring through the dark in the direction of the door, hearing the faint click as the bolts slid back into place. What had he wanted? Why had he come and just looked at her, at this time of night?

To reassure himself? Make certain she had not escaped? If he was still uneasy about that possibility, she had work to do with him. He had to be reassured, relaxed, the thought banished from his mind. If she couldn't accomplish that, Moira knew, there was no chance at all of attempting an escape on her own. She'd be reduced to a passive victim, with nothing but to wait, and hope.

She had work to do, to calm his worry about her...

In the tower room below her cell, Bruno put the lamp down on the table beside his bed. He got out of his slippers and dungarees, but continued to stand for a time, looking at one of the two objects on top of the small bureau: the carved stone figure, small and dark, of the prehistoric goddess.

It was so old, and oddly beautiful. And so evil . . . He picked it up, and stifled a sudden impulse to smash it against the wall. Instead, he opened the top drawer of the bureau and put the little statuette away, inside.

He looked for a moment at what was left on the bureau: a fading photograph in a frame. It was a picture of a very pretty girl of eighteen. His mother, dead before he'd known her long enough to remember. All he had of her was the photograph, and what he'd been told. About the *way* she'd died. He'd been almost two years old when it happened—he *should* be able to remember . . .

Bruno shut the drawer and went back to his bed. He switched off the lamp, and lay there in the blackness, forcing himself back down into sleep. But when the sleep finally came, it brought another dream: this one of a figure who stood over him, beside his bed. It might have been his mother—or the dark goddess.

2

Below Sawyer the black pool surged and foamed like an underworld beast struggling to rise up out of its pit. The crescendo of the underground waterfall reverberating within the confines of the cavern might have been its howling. Neyroud had to shout to be heard as he pointed his flashlight down at the jagged rocks projecting from the turbulence at the bottom.

"That is where we found Martinot's body." In his sixties, Neyroud still didn't allow his plumbing business in Barcelonnette to interfere with his passion for rock-climbing and exploring caves. He'd led the first search team in, after Professor Borelli had reported the failure of Martinot and the two women to emerge from the cave system. "The three of them must have fallen from this part of the ledge. About where we now stand."

Sawyer moved his left leg slightly. Under his boot the rough surface of the ledge did feel slippery.

Neyroud swung his flashlight beam to the hole where the subterranean river fought its way out of the cavern bottom. "The two women were swept away through that. The scuba divers who went in couldn't get far. Too much danger of being torn from their securing lines. And there was no point in taking the risk. The women couldn't have survived in there."

As outlined by Neyroud it was that obvious, and final. It hadn't happened that way, Sawyer knew. But the assumption that it did was natural, unless you had a reason to question the validity of the "accident." Sawyer took a last look at the parts of the watery cavern revealed by their head lamps and the flashlight. The place had the dismal beauty of a Doré pocket in hell.

"You said there's another way out," Sawyer shouted.

Neyroud nodded, wiped a hand across his steel-rimmed glasses, and turned away from the drop. Sawyer followed the tall, skinny figure along the ledge. Behind him was the opening through which Martinot had entered the cavern with Moira and Christine Jonquet. Neyroud left the ledge by way of the other opening. Sawyer went in after him.

They began to climb immediately, crawling up inside low passages, squeezing through narrow fissures within the living rock, snaking on their bellies through low, branching tunnels. It was less comfortable than the way down which Martinot had used; but in less than half an hour they were out.

They emerged from a crack in the convoluted rock formations on a hillside above a rugged, pine-forested valley cut through by the swift Ubaye River. Sawyer scanned the region, searching for something. On the other side of the river, topping a green-covered rock mass, an old chapel tower pointed a thin finger toward God. To the left a narrow waterfall dropped down a succession of cliffs and became a stream that spread out like lace among the rocks as it reached for the river. Beyond the highest cliffs rose three bare peaks: one sharply pointed, another heavily rounded, the third looking like a giant's castle.

Neyroud nodded in that direction. "We call those The Three Bishops, I don't know why. The east face of the pointy one makes an interesting climb." He switched off his head lamp.

Sawyer did the same, and took off the hard-hat Neyroud had lent him. But he kept on the muddied coveralls. In spite of the strong morning sunlight the air was chilled by the altitude and downdrafts from the surrounding Alps. The people of this region called it "The High Earth." Unable to find what he was looking for, Sawyer asked Neyroud: "Where's the ravine where we entered the cave?"

"The other side of this hill, behind us. We're more than a mile from it here."

So it would have been a simple matter to bring Moira out of the cave system by this route, without being seen by Professor Borelli, waiting near the other entrance. *If* Borelli hadn't been part of the plan.

Sawyer pointed down at a dirt road on the near side of the river. "Where does that lead?"

"To Barcelonnette, in that direction." Neyroud pointed. "The other way, it goes past some farms and joins the road to Seyne."

They could have taken Moira in either direction. And then to any part of France, if she really was still inside the country.

Neyroud was studying Sawyer thoughtfully. "If you are thinking that the two women somehow got out of the cave, you really must give up the hope." He shook his head sympathetically. "Believe me, there is no way out of that hole where Martinot died. I was one of the men who got Martinot's body up. Even with rope ladders, and others hauling us on lines, the force of the water made it extremely difficult."

He looked at his watch. It was after ten. "Time to get back to town, for me. My customers will be crying."

Sawyer sat down on a humped rock and got out a pack of cigarettes. "Let me rest a bit, first. I'm tired from all the climbing around in there, even if you are not."

Neyroud grinned. "I'm used to it." He accepted a cigarette from Sawyer, and sat beside him.

Sawyer took a cigarette for himself, and lit both. "I wonder how Gaspard Martinot knew about this cave?" His tone was that of a man merely making conversation, to pass a little time. "He lived in Sospel. That's a long way from here. Two hours' drive."

"But he was born here," Neyroud told him. "In Barcelonnette. He lived here until after the war. In the war, we used the caves around here to hide in, from the Germans."

"You and Martinot were part of an underground resistance group?"

"There were a number of groups in this region. Only loosely united; sometimes even opposed to each other. I belonged to one group. Martinot was part of a different one." Neyroud hesitated, seeming to remember something that bothered him. But all he said was: "We all used the caves, from time to time."

Sawyer sensed a holding back. He drew on his cigarette, gazing at the peaks of The Three Bishops. "This is beautiful country. Why did Martinot go away, after the war?"

Neyroud shrugged. "All of his family had been wiped out in the war. He had no one left here." Again the hesitation; the sense of holding back was stronger. "Maybe the memories troubled him. The things that happened here at the end of the war . . . It was a bad time. You can't imagine what it was like."

"I know what it was like," Sawyer said.

Neyroud shook his head. "You can't. You can read about it, but you can't *know*. You're too young; and you are American."

He'd shut up like a clam. There was only one way to pry him open, Sawyer knew. The French reputation for being unfriendly came from the fact that strangers made them uneasy. The cure was to open up your own life to them, with as many intimate details as possible. After that the French were trapped by their own psychology, because it was impossible for them to go on regarding you as a stranger. Sawyer had used the method before. It seldom failed.

"My father was a young American, too, at the time," he told Neyroud. "He's buried down in the Roya Valley. In a village called Tende. He was buried by the only survivor of a little resistance group my father had joined."

"Ah?" Curiosity opened the clam, just a little. Sawyer went on with it: the story of his father, a gunner who'd bailed out of a burning bomber, and landed in the woods near St.-Martin-Vésubie. "He was picked up by a group of resistance fighters, and stayed with them awhile. There was a seventeen-year-old girl named Babette with the band. She and my father fell in love; you know how fast those things happened in those times. They were married secretly, in a cave much like this one. I was probably conceived in that cave."

"So—then you are actually *French*," Neyroud said. For the French, you were whatever your mother was; one could never be absolutely *sure* about your real father.

Sawyer didn't argue the point. He fed Neyroud more details: The SS units hunting the area had finally located the resistance group. Sawyer's father and mother escaped to the south; finally reaching Marseilles, where they were almost caught. They would have been, except for a gangster involved with black-market smuggling, who decided Babette was too young and pretty—and pregnant—to die in a Gestapo torture cell. He smuggled the two of them across into Spain.

Sawyer had been born there. But by then his father was gone: back with the U.S. Army, which had decided his experience with the French resistance made him of special usefulness. They dropped him back in southern France, to help get the resistance groups ready for the Allied invasion. He went hunting for a resistance group to start with, and found one, the day before they walked into a German ambush. They all died, except one man who survived wounds so terrible the enemy thought him dead.

"It is odd," Neyroud confided after a moment. "Though I am so much older than you, we both lost our fathers in the same war, and not far from each other. And your mother? She is still alive?"

Sawyer nodded. "She married again. A good man, we get on well. The last few months they've been living in Japan. The shipping company he works for sent him to represent them there."

"Where were you raised, then?"

"In France, part of the time. The rest in America, with my grandparents. Chicago. My grandfather was a cop there, until he retired. My mother thought I should know my father's country, and family. I shuttled back and forth."

"Interesting, to be brought up that way—in two such different worlds."

Sawyer studied Neyroud, and decided he was ready. "I sometimes visit my father's grave, down in Tende. And talk with the man who escaped, when he was killed with the rest of the group . . ." Sawyer dropped the butt of his cigarette and ground it out under his heel. "So you see, I do know what it was like in those days. Whatever happened to make Martinot leave here, for example, I doubt that it would surprise me."

"I suppose not. But I tell you, some things are difficult to stomach, even for those of us who were through the worst. Martinot, he was always a wild boy. But brave, in the war. Too brave, maybe. The Germans, he hit them hard, and they searched for him hard. When they couldn't find him, some of the SS slaughtered his whole family, in retaliation. After that, like some others I knew, victory was not enough for him. He wanted vengeance, too."

178

Sawyer gave him another cigarette, and lit it. "I know rough things were done then, at the end. A lot of people had scores to settle."

Neyroud took a deep drag, and squinted against the smoke curling from his mouth. "There was a local girl—she had been the mistress of an SS officer stationed in Barcelonnette. While the Nazis were lording it over us. This officer, he was killed in the German retreat. The girl was left behind, alone. Guilty of collaboration, no longer protected . . . Some of Martinot's group kidnaped her, to punish her, they said. They all raped her, of course. Many times. But for Martinot, that was not enough. In the end, when the others had finished, he killed her. At least, that is what one heard. It was never officially investigated, you understand."

Sawyer nodded. "A lot happened then, that everybody figured it was better to bury, with the dead."

"Exactly." Neyroud jerked a thumb at the cave behind them. "It was in there that they held the girl. And there she died. Perhaps, by Martinot's hands. Anyway, that is what everyone here believed. So he went away, and never came back."

"Until now—to die in the same place as the girl."

"Yes. Sometimes, I think, Destiny likes to play unpleasant little jokes with men's lives—don't you agree?"

3

On his return from America to France, Sawyer had stopped in Paris only long enough to pick up his car, make two phone calls, and inform Alain Gassin that he was taking a few days' leave from Audubon Research Consultants. He didn't tell Gassin more than that. Eventually, he would have to, because the company's extensive resources could save him considerable time in the search for Moira. But even then, the need for secrecy would make Sawyer extremely careful about what he told, and how he used those resources.

And first, Sawyer had to find the basic openings into which the preliminary line of inquiry should be directed. To determine this he needed certain information, from three primary sources. The first had been Neyroud. The second was Professor John Borelli.

From Barcelonnette, Sawyer drove south and east to the upper Roya Valley. It was an area he knew intimately, both in reality and in a lifetime of imagining. He hadn't been back there in almost five years. It was strange that it should be Moira who was drawing him back now.

The drive took him two hours. At the same time, it took him back more than three decades—to a war he had never known and a father who had never known him. It was a region in which it was impossible to avoid thinking of both.

They remembered their last war, in those mountain villages along the upper Roya River, in the southeastern reach of the French Alps. It was one of the last places liberated from the German forces. On hearing that the Americans, British, and Free French had landed on the south coast of France, the people of the area mistakenly believed the troops would reach there in a few days. The resistance groups emerged from hiding and attacked the Germans in the open, much too soon.

The Nazi fanatics among the occupying forces—the SS troops, the Gestapo, and their vicious French helpers, the Milice—had always wielded their power with arrogant sadism. When they realized their war was lost they retaliated with vindictive savagery against the villages, like a dying snake lashing out one last time. Many among the regular German Army did what they could to stop the mass torture and slaughter of the populace. But most of the time they were too busy fighting off attacks, and trying to organize an orderly retreat, to interfere.

The street names in these villages were like scars of old wounds that still give bitter pain: "Rue Maurice Sassi—Died for France." "Rue Louis Monello—Murdered by the SS, Age 17." "Rue Lieutenant Kalck." "Rue Jean-Pierre Pannunzio—Martyr For The Resistance."

Then there were the little stone memorials on walls of narrow lanes and tiny squares, each adorned with fresh flowers once a year: "Antoinette Siccardi—Shot Here by the Milice. Never Forget." "Olivier Cavalucci —Died In Attack on SS." "Rose Lautier—Tortured to Death By The Gestapo." "Lucie Giovanoni—Died In Deportation, Age 2." "To Our Children Killed Or Lost In The Second World War—In Passing, Bow in Respect For Their Sacrifice."

Most of the family names were Italian, because the upper Roya was close to Italy and most was once part of it. But all the first names were French. Because though some of the old people still spoke better Italian than French, all considered themselves citizens of France. They had given their blood, and the lives of their children, to prove it.

They had lost many more in the First World War than in the Second. The Gioannis alone—a family spread between the neighboring villages of Fontan and Soarge—lost nineteen boys in the First War. But they died far away, in the Marne and Verdun. Only three Gioannis were killed in the Second War—François, Etienne, and Madeleine; but all three died right there, in the villages. Everyone saw it. No one forgot.

Professor John Borelli's mother had been a Gioanni. That made him a Gioanni, in spite of never having met any of his relatives in the upper Roya before. The village of Soarge was less than ten miles from the Valley of Marvels, where Borelli had been investigating the prehistoric symbols carved on remote canyon walls. It was only natural that he would settle in with part of the family in Soarge, during his recuperation from the illness that had begun the day Moira Rhalles disappeared.

The house in which he was staying was in a crooked stone passageway where the least ancient object in sight was the metal street sign: "Rue Lt. Jean Revelli—Died For France." Borelli wasn't there, but Madame Gioanni told Sawyer where to find him. He walked back to the corner and turned into Rue Jeanne d'Arc. Soarge was built into the slope of a mountain, and its streets were steep, crooked, and too narrow for cars. This one twisted down and became a dark tunnel burrowing underneath the floors of a dozen attached stone houses. There was just enough room for Sawyer to pass a donkey struggling upward under a load of firewood, pushed from behind by a woman who looked, in the darkness, as old and crooked as the street.

Sawyer emerged into blinding sunlight on the Esplanade Général De Gaulle, at the bottom of the village. One side of the esplanade ended at the edge of cliffs dropping to the river twisting through a tight bend far below. Fragile, shrunken old men in old dark suits sat on iron benches warming their thin blood in the hot sun.

On the other side of the esplanade a burly man sat under the shade trees, wearing faded jeans and a sports shirt. He was engrossed in a book, glasses perched on the tip of his large nose. He looked up when Sawyer spoke to him, pushing his glasses back onto the bridge of his nose. "Yes, I'm Borelli."

"My name is March," Sawyer told him. "I'm a journalist, with the European Magazine Syndicate." He gave Professor Borelli a business card.

Borelli glanced at the card, gave it back. "I've already talked to quite a few journalists, if it's the cave tragedy you're interested in. I can't add much to what you've probably read in the newspaper accounts."

Sawyer sat down on the bench beside him. "I'm af-

182

ter a different angle on it. The perils of archaeology —or all the discoveries that've been made since France became so cave-conscious." His smile was disarming. "To tell you the truth," he admitted, "I'm not sure what I'm after. I'm just fishing, for anything that would make a salable magazine article."

Borelli laughed. "We've all got to make a living, somehow. How'd you know I was here?"

"I went looking for you in the Valley of Marvels. Your group there told me you'd been sick . . ."

"I'm not *sick*. I had some kind of food poisoning. It's just left my insides queasy."

"I understand it started the day Moira Rhalles died. With Martinot and the French girl, Christine Jonquet."

Borelli nodded, sadness darkening his face at the memory. "Right after breakfast, before they went into the cave."

"Food poisoning doesn't usually last that long. If you've still got it, it's serious."

"No, I've seen doctors, had all the tests. It's only a lingering aftereffect. I'm getting over it, but it's taking time. I just have to stick to bland food, and not much of it at one time or my insides get upset." Borelli shrugged. "Well, you're certainly not interested in hearing about my stomach troubles."

Sawyer was, but he let it pass for the moment. "I read that it was a small Stone Age sculpture of a cult goddess found by Gaspard Martinot that caused you to investigate the cave."

"Yes. A Venus figure. As you probably know, they are extremely rare. So it was quite an exciting find. This one was exquisitely carved, out of dark stone."

"How'd Martinot happen to show it to you?"

"It was Christine Jonquet he showed it to, first."

"She wasn't part of your dig group, was she?"

"No, but she knew Moira. She was taking the three-year course in museology at the Louvre School in Paris. A couple of months ago—sometime in late February, I believe Moira said—she went to America for a few weeks, to look over museums there. She came to Philadelphia to see our archaeological museum at the university, since it's one of the best in the world. That's where she and Moira met."

A man who has spent most of his professional life watching other people, studying their movements and expressions, had to develop techniques to keep it from being obvious. Normal people didn't observe others in the same way; they were too embarrassed, and too conscious of their own image. Sawyer's visual assessment of the archaeologist was achieved through short, occasional glances. For the most part he gazed at the wooded mountain slopes rising from the other side of the river, listening for undertones in the voice.

"Moira was arranging a display of flint tools from her last dig in Nubia," Borelli explained. "Christine Jonquet began asking her questions. Like most teachers, Moira was always interested in students who were both curious and knowledgeable. They talked for almost an hour."

"They kept in touch, afterwards?"

"I don't believe so. It was just happenstance: the Jonquet girl was driving through this area, on her way south to the Riviera. She stopped in St. Dalmas for gas. That's the nearest village to our dig area, and there's a bistro next to the gas station where we go at times for a break. She came in for a coffee, and she and Moira recognized each other. They were both surprised, and delighted, naturally."

"Naturally." Sawyer had his own thoughts about how much of a surprise the "chance" meeting had been for Christine Jonquet.

"It was evening when she went on her way. She stopped overnight in a hotel in Sospel. Near the hotel was the antique shop owned by Martinot and his wife. Christine visited it in the morning. Martinot was excited to learn that she was a student at the Louvre. He told her he had found something, and wanted to know what she thought about it. Well, when she saw what it was, *she* became quite excited. She drove back up to tell Moira, who consulted with me."

"And the three of you went back to Martinot in Sospel."

"If it really was a genuine Venus figure he'd found, it could be the discovery of a lifetime, for Moira and myself. We examined it, and were both convinced it was genuine. But it was necessary to find confirming evidence, in the cave where it was found."

"Did Martinot explain how he'd happened to be in a cave all the way over in Barcelonnette?" Sawyer asked. "That's a two- or three-hour drive from Sospel."

"Caving has become a favorite weekend sport for many Frenchmen ever since the discoveries at Altamira and Lascaux. Martinot told us he'd been caving all over southeastern France for years. It was only the previous weekend that he'd explored the cave where he discovered the Venus figure. A tragic discovery, as it turned out."

Borelli fell silent, brooding over it. Sawyer waited, not pushing him. He spotted a shepherd's stone building among the trees on a high slope across the river. His eyes moved, scanning the slopes, trying to locate the shepherd, and his flock.

"Martinot was as anxious as we to prove it was authentic," Borelli resumed somberly. "Since he hoped to sell it for a good price. He agreed to take us to the cave. There are no roads for ordinary cars near it, so we went in his jeep. To Barcelonnette first, where we stayed overnight at the Hôtel des Alpes."

"That where you got hit by the food poisoning?"

"I felt it immediately after breakfast, as we were leaving the hotel. But all I'd had was coffee and rolls. Perhaps it was something in the dinner the night before, though none of the others got sick. The only thing I ate that they didn't was a candy bar. The

185

doctor says that's a possibility, but not likely." Borelli shrugged helplessly. "Whatever did it, the cramps that morning were not pleasant."

"But you went along to the cave, anyway."

"I've had a delicate stomach all my life," Borelli explained. "So at first I just assumed it was some of my old trouble starting again, and I know the remedy for that. I got some medicine from the local pharmacy and took it before we started out. It controlled the cramps, but by the time we reached the cave area my legs were getting too weak to go in with the others."

"Luckily for you." Sawyer glanced at Borelli then, and saw nothing in his face but lingering sadness. "According to the papers you waited out there almost three hours before going in to see what was keeping them. That right?"

The archaeologist nodded. "I didn't go in far. I was feeling better at that point, but exploring caves one doesn't know alone is foolhardy. I called, but they didn't answer. Finally I left them a note at the cave entrance, and drove the jeep back to town for help. A local spelunker who knew the cave led a search group. I didn't go with them because the cramps had come back, more violently than before. About the rest —the finding of Martinot's body, and the failure to find the bodies of Moira and the French girl—I only know about that from the papers. By then I was in a clinic having my stomach pumped out."

Sawyer had located the sheep; a long line of them moving along a high ridge. He still couldn't spot the shepherd. "Did the clinic find out what caused your sickness?"

"Just that it was some kind of food poisoning. They couldn't pinpoint *which* food was the culprit."

If Borelli had had any part in the plot to snatch Moira, Sawyer could think of no reason he'd still be pretending to suffer aftereffects of food poisoning so long after the pretense had served its purpose. If his illness was not a fake, he'd had no part in the plot. This fitted Sawyer's impression of the man. But he was not relying solely on that impression.

An investigation firm in Philadelphia was at that moment engaged in a complete check of Professor Borelli's background and recent extracurricular activities. *Not* the same firm Sawyer had given the cassettes to, after wiping names and certain words from them. If he gave too many parts of this to a single firm, someone could put them together, and draw correct conclusions about the true nature of the investigation.

Sawyer asked Borelli: "What happened to the statuette Martinot showed you?"

"Vanished. I know he took it with him to Barcelonnette. Apparently afraid we'd slip back during the night and steal it from his shop." Borelli's tone was understanding. "Perhaps he had it in a jacket pocket, when he fell inside the cave—and it was washed away by the force of the river down there. At any rate, it's gone." He sounded almost as sad as he had about Moira.

"The original reason for going into the cave, you said, was to find other prehistoric remains. I suppose you've been in no shape to go back there, since?"

"I haven't. But several of my young student-assistants from the dig have. With the caver who led the rescue effort. They explored the cave thoroughly. But found absolutely no supporting evidence to indicate that the Venus figure might have come from there."

Sawyer eyed him then. "Is it possible the figure was made recently?"

"A fake? It could have been. Though I'm fairly sure it wasn't."

"But you can't be certain, can you? As I understand it, an object made of stone can only be dated by what it's found *with*. By amino-acid tests to date pollen in any earth clumps clinging to it. Or radiocarbon dating of organic matter, like bones or wooden objects, found in the same spot. Right?"

Borelli nodded. "Is archaeology a longtime interest, or did you just bone up on it before coming to see me?"

"A little of both," Sawyer answered honestly. "So, since you had no way to confirm the figure's age, it *could* be a forgery."

"If it was, it was done by someone very good at it. Good enough to fool both myself and Moira Rhalles. There is more to my profession than scientific testing, you know. You acquire a *feel* for these things." Professor Borelli shook his head. "I don't believe it was a forgery. My assumption—and it is only that, a guess—is that it was stolen. And Gaspard Martinot was trying to peddle it for the thieves, passing it off as his own discovery."

Sawyer said slowly, "From what I've read, there are only about thirteen known Venus figures of that kind and quality, anywhere in the world. Wouldn't you have heard about it, if one of them were missing?"

"Of course," Borelli acknowledged. "That's the thing which really puzzles me. I don't know of *any* Venus figure that has ever been discovered, and later stolen."

Sawyer took a moment to digest that. "How big was the one Martinot showed you?"

"About the size of my hand. I measured it. Exactly nine inches tall. And so lovely . . ." Borelli's eyes had become dreamy with longing. "Dark stone, but not quite black. There are two main types, you know. Most are extremely obese. The other type is slimmer, more graceful. This was one of the latter. Long, slender figure. The usual emphasis on breasts, butttocks, and pelvic region, of course. But not grotesque. Very like the one found at Gagarino. The heads on most of these statuettes are merely featureless knobs. But this was a rare type, resembling the Brassempouy Venus figure. Same stylized hair and individualized face. Her features were quite weathered, but somehow that only added to her beauty."

Sawyer took a moment to fix each facet of this description in his mind.

Borelli glanced toward the old men sitting in the sun. "Seeing *them* there all the time, I begin to feel I'm absorbing all their years. On top of my own, which are quite enough." He looked at his watch, then hopefully at Sawyer. "Are you by chance traveling in the direction of St. Dalmas when you leave here?"

"As a matter of fact, I am."

"Some of my group should be at the bistro there soon. I need to see young people, from time to time. To feel I'm still among the living. If you'll drive me, we can talk more on the way."

"Fair enough." Sawyer stood up, and waited.

Borelli smiled gratefully, made a small fold in the page he'd been reading, closed the book, and walked slowly with Sawyer to the parking area at the foot of the village.

Below Soarge the narrow car route twisted down the mountain slope to a two-lane road along one bank of the Roya. Sawyer turned north onto it, following the sharp bends of the river carving its way through tight rocky gorges.

"I'd like to know more about those little statuettes," Sawyer told Borelli. "The kind Martinot showed you. The accounts in the papers were highly romanticized."

"It is impossible," Borelli stated firmly, "to *over*romanticize a Venus figure. Just consider what they are: the first manifestation of the religious awe and terror of the first true men. Whispers from the retreating cold of the last ice age. Fashioned by the race that wiped out the Neanderthal Men, and became our ancestors."

"And these statuettes are about twenty thousand years old, is that right?"

"Perhaps *twice* that age." Borelli's voice held the respectful hush of a novice in a cathedral. "Venus figures have only been found with artifacts of the Aurignacian period, and we're not sure how long that period lasted. Aurignacian artifacts have turned up in the Abri Pataud excavations, in the Dordogne, which are apparently thirty thousand years old. And there's a Hungarian cave where they've found some that give a radiocarbon dating of *forty* thousand years."

Professor Borelli raised both hands expressively. "So what can one say about the age of a Venus figure? Except that she is incredibly old."

Sawyer shot him a sidelong smile. "And incredibly romantic."

Borelli quietly agreed: "Incredibly."

"What does she represent, exactly?"

"Exactly—everything. I say that advisedly. *Everything*. In her benign aspect she represents birth, life, sexual desire, fertility, growth, hope. In her terrible aspect she is decay, destruction, disease, darkness, and death. She is mother and destroyer, the womb and the grave."

The man beside Sawyer radiated intense excitement as he warmed to his subject: "She has been called The Great Mother, and also The Eater of the Dead. And so many other names: the Great Goddess, the Queen of Death, the Earth Mother. In essence, what she represents *is* the Earth—out of whom everything is born, by whom everything is nourished, into whom everything ultimately sinks in death, to provide food for rebirth."

"And her statue is always found in caves."

Borelli nodded. "She is also associated with caves as a symbol. Many primitive people believed—and some still do—that caves are passages through which the first humans emerged onto the surface of the world. Each newborn soul still travels those same passages, out of the region of death, into the world of the living. And on dying return the same way, through the cave passages from this world back down to the underworld. The goddess is a personification of that two-way labyrinth between death and life, in addition to her other meanings."

As Professor Borelli told it, she'd represented *so much* that the civilizations which inherited her memory couldn't take her whole. Couldn't accept, for example, that she was both Good and Evil. They'd begun subdividing her various attributes, portioning them out among different gods and goddesses of smaller scope.

Sawyer could not predict how much of the background information would prove to be of use. But some of it would, because it was the lure that had been used to seize Moira. He listened carefully to everything Borelli told him, registering each point that was pertinent to the original goddess:

The Sumerians had made her into twin sisters: Inanna, goddess of heaven and light; Ereshkigal, goddess of hell and darkness. Two faces of the same goddess. In Egypt, the two aspects were again divided between sisters: Isis and Nephthys.

"You might say her various subdivisions are the history of religion," Borelli pointed out. "The Greeks and Celts with their triple moon goddesses: Selene, Artemis, and Hecate—for heaven, earth, and hell; Morrigan, Macha and Badh—for birth, growth, and death. Even Christianity is a continuation of the Earth Mother. With her bountiful aspect given to God and the angels; her fearful qualities to Satan and his devils."

Sawyer swung around a slow truck. "And she never got put back together again."

Borelli smiled briefly. "Some religions came close. Ancient Crete had the Mother of Mysteries, whom you've probably seen pictures of: a beauty with bared breasts, holding a snake in each hand. And India has Kali. Just look at some of her statues: enticing body, frightening face; hands offering gifts and comfort, and brandishing knives and skulls."

Professor Borelli fell silent for a moment. "But—all of it started with the little statuette out of the ice age. Probably our first deity." He stared ahead through the windshield, and grimaced angrily. "I even held her in my hand. And now she's lost. Forever."

4

When Sawyer dropped Professor Borelli off in St. Dalmas, it was three o'clock in the afternoon. In Italy, the plane carrying Charles Lang from Washington had just landed outside Rome.

Lang took a taxi into the city, and registered in a small hotel at the end of the Via Flaminia, overlooking a narrow bend in the Tiber. His room was large and simply furnished. From the single tall window he could see the Milvian Bridge, spanning the river.

Lang stood for a time gazing down at the low, solid stone bridge. On it Constantine the Great had fought the battle which had made him Emperor of Rome. Before the battle Constantine swore to God that if victory were his he would show his gratitude by making Christianity the sole, official religion of the Roman Empire. It was because of what happened on that bridge, one day in A.D. 312, that Europe and America were Christian.

So much, thought Lang, for those who scoffed at what one man could do to alter history.

He turned from the window and went into the bathroom to burn the passport and flight ticket he'd used between Washington and Rome. He had another passport on him, which gave him another name and was stamped to indicate that he had flown from New York to London almost two weeks ago. He also had substitute flight tickets, according to which he was a normal American tourist doing Europe on a fast three-week vacation.

The tickets, stapled together, showed clearly that he had spent four days in London, four in Paris, three in Nice—and was just finishing his three scheduled days in Rome. On the following day he was booked to Budapest; after which, according to his tickets, he would fly to Vienna, Copenhagen, and back to New York. There was nothing on Lang to reveal what he really was, or that he might have any reason other than sightseeing for being in Europe.

Lang flushed the last of the ashes down the toilet, and went to the phone to confirm his seat on the following morning's flight from Rome to Budapest.

ELEVEN

1

After leaving Professor Borelli in St. Dalmas, Sawyer continued to drive north, toward Tende. The man he had sent for should be there by now, waiting for him.

The road stuck to the river all the way, following every twist of the Roya through its narrow gorges. It passed high ruins of one stone and brick railroad bridge after another. All of them had been blown up by the retreating German Army, to slow the pursuing Allied troops. There hadn't been a train through this area since. Other reminders were the man-made holes and reinforced concrete bunkers in the cliffs and slopes on either side: entrances to the underground fortifications that honeycombed the mountains this close to the Italian frontier. They hadn't been much more useful than the Maginot Line, along the German border. All that was left inside them were miles of useless tunnels containing nothing but rusting metal and muddy water.

Road and river followed a long sweeping curve together, and at the end of it the walls of the last gorge fell away from each other. They joined the sides of a short, bowl-shaped valley surrounded by round-humped green mountains. On the far side of the bowl the village of Tende appeared, all at once. It was spread out against a curving cliff like an upright gray and black fan; merged stone houses and slate roofs rising on top of each other.

It was crowned by the last vestiges of a fortress-castle destroyed three hundred years earlier: a massive round tower and a single tall shard of another, outlined against the sky. The castle area between them had become the Tende graveyard, tombs and gravestones piling above each other against the cliff in an upward continuation of the village.

Beyond the tombs at the very top rose range after range of the Alps. Among the highest mountains the strong sunlight reflected from patches and fingers of dazzling whiteness: glaciers, left behind by the same retreating ice age which had produced the little goddess who had lured Moira to the cave.

Sawyer parked his car on the Place de la Résistance, beside the stone pillar listing Tende's dead in both world wars. *James Sawyer*—it looked odd, among all those French and Italian names. His son, ten years older than James Sawyer had been when he'd died, stood for a moment staring at the name. Then he turned away.

Tende was the last stop before the Italian frontier. Like most border towns, it had more bistros and hotels than its size would otherwise warrant, concentrated along the newer section flanking the road that continued into Italy. Sawyer went past them to the post office. Inside he placed a call to the Paris number of a business security firm which specialized in banks and insurance companies. He asked the switchboard operator there for Gérard Beaufils.

Beaufils came on sounding harried but amused: "You certainly expect quick service."

"You don't need much time these days, with those centralized bank computers."

"It is not *so* simple. But, I do have the answer for you, as it happens. The man you asked about—this Gaspard Martinot—he and his wife had a joint checking account in the Crédit Lyonnais in Sospel."

"Had?" Sawyer sounded mildly puzzled.

"He died recently, according to the bank manager. You didn't know?"

"No, but don't expect a bigger fee for the information. It's not pertinent to our inquiry." Sawyer had not told Beaufils the nature of the inquiry, and was not worried that he might get curious about it. That was one usefulness of private firms. They probed only as far as you went on paying them to. They'd never dig further, unless they smelled big money at the other end.

"Martinot's widow still has the account," Beaufils went on, as though referring to notes on his desk. "But there's not much in it after paying his funeral expenses: 312 francs, 70 centimes, as of this morning. There never was much in it, at any one time. They made small deposits fairly regularly, normal income for a little antique shop in the country. Both of them made withdrawals from time to time; again, small accounts, consistent with normal modest living expenses. At no time did either of them make any unusually large deposit in this bank."

Beaufils paused. Sawyer smiled dully at the phone. "In *this* bank," he repeated sourly. "Don't string it out, Gérard. I've got other things to do, if you haven't."

There was a chuckle at the other end of the line. "Martinot has a savings account at the BNP in Peira-Cava." That was a ski-resort town an hour's drive northwest of Sospel. "Apparently he came into a bit of money he didn't want his wife to know about. She hasn't contacted the bank there. BNP wasn't even informed that Martinot is dead."

"When did he open the BNP account?"

"This year. Early in March. With a deposit of five thousand French francs. In cash." With the current exchange, that came to more than a thousand dollars. "There has been only one other deposit since he opened the account," Beaufils went on. "The same amount. Five thousand, again in cash. Late in April."

Sawyer got out his little notebook and opened it. "I'd like the exact dates of both deposits." He marked

196

the dates in his notebook. The last deposit was dated two days before Moira had gone into the cave with Martinot and the French girl.

"That's it?" he demanded. "No other bank accounts anywhere else, for either Martinot or his wife?"

"Not in France, at any rate."

"Thanks, Gérard. I'll send you a check."

"You don't need anything further on Martinot?"

"No," Sawyer told him. He did, but not from the same source.

2

Gustave Jarno, the only one who'd survived the ambush of the resistance group in which Sawyer's father had been killed, had died five years ago, never having entirely recovered from his wounds. But the bar he'd owned in the medieval section of Tende was still there, run by a couple Jarno's widow had sold it to before returning to her family in Dijon. It was there that Sawyer had set his rendezvous with Fritz Donhoff.

Sawyer took the Rue Colonel Lonardi up into the old town. It was a climbing tunnel-passage of cobblestone ramps and steps that changed direction five times in thirty seconds. There were no separate houses. They were all grafted to their neighbors: above, below, and on several sides. This made the old section a compact unit when viewed from outside, but a confusing maze to thread through, with the haphazard passages cutting under house floors, between walls, over roofs.

The bar was in a very small square near the top of the maze, under the great round tower at the base of the cemetery. The square echoed with the sound of the fountain at one end: three plain metal spouts pouring water into a large, eroded marble tub. The other end of the square was open, overlooking a jumble of dark slate roofs tumbling down toward the Roya River. The air was permeated with the odor of manure and wet hay, from the donkeys stabled in the bottom rooms of the joined stone houses on the third side of the square. Donhoff was waiting for Sawyer on the other side, at one of the two tables in front of the tiny bar.

A big, heavy-set man with glossy white hair and large, baggy eyes, Fritz Donhoff was an anachronistic holdover from a totally different Europe which had disappeared between the wars. He dressed like a Thirties dandy: dark velvet suit with a red carnation in the lapel, an opal stickpin in his flowered tie, pearl cuff links, and a large gold ring in the shape of an eagle's head on the little finger of his left hand. In spite of all the decorative paraphernalia, Donhoff managed to convey an old-fashioned dignity and impressive calm.

He raised a large, plump hand in greeting as Sawyer joined him at the table. "Perfect time. I just got here, myself." Donhoff's voice was habitually soft and gentle, and his French was so good that most people assumed he'd been born in France. He *was* a French citizen, now. But he was from Bavaria, where he'd been a detective with the Munich police when Hitler had come to power.

"I appreciate your coming this far from Paris on short notice," Sawyer told him.

"We are friends," Donhoff said simply. "And you did say it was a personal matter." His smile was warm, somewhat shy.

By 1938 the vengefulness of the Nazi Party, which he'd scathingly denounced whenever the subject came up, had forced him to flee from Germany to save his neck. He'd gone to Paris, that second home of all exiles, and lived the drab exile life of bleak rooms and ill-paying jobs, mostly as a waiter. When all German nationals in France had been put in detention camps at the beginning of the war, Donhoff had been hidden by a cop who knew his anti-Nazi record. Later, when his fellow Germans had marched triumphantly into Paris, Donhoff and his police friend had both vanished into the underworld of the Resistance. By the time he'd emerged at the end of the war, he'd come to be known as The Executioner, because of the number of Nazi collaborators and Gestapo agents he had murdered.

It was said that several nights after the war ended Fritz Donhoff had walked out on the Pont Neuf and dropped the pistol he'd used into the Seine. At any rate he had never used a gun again. And he hadn't returned to his native Germany, applying instead for French citizenship, which had been bestowed on him as a reward for his work with the Resistance. That work had also given him a great many useful connections in the veterans' organizations of the Resistance throughout France. This, plus his police experience, got him a job as investigator for a large Paris law firm. But he hadn't stayed there long.

After the war millions of displaced persons had wandered over Europe, searching for some surviving member of vanished families. And there were thousands of families seeking loved ones torn from them, and lost. Husbands and wives, sisters and brothers, parents and children—all desperately hunting for each other. Some had come to the offices of the Paris law firm for help. That had been the start.

Fritz Donhoff had begun combing Europe and the Middle East, checking records, consulting refugee officials, establishing contacts with police in all countries in the process of his searches. In many cases the people sought turned out to be dead. But there were survivors, and Donhoff established an exceptional reputation for finding them. He never returned to the law firm.

Finding missing persons was still Donhoff's specialty. Which entailed tracing people's movements, and tracking down every facet of their backgrounds. There was no one in Europe who was better at it, in Sawyer's opinion.

A handsome blond woman with a powerful figure came out of the bar and asked what they would like. Her smile was pleasant and her French had a strong Dutch accent. Donhoff ordered a glass of local red wine. Sawyer asked for a coffee. When she went inside, he glanced around the square. The other table was empty. There was no one close enough to overhear them.

"I've got a delicate problem on my hands," he told Donhoff. Point by point, he began to outline what had happened to Moira Rhalles and her husband.

Sawyer held nothing back. Most of the people he used on this job would be told only as much as was necessary for the narrow assignments he gave them. But investigators with partial knowledge could deliver only partial information. To be sensitive to which piece of information might be useful, to know how to fit the different pieces from different sources together, it was necessary to know the whole thing.

If Sawyer were the only one with the whole picture, it was going to take too long to push the search through the several channels required. He needed help, to move it faster.

Sawyer could not estimate how much time was left. He did not know about Lang, working from the opposite direction, cutting steadily into that time. But he did know it could at any moment become too late for his efforts to matter. Rhalles might crack. Moira's snatchers could panic. Any of a dozen things could abruptly go wrong and end Moira's life.

There were only three people with the ability to help whom Sawyer was certain he could trust with the whole story. Donhoff was one of them. Even if he refused the assignment, what he learned would go no further. Sawyer knew that, better than he knew himself.

Donhoff listened to him without interrupting, his great, baggy eyes intent on Sawyer's face, the methodical mind behind those eyes at work on what he said.

Sawyer paused when the woman came out with their orders. Donhoff sipped his wine and smiled his pleasure at her. Sawyer stirred sugar in his coffee and waited for her to leave before resuming.

But it was Donhoff who spoke first: "Pierre-Ange, I don't know if trouble finds you or you find trouble, but you're in it again."

"I know. It can't be helped."

"If this gets out, you are a ruined man. Do you know *that?* Espionage and high-level treason. And you're an accessory, since you're concealing your knowledge of it. That can get you twenty years in an American prison, if your country finds out. If you manage not to be dragged back to America, you'd become a stateless person. And probably unemployable, considering the pressure your country can bring to bear."

"That's what happens *if* I get caught at it," Sawyer pointed out sourly. "On the other hand, there's what happens to Moira Rhalles, if I do nothing."

Donhoff eyed him thoughtfully. "Yes, that's it, of course." There was sad understanding in his tone. "Always, it has been someone you care about who pushed you in the soup."

That, Sawyer admitted to himself grudgingly, was the truth. His grandfather had gotten him onto the Chicago police force, in the first place. Sawyer's unique background had made him a natural from the start for work as an undercover cop. Posing as a minor French criminal in hiding from the French police. His success, especially in the narcotics scene in Chicago, had resulted in an offer to become a federal narc.

That had been a beauty of a job: mostly in Europe, with good pay and a great expense account, which could be made greater by trading his dollars on local black markets. His future had been rosy.

Then his grandfather had contacted him: the daughter of a close friend of his was in a Mexican prison, with her boy friend, on a marijuana rap. According to her father, she was being treated horribly there. Sawyer's grandfather wanted him to see what he could do about getting her out, or at least making her situation more bearable.

Sawyer had wangled a leave "for personal reasons," and gone to Mexico. Federal narcs there had managed to get him into Lecumberri Prison as a privileged visitor. What he'd found was even worse than he'd expected. The girl, eighteen years old, had been raped and sexually tortured so often by certain guards that she was close to suicide. Her boy friend had been beaten so badly he'd never walk straight again. The other young Americans in the prison had all been subjected to regular, brutal abuse. Some of them had complained secretly to a visitor from the State Department. After he'd left, those who'd talked had been beaten unconscious.

Sawyer had gone to see the State Department man, who warned him to mind his own business. It was, other narcs told him, part of a deliberate policy begun in 1969, when President Nixon had been under pressure to "do something about dope." Instead of going after the big leaders of the drug racket, Nixon had pressured Mexico into grabbing as many vacationing Americans as could be caught with a marijuana cigarette, and going "real rough" with them.

Sawyer had leaked it to the news media, and gotten fired. It had been tight for a while, until he'd landed the job as Senate investigator. Which had been even better: just as good pay and expenses, more prestige. Until he'd had to do a crude cover-up job for a slimy Marseilles gangster who in a decent moment, before Sawyer had been born, had saved the lives of his parents.

Fritz Donhoff knew his story: "You lost the narcotics job because of your grandfather. You lost the

Senate job because of your mother. Now, it's the woman. Moira Rhalles. I suppose you're still in love with her?"

"I care about what happens to her," Sawyer snapped. "And that's enough. Now shut up and listen to the rest."

He told the rest, in detail, including his conclusions about what had really happened: "It starts with that little statuette of the goddess, the Venus figure. The enemy—whoever kidnaped Moira—had it. Whether it was looted from a dig or museum, or an extremely good fake. Either way, it's a lead."

Donhoff nodded. "You have to try to trace where it came from, originally. How it got from there to the kidnapers. And how it got from them to Gaspard Martinot. Who is another lead for you, since he was certainly part of the scheme."

"Had to be," Sawyer agreed. "Though I don't think he had any idea of what the scheme really was. If he'd known how big it was, involving kidnaping, he'd have realized they had to leave him dead in the end. To indicate that Moira was dead too, and prevent him from talking. He probably thought he was just part of a little con job, to pass off a fake Venus figure as real.

"Which brings up another interesting point: whoever hooked him into the scheme must have known him. Or at least known enough *about* him, to know he'd be *willing* to take part in a con job, if they paid him enough. Also, someone—maybe the same someone who knew Martinot wouldn't mind taking part in a swindle—had to know about the cave. And Martinot's familiarity with that cave."

"You've got two dates," Donhoff put in dryly. "The dates when Martinot made those deposits in his secret bank account in Peira-Cava. Which were undoubtedly his first two payments from that *someone* you're interested in. A check of all the hotels in the areas of Sospel and Peira-Cava just might turn up the name of the right someone, staying at one of them on those two dates."

Sawyer smiled. "You're getting ahead of me, Fritz. Let's go back to what happened, step by step: first, the kidnapers getting the statuette. Then, one of them takes it to Martinot, and cons him into helping with what he thinks is just an archaeology swindle for profit. That brings us to the next possible lead: Christine Jonquet—checking out her background, where she's been, what she's been doing, who she's been doing it with."

He paused, and then added: "And where she might be, now."

Fritz Donhoff took another small sip of his wine. "You don't think she died in that underground river." It wasn't quite a question.

"Do you?"

"No. Or they would have left her dead in that cave where she would be found. As they did with Martinot. As further proof that Moira Rhalles must be dead, too."

"Exactly. But they didn't. So Christine Jonquet was in on it—a lot deeper than Martinot. If I'm right, it lines up this way: they sent her to America for the purpose of making Moira's acquaintance in that museum in Philadelphia. So that later she could *happen* to run into Moira again, in St. Dalmas. After which she could happen to find out hat Martinot, down in Sospel, happened to have a Venus figure."

Donhoff was watching his own long, plump fingers trace designs on the table, deep in his own thoughts. "Christine Jonquet might possible be the same *someone* who originally contacted Martinot."

Sawyer considered it. "It's possible, but it doesn't feel right. I think they'd use a man, to talk to a man like Martinot about joining in a swindle. Either way, she went back to Moira—and John Borelli—to tell them about the Venus figure. Now, I don't think Borelli was part of the scheme. I'm having him checked. But until proven wrong, I'm assuming he was an innocent dupe. They wanted him along—just so there'd be someone who knew they'd gone into the cave, and who would get worried when they didn't come out."

"And," Donhoff added, "to tell what had happened, as far as he knew it. Which would be the version they wanted known."

"Right. So Christine Jonquet slipped a little poison in Borelli's breakfast, just enough to make sure he'd be in no condition to go into the cave with them. That left the three of them to go in: Moira, Christine Jonquet, and Martinot. With Martinot thinking he was leading them to some phony evidence which would have been planted to authenticate the Venus figure he'd claimed to find in there. Instead, they were waiting to crush in his head. Making sure he was dead before wedging him in the rocks at the bottom of the waterfall, where the search party would find him. After which, they took Moira out the other way. With the help of Christine Jonquet, if I'm right."

Sawyer paused again, his eyes fixed on Donhoff. "I need help with this," he said evenly. "Your help, if you'll give it."

Donhoff didn't answer right away. He leaned back in his chair, thinking about it, gazing at the view framed by the open end of the small square: the mountain ranges changing from green to dark blue to misty gray as they receded into the distance. Sawyer waited tensely for his answer, not pushing it, looking down toward the bottom of the village. He couldn't see the war monument from here. But he could see the railroad station, waiting in vain for a train ever since the same week in which James Sawyer had died.

The orange-tiled roof was still intact. But the overhead electric lines that had run past it were gone, and the tracks were brown lines of rust. The railway bridge crossing the river near it had been only partially destroyed. The rest now supported a green jungle of bushes, wild grass, and small trees.

"We'll have to be careful who we use to help," Donhoff said finally. "And what we tell them."

Sawyer smiled at the "we." Donhoff was in. But Donhoff had more to say: "Especially, we'll have to be careful about your boss. Gassin is a very smart man. And extremely interested in what any of his employees are up to. A reasonable interest, since so many people in industrial espionage seem prone to double-cross each other and the people they work for at the drop of an extra few francs."

"Don't worry, I intend to be careful."

"Extremely careful," Donhoff emphasized somberly. "Gassin loves that firm he has built. And much of its continuing success depends on the strength of his connections with various branches of our government. Including our police and intelligence people. If he found out about what we're involved in, he could increase the strength of those connections by passing it on to French intelligence. Which would pass it on to American intelligence. First, for the pleasure of making them look incompetent. Secondly, for the very large favor they would owe us in return."

"I know the danger," Sawyer assured him quietly.

Donhoff continued in the same tone: "On the other hand, if Gassin found out and *didn't* pass it on . . . and then they found out . . . they would be quite furious with him. Certainly enough to damage his business. Perhaps enough to destroy it. I don't think he would be prepared to risk that, do you?"

"Alain Gassin is my problem," Sawyer told Donhoff firmly. "I'll handle it."

"I hope that you can." Donhoff watched Sawyer's face. "Does Gassin know you are the father of his daughter?"

Sawyer held onto his temper. "I'm *not*," he said flatly.

"Ah?" Donhoff appeared ready to drop it. Instead he said, carelessly: "His wife—is certainly a remarkable woman."

Sawyer grimaced.

Donhoff said softly: "I'm sorry if I've made you angry."

"Not angry. Just irritated. First Moira, now Annique—you have the curiosity of a village gossip."

"I have the curiosity," Donhoff said with dignity, "of a man who cares about what is happening to his friends." He finished off his wine, and put the empty glass down with a gesture of finality. "Well, let's get to it. You have three leads open to you at this point: the statuette of the goddess, Christine Jonquet, and Gaspard Martinot. Since you had me come down here to tell me about it, I suppose you want me to take Martinot."

"That's right. At least at this point, until you've squeezed out everything there is to get on him. His background, who he was in contact with, who knew enough about him to use him in this scheme. You know all this better than I do."

"I know that taking his widow the good news about that money waiting for her in the Peira-Cava bank should put her in a pleasantly talkative mood, for a start."

Sawyer got out his notebook and tore from it the page with the dates on which Martinot had made the deposits. "And there's the matter of finding out if somebody interesting checked into some local hotel, on these two dates, one month apart. If you have trouble getting the police down here to co-operate, I can help."

"I never have trouble with the police, anywhere." Donhoff took the paper, folded it neatly, and slipped it in his pocket. "But they are notoriously slow, as you know. Especially when it comes to systematic filing of all those hotel registrations. A check like this could take a week, or more."

"We don't have that kind of time. It has to go faster." Sawyer took an envelope from his inside breast pocket. "Expense money. Buy yourself extra co-operation. And extra assistants, on a one-day basis, when you need them."

"That should speed it up," Donhoff agreed.

Getting out his pen, Sawyer wrote a telephone number on the envelope. "If you get something, this is the number to call in Paris. It's a safe number; at least nobody would have had any reason to bug it, as yet. If it gets tapped, I'll let you know. And if I'm not there, and I probably won't be, you can leave a straight message with whoever answers. *Don't* call me at ARC—I don't want Gassin or anybody else there to know you're working on something for me."

"Sensible." Donhoff took the envelope and snuggled it into the inside pocket of his jacket as Sawyer put down money for their drinks and stood up. He pushed back his chair and got to his feet. "And—well, you do know my rates."

"And your address. You'll get the check once a week."

They went down through the old town together. Before they parted, Donhoff asked Sawyer: "Do you ever pray?"

"No."

"Neither do I, but perhaps we should start. We are going to need luck."

3

Lang spent his first hour in Budapest playing tourist and checking for surveillance. He began by strolling the streets of the Inner City, pausing occasionally to take pictures of interesting buildings. A camera was an excellent antisurveillance tool. It enabled Lang to stop and look systematically in all directions, without appearing to do anything stranger than searching for camera angles and subjects worth shooting.

The hodgepodge of building styles provided Lang with enough excuse for this. Interspersed among the drab stone buildings of the Twenties and featureless modern glass-and-steel structures were baroque, neoclassical, and art nouveau façades, from the days when Budapest was the second capital of the Austro-Hungarian Empire, with occasional Oriental touches from the century of Turkish occupation. Lang stopped to photograph a number of the more ornate examples.

The camera he was using was a Nikon F2; the attached lens an 80-200mm f/4.5 Nikkor. But it drew no special attention from anyone. Budapest had gotten used to tourists lugging expensive cameras. Most of these tourists were prosperous functionaries from other countries within Russia's Comecon community. For Communists who could afford the trip, Budapest was the favorite holiday town. Since Hungary had learned its lesson, and now carefully toed the Soviet political line, the atmosphere of its capital had been allowed to return to its traditional easygoing love of good living. The superb food in its restaurants, gaiety of its nightclubs, and relaxed sexiness of its pretty women made it the next best thing to actually going outside the Iron Curtain.

By the time Lang reached Liberation Square, he was quite sure there was nobody tailing him. Turning into the rococo Paris Arcade, he paused several times before its shopwindows, checking behind him one last time.

When he emerged from the other end of the vault-roofed passage, he was on Petofi Sandor, a narrow, crowded shopping street. The Volkswagen Lang had rented at Ferihegy Airport outside Budapest was parked there, two blocks from the arcade.

Lang passed the car at a slow stroll, his restless hazel eyes flicking to doorways and second-floor windows. If the car had been put under observation since he'd parked it there, he couldn't detect it. Half a block further on, across the street, was the building occupied by the CIA's Hungarian informant, and also by the mysterious Pole who acted as a relay station for the messages the NSA had so far been unable to decode.

The building was six wide stories of solid gray stone. It was topped by a slanting green tin roof, a replacement for the original orange-tile covering hit by a blockbuster when the Russians had fought their way into the city near the end of the Second World War and liberated it from the Germans. The next armored Russian entrance into the city, to crush Hungarian experiments with freedom of thought in 1956, had obliterated many of the 1890s statues which had decorated the façade.

But some remained: a fat baby angel over the entrance door. A muscular naked couple exchanging a cool kiss between two tall third-floor windows, their legs disfigured by shrapnel. A huge Medusa face at the fourth-floor level, with streaks of grime forming long black tears below the glaring eyes. At the very top, just under the green tin roof, a dying Cleopatra sprawled. She wore only a headdress, which was necessary to identify her as Egyptian. Her thick, solid figure, especially the big, gloriously rounded breasts between which she clasped the asp, was unmistakably Hungarian. Her left leg was stretched horizontal and the right one raised to frame a small round window under the knee. Her hair flowed out to form a ledge under an identical window. Behind those twin windows lived the CIA's man.

Lang continued to check for surveillance as he approached and crossed the street. His nerves were tensed, ready to divert his approach into a stroll-past if anything triggered its sharply attuned warning system. Nothing did. Lang went in under the baby angel, through a dingy corridor of cracked tiles smelling of decades of boiling cabbage. At the other end, inside the heart of the building, was the bottom of a large courtyard like a squared-off abyss, six floors deep.

There were interior wraparound balconies with wrought-iron railings at each floor. The lowest was supported by fat columns with Doric capitals, the original white of their stone obliterated by brown stains and black dust. Parts of the topmost balcony were roofed with wooden trellises from which bright green ivy grew in a sunlight which did not penetrate to the depths of the lower floors. Each balcony led past six to ten doors, the entrances to apartments, single rooms, and business offices. At opposite end of the courtyard rose exposed wrought-iron elevator shafts. The elevators inside were cages of dark wood and pebbled glass, still bearing bullet holes from either the Soviet army which had liberated the city or the subsequent one which had subjugated it. Perhaps both. Lang got into the elevator beside the entrance corridor and rode it to the top floor.

Getting out, he walked along the balcony until he found a wooden door to which was tacked a square of paper with the name typed on it: Koroly Zoltan. The low, wide window next to it had closed wooden shutters. There were matchbox-size chinks between some of the warped slats, but only darkness could be seen behind them. Methodically, Lang did a last scan of the courtyard before knocking on the door.

Though he had been told what to expect, Lang took a second to adjust to the man who opened the door. It was not only that Zoltan was a dwarf. The top of his head, on a level with Lang's waist, was wide and flat, sparsely covered with black down. From the broad forehead his face tapered down in an inverted triangle to a sharply pointed chin. The rest of him was less disconcerting: the thick torso almost normal, accentuating the extremely short muscular arms and stubby legs. He looked in his forties, though Lang knew he was only twenty-five.

Zoltan tilted the misshapen head to look up at

Lang, and started to ask nervously in Hungarian what he wanted. Then he saw the "W" penciled on the airline tag still attached to the neck strap of Lang's camera. After a swift survey of the courtyard, his tiny hand seized Lang by the wrist and yanked him inside with surprising force. Zoltan shut the door and reached up to lock it before turning on Lang furiously.

"What the hell are you doing here?" he snarled in an accented English that would not have been surprising from a New York cabdriver. "You people ain't even supposed to know where this place is."

He was referring to the CIA couriers who picked up his intercepts of the coded messages. Since the experienced agents they'd had available were too well known to the Hungarians, the case officer running this operation from the Vienna field station was using new operatives. They could not yet be trusted with too much information or proximity to a precariously positioned resident agent like Zoltan. The operational routine was for the couriers to wait at a certain bench in the heavily wood park on the Danube's Margaret Island, just before dusk. If Zoltan had a cassette for them, he would slip out of the bushes behind the bench and drop it in the flight bag left open beside them, with the marked airline tag prominently displayed.

"I'm not one of the delivery boys," Lang told him in Hungarian. "So relax. I'm an experienced field officer, my face isn't known in this area, and I wasn't followed here."

"May God bless your optimism." It was a standard Hungarian response, not an avowal of faith. Zoltan hurried to the other end of the room and climbed up on a studio bed against the wall under the twin round windows. Parting one of the gauze curtains that kept the room dim, he peered down into the street below.

Lang looked around the apartment. Two open doors

showed a tiny kitchen and equally small bathroom. The room they were in was quite long and fairly narrow. The street end was Zoltan's sparse living quarters: the studio bed, a bureau, a portable phonograph on an open cabinet stuffed with records and magazines, and a low coffee table, big and square, with cushions on the floor around it. There were no chairs. On the coffee table were a dozen jars of ceramic paints, a bottle of turpentine and some rags, an assortment of paint brushes in a large glass, and a lot of plates and small vases. Some were plain white, others painted with typical Hungarian folk designs. Decorating ceramic ware had been Zoltan's only source of income before getting on the CIA's payroll. It was still his cover job.

Much of the courtyard end of the long room was taken up by a number of large, unwieldy looking electronic units. All but one of these units were linked together and added up to the very latest development in medium-range directional eavesdropping equipment. Operational at distances up to four hundred feet, it utilized a laser beam focused on a windowpane to pick up speech-caused audio vibrations inside the room behind the window. The laser "gun" itself was a shotgun-like affair mounted on a solid tripod and angled downward through Zoltan's open courtyard window. Its snout fitted into one of the small gaps Lang had noticed between the slats of the closed shutters.

The other electronic unit was a receiver tuned into a cable-strand tap that had been placed on the line of the telephone being used by the Polish "businessman" for the mysterious coded messages. The tap was connected to the line under a street two blocks away, and could not be detected by even the most sophisticated antibugging sweep of the Pole's office—or the entire building.

The job had been done by an NSA specialist brought in from Fort Meade, after a utility agent had turned up the pair of numbers of the Pole's telephone line. Later, when the "need-to-know" category of what was transpiring in the Pole's office was upped, the same specialist had returned to assemble the laser directional equipment which had been smuggled piece by piece into Hungary. All of these complicated devices finally funneled down to a very simple unit: the hookup to an ordinary cassette-tape recorder resting on the floor of Zoltan's apartment.

Zoltan, still standing on his bed and peering down through one of the small round windows, said nervously: "There's a car down there across the street that I haven't seen parked around here before."

"If it's a new gray Volkswagen," Lang told him, "it's mine."

"It is—and I'm still scared. I shouldn't be in this kind of business. I'm too frightened all the time." Zoltan let the curtain fall back in place and hopped down off his bed. He studied Lang for a moment, taking in his red hair, blunt features, and stocky build. "Your parents were Hungarian?"

"No. I just studied the language in school."

"Then my congratulations. You speak it very well. Not that it's difficult. A simple, crude language, easy to learn. But who would want to? Except a born Hungarian, who can't help it."

Lang shrugged and smiled faintly. "I did." He turned to move around the barrel of the laser gun to the shuttered window.

"Be careful!" Zoltan snapped at him. "I know how to turn that junk on and off, that's all. I can't readjust it, if you disturb anything."

"I can," Lang reassured him. But he was careful. Stooping, he squinted through a gap between two shutter slats. "Where is the Pole's office?"

"On the other side of the courtyard, across from us. Next floor down. He has the only window there with venetian blinds. And no shutters."

Lang located the window Zoltan meant. The venetian blinds were closed, concealing the room inside. "Does he live there, as well as using it for an office?"

"No. He's never there at night. Comes at eight-thirty every morning. On the dot. Goes out to lunch at twelve-thirty, comes back at one-thirty. Leaves for good at six in the evening. That's if the courier doesn't show up. If he does, the Pole leaves for the day right after the courier goes away."

"Has their courier showed up there this morning?"

"No," Zoltan told him. "Means he won't until this afternoon. If he comes today. The Pole went out for lunch fifteen minutes ago."

"This courier always the same man?"

"Always the same."

Raising his camera, Lang focused it through the chink in the shutter, at the door beside the window with venetian blinds. Setting the speed at 125, he adjusted for distance and light. "I'm going to try to get a picture of him," he explained to Zoltan. "And the Pole."

Zoltan started into the kitchen, hesitated in the doorway. "You want to have lunch with me? I'm making soup."

"Thank you, if you're sure there's enough."

"I wouldn't invite you if I didn't have enough," Zoltan growled. "Americans!" He gestured Lang to the coffee table, and disappeared inside the kitchen.

Unstrapping the camera from around his neck, Lang put it down carefully on the floor under the window. He walked to the kitchen doorway. "What if one of them comes while we're eating?"

"Then we'll hear them, in plenty of time." Zoltan lit the gas burner under his soup pot. "Noisy elevators, didn't you notice?"

"There's a stairway, too. They could use that."

"They could, but they never do. Neither of them. Lazy, like the rest of us." Zoltan got a long spoon and reached up to stir the soup.

Lang leaned against the side of the doorway. "The

name the Pole uses here—Stefan Tozinski—does he use the same one where he lives?"

"I don't know. I don't know where he lives." Zoltan looked up and caught Lang's slight frown. "Did you expect me to *follow* him?" he demanded irritably. "Maybe you think I look inconspicuous enough to follow somebody without being noticed?" Zoltan returned to stirring the soup.

"You're probably right," Lang said, trying to mollify him. "Too risky. I suppose the same thing applies to the courier—you don't know where he comes from, or where he goes."

"I do not," Zoltain stated flatly. He looked at Lang again. "If it's any help to you, I do know the car Tozinski uses between here and wherever he lives. I saw him drive off in it once. Big black Mercedes-Benz, with Polish plates."

Lang looked at his watch. There were still almost forty minutes to go before the Pole was due back. "It does help." Tozinski might have used his car to go to lunch. But maybe not. "I'll be right back," he told Zoltan, and went out quickly.

There was no black Mercedes-Benz with Polish plates along the street in front of the building. Lang circled the block without finding it. Moving fast, he went around the next block, and there it was, parked in a side street. Hurrying back to his rented Volkswagen, he drove around past Tozinski's car, shoehorning into a tight space he'd spotted two thirds of a block ahead of it. Then he went back to rejoin Zoltan for lunch.

Zoltan had moved some of his ceramic paint jars to make room for their meal on the low coffee table: two big bowls of the soup, with slices of crispy bread liberally buttered. The soup was delicious, and Lang said so. Zoltan cracked his first smile, pleased. With his normal torso, when they were both sitting on the floor cushions their faces were on the same level, which seemed to make him less aggressive.

"Let's talk American for a while," he told Lang. "I can use the practice."

"Okay. Where'd you learn?"

"New York. I was there two years. My uncle has a little ceramics business there. Went in '56. So I went to work for him." Zoltan took a spoonful of soup, studied Lang briefly, and then added carelessly. "I figured I'd go away and give my mother a break. She really can't stand having to look at me. Thinks the way I am's her punishment for sin. I'm a bastard, you know."

Lang said carefully: "Why did you decide to come back here?"

"My uncle's business started to go sour, and he couldn't really afford to pay me anymore. And my Green Card, my permit to work in the States, was running out. Then along comes this smooth guy from your government; takes me out to dinner in a really top restaurant, sweet-talks me, and tries to recruit me. To come back here and just sort of keep my ear to the ground for your people. For not bad dough, which'd get a lot better if I turned up something. So I figured what the hell, why not? I'm not doing anything against my country. Just against the present government, and who gives a damn about their governments anymore? You know what Talleyrand said about being a traitor?"

Lang nodded. "He said treason is merely a matter of dates."

"Right on. What'd you know, another book reader in the house. Anyway, to tell you the truth, I wasn't all that happier in New York. Here or there, I'm still a freak. And a freak without money might's well crawl in a hole and die. At least with dough you can buy hookers, no matter what you look like."

"Have any trouble getting Hungary to let you back in?"

"Nah. The government was delighted. They like having people who go away come back. Shows everybody the life here must be better. Which as a matter of fact it is, outside the politics. And who gives a fuck about politics? I got troubles of my own."

There was the noise of one of the elevators cranking into operation. Zoltan and Lang got up and went to peek through the shutters into the courtyard, Lang snatching up his camera. But it was only an elderly couple, getting out of the elevator at the fourth floor and going along the balcony to the office of an eye doctor. Lang and Zoltan returned to the coffee table.

Their meal was interrupted three more times by the sound of the elevator. But each time it turned out not to be either Tozinski or the courier. Lang questioned Zoltan carefully about the Pole, without learning anything important that he didn't already know.

There were three main questions needing answers: What was in the long coded messages? Where did they come from? Where did they end up, after being telephoned to the still-untraced number in Warsaw?

The first question was basically NSA's nut to crack. There were agents in Warsaw working on the third question. Lang might be able to turn up something that would help them, by tailing Tozinski. But that was a very secondary reason for his being here now.

His main concern was the second question: Where did the code messages come from? Obtaining an answer to that, at this stage, entailed learning more about the courier who brought the messages to Tozinski, and shadowing him. Finding out who and what he was, where he came from, where he went, who his contacts were, where he picked up the messages, and who from.

"What's the routine with the courier?" he asked Zoltan. "Everything, step by step."

Zoltan shrugged. "It ain't much. On days he shows up, which ain't every day, he gets off the elevator, walks to the Pole's door, and knocks. Tozinski opens

218

up, the courier goes inside across there, they shut the door."

"By then you've got your listeners tuned in. What do they say to each other?"

"Again, not much. Hello, how are you, lousy weather—like that. Just small talk. Then they make the call . . ."

"What language do they use with each other?" Lang cut in.

"German."

Which didn't mean that Tozinski wasn't really Polish. It certainly meant that the courier wasn't, though not necessarily that he was German. German was the common language used by people from different Eastern European countries in talking to each other. The courier could be a Bulgarian or a Czech. Or a German.

Lang put his next question: "How long does it take, between the time the courier goes inside there, and they place the call to Warsaw?"

"Not long. Few seconds, maybe. They say hello to each other, and right away Tozinski picks up his phone, dials the long-distance operator, and asks for the Warsaw number. Then they wait, not saying anything, until the call goes through."

This was the first piece of important information Lang had so far gotten from Zoltan. It meant that the message the courier delivered here was already in code. There wasn't enough time, between his entering the Pole's office and the placing of the phone call, to do the encoding. Lang would have to tail the courier back to the point where he picked up the message. And continue to back-trail the message, to the point where it was encoded. At that point he would have a chance to get his hands on the clear message, before it was rendered into code. And knowing what the messages were all about might reveal their source.

"What do the people at the Warsaw end say when they pick up the phone?" Lang asked Zoltan.

"Nothing. Not a damn thing. You just hear the click when it's picked up. Then, right away, the dots and dashes start going through the line from Tozinski's office. No talk, just dots and dashes, sometimes for over an hour. When it's finished, Tozinski hangs up his phone without a word. And that's it. He and the courier say goodbye to each other, see you next time. No shoptalk. Not even when he'll come again. The courier goes away. Just like he came. And that's all I can tell you. Because there's nothing else to tell."

"Beside the courier, does anybody else ever come to Tozinski's office?"

"Nobody else. And no phone calls, outside of the ones with the code. He doesn't get any, or make any. He just stays inside there by himself, all morning and then all afternoon if the courier doesn't show, and waits. I don't know what he does with himself all that time alone in there. Sleeps, maybe. He doesn't even play a radio. Nothing."

The noise of the elevator drew them to the shutters again. Lang, peering between the slats, saw a very tall, thin man in a respectable business suit get off the elevator at the fifth floor.

"That's him," Zoltan hissed. "Tozinski."

Lang already had the camera in his hands. He managed to snap three fast pictures before the Pole reached the door to his office. Then, through the magnification of the telephoto lens, Lang carefully observed every move of Tozinski's unlocking the door and going in.

There was nothing to indicate that Tozinski was deactivating any alarm system he might have set before going out. If there was no break-in alarm it probably meant there was nothing in the Pole's office worth breaking in for. But Lang would still have to check it out.

Zoltan had turned on both listening systems. Lang picked up one of the earphones and heard the sounds of Tozinski's shoes on an uncarpeted floor. Then that stopped, and there was a scraping noise, possibly a chair being shifted, with a man's weight on it. After that came small sounds Lang couldn't identify. They continued, but less frequently; seconds and sometimes minutes between them. Other than that—nothing.

Lang and Zoltan settled down to wait for the courier.

TWELVE

1

"I would be lying if I told you I was upset when I heard Christine was killed. After all, I hadn't seen her in two years. I was surprised, of course."

"And a little relieved?" Sawyer suggested.

"Can you blame me?" Jonquet's tone was defensive. He avoided Sawyer's eyes, looking down at the half-finished drink cradled between his hands as though he were trying to draw security from it. "You know what a bitch she turned out to be. And crazy. I mean, that's the only explanation I could come up with for the way she treated me."

"It *was* strange," Sawyer conceded.

He didn't mention another possible reason he could think of for Christine Jonquet's behavior: that she had left Jonquet because she had achieved what she'd married him for, French citizenship.

Sawyer had spent most of the morning and early afternoon getting to know more about the girl who had vanished in the cave with Moira Rhalles, and finding her husband. It had begun at 9 A.M., with the dossier waiting for him in the Information Analysis Department at ARC, the initials on the entrance of the building that was the Parisian headquarters of Audubon Research Consultants. The dossier consisted of only a single sheet, but it contained food for thought.

Christine Bieler Jonquet. Age: 24. Occupation: Student, at the Louvre School. There were copies of two photographs with the dossier: one from her school

of poverty, and painfully unsure in his personal relationships.

By the time Sawyer got to Jonquet, he knew enough to cut away Jonquet's initial hesitation in discussing his relationship with his wife. He was a heavily built young man with chunky features and restless eyes that failed to conceal the basic lack of self-confidence. Sawyer had taken him out to a bistro on the Place de la Bastille, bought the drinks, and proceeded to open him up. The tool he used was a cruel one: there were people in the neighborhood where he'd lived with his wife who believed he'd married her for her money, and she'd left him when she realized it. That forced Jonquet into the position of having to justify himself. Sawyer, having gotten him started, sat back, sipped at his drink, and waited.

Like many people, Jonquet became nervous with long silences and was impelled to end the waiting himself. "It wasn't like they say. Not at all."

"No? How was it?"

"I didn't go after her, for her money or anything else. *She* came after *me*. Right from the start."

"Where was that?"

"The Louvre. I was taking pictures there—on assignment for *Paris-Match*. Christine came over and started to talk to me, just like that. She said she needed some pictures taken of her and could I come to her place that evening and do it. I told her what it would cost, and she said it sounded fair—so I went."

"I understand she had quite a nice apartment."

"A dream. And it turns out, after I take some pictures of her, that she expects me to stay for dinner. She already had it prepared. Delicious, and with top wine." Jonquet hesitated.

Sawyer nudged him: "So you made a pass."

"*She* did. Starting with half-joking about also wanting me to take some pictures of her in the nude. And then one thing leading to another . . ." He hesitated again, but this time he needed no nudging: "I'll say one thing honestly, she was wonderful in bed. I don't claim to have that much experience with women, but Christine was . . . very passionate. After that, we started seeing each other every night. If I didn't go to her place, she'd come to mine. She acted like she was wildly in love with me." Jonquet's voice had become bitter.

"So you finally moved in with her."

Jonquet gave an uneasy shrug. "My place was a hole. Hardly enough room to turn around in. The toilet out in the hall. It made sense, her place was more than big enough for the two of us."

"Where did she get the money to pay for an apartment like that?" Sawyer asked him.

"Her parents had money. Christine inherited when they died. Plane accident."

"Did she have any relatives still living?"

"She mentioned some, in Stuttgart. I never met them."

"I suppose she was the one who proposed marriage?"

Jonquet nodded. "I couldn't think of any reason not to. After all, she wouldn't be any added financial responsibility for me."

"Quite the contrary."

"That's right." Jonquet's voice was bitter again. "So—I married her."

Changing her name from Bieler to Jonquet, and enabling her to become legally French without the years of waiting otherwise required.

"What went wrong?" Sawyer asked him.

"I don't know. I told you, I decided afterwards she must be crazy. Two weeks after we were married, she packed and moved out. No real reason. She just said she was fickle that way, quickly bored . . ." Jonquet finished off his drink, stared down at the empty glass he held. "And . . . well, she'd had enough of me."

"Where did she move to?"

"I don't know. I don't know if she even stayed in Paris. I never tried to get in touch with her again. Why should I?"

"But you didn't get a divorce."

"A divorce costs money. I figured she'd take care of that, sooner or later. Now, it isn't necessary."

"You never saw her again?"

"No. Thank God."

Sawyer questioned him about friends who might have stayed in touch with her. But if she had had any other friends, Jonquet didn't know about them. After persistent prodding, he finally was able to come up with only one name that held any possible interest for Sawyer:

"Clarissa Koller—she's from Germany. She has a little art gallery on the Rue de Seine. Or she did. Christine and I dropped in there one day, just in passing. They were surprised to see each other in Paris. It turned out they knew each other in Germany. Stuttgart, I think. But they were just acquaintances, not old friends. Christine wasn't interested in seeing her again."

Sawyer went to have a talk with Clarissa Koller.

2

He found the gallery but Clarissa Koller wasn't there. Her assistant told Sawyer she was visiting friends in the country near Chantilly, some twenty-five miles outside Paris. Sawyer managed to pry the phone number from her assistant, and went to the nearest post office to make the call.

Clarissa Koller's voice was heavy and warm, the Germanic accent not unpleasant. But Sawyer didn't want to question her over a phone line. You could miss things, if you weren't watching the other person's face. She told him she would be back in Paris by nine that night, if it was urgent. Sawyer told her it was, and got the address of her apartment.

From the post office, he went to his apartment building on the Rue des Lions in the Marais, to check on whether the afternoon mail delivery had brought either of the two items from America he was waiting for. The building was a three-story eighteenth-century town house that had been renovated and divided into small apartments. Sawyer's took up all of the top floor, but his mailbox was with the rest in the ground-floor passage.

He didn't expect any of the mail in his own box to be of interest, but there was a penciled note that was. It said only: "They're here."

The smallest apartments in the house were on the ground floor, four one-room-kitchenette-and-bath affairs. Sawyer walked through the passage and knocked at the one at the end, behind the staircase.

Olivier called from inside: "Come in, it's not locked."

The room within was large enough not to be crowded by the bed, bureau, table, TV, and hi-fi. Oliver Verger was a lean kid of eighteen, with wide, bony shoulders and the face of a young Edgar Allan Poe, dominated by dark, melancholy eyes and framed by thick wavy hair he never combed with anything but his fingers. He put aside the soldering iron with which he was rewiring the hi-fi amplifier and looked at Sawyer. "You know I never lock it during the day."

Sawyer shut the door behind him. "You might have had company."

"Like that present you sent me last week?"

"That was a bonus for your help with the Bernier Chemicals investigation. You earned it."

"She was nice. But I can't afford whores that nice on my own income."

Sawyer shrugged carelessly. "There are girls you

228

don't have to pay for out there. Go out and look around."

Olivier grinned. "I figured that was the idea when she showed up." He patted the armrests of his wheelchair. "Get me turned on to the idea of finding myself what you'd call a normal life again."

"It's not a bad idea."

When Olivier stopped grinning some of the melancholy seeped back into his dark eyes. "I know it's not. Just give me time, don't rush it."

He was the son of Sawyer's mother and her second husband, and he'd had a passion for all kinds of sports. One of them had been rock-climbing. He'd been fifteen when he fell from the face of a cliff in the Verdon Canyon. There had been four operations on the smashed leg and hip since, and he still couldn't walk without crutches and probably never would.

Sawyer had begun using him on assignments five months ago, at first just to hang around bistros and pick up needed information. "Everybody feels guilty around cripples," he'd explained without softening it. "Because they're whole and you're not. They'll want you to know they've got problems, too. Closemouthed types I'd have trouble opening up will tell you their whole life and anybody else's in the first fifteen minutes—if you go at it the right way."

From the start, Olivier's results exceeded his expectations. Sawyer had since begun training him in the difficult skills of combing fragments of related information out of public archives and filing systems. Always, he'd earned whatever Sawyer paid him out of ARC's supplementary informants' expense account.

"What have you got for me?" Sawyer asked him.

Olivier spun his wheelchair around to the table and picked up two envelopes with U.S. airmail stamps. "Looks like both items you were waiting for."

One was the report from the firm he'd given Moira's tapes to, after carefully wiping out anything that told who or what was involved. The report was negative.

The cassettes were a popular Swiss brand, sold all over Europe. Extreme amplification and audio-separation techniques had failed to reveal any background sounds that might have contained a hint of where the tapes had been recorded.

The other report was from the firm to which Sawyer had given the job of checking out Professor Borelli. With all the available computerized files on people regularly assembled by insurance companies, the IRS, credit-checking firms, and various other government and private agencies, it had been mainly a matter of collating the right ones, plus some intensive checking to bring them up to date. The envelope contained a detailed dossier of Professor Borelli's life, career, habits, associations, problems. It contained items Borelli would not have liked being passed around: an arrest for a drunk-driving accident when he was twenty-two, a rotten marriage, the patronizing of homosexual bars.

But Sawyer could find nothing in any of it that changed his feeling that Borelli had not had any conscious connection with Moira's kidnaping.

"No calls from Fritz Donhoff?" he asked Olivier.

"Not yet. He hasn't really had enough time to come through with anything, has he?"

"We don't *have* time," Sawyer growled. He burned both documents, and went back to ARC to find out what Information Analysis had managed to dig up, to help him trace the background of the mysterious statuette of the Stone Age goddess.

3

The building owned by Audubon Research Consultants was an imposing seventeenth-century mansion along the Quai d'Orléans on the Île St.-Louis, its windows on one side commanding a view of the Seine

230

and the rear of Notre Dame. People customarily said that Alain Gassin had built the enterprise contained in that building up out of nothing. What they meant was that he had started with very little money. But he'd had everything else necessary. Most important, he'd started with more and better high-level connections than anyone else in the business.

First of all, Gassin came from an old military family which, while not wealthy, had solid prestige going back over generations. His father had become a military adviser to De Gaulle in London during the Second World War. Unfortunately, Alain Gassin and his mother hadn't managed to reach London and join him. The Nazis had seized them, and in retaliation against his father had sent them to a detention camp in Austria. An officer in the camp had helped the boy celebrate his tenth birthday by tying his ankles to a ceiling pipe and letting him hang upside-down there for the entire day.

Sawyer doubted that anyone else knew of that event in Gassin's life, and what it had done to him, other than Annique and himself. The boy had returned to France after the war in appalling condition. But his health had fully recovered, and if the experience left any marks on his mind or spirit they didn't show in his subsequent schoolwork. He was an achiever.

On graduating at twenty-three from the École Nationale d'Administration, Gassin had automatically become part of the network of ENA alumni, an elite mafia of administrative talent spread through every area of big government and corporate business. Men loyal to the old school tie, and indispensable in running France. One ENA man, in a five minute discussion with another graduate could accomplish objectives that would ensnarl anyone else in several months of red tape.

Sent on graduation into the DST, France's equivalent of the American FBI, within three years Gassin had become chief administrative secretary to the director. Then he had startled everyone by resigning from the government and going to India. No explanation, except it was something he felt a need to do. After two years in a remote hermitage east of Bombay, he had returned. Still no explanation, and no apparent change in the man—except that he no longer had a taste for being a cog, no matter how powerful, in the machinery of government. He wanted something all his own.

Gassin had started ARC from one rented room in the same building on the île St.-Louis. The firm had gradually expanded into other rooms as business prospered through his connections with the network of highly placed ENA graduates in government and business. There was one other large plus factor in the success of Audubon Research Consultants: Annique Jourdan, undoubtedly one of the best research directors in Europe.

Gassin had lured her away from Interpol with the offer of a full partnership. Two years later they had sealed the business partnership with marriage. As their company expanded, and Gassin staffed its specialized departments with other top talent lured from government and private security agencies, his wife had built her Information Analysis division into a computerized data bank so formidable that on occasion both the Secret Service and the DST had to come to her for facts unavailable in their own archives. Which put her in a position of being able to raid their file systems in return. By the previous year, Alain and Annique had been able to purchase the whole building, and ease out the last of its non-ARC tenants.

Sawyer entered by way of the small drive-in courtyard, nodded to the armed guard on duty in the foyer, and climbed the marble inner stairway to his offices on the second floor. There was a note waiting for him: Gassin wanted to see him, urgently, if he chanced to come in before 5 P.M. Sawyer consulted his watch. It was a few minutes before five. Deciding it was better to find out what was on Gassin's mind than avoid him, Sawyer went on up the stairs to Gassin's top-floor suite.

In the luxurious little V.I.P. waiting room the former military security officer who served as Gassin's private secretary shook his head regretfully. "I'm afraid you are too late. The director is just leaving. There's an emergency conference tonight in Sophia-Antipolis."

Maximum security was the main reason for the existence of the fenced-in Sophia-Antipolis Center down near Antibes: to provide a place where the international corporations that maintained headquarters inside it could accomplish their research and long-range planning without danger of leakage to rivals. Gassin had helped to organize that security, and ARC was still responsible for keeping it effective.

"Fine," Sawyer said, and started to leave, "I'll see him when he returns."

But at that moment the door of the inner sanctum opened, and Gassin strode out carrying a slim black briefcase and an air of anxiety.

Alain Gassin the handsomest man Sawyer knew: tall and slim, with a lean, elegant face and hair a beautiful blend of silver and gray. He dressed British, like many upper-class Frenchmen. But the sharp Cartesian logic of the mind was distinctly French. And he had the slow-moving observant sureness of one steeped in the usages of power.

He stopped when he saw Sawyer. "Good, you're back. We've got a problem in Sophia-Antipolis, and they're waiting for me. Bentrell Instrumentals thinks it has sprung a leak. I don't think the leak is down there. But we have to check it, full-scale. You can come with me. Buy you a toothbrush on the way."

"I'm *not* back," Sawyer told him. "I only came in

to pick up something. You can take Reshevsky with you." Reshevsky was Sawyer's chief assistant in the investigative branch of the company.

"He's already on his way there, for the preliminary analysis."

"He's a good man."

"But not as good as you, or I'd give him your job. Reshevsky is clever enough, probably more clever than you. But he lacks your killer-feel, that tells when you're near something that might be vital. He doesn't get enough educated hunches that turn out right. Without that kind of ESP, an investigator is slightly crippled."

"I can't go with you Alain. I explained . . ."

"When *will* this personal matter of yours be cleared up?"

"I've got one month of vacation overdue," Sawyer pointed out. "Now, I don't expect to be out that long, but . . ."

"I sincerely hope not. You know I don't like my department heads taking the month all in one chunk. There's just too much going on here for that."

"Sir," Gassin's secretary interrupted quietly, "it's a few minutes past five. Your car is waiting."

Gassin put a hand on Sawyer's shoulder. "Walk downstairs with me."

He kept the pace slow as they started down the steps. "I wouldn't mind your absence quite so much, Pierre-Ange—if you weren't so secretive about this *personal* matter."

Sawyer's smile was small and hard. "I'm not working for a rival firm. Get that out of your head."

"I know you wouldn't do that." Gassin's tone managed to convey sincere trust and at the same time a hint of what could happen to Sawyer if he were lying.

Irritation pulled at the corners of Sawyer's mouth. "It's nothing against you, Alain. The friend I'm help-

234

ing begged me to keep it to myself. That's absolutely all there is to it."

"But you did tell Annique something." Gassin shot a sidelong glance at Sawyer. "I understand you have her doing some work on this personal matter of yours."

"Because there's no other safe way to get certain information I need."

"And because you know you can trust her." Gassin nodded. "And of course you can. She wouldn't even give me a hint." His smile seemed philosophical. "She is a strong woman. But then, they all are. We men make jokes about women the same way soldiers make fun of generals, or slaves of their masters—to lighten our servitude."

They had reached the small entrance courtyard. Gassin's Rolls was waiting, his chauffeur holding open the rear door. Gassin's gesture sent the man hurrying around to the front to get back in behind the wheel. It had been a slight, two-finger gesture. Gassin had learned that at ENA: a man's ability to command could be gauged in inverse ratio to the size of gesture and volume of voice required for him to have a command obeyed.

"We're having dinner alone together at home, tomorrow night," he informed Sawyer. "Why don't you join us?"

Sawyer shook his head slightly. "Can't. Too much to do."

Gassin regarded him thoughtfully. "You haven't come by in quite some time. Since Katie was born. There's no reason you shouldn't, you know."

Sawyer's face and tone had no expression of any kind: "I guess not."

Katie was Annique's daughter. Gassin couldn't be the father because, although his present mistress and past ones attested to his virility, he was sterile.

"Katie's two now." Gassin's voice softened, and an

unaccustomed warmth crept into his eyes. "You ought to see her. She's the sweetest little creature . . ."

Sawyer put a hand on the open rear door of the Rolls. "Better get started, or you'll be late."

The look Gassin gave him was faintly pitying. "True. Well, get your personal matter over with, and come back to work." He climbed inside with his brief-case. Sawyer shut the door and watched the Rolls pull out.

It had been easier than he'd expected. Too easy. Sawyer worried about it as he went back inside.

Annique Gassin's management office was on the third floor. But most of the actual work of her department was done in the basement area. Sawyer went down the steps and spotted her through the window in the locked basement door. She was getting a large accordion envelope from the man in charge of her data systems, at the near end of a bank of file cabinets. A tallish woman in her thirties, with a marvelous figure and a healthy, cheerful face. She wasn't a beauty, but women who were kept wondering what she had that they didn't, other than her relaxed femininity and gourmet appetite for living.

Sawyer knocked, and a computer programmer who was nearest opened up for him. Annique grinned when she saw him. "Just finished collating your material." She had a husky voice that could still do things to him. And she knew it. Motioning with the envelope, Annique headed for one of the cubbyhole offices behind the archives. Sawyer followed her in and shut the door.

Annique dropped the envelope on the desk and turned to give him a light hug and a kiss on the mouth. She smiled at his stiff face. "It's all right," she told him gently. "Nobody's watching."

His expression didn't change much, except for a slight deepening of the lines alongside the bridge of his nose. "When was this room scanned last?"

"Less than an hour ago. No bugs, no taps. It's clean."

"What do you have for me?"

Annique went around the desk and sat in the hard-back chair, unlocking the drawer as Sawyer sat on the edge of the desk. "First of all," she told him, "you can forget about your statuette having been stolen from a museum or collection. None are missing, anywhere. None ever have been stolen, except one that vanished in Berlin in '45. But that one turned up again a year later. Even if a copy was made it wouldn't be the one you're interested in. Wrong kind of figure, wrong size, and just a knob for the face—no features at all.

"That leaves you with two alternatives: either it was a well-done fake, or else it's a real one looted from an archaeological dig before it was officially spotted and its existence recorded." Annique took five file folders from the drawer and spread them neatly on the desk. Each was numbered. She tapped the first one. "Here are your art forgers. You're not interested in paintings, but I've given you a rundown on the best painting forgers on the chance they might know something about other people in the racket that would be of use to you. There aren't many sculpture forgers. In fact, I've only come up with two who could have done a fake of your statuette good enough to fool an expert like Professor Borelli."

Annique indicated the other folders. "These have to do with your other alternative: people involved with archaeological loot. The first has names most of which you probably already know—police in various countries who do or have done special assignment work in locating missing archaeological work.

"The other three," she went on, touching each in turn, "are divided into buyers, sellers, and transporters. There are an increasing number of people with the money to buy, who only want archaeological loot. But among the sellers and smugglers it's strictly a sideline, not a speciality. They're the same ones involved in other art robberies. In the sellers' folder I've included the looters, the criminals who handle the actual stealing part."

"That's complete enough to start from," Sawyer acknowledged. "Thanks, I appreciate it."

Annique leaned back in the chair and smiled at him, showing her teeth a little. "You could reward me with dinner, tonight. Alain won't be back until tomorrow. I could come to your place."

He had asked her to divorce Gassin and marry him, when she found she was pregnant.

She'd been a bit surprised: "But you know I can't get a divorce. I'm a Catholic, and so is Alain. Even if I would, he would refuse." The rest was said quite matter-of-factly: "Anyway, I wouldn't do it. Because you don't love me. You're only disoriented by the thought of becoming the father of my child. But there's no reason we can't go on as we have. That does work, for both of us."

He'd said no then, and he hadn't changed. "I can't tonight. Too much work."

"You *never* can." She was still smiling at him, the eyes knowing and a little sad.

Sawyer began putting the folders in the large envelope. "What happened to Durey?" That was the name of her current lover, a pretty good newspaperman.

"He's still around," Annique said carelessly. And then, not carelessly: "I was talking about seeing *you*."

He picked up the last folder. His voice was good-humored but his face was stiff. "I just can't handle it, Annique."

"That's a shame." There was real sympathy for him in her look. "You may be half-French, but that American side keeps cropping up, doesn't it? Sooner or later, the Puritan in all of you comes out."

This time he smiled at her. "Sooner or later."

Sawyer took the filled envelope up to his own office and spent the next several hours reading and analyzing the material inside the folders. The fact that archaeological looting and forgery were still a relatively small branch of art-related crime enabled him to cull from Annique's lists a manageable number of people to be checked further. One possibly fruitful lead which he abstracted from the material was the method used by a few of the archaeological looters to obtain access: they had worked briefly at the dig sites, as laborers.

He decided he would have to hand Annique another large order, in the morning: to establish a list of digs in areas where a Venus figure *could* have possibly turned up and gone unreported. Then to do a computer comparison with the names of looters, to see if any of those names turned up as workers at any of those digs. It was an extreme long-shot, but potentially productive.

When he left, Sawyer took all the material with him. It was dark outside by then. He went to Balzaar to have a quick meal before going to his meeting with the woman who had known Christine Jonquet in Germany.

4

In Budapest, Lang had been following the Pole for three hours. The courier had not shown up that afternoon, and Tozinski had left his office promptly at 6 P.M. Lang, observing from Zoltan's apartment across the courtyard, had again failed to spot any indication of the Pole setting an alarm system in the office before leaving.

Going out of the building, Tozinski walked briskly for several blocks, to Vörösmarty Ter, the most popular square on the Pest side of the Danube. Lang stayed well behind in following him. But the Pole never looked back. Whatever he was, he was not worried about surveillance. This could have been merely because he felt at ease, being a person with some authority in a friendly country. But it also probably meant that he didn't carry *enough* authority to know of any reason to be worried.

Tozinski joined a plump, gray-haired woman waiting at one of the sidewalk tables in front of Gerbeaud, the big, flossy café-pastry shop facing the square. Lang watched him give the woman a brief peck on the cheek before sitting down. There was no mistaking the dutiful way the kiss was given and received: they'd been married a long time.

Lang took a table close enough to keep them in sight, far enough so they wouldn't get to know his face. He pretended to have trouble ordering black coffee from the waitress who didn't understand his English, until a German at the next table translated for him. The people at most of the other tables were gorging themselves on cakes and coffee topped with generous heaps of whipped cream. But Tozinski and his wife ordered apricot brandies, and dallied over them.

They had the look of people with nothing of special interest ahead of them that evening. And though they remained at their table over an hour, Lang failed to see anybody make contact with them, even obliquely. The woman took small clothing items out of a shopping bag and showed them for her husband's approval. He nodded without enthusiasm at each item. Most of his attention remained on pretty girls meeting their boy friends near the giant figure of Mihály Vörösmarty, in the middle of the square. Not *too* near, because scores of pigeons were streaking the statue of the famous poet with their white excrement. Budapest intellectuals claimed the pigeons were the condemned souls of literary critics, still practicing their profession.

Tozinski and his wife passed the statue when they

left the square. Lang followed them to the Karpatia, a restaurant behind a Franciscan church left over from the eighteenth century. Two hours later they were still there at their table near the four-piece orchestra, having second desserts and coffees while they continued to enjoy the gypsy music.

Lang, at a table in the rear of the restaurant, was now convinced that the Pole was just a utility relay station, with no knowledge of what was being relayed through his office. He was too entirely unpreoccupied to be a man with weighty responsibility. Tozinski's wife, Lang figured, knew even less; probably not even where the office was located, since she hadn't picked him up there.

It was getting on toward ten o'clock when they finally paid their bill and left. They crossed the now dark and empty Petofi Sandor Street, and got into the Mercedes. Tozinski's wife drove the car, across the Chain Bridge, past what was left of the wall of the old city of Buda on the other side of the Danube. Lang turned off the headlights of the Volkswagen for two short periods as he trailed them into the Buda hills. He was a safe distance behind, with the lights off, when the Mercedes turned into a fairly new residential area of two-floor houses, most of them divided into separate upper and lower apartments, each with a small garden around it.

Lang turned on his low lights and turned in after them, but slowly. Ahead of him, the Mercedes was already parked in front of a house where lights showed in the upper windows, but the ground floor was dark. He drove past without slowing, and went on for two blocks before turning a corner and parking. After waiting there a few minutes, Lang got out and walked back toward the house where the Mercedes was parked.

Lights were on inside some of the ground-floor windows now. Lang glanced around, saw no one, and entered the front garden in a low crouch. When he reached one of the lighted windows, to the right of the entrance door, he raised up cautiously, just enough to see over the sill. Inside was a large kitchen, empty. The window on the other side of the entrance door was dark. Lang moved around the corner to a lighted window in the right side of the house.

Inside was a small living room. Tozinski was in there, selecting a book from a wall shelf while his wife got a record and put it on a player sitting on a side table. Music was not one of Lang's interests. He knew it was something classical he could hear through the window, but couldn't identify it further. It wasn't important. What was important was the way Tozinski got out of his shoes, slid his feet into slippers waiting before a cushioned wing chair, and settled down comfortably with the book he'd selected. And the way his wife picked up a half-finished wool pullover and two balls of wool from the coffee table, took them to the sofa, and resumed her knitting.

There was a feeling of permanence here. The communications line, in which Tozinski was a link, was no hastily improvised, short-term thing. It was part of a major, ongoing operation. Important enough to justify not only Tozinski's making himself at home here, but bringing his wife along with him.

The growing sense of being onto something major sharpened Lang's appetite for it. Going to his hands and knees, he crawled under the living-room windows, to a dark window toward the rear of the right side of the house. Light reflecting in from the living room through a partially open door showed a bathroom. Lang went around the rear corner of the house, and rose up off his knees to peer into an unlighted back window. It was murky inside, but after a few seconds Lang made it out: a small bedroom.

Next came a back door. Lang paused. There might not be anything of interest inside the house, but it was a possibility. He doubted that he'd be sticking around in Budapest long enough to wait for the house to be empty so he could do the search himself. But someone might have to, eventually. Since he was already there, he might as well do the preliminary survey for whoever did wind up with the entry assignment.

It didn't take long. With a fingertip, Lang examined the crack between the back-door lock and the doorframe strike. He judged that there was not enough space to insert a celluloid strip and apply pressure effectively. But his examination of the lock itself was more fruitful. It was a basic pin-tumbler lock. All it would require was a small insert tension tool and a pick, and the lock could be opened in a couple of minutes without leaving a mark.

Lang moved on to the next rear window. A bigger bedroom. He went around the corner, along the other side of the house. There were no lights behind any of the windows on this side. One was a second window for the big bedroom. He moved on to the next window: a dining room.

He was turning from it when a flashlight snapped on behind him and a nervous male voice ordered in Hungarian: "Put your hands up. What are you doing?"

Lang completed his turn, and found himself facing a young uniformed policeman holding the flashlight in his left hand and a revolver in his right, both aimed squarely at him.

With a sharp effort, Lang controlled the flinching of his nervous system. He had committed an elementary blunder, in failing to check every few seconds for surveillance. The cop's voice hadn't been loud, but could become so—loud enough to be heard by Tozinski and his wife inside. Lang moved to forestall that. He wasn't supposed to know Hungarian but the cop's gesture with the gun was unmistakable. He raised both hands obediently. Shoulder high.

"I'm an American," he told the cop, trying to get frightened confusion into his voice and still keep it low. "An American, understand? I'm lost, trying to find my way back into the middle of the city. I was just going to ask the people in here . . ."

The cop didn't understand English and was only bewildered by it, which was Lang's first objective. But he did get one word: "American? Why are you here? What were you trying to do?"

Lang shot a glance toward the street. No patrol car. This was a lone foot cop. That was the only element in Lang's favor, because there was only one thing left to do at this point. Anything else, and his mission was destroyed, completely.

It didn't matter whether he talked English or Hungarian to this cop. He was going to wind up at the local police station, and then somewhere they could come up with an interpreter. Nor did it matter if they finally accepted his story that he'd had no criminal intent here, and let him go without even suspecting he was an intelligence agent. Because at some point they were going to check with Tozinski, to find out if anything had been stolen from his apartment. And Tozinski would tell his superiors about an American caught prowling around his house.

The slightest possibility that their operation had been breached would make the enemy institute a total change in its entire communications system. And the only lead into it that American intelligence had would be lost.

Even if he could escape this cop, he would report it. And the end result would be the same.

Lang didn't think all of this through. There was no time for that, and he didn't have to. He just *knew* it. And knew what he had to do about it.

"I'm not a thief or a peeping Tom," he babbled, quietly. "Ask anybody, I'm just a tourist, an American tourist . . ."

The cop continued to be bewildered by the language he couldn't understand. But he got the note of cringing helplessness in the voice, which inclined him to underrate what he had here. He carefully tucked his flashlight under his right armpit, so it still shone on Lang. The revolver in his right fist stayed steady on Lang's stomach. But he had relaxed enough so that his finger was no longer quite touching the trigger. And part of his attention was on what his left hand was doing, reaching behind him to unclip handcuffs from his belt.

The hard bone of Lang's left forearm snapped down across the cop's right wrist, at exactly the place to spring his hand open and send the gun spilling to the grass. Simultaneously, Lang's right forearm clubbed viciously into the cop's throat, smashing the start of a shout into a strangled whisper.

With no pause at all and with his right forearm still across the throat of the other man as he fell backward, Lang's whole body twisted forward and pivoted behind his back, falling with him. When they struck the ground together Lang's left arm was already up in place, elbow jammed high into the man's spine, hand grasping the back of his skull. His right hand seized his left wrist, and his right forearm used the extra leverage to tighten the strangling presssure across the cop's throat.

Lang got all the strength of his shoulders, arms, and hands into increasing the pressure, while his legs clamped around the other man to hold him down. Now not even a whisper could escape the cop's throat. He thrashed his legs and twisted his body back and forth to get free of Lang. But he couldn't break the leg clamp. Too much of his strength was going into trying to pull away the arm pressing relentlessly into his throat, denying him air and swelling his brain with trapped blood.

That was no good; the stranglehold couldn't be broken that way, no matter how strong you were. The only way would have been to reach for a sensitive point on some part of Lang, and apply enough counterpain to spring Lang's arms loose. But the young cop didn't have training or experience in that kind of fighting. He kept clawing uselessly at the human bar remorselessly tightening for the kill, his struggle weakening with startling swiftness.

There was a dull cracking noise inside his throat. Abruptly, he went limp in the grip of Lang's arms and legs. He continued to twitch for a time, but with no conscious motivation behind it. When he was still, Lang continued to lie there holding him, gritting his teeth to quiet the sobbing of his breath, working to clear the dizziness from his brain.

He turned his head and looked at Tozinski's house. No lights had gone on behind any of the windows on this side. So they hadn't heard. They must still both be in the living room on the other side, where the music from the player would have helped prevent their hearing.

Lang disengaged himself from the limp corpse, and crawled to the fallen flashlight. Snapping it off as he picked it up, he searched for the gun. It took a while. Crawling back to the dead cop, he stuck the gun in his holster and tied the flashlight by its cord to his belt.

His stomach was churning. He didn't like what he had done. He was not a Moran. But there'd been no option, as he saw it. It had been a tactical necessity.

Lang studied the street out there. There was no one in sight, and little light along it. Gripping the cop's wrist, he pulled the limp arm across his shoulders, and heaved to his feet dragging the dead man up with him. Then he ducked down quickly, yanking the wrist sideways. All of the dead man's weight fell across his shoulders.

With a concentrated surge of effort, Lang straightened with his burden, and moved out to the street. He turned in the direction of his parked car. His progress was slow, both because of the weight he was carrying and the need to stick to shadows. When he reached the Volkswagen, he was panting.

There was no need to carry the dead man further

246

cause I had a friend there. But it wasn't my kind of city; too ugly-rich industrial. So I moved to Hamburg, started a gallery. I did fairly well with it, but then I made several selling and buying trips to Paris, and fell in love with it." She shrugged and smiled. "And —well, here I am."

Her smile was open but had an odd vulnerability. She was a woman whose ego had had its share of bruises and burns, and the smile showed it.

Sawyer said, "Jonquet was under the impression you and his wife knew each other from Stuttgart, where she was from."

Clarissa Koller shook her head. "No, and anyway that's not where she's from. She was born in East Berlin, like me. That's where we knew each other from."

Sawyer experienced the tingling pleasure of a stalker who finds a sign he's on the right trail. He'd sensed it in Barcelonnette, become increasingly sure with Christine Jonquet's husband. Now he was certain: she had been part of the kidnap plan, and she was still alive somewhere, waiting for him to track her down.

"How well did you know her?" he asked quietly.

"Hardly at all, though we lived in the same apartment development, right down the hall from each other. And one year while I was still teaching art, I had her in my class. A good student, hard-working and intelligent, but oh God so deadly serious all the time. I don't think *anybody* knew her very well. She was that kind of girl—reserved, completely introverted, no small talk. The only person she was close to was her mother. Her father died a few years before I tried to get out and got caught."

"No boy friends?"

Clarissa Koller thought about that. "Maybe one. There's a coffee-house on the corner across from the development where we lived. The few times I ever saw here there, she was always alone. But the last year, she was there several times with a man. She was quite animated with him, I never saw her that way before. I don't know where she found him—he was French, not German. You could hear it in his accent. I stopped by their table once because I was curious about what he was doing in the East, but I didn't get any straight answer."

"You didn't happen to get his name?"

"No, it didn't come up."

"What did he look like?"

"You certainly are curious about a lot of old incidentals, for an ordinary insurance check. Is there something fishy about the way Christine died, or something?"

Sawyer's laugh was relaxed, good-natured. "No—it's just, *I'm* curious. Personally. Why do you think I became an investigator in the first place? And Jonquet said some pretty bizarre things about her. He really hated her, in the end."

"*I* wouldn't have wanted to be married to her. All that reserve, it had to be hiding something strange. And no humor at all. *Deadly* serious—except with this Frenchman."

She was silent for a moment, thinking back, frowning. "He was about your age, give or take a year. But much shorter. Stocky build. Almost as serious-looking as she was . . . I don't remember hair color or anything special about his features. Except, he had a funny gray patch on one cheek. A birthmark, I imagine."

"And you think he was her boy friend."

"Well, she did act differently with him." Clarissa Koller paused, remembering. "I'd say she was in love with him—I don't know why. It takes all tastes. From what I could see, to me he looked stronger than boredom."

She straightened out her legs and crossed them. They were shapely legs, firmly plump. When Sawyer looked up he saw she was smiling again, with that same peculiar unsureness. He smiled back, and after a moment her smile became less vulnerable, more re-laxed.

"Was she political?" he asked her.

"Not that I know of. I was surprised to find she'd come out to the West. Christine—I didn't think she was the type."

"She left after you did?"

Clarissa Koller nodded. "I left five years ago, in-cluding my year in prison. She was still there then."

"When she dropped into your gallery with Jonquet, did she mention *how* she got out?"

"No. We didn't actually get to talk much. She was in a hurry to leave, and as reserved as ever. I asked after her mother and she said she was fine, still in East Berlin. She said she liked one of the pictures I had on display, for an abstract. Classical painting was all she ever really liked. That's another way she was different. Most of the young art students were crazy about abstract, eager to talk about the latest work in the West."

Sawyer questioned Clarissa Koller further, without learning anything more except that Christine Jon-quet's maiden name *was* Bieler. And he took down the address of the apartment development in Berlin where they had both lived.

He gave her Olivier's number as he left, in case she thought of anything else. She remained in her doorway and watched him go down the steps, not closing the door until he was going out of the build-ing.

Sawyer made the call from the first bistro he came to, reserving a seat on an early flight to Bonn the next day. That was the logical next step: to find out what the Ministry for Inter-German Relations there could tell him about how Christine Jonquet had gotten out of East Berlin.

Then he drove home to get some sleep. But Olivier was waiting up for him, with a message: Fritz Donhoff had called, and left a Sospel number. Sawyer phoned the number.

Most of what Donhoff had for him was negative: first, the check on hotel registrations in the area. He had a number of people working on it. So far they hadn't found a name registered on both dates of Martinot's bank deposits, and only those two dates.

Second, Martinot's wife. She had been surprised, and delighted, to learn about the money in her dead husband's secret account. She hadn't the faintest clue to where the money could have come from, and knew of no unusual contacts he'd had with anyone who might have been the source. Also, she had never seen her husband with Christine Jonquet, and had never heard of her before the cave accident. Martinot had never mentioned the cave to her; and if he'd had anything like the goddess statuette, she hadn't known of it.

Third, Martinot's friends—in Barcelonnette, and then down in Sospel: he hadn't had any. No one close enough to confide in, or who knew anything about him that was of use for their investigation. Donhoff had consulted the Resistance veterans' organizations in both towns, and gotten little.

"Nobody knows what he was up to lately," Donhoff explained, "because no one cared to be that close to him. They just didn't like him much. The way he killed that girl bothered everybody in a way they never quite got over. Although they did defend him, when the girl's father tried to get the law to charge him with her murder."

"Why did they defend him if they didn't like him?" Sawyer interrupted Donhoff.

"Because Martinot was also something of a Resistance hero, before what he did to the girl. And because her SS officer—by whom she even had a son, incidentally—had been involved in a number of extremely unpleasant atrocities in this area. So the

252

charge against Martinot never got to court. Bruno took her boy and left the area in disgust."

"Bruno?"

"The father of the girl Martinot killed. Her name was Marie-Anne Bruno."

There was no reason why the name should have meant anything to Sawyer at the time.

THIRTEEN

1

The Budapest courier showed up shortly after ten the next morning. Zoltan, peering through two of the lower slats in his apartment shutters, identified the man as he got out out the courtyard's front elevator on the fifth floor. Lang snapped two pictures of the courier walking quickly around the fifth-floor balcony to Tozinski's office.

Lang's examination of the Pole's office the previous night had turned up absolutely nothing connected with the enemy operation which used the communications line which passed through that office. Nevertheless, he considered his break-in to have been productive, since it almost certainly ruled out any need for more intensive surveillance on Tozinski.

Even the lock on the office door had been indicative: a simple tension tool and a tiny pick had opened it. As Lang had anticipated, there had been no alarm system rigged to the door. Inside he had found a single office with a small connecting bathroom. The office furniture consisted of a desk, two chairs, and a studio couch. Nothing else; no address book, no papers in the desk drawers or anywhere else Lang had searched. On the desk were the telephone and a Japanese-made cassette-tape player, with nothing on its spools. Lang had examined a number of cassette cartridges that had been dumped into a wastebasket. But they'd been common brands sold internationally, and all had been emptied of their tapes. In the bathroom

254

Lang had found traces of ash, possibly from burning the tapes.

The only other items he'd found were a cheap chess set and board, and eleven books of chess puzzles and famous matches. Which explained how Tozinski spent his days in the office, and the faint sounds Lang had heard over the laser eavesdropper. Lang had relocked the office door on leaving, gone to his room at the Hotel Astoria, and had six hours of solid dreamless sleep before returning to Zoltan's apartment at eight this morning to begin the day's watch.

The courier who knocked at Tozinski's office door a few minutes after ten that morning was a short, broad-shouldered man with a shaved skull and an ill-fitting brown suit. He carried no bag of any kind; so if he had a tape for Tozinski it was in his pocket, and that was all he was carrying. No encoding machine. And there was none in Tozinski's office. That finalized what Lang had already assumed from Zoltan's description of the timing of the courier's visits: the encoding was done somewhere further back along the line.

Zoltan had his recorder and both listening setups operating by the time Tozinski opened his door. Lang took up one of the earphones and heard quite clearly as they exchanged formal greetings in German without mentioning names. Lang watched the courier step inside and the door close as he heard Tozinski ask after the courier's health. The courier's German was better than Tozinski's, with an Austrian inflection. He said he still couldn't shake his cold.

There were small sounds that could have been from a cassette being put in the machine. Tozinski's phone was picked up and dialed, and a long-distance operator came on. Tozinski asked for the Warsaw number.

The call took several minutes to get through. Tozinski and the courier waited without speaking. Warsaw picked up on the first ring. Still no voices. There was the whirring of Tozinski's player, and it began transmitting the coded message in series bursts of high-speed dots and dashes. Lang checked his watch.

The transmission continued for fifty-three minutes. When it ended there was only a brief whirring sound, and then Warsaw disconnected. Quickly, Lang put down the earphone, snapped off Zoltan's recorder, and took out the tape cassette which had recorded the message. He slipped the cassette into his pocket as he went out of Zoltan's apartment. Watching To-zinski's office out of the corner of his eye as he headed in the direction of the front elevator, Lang detected no one peeking out through the closed venetian blinds. He bypassed the elevator and started swiftly down the steps before the door of Tozinski's office opened.

When the courier came out of the building en-trance, Lang was already in his rented Volkswagen halfway down the block. The courier glanced up and down the street, but not like a man checking for sur-veillance; rather like someone searching for a taxi. There were no cabs in sight. The courier headed along Petofi Sandor in the direction of Kossuth Lajos Street.

Lang had to make a U-turn to drive in the same direction. By the time he completed the turn, the courier had disappeared through the shopping crowds. But Lang was fairly sure where he was going. Ma-neuvering the Volkswagen around a slow delivery van and cutting off an oncoming car, Lang reached Kos-suth Lajos and turned into Liberation Square. The courier was crossing the square to the taxi stand, dodging traffic.

The taxi the courier got into worked its way out of the narrow streets of the Inner City to Kalvin Square, and headed up Ulloi Avenue toward the out-skirts of Budapest. Heavy traffic all the way made it easier for Lang to stick close to it without becoming conspicuous. Outside the city, the taxi turned onto the highway to Ferihegy International Airport ten kilometers away. Lang eased back and let a number of cars get between the Volkswagen and the taxi as he followed.

At the air terminal Lang double-parked while the courier was paying his fare, and got inside first. The courier strode in a moment later and went to the Austrian Airlines counter to confirm his reserved seat on the next flight to Vienna, leaving in three quarters of an hour.

Lang waited until the courier strolled away toward the bar, then tried to get a seat on the same plane. But it was fully booked. The best they could do for him was a seat on a flight leaving for Vienna in three hours. Curbing a sharp surge of impatience, Lang nodded, getting out his passport and credit card.

It was, he reminded himself, only a delay, not a setback. Nothing was lost, except a little time: a day or two. The same courier made the same trip whenever there was a code tape to deliver to Budapest. The delay gave Lang time to organize the Vienna end, have the station develop his pictures of the courier, and make copies for a surveillance team which would be set up at Vienna's airport. The next trip the courier made, the team would spot him. By the time the courier returned Lang would be in position, ready to tail him.

He had reason to be satisfied with his progress at this stage, Lang knew. Outside of the one foul-up of allowing himself to get tagged by that young cop—a foul-up which he had corrected—the assignment was well begun.

2

Moira sat cross-legged on her bed, engrossed in the book Bruno had given her yesterday, when he unlocked her cell door and came in. A fat shaft of morning sunlight from the barred window warmed her face when she raised it from the book to give him a welcoming smile. He had another book with him, a thick volume with a stained old-fashioned binding. In his other hand he carried the cassette-tape recorder, but Moira did not lose her smile.

"This is a tremendous work," she told him, patting the opened book resting on her crossed legs. "I'm fascinated with it."

She didn't have to exaggerate her enthusiasm. It was the most complete study she had ever come across of Gislebertus, the French Romanesque sculptor; an English-language edition, with detailed photographs of the sculptor's ten years' work at the St. Lazarus Cathedral in Autun.

Bruno nodded, and Moira could see he was pleased, though he didn't smile. It showed in his eyes. "I once spent quite some time, studying that book . . . in a German translation. You are lucky I was able to find the English version, in a bookshop near here."

"I appreciate it." And she did, for more than one reason. It confirmed her belief that she was still in France. Probably not far from Autun, since it was unlikely that an English version of such a highly specialized work would be readily available anywhere else on the Continent. Certainly not in a German bookshop.

Moira knew that Bruno was intelligent enough to realize she might draw some such conclusion. But he'd gone and gotten this book for her anyway; because it was a favorite of his in the field of art, in which they'd discovered a shared interest. It was another proof that he was responding to her determinedly improved attitude since the ordeal of the tape recording she'd refused to make. He had relaxed enough not to care if she guessed where she was. As long as she was sensible enough not to bring it up directly, which would tighten him up again.

"The illustrations are fabulous." Moira turned a few pages to a full-page photograph of a detail from the lintel of the cathedral's tympanum: a sculpture of two huge hands with clawed fingers seizing the screaming head of a damned soul. "Especially the big ones, like this."

Bruno put the recorder and the other book on the bureau and came over to her bed to look down at the picture. "Oh yes—*The Stranglehold of Hell.* Beautiful."

"In a *horrible* way."

Bruno gave a slight shrug. "High horror was one of the specialties of Romanesque and Gothic artists. A compensation for having to do saints most of the time."

"I know," Moira said wryly. "Depicting the souls of the damned in torment gave them a chance to get all the sick sex and sadism out of their systems. So many of the hell scenes in old churches are sheer pornography."

"..." Bruno conceded s... *asked him. the book* ... Gislebertus' work. He w... He didn't desecrate his talent with filth. No question, Gislebertus was the best of the twelfth century. Nobody else came near him—not at the Saulieu church, not even at Vézelay. And Grivot, the abbé who wrote this work, has studied him longer than anyone."

Moira appeared quite relaxed, enjoying their discussion. But all her senses were concentrated on trying to read every nuance of Bruno's voice and expression. It was vital to develop further what she had already succeeded in establishing: a special feeling of intimacy between them. This depended on her ability to remain sensitive to the faintest responses from the secret places inside this man. His response to the book on her lap provided her with another means of penetrating his defenses, and she stayed with it a while longer, but cautiously:

"Yes," she agreed, "he does know what he's writing about. But he's not as specific as he could be in his descriptions of some of the capitals. Like this one

. . ." Moira turned back to a picture of a sculpture showing a small man brandishing a knife on the back of a large bird. "All the text says is that it's a man riding on a water bird. But why the knife?"

Bruno's nod made her think of a teacher pleased with the alertness of a pupil. "Abbé Grivot was being too cautious there. I read another book where he took the chance and gave an educated guess. There's an ancient legend about a land of pygmies always at war with their chief enemies—flocks of cranes. That's what this is: a pygmy fighting a crane."

Moire looked at Bruno with genuine interest as she closed the book and got off her bed. "You keep surprising me. How do you know so much about art?"

For a moment she thought he was going to smile. But he didn't. "It was necessary at one period in my life to know something about it—for my work. And then, I became interested in knowing more."

"What kind of work was that?" Moir

But he didn't reply, gesturing instead he'd put on the bureau with the cassette machine. "This one is about the art of Pompeii. I haven't read it, and much of the information certainly won't be up-to-date, since it was published in 1902. But books in English are not easy for me to find."

"I do appreciate it," Moira assured him. And then indicating the recorder and keeping it light: "I see it's time for me to sing my song again."

He stared at her blankly. "Your song . . . ?"

"Just a stupid joke." Humor, she had learned, was an alien planet for this man.

He took from his pocket a folded sheet of paper. She took it from him and unfolded it. On it were printed the words she had to say. Moira made a point of not allowing any trace of resistance or hostility to creep into her tone: "Well, I suppose we should get it over with."

"Yes. The tape must get started on its way very soon."

Moira turned on the recorder herself, picked up the small mike, and read the words into it: "Hello, Alex, how are you?" She thought of him and let the warmth into her voice. "I really hope you are well, and behaving yourself. I'm still all right. I read in the papers yesterday that the Italians just released the first interpretations of the Sumerian tablets from their dig in Syria. Including one with a reference to a trade treaty with Egypt in 2300 B.C. Be good, Alex, and I'll talk to you again soon."

That was it, word for word. She hadn't changed anything in it, by omission, alteration, or inflection.

Bruno looked approving as he snapped off the recorder and picked it up, taking the microphone from her. "Good. Now I have to go."

He was turning toward the door when Moira asked: "Have you thought anymore about letting me outdoors from time to time? I really wouldn't give any trouble. And you could watch me. Or Lorenz."

"I have thought about it. But there would be only one way I could take such a risk." Bruno stopped, seeming embarrassed again, as he had when she'd referred to pornography. "I . . . it would be necessary to use handcuffs. And I would have to get a chain. I'm sorry, there is no other way."

Moira's laugh had nothing in it but good-natured relief. "I wouldn't mind—not at all. If that's all it takes for me to get out in the sun a bit, bring on your chain and handcuffs."

"Then—perhaps tomorrow." He stepped out of her cell.

Moira picked up the new book from the bureau. "And thank you, again, for the books. I'm sincerely grateful to you."

Bruno paused with his hand on the door, looking at her expressionlessly, all thoughts and feelings hidden. Then, without speaking, he shut the door, closing her in. She listened as he slid the bolts in place on the outside.

3

Sir,

You're probably safe from want now and haven't any personal or family problems. Your life is probably pleasant and you enjoy your work. But what about tomorrow? In six months' time, within a year?

Perhaps you'll be then trying to cope with unexpected problems. Perhaps you'll be jobless or you won't enjoy your job any longer. Perhaps you'll have problems within your own family. Or you'll be up against the law.

You never can tell, can you?

Undoubtedly you'll then be happy to find a roof and a home for shelter; to become a full member of a community which will welcome you, advise and help you to weather through your troubles.

All that is offered to you by the FOREIGN LEGION.

No identification papers will be asked for. Your intellectual level is of little importance. It is not necessary to know the French language as you'll learn to speak it during the time of your 5-year contract. You can apply for French citizenship after 4 and a half years of service and thus acquire the French nationality.

If you want more detailed information, please take this introductory letter along to apply to one of the addresses appended.

Yours very sincerely,
The Foreign Legion Information Service

Lorenz had served only two years of his contract with the French Foreign Legion, before he'd been forced to desert after killing his sergeant. But he still kept the letter which had recruited him, stained and shredded over the years since, folded inside the wallet he carried in the right-hand pocket of his jacket.

The cassette tape which Moira Rhalles had recorded was in his other pocket as Lorenz drove north to Paris. And a bitter resentment at Bruno, for never allowing him the pleasure of toying a little with the girl, burned like acid in his guts.

Lorenz was accustomed to the acid of bitterness. He'd felt it toward almost everyone for a very long time, and he knew it to be justified. If Germany had won the war, his services as an underofficer in the Waffen SS would have earned him an enviable secure future. But they had lost, and at sixty what was he? Nothing. Why? Because the West German Government had traitorously assisted Germany's former enemies in tracking down and punishing what they called "war criminals."

Lorenz had been charged with two such "crimes": In Italy, he had supervised the burning of a village where a Wehrmacht dispatch rider had been murdered, and the killing of every inhabitant. In Belgium, during the final retreat, he had personally crushed to death six captured American paratroopers, chaining them to the ground and driving a tank back and forth over them. To escape trial on these charges, Lorenz had had to leave his native Augsburg and wander through Europe like a hunted animal. Then he'd run into a former SS comrade in similar trouble, who'd given him the Foreign Legion recruiting letter.

The French had had a use for them, first in Indochina, and then in Algeria. For their talent as killers, and their experience in torturing information out of captured enemies who failed to respond to normal rough interrogation. Lorenz had enjoyed his service with the Legion; it had provided him with a needed means of releasing the bitter anger. But then he'd had the misfortune to kill the sergeant.

It had begun as nothing more than a stupid drunken brawl in an Oran bar; the sort of thing Lorenz liked to provoke when he had enough liquor in him. But the sergeant had been younger and stronger; and as long as Lorenz stuck to accepted barroom-fighting tactics he'd taken a beating. Then the thing had happened: the explosion which sometimes shook him and over which he had little control, though it always gave him pleasure. Three seconds later the Legion sergeant had been dead on the floor.

Lorenz had fled to Algiers, where he'd tried to find refuge from French military law by joining the Algerian rebels. He had found himself talking, finally, to a former Gestapo counterespionage expert who was acting as secret adviser to the rebels for his present employer: the East German Government. The man had explained to him that the Communist government of East Germany had some time ago decided to forgive any "war criminals" who had skills that could be of use to them. Possibly, Lorenz had such skills.

Flown to East Berlin, Lorenz had been subjected to a long series of psychological tests and interrogations which he'd considered childish. Nevertheless, the psychiatrists conducting these tests had established, over several weeks, a number of facts about Lorenz which he had never consciously confronted before: that he considered the world divided into two groups —natural victims who got hurt, and survival types who did the hurting. And that since he did not want to be in the first group, he enjoyed considering himself part of the second group. That he had a fear of dying, which was considerably relieved whenever he saw others die, while he survived. That surviving amid death made him feel he was an immortal, who could never die. And that this feeling of intense *aliveness* he experienced was at its strongest when he himself was responsible for the death of others.

Lorenz had finally been accepted into the reasonably well-paid security of the East German secret service, without ever knowing that the series of tests he had passed had originally been devised for the KGB by Irina Frejenko.

It was getting dark when Lorenz entered Paris, by way of the Porte d'Orléans. He drove to the Rue St.-Jacques, which had once formed the final length of the road the Caesars had built from Rome to Paris, and followed it in the direction of the Seine. Parking behind the Sorbonne, Lorenz walked back to the Rue Soufflot and bought a copy of *Le Monde* at a corner newstand.

Glancing at his watch, he saw that he still had almost an hour to wait. Taking the newspaper with him, Lorenz went to one of the student bistros lining the street. He ordered a sandwich and beer, and settled down at an outside table where the noise of the bistro's jukebox and pinball machines was not quite so annoying. He finished his sandwich and had two more beers while waiting. Once, he tried to make sense of the headlines in the paper he had bought; but written French remained incomprehensible to him.

At five minutes before nine, Lorenz got up and paid his bill. As he crossed the street, he took the cassette Moira Rhalles had taped from his pocket and slipped it inside his folded newspaper. Entering the bistro on the other side of the street, he ordered a coffee. The bistro was nearly empty this close to closing. There was a long padded bench along one wall, with small tables in front of it. Lorenz sat down there, behind one of the tables. He placed the folded newspaper on the bench beside him, touching his left leg.

At exactly nine o'clock an attractive woman of about fifty entered the bistro. Lorenz appraised her superb figure approvingly as she asked the barman for an iced lemon-and-water. His approval turned to surprise as she turned from the bar and he recognized her. She brought her drink over and sat down on the bench beside him, behind the small table to his left. That was the place the man who always took the pickup from him was supposed to sit.

He had only met her that once, at 22 Normann-strasse, the State Security headquarters building in the Lichtenberg district of Berlin. Stryker, Lorenz's immediate superior in East Germany's SSD, had introduced them, and then left them alone together. She was the woman who had explained the details of his job in this operation.

Irina Frejenko asked him pleasantly: "If you are through with your paper, could I look at it for a moment?" It was part of the pickup formula, exactly according to ritual. "A friend told me there is an interesting review in it by an Argentine exile."

Lorenz was still looking at her, puzzled, having difficulty adjusting to the unexpected change from his usual contact.

"The man you expected had an accident," she told him, very softly. "He's in a hospital. I'll be your contact here until further notice."

Lorenz nodded, accepting the change, and began his part of the ritual: "You can keep the paper. I've finished with it."

"Thank you." She took the folded paper and put it on her lap, with the tape-cassette concealed inside it. "In that case I'll take it along and read it when I get home."

"You're welcome." Curbing his curiosity about her, Lorenz finished his coffee and left the bistro.

When he was gone, Irina Frejenko looked at her wristwatch. She still had ten minutes to wait. Sipping her drink, she gazed blankly in the direction of the bar, struggling against the feelings of insecurity and homesickness that continued to assail her.

It had been one of those unexpected accidents Jorgen had warned her could throw everything awry. And it couldn't have had a more unpredictable—even ridiculous—cause. The man in control of the Paris junction of her operation had taken his dog for a walk on a leash. Another dog had run over to play with his, and the agent had gotten his ankles tangled in the leash. It hadn't been much of a fall, but he'd landed on one knee and broken it. His kneecap had been operated on yesterday. Even if it healed without complications, it would be several months before he could expect to walk without crutches.

Irina Frejenko was in Paris because there was no one else who could be sent on short notice to replace this particular agent. He'd been the *only* person in her organization who was connected to two main arms of the operation: the one leading to Alexander Rhalles, and the other leading to Moira Rhalles. He'd also been the single connection to the trained assassin who waited in Paris for an order that would become necessary if the operation went wrong: to make certain that Moira Rhalles was disposed of before anyone else could find her.

"I'll leave it up to you," Vasily Pokryshkin had told her in his Lubyanka office. "Can you think of anyone *you* would feel comfortable about sending immediately to take over from your Paris control?"

"No," she'd had to admit. "I'll have to go."

"It won't be for long," Vasily had assured her. "Perhaps a few weeks, at the most. I need time to find an experienced man who can be trusted to exercise complete authority there without supervision, detach him from whatever other important operation such a man would undoubtedly be involved in, and brief him thoroughly. Both on his part in your organization, and its potential dangers."

"Vasily," Irina Frejenko had warned him, "be *very* careful about whom you choose for this."

"That," he'd replied soberly, "you do not have to tell me."

She finished her drink and glanced at her watch. It was time. She picked up the folded newspaper containing the cassette Moira Rhalles had taped, and left the bistro. Behind her, the owner began turning off his lights. Turning up the Rue Soufflot, she approached the Pantheon, with its big illuminated dome looming into a cloudy, dark sky. She walked to the left around the building, slowing her steps.

Her timing was exactly right. In the parking space between the end of the Pantheon and the St. Geneviève Church, a man was getting into a white Renault that had a torn sticker from the Val d'Isère ski resort pasted to its rear window. He wound down his window and started the car, letting the motor idle.

Irina Frejenko walked quickly to the Renault. She recognized the face of the man inside at the wheel, though he had never met her. "Excuse me," she asked, "can you tell me the way to the Rue des Écoles?"

He looked startled and worried, as Lorenz had. Holding the newspaper in her straight hand, Irina Frejenko leaned down and rested it on the lower part of his open window. "I think your left tire will have to be replaced soon," she recited to establish herself. And softly: "Your usual contact had an accident. I am replacing him until further notice."

She let the cassette slide from the paper and drop in his lap. Then she straightened, holding the paper, and said, "Thank you." Walking away in the direction of the Rue des Écoles, she heard the Renault drive off behind her. She kept going until she reached the Seine, and then strolled for a while along its Left Bank quays, trying to lull her nerves. But the beauty of the lights on the night-dark water only intensified her homesickness—and loneliness.

She had tried to persuade Vasily to let her bring Valentin with her. The answer had remained No—regretful but firm. And she understood, of course. Her husband had to remain behind as a hostage, just in case. Though she regretted that decision she could not resent it, because she understood too well the fears that dictated it.

Irina Frejenko reached the Pont Sully and turned

onto it, walking across the river to the apartment she'd sublet for the month.

It was on the Rue St. Paul in the Marais, two blocks from the building where Sawyer and Olivier lived. In his one-room apartment on the ground floor, Olivier had just gotten a phone call from Fritz Donhoff, with news of the first real break in his investigation.

4

Fighting against encroaching weariness after the long day of plodding, unrewarding work, Donhoff gripped the wheel of his big Citroën DS and concentrated on not going off the hairpin turns of the dark, narrow mountain road. Up ahead of his car, the red taillight and deep-throated roar of Titine Delisio's motorcycle led the way.

She had beaten the police clerks of the Préfecture in Nice to it. Donhoff was paying two men in the Préfecture's central records department to check the hotel registrations for the entire Alpes-Maritimes area. But it was a large region with an enormous number of little village hotels, and nobody had yet found a way to make the collection system foolproof. Donhoff knew that registration cards were lost all the time, by the hotels or in transit to Nice. Those that did reach the central records department, which lacked funds for an adequate staff or efficient data-processing equipment, piled up and added to the confusion.

So Donhoff had also hired three neophyte employees from the largest private investigation agency in Nice, to contact hotels in person. He'd assigned each a different territory to cover. Titine Delisio had gotten a wide area south of Sospel, where Martinot had lived, and Peira-Cava, where he'd made the two secret bank deposits. Racing up and down the mountain roads on her motorcycle, she'd hit more back-country hotels than the other two operatives combined.

She'd struck pay dirt in the village of Peille: a Belgian had stayed at the Hotel of the Fountain for two days, at two different periods a month apart. The dates of his registration coincided with the dates when Martinot had made his two large deposits.

"You don't have to waste time checking it out again," Titine had told Donhoff resentfully before leading him up there. "I asked all the questions and I didn't forget any. You won't find out anything I didn't already get."

"Probably." Donhoff had made his tone as kindly as possible. "But you *are* young and inexperienced. I have to make certain."

Donhoff followed her into a short mountain tunnel. Emerging at the other end, he saw the lights of the stone village, perched on a rugged slope on the other side of a deep ravine. The motorcycle led him around a long curve, up over a short bridge, and down into Peille on the other side. The road ended in a parking square overlooking the ravine, just inside the edge of the village.

Titine Delisio took off her motorcycle helmet and shook out her dark curls as Donhoff climbed from the Citroën. She was a short, wiry Corsican; a tough, sentimental, vivacious girl with sly, rancorous humor and sudden moodiness, both bubbling close to the surface. And her hard black eyes were still resentful as she led Donhoff down a narrow passage to the heart of the village: a small square, hemmed in by ancient stone houses and centered around a Gothic fountain shaped like a giant tulip.

The hotel consisted of five rooms on a single floor above the "Cafe of the Fountain." Its reception desk was the tobacco counter at one end of the café's bar. The owner was a fat, earthy woman named Madame Sorel. She greeted Titine like an old friend, poured short brandies for both of them, and let Donhoff examine her registration ledger without a trace of reluctance.

The man who had stayed there on both pertinent dates was registered as Maurice Ruyter. His Belgian passport had listed his occupation as Bargemaster, and his home address was in Antwerp.

"You said he was a stocky man in his mid-thirties?" Donhoff asked Madame Sorel.

She nodded. "Very strongly built, as I told your friend. Pale gray eyes. Tough face, but not unpleasantly. With that funny gray birthmark on his cheek."

"You remember him quite well."

"You know how it is in places like this. We don't get that many people in the hotel, out of season. And when one of them comes back again like he did, well, naturally you're pleased to see him. It means he liked your food, the ambience of your place." Madame Sorel laughed suddenly, almost girlishly. "And besides—this one had the kind of deep, rough voice that spoke to my hormones."

Donhoff questioned her carefully. She told him that the man registered as Ruyter hadn't had any visitors while he'd stayed there, either time. Hadn't gotten into conversations with anyone. Had taken his breakfasts and dinners there, but had spent the rest of the day, both times, off somewhere driving around the country. Just sightseeing, he'd told her. She remembered that he'd driven a blue Renault, but not the license number.

All of which Titine Delisio had already gotten, along with Ruyter's passport number and address in Antwerp. Fritz Donhoff was unable to get anything else, and he turned to look at her smug-sullen expression with an approving nod. "You're right, there was no need for me to come. You didn't miss a thing."

Her expression instantly changed to eager, unconcealed pleasure. "I'm new at this, it's true, but I really do have talent for it. You'll see."

"Unfortunately," Donhoff told her regretfully, "I'm

afraid I won't have any further use for you or the others. At this point, at least."

Abruptly, her face clouded with disappointment.

He turned back to Madame Sorel. "Can I use your phone to call Paris."

"Of course." Madame Sorel got a phone from behind the bar, put it on top, dialed the operator, and asked for time and charges.

Donhoff took the phone from her and gave the operator Olivier's number in Paris.

Olivier picked up on the third ring. "Yes?"

"This is Fritz Donhoff. Is this line still safe?"

"Pierre-Ange checked my phone and did a bug-detection sweep of the apartment before he went," Olivier answered. "He left me the checking equipment, *and* a neon audiodisrupter to louse up long-range bugging. I've been using both, so this end should be clear."

"Where can I get in touch with Pierre-Ange?"

"Right now I don't know. He *was* in Bonn, talking to the people in the screening bureau at their ministry for Inter-German Relations. But the last I heard from him, he was on his way to Stuttgart. He has a lead on a man who knows how Christine Jonquet got out of East Berlin."

"When he calls again," Donhoff said, "tell him I have a lead too." He explained briefly about the man registered as a Belgian named Maurice Ruyter.

Olivier became excited about the gray birthmark on Ruyter's cheek. He told Donhoff about the Frenchman Clarissa Koller had seen with Christine Jonquet in East Berlin—who'd also had the gray birthmark. "Annique Gassin is already running a check, to see if any kind of record exists on a man of that description."

"Better and better." Donhoff felt his own excitement quickening. "I'll start up to Antwerp in the morning, to see what I can find on him there."

Donhoff paid for the call, thanked Madame Sorel, and walked out wearily.

Titine hurried out after him. "Why wait until to-morrow to start for Antwerp?" she demanded tensely. She knew nothing of Donhoff's reason for wanting the information she'd ferreted out for him, but she did know it was something urgent. "If you start out now, you could *be* there in the morning."

He stopped and smiled at her. "How old are you, little one?"

"Twenty-two," she told him defensively. "What has that to do with it?"

"Well, I'm almost seventy. Lately, I only need about five hours sleep a night—but those five hours I do need. And right now I am very tired. Understand?"

"No. There's plenty of room in the back seat of that car you've got, for you to curl up and go to sleep. While I drive you up."

Donhoff laughed softly, enjoying her spirit.

She did not laugh. There was too much anxiety in her eagerness. "Look, you're famous in this business. If I can help you for a while, it'll do me good later. I won't even charge for driving you. Just if it turns out you need me for other things. And you will. I'm good, you'll see."

Donhoff considered it. He did not relish the prospect of spending the night sleeping off-and-on in the back of a moving car. But the time element in this investigation *was* vital—if they were to have a chance of finding Moira Rhalles while she was still alive.

"What about your motorcycle?"

Now she laughed, delighted. "I can leave it in the back of the cafe." She rushed back inside to arrange it.

Five minutes later she was barreling the Citroën along the dark mountain roads in the direction of the expressway to the north, while Donhoff loosened his collar and settled down on the wide seat behind her. It was a few minutes before ten o'clock.

In Washington, D.C., the time-zone difference made it a few minutes before four o'clock in the afternoon.

5

At six in the evening, Alexander Rhalles left the White House on foot and walked up Sixteenth Street. What he was about to do now, what he had done two hours ago in the President's study off the Oval Office, and what he intended to do later this evening—all added up to three transgressions against the people Jorgen worked for. Surges of panic tore at Rhalles. He deflected them with cold anger, and kept walking.

Under intense pressure you had a choice, he knew. Either you gradually broke apart under it, or you hardened until it couldn't get inside you. Rhalles was getting harder. The technique he used was similar to that of an actor who thought his way inside a character he must play, until he became that character. In Rhalles' case this was easier because the character was his own, before Moira. He had created his "iceberg" personality long ago for the purpose of fending off the world around him. He used it now to survive without destroying Moira.

At L Street Rhalles entered a Chinese restaurant next to an old corner hotel. He took a table in the rear, with his back to the wall. From this position he could observe both the main entrance and a side door leading into the lobby of the hotel, to which the restaurant belonged. He did not immediately pick up the menu given to him by the waiter, but watched both doors. When a couple of minutes had passed with no one following him in, Rhalles glanced through the menu.

After giving his order to the waiter, Rhalles asked where the bathroom was, though he knew the answer.

The waiter pointed to the side door. "Go into the lobby and to the left, you'll see it."

"Thank you. You can bring my order, I'll be right

back." Rhalles went through the door into the hotel lobby and turned to the left past the reception counter and a newsstand displaying nothing but a wide variety of vividly colored girlie magazines. Beyond that were the bathrooms, and two public phone booths.

Stepping inside one of the booths, Rhalles shut the door, dropped in a coin, and dialed long-distance. He told the operator he wanted to place a collect call to Paris, gave the number he'd gotten from Sawyer, and identified himself as Mr. Samuel Otto.

Olivier's voice came on sounding sleepy. He accepted the call, and when the operator went off he said: "Hello, Mr. Otto, what is it?"

"I'm sorry if I've wakened you. I realize how late it is there, but . . ." Rhalles paused, and chose his words with care. Sawyer had warned him about the vulnerability of transatlantic calls, and that the NSA computers were keyed to pick up on certain words and phrases. "I'd like to talk to Pete, if he's around."

"I'm sorry, but he's not. Any message, when I hear from him?"

"I want to know how he's coming along. I don't suppose you could tell me anything about that?"

In Paris, Olivier hesitated, and then told a lie followed by a truth: "Well, as you're aware, sir, I don't know the details of this sales campaign. But he said that if you called, to tell you that it's progressing better than he'd expected. He's following up one very promising prospect now. And a few hours ago I heard of a second one. So he said to tell you—his exact words: Sit tight. Don't worry. Hold on."

"I'll hold on," Rhalles said grimly, "don't worry about that. Just get me results."

His order was waiting on the table when he returned to the restaurant. Rhalles sat down and began to eat, though he had little appetite. He couldn't afford to indulge his nerves. He had to eat normally, sleep normally, and stay well. Which required him to believe, with absolute conviction, that the machinery he'd set in motion was going to achieve its objective: he would soon have Moira back.

"Think positive, baby," she'd warned him, "because what you think gives off waves that influence what happens. So the next time you start indulging that old pessimism of yours, I'm gonna kick your beautiful ass, hard."

A passing waiter gave Rhalles a curious glance, and he realized he was grinning idiotically to himself. He swallowed the grin, but kept it warm inside him.

It was part of their running argument, between his Darwinism and her belief that the development of man, and the universe, was *willed*. She had never managed to convince him, but he acknowledged that the notion was emotionally attractive: "That's why you believe in it—because you want to."

"Because it makes sense," Moira countered. "Why did we graduate from small cells floating around in the ocean, to creatures capable of sending machinery to Mars?"

"It's called natural selection, you pagan."

"Chance encounters and random accidents of heredity over thousands of years? Bullshit. Something in those cells reached out to achieve the development, and every step of the way that something in us *determined* to continue the trip. And here we are."

"I was always determined to wind up with a beautiful blonde," Rhalles complained, "and look what I got."

"I've *always* been a beautiful blonde, in my heart."

"Which is why you've always had more fun?"

"You said it."

It was getting dark when the cab dropped Rhalles at his house in Georgetown. He turned on the lamp in his study and closed the blinds, before sitting down to talk into the tape recorder. He told about his conversations with the President that day; about discussions he'd had with the presidential Press Secretary and with a State Department planning adviser; about the conference of Pentagon chiefs he'd attended in the Cabinet Room.

As always, Rhalles carefully left out certain vital items. Increasingly, he was leaving out more. He had convinced himself that he could do so without harming Moira. First of all, if they did learn of what he'd left out, from other sources, they couldn't be certain he'd left these items out deliberately. There were a great many secrets he wasn't party to; either because they were kept from him, or he just didn't happen to be around when they were discussed. And certain deletions could be blamed on normal memory lapses.

Secondly, they wouldn't kill the goose that laid so many golden eggs for them, even if there were a few other eggs withheld. If they destroyed Moira, he would cease being the source of *any* information for them. They would not be so stupid. As long as he was careful to give enough information to keep them reasonably satisfied.

Rhalles ended the tape with a final bit of information which contained a further exercise in deviousness on his part. He began it with an interesting item they wouldn't know yet, to sugar the rest: "The day after tomorrow, the President will leave for Florida, ostensibly for a three-day rest. Actually, though it won't be announced until later, he is going there to have meetings with representatives from six Latin American countries—to discuss means of strengthening the naval defense system of the American continent, especially in the Caribbean and Canal areas."

Rhalles did not alter his tone as he added the rest: "I attempted to persuade the President to take me along, saying it would be an interesting experience for me. But he was not responsive to my suggestion, and I could not persist without arousing his suspicion about my motives."

That was not true. The President had asked him to go along, but had accepted his excuse that he was too involved with his own historical work to leave at this point. Since they had been alone in the President's study when this conversation had taken place, Rhalles couldn't see any way Jorgen's people could find out the truth. The possibility that the President might mention it to someone else, who chanced to be another one of their pipelines, was remote. And Rhalles badly needed the few days of relief from part of the pressure on him.

It was shortly after ten that night when Rhalles left the house with the tape cassette in his pocket, sealed in a small plastic bag of the sort used for storing vegetables. He drove haphazardly for ten minutes, watching his rear-view mirror, before stopping at a phone booth to make the call. As always, whoever picked up the phone at the other end did not speak. Rhalles said: "I have a delivery," hung up at his end, and got back in his car.

The pickup spot scheduled for this date, on the list hidden in his study, was across the line, in Maryland. Rhalles drove out of Washington on MacArthur Boulevard. When he was out among scattered suburban communities separated by wooded stretches, he pulled over to the side of the road and stopped. He stayed there for several minutes, until he was sure nothing had been following him. Then he switched off MacArthur, down to Canal Road, and followed it out through the dark countryside along the narrow canal and the Potomac River.

The roadside sign that marked his crossing into Maryland read: "Maryland Welcomes You—Please Drive Carefully." Rhalles slowed and began to keep a careful check on his mileage. He passed the next sign: "Keep America Clean—Do Not Litter." Inevitably, from that point on, the side of the road became strewn with beer cans, broken bottles, and bags of garbage thrown out by passing motorists. It was impossible for some Americans to resist a sign like that.

Exactly five miles beyond the antilitter sign, Rhalles stopped the car off the side of the road. There was no building in sight, and no road lights within range. To his left across the road bushes and trees flanked the canal and a horseback riding path, silent, empty, and dark. Beyond that was the black width of the Potomac, and the state of Virginia on the other bank.

The side of the road Rhalles was on was made even darker by a bushy slope that rose from it for about a hundred feet to a densely wooded crest. Rhalles waited until there were no other cars on the road before he got out.

At the top of the slope above him, Jorgen stood against the trunk of a tree, merged into its shadow, watching Rhalles begin to search the ground. He had never before come to a pickup spot while Rhalles was still there, but this time he had a reason. Raising binoculars equipped with night lenses, Jorgen did one final survey of the area. When he was satisfied they were not under observation, he lowered the glasses and started silently down the slope.

At the bottom, Rhalles ducked down in the shadow between his car and the slope as the headlights of a car approached. He stayed down until the headlights passed and he could no longer see the taillights. Then he moved on in a crouch toward the stone he'd spotted. It was flattish, about the width of three hands, and there was a faint streak of phosphorescent paint on it. He raised the stone and was about to place the wrapped cassette under it when he heard a noise on the slope just above him.

Rhalles jerked upright in alarm, and saw the murky figure of a man coming down out of the bushes toward him. Then the man was closer, and he saw it was Jorgen. Rhalles stared at him, surprised but starting to breathe again.

Jorgen held out a hand. "I'll take the tape," he said coldly.

Rhalles gave it to him. "What are you doing here? You scared hell out of me."

"I've come to tell you that you'll be receiving another message from your wife tomorrow—and it may be the *last* you'll ever hear from her." Jorgen spoke with an undertone of fury barely contained. "I've just heard from my employers. They say you're cheating them. You've been withholding information you knew about—far too much of it."

Rhalles exerted tight control on himself, and answered anger with anger: "They're crazy! That's just not true."

"They *know* it's true. I *warned* you they have other sources. They want to terminate our arrangement—and that includes your wife."

Rhalles felt his legs going weak, and there was acid in his throat and stomach. But his voice stayed firm: "Their other sources are *wrong*. I haven't held anything back."

"Please stop lying to me. They wouldn't have any reason to say so, if it weren't so. You've been concealing information you agreed to deliver. I had a great deal of difficulty in talking them out of terminating—by promising them that it wouldn't happen again."

None of what Jorgen was saying was true. He had heard nothing, from anyone, about Rhalles withholding information. But his experience and grasp of human nature both told him that Rhalles was bound to be doing exactly that. It was routine, something to be expected. And Jorgen's purpose in coming here was also routine: to frighten Rhalles so badly that he would withhold less in the future.

"It won't happen again," Rhalles told him angrily, "because it never has happened. I've told everything I know."

Jorgen had to admire the man's control. He had been in these situations before. Rhalles had not, but he was conducting himself with a resilience not indicated in Irina Frejenko's psychological evaluation. Jorgen had always found it interesting, the weak ones who unexpectedly toughened under stress.

He made his voice calmer, kinder: "Please, Mr. Rhalles, remember what I said during our first talk together. The three of us are in the same boat—you, your wife, myself. If you continue as you have been, all of us are finished. You must be more careful from now on."

Rhalles stood before him stiffly, the face a mask. "All right, you've told me. And I still tell you, it isn't true."

"It *is* true, Mr. Rhalles. We both know it is. Just don't do it again."

"Is that it?" Rhalles demanded steadily. "Can I go?"

"Yes."

Rhalles turned and walked back to his car. He got in, shut the door, turned on the lights and motor, and then sat for a second gripping the wheel. It was guess-work and bluff, he told himself; by Jorgen's superiors or Jorgen himself. But he *was* shaken.

Jorgen watched Rhalles make a U-turn and drive back toward Washington. Putting the tape cassette in his pocket, he climbed up the high slope. His car was parked behind the crest, in a narrow paved lane that called itself Potomac Avenue. Jorgen got in the car, drove up to MacArthur Boulevard, and took it into the city.

The apartment he'd rented was on the second floor of an old three-floor brick house in the Columbia Road area north of Dupont Circle——a neighborhood of mixed incomes and mixed races with a relaxed live-and-let-live feeling among its crowded inhabitants. A neighborhood where Jorgen had no trouble remaining inconspicuous.

The living room was fairly large, with bay windows and a high ceiling. Jorgen turned on the lights and pulled down the shades. His cassette player rested on one end of a large table, with a cord running down to a stop-and-go foot pedal. The rest of the table was taken by the encoding machine, the bulky apparatus which had been delivered to him from a submarine on the Florida shore.

Jorgen put the tape cassette he'd gotten from Rhalles on the player, put on the earphones, and sat down in front of the encoder. He turned on the encoder and the cassette player, and put his foot on the floor pedal. The Rhalles tape began, and Jorgen commenced typing.

It was a normal-looking typewriter keyboard, all the keys normally labeled. When Rhalles' voice said, "The President believes the present naval program is an error," Jorgen did not change a word in typing. It was the electronic encoder surrounding the keys that changed the letters into dot-and-dash codes—altering the code for each letter as soon as it was used. When Jorgen typed "error," the code for "R" changed three times in the course of that single word.

The only danger was that he must not make a single typing mistake. This made it necessary to stop the Rhalles tape after every few words, so he could type them out slowly and carefully.

Jorgen was glad he'd taken the two-hour nap earlier. He had a full night ahead of him.

6

Benjamin Scovil was on the couch in the living room of his Baltimore home, listening to the code tape he had brought with him earlier that night from Fort Meade. At the same time he was listening to a record of piano pieces by Erik Satie, letting his mind drift with the music, not paying strict attention to the tape but not shutting it out completely.

His wife appeared at the top of the staircase in her

pajamas. "It's getting late, Ben. I guess you're not coming to bed tonight."

"Later, maybe," he answered dreamily, not letting his attention focus on her.

"Well, happy inspirations." His wife went into their bedroom and closed the door.

Scovil stretched out on the couch, listening to Satie, the dots and dashes from the tape forming a background he was barely aware of.

So far the decoding machines at Fort Meade, the computers and human logic, had failed with the Budapest tape. Now Scovil was trying to give his subconscious mind a shot at it.

Pure logic, and consequently the computers which were a logic tool, could not match instinctive groping in certain situations. Scientists had discovered, for example, that the most sophisticated computer could not beat even an amateurish player at chess. Because the human mind worked, Scovil knew, not by straightforward logic, but by intuitive jumps. After the fact, logical analyses could be used to prove out the jumps, which reached in seconds answers that would have required years for a machine.

That was what Scovil was looking for now: an intuitive jump. What his wife called inspiration.

The record had ended. Scovil got up and started it over again. Turning off the lights, he stretched out once more on the couch and closed his eyes. Listening to the blending of piano music with the dots and dashes of the code tape, he allowed his conscious mind to sink away into the oblivion of sleep.

Maybe when he awoke, his sleeping brain would have presented him with a key to unravel the code on the tape.

FOURTEEN

1

Sawyer got off the subway at Uncle Tom's Cabin. As he came out into the cool early-morning air, a jet shrieked down to a landing at Tegel, the only international commercial airport in Europe inside the heart of a city. There was nowhere outside to put it. In any direction, where West Berlin ended enemy territory began.

Leaving the Onkel Toms Hütte U-Bahn station behind, Sawyer headed for the address he'd been given on Uncle Tom Street. Germany had just been rediscovering the American Civil War novel when this neighborhood had been built. The street was lined with the trees which softened so much of Berlin's basically stark look, and there were pretty little gardens behind the solid two- and three-floor houses. The house he entered had one apartment on each floor. Sawyer climbed the steps to the top floor and knocked.

James Gordon opened the door and said in fairly decent German: "Hello, can I help you?" The voice had an odd sound, coming out of the thick, stiff bandages entirely masking his face except the holes for eyes, nose and mouth.

"I'm hoping you can," Sawyer told him in English. "I'd like a few minutes' talk. My name's Sawyer. Kurt Meier down in Munich sent me. You can phone him and check at my expense, if you want."

"No need," Gordon said. "I'm out of the body business now. So I've got nothing to worry about anymore. Come on in."

284

The living room was pleasantly furnished, with three tall windows letting in a lot of morning sun. "Nice place you found," Sawyer commented as Gordon shut the door.

"Yeah, and even nicer because the rent's practically a steal. They've got so many old people in Berlin the city government gives all kinds of financial come-ons to attract young couples. That's how come we decided to move here after . . . I guess Meier told you what happened to me."

Sawyer nodded. Gordon was an American helicopter pilot married to a German girl. In the five years since he'd gotten out of the U. S. Army he'd had a varied job career in Germany, including occasionally using a chopper to smuggle escapers out of the East. Two months ago he'd set down for a scheduled pickup and found a bunch of Communist troops waiting for him. He'd managed to lift off fast, but the chopper had been riddled with machine-gun fire. It had made it back over the line to West Germany and then crashed. Gordon had crawled out of the wreckage engulfed in flames.

"Sit down, make yourself comfortable," Gordon said, indicating a wing chair by the windows. "My wife's out shopping, but I can make you some coffee if you haven't had breakfast yet."

"No thanks, all I want is answers to a couple questions." Sawyer sat down with a relieved feeling that today might turn out better than yesterday had been. He'd gotten what he'd needed, but it had been frustratingly slow going.

First there'd been the two hours of waiting at the Inter-German Relations Ministry in Bonn, while they tracked down their screening bureau's entry file on Christine Bieler. There'd been two other names in her file. One was her uncle, a Stuttgart businessman who had paid for her escape, and with whom she'd proposed to live. The other name was James Gordon. That was unusual. Escapers from the East seldom named the body movers who got them out. People engaged in what Germans called "the body business" were in enough danger without having their activities advertised.

Sawyer figured Christine Bieler had named Gordon to back up her claim to be an escaper; not a sleeper sent out by East Germany to settle in and wait until such time as she was needed.

From Bonn, Sawyer had gone first to Stuttgart, and learned nothing. Except that Christine Bieler had stayed there less than a week before moving on to France, and that her uncle had died two years ago.

The last address Sawyer had had for James Gordon had been in Munich, the chief center for the body business. But he'd arrived in Munich to find Gordon was no longer there. Others involved in the shadow world of the people smugglers had been understandably reluctant to tell him anything. There were too many agents around working for the East Germans, and what had happened to Gordon showed what could result from their snooping. Sawyer had finally made contact with Meier through a detective in Munich's vice squad. But by then it had been midnight, and he'd had to wait for the first morning plane to Berlin.

Gordon sat down in another wing chair and opened a box of cigars on an imitation-marble coffee table. "Want one?" When Sawyer shook his head Gordon said, "You're right, it's too early in the morning to smoke. But I need something for the nerves, and it's either smoke or drink."

Sawyer watched him place a cigar in the mouth hole of his bandage mask, and light it. His hands were disfigured by brutally livid burn scars.

Gordon caught Sawyer's glance and said, "We're hoping when these bandages come off my face won't look like my hands, anymore. If that works out right, then we can get around to the plastic surgery on the rest of me." He took a short drag at the cigar, blew smoke out of the mouth hole. "Okay, shoot. What d'you want to know?"

"Three and a half years ago you smuggled a girl named Christine Bieler out of the East. Remember?"

"Sure, I didn't fly that many trips. Nice quiet girl. And a nice simple job. I was supposed to pick her up at an isolated spot in the country north of Plauen, and she was waiting when I got there. All alone; no ambush party that time. I flew her back over the frontier and let her off outside Kulmbach. Then I returned the chopper to Munich and picked up my pay. Five thousand bucks, for a few hours' work. Seemed more than reasonable, at the time."

"What did she talk about on the trip?"

"Not a damn thing. Like I said, a very quiet type girl. I can remember every word. I said, 'Get in,' and she said 'Thank you,' very calm. Later I said 'Here's where you get off,' and she said, 'Thank you very much.' And nothing in between."

"What did her uncle tell you, when he hired you for the job?"

"I don't know her uncle," Gordon said, "or anything else about her. Sorry. The job was set up and passed on to me without trimmings, by a body broker named Franz Heidegger."

Sawyer sighed wearily. "And he's back in Munich."

"No, as a matter of fact you're in luck there. He *was* in Munich. But last year he moved his operation up here, to Berlin."

"That's better. Where do I get in touch with him?"

Gordon hesitated. "I'll have to check with Heidegger, first." He stood up, walked to a phone on a small desk, unplugged it from the wall and picked it up. "I'll make the call from the bedroom. Wait here." He carried the phone past the kitchen and down a short hallway to the bedroom, shutting the door behind him.

Sawyer lit a cigarette and gazed through the windows at a high hill rising above the roof line of the houses across the street, its humped crest covered with neatly trimmed bushes and young trees. It was a personification of Berlin: an artificial hill, created by piling up bomb rubble, covering it all with dirt, and planting.

Gordon opened the door and called, "Okay, he'll talk to you."

Sawyer crushed out the cigarette and went down the hall. Gordon stood by a bureau holding the phone. Sawyer took it and said: "Heidegger?"

"Yes, Mr. Sawyer. Jimmy says you are recommended by Meier."

"I'll pay for the call, if you want to phone Munich and check."

"I intend to, Mr. Sawyer. If Meier confirms, I can meet you at the Three Bears on the Kudamm. Do you know it?"

"Yes," Sawyer told him. "When?"

"As soon as I've made the call. Say half an hour. I'll be the small, distinguished-looking gentleman carrying a cane with a silver handle in the shape of a lion."

2

"I consider myself a rescuer of lost souls," Heidegger informed Sawyer as he had his breakfast. "But Bonn is making it increasingly difficult for people in my profession to continue. The government is terrified that the Communists surrounding us will retaliate with something even more final than the Wall."

Traffic poured past them on the Kurfürstendamm, Berlin's Champs-Élysées, which ended at a stark version of Manhattan's Central Park South, facing the Tiergarten. Sawyer sipped coffee and regarded the man across from him at the sidewalk table under the canopy in front of the Drei Bären. Heidegger was in

288

his forties, a short, chubby man in a sober business suit. He had a round, good-natured face with clever eyes and a narrow slit of a mouth that was not at all good-natured.

"Bonn keeps making these noises about bringing people out *legally,* under the Freedom-Purchase Plan. But twenty times as many have gotten out by means which Bonn calls illegal. Yet Bonn acts as if we are criminals."

"Except," Sawyer pointed out mildly, "they do usually look the other way when you work."

"Less and less, lately. And they make it especially difficult, here in Berlin. I've begun to invest in massage parlors, to make up the difference. My income was much more solid in Munich."

Heidegger took another forkful of sausage and eggs, chewing thoroughly before washing it down with a long sip of his Bloody Mary. "But, I'm a Berliner— and I couldn't stand being away any longer. This is the only civilized city, the only interesting people. The rest of Germany is just too boring. And the Germans! You know what we say about Germans—they have beer for blood and potatoes for brains. There are exceptions, of course. But they are punished, for being different. Finally, all the exceptional ones have to leave Germany, or come to Berlin."

"Like you."

The body broker grinned. "You find me arrogant, yes? I am, of course. All Berliners are. We have to be, to fight the claustrophobia of that Wall around us —and the fear. It's much like the atmosphere in your New York. I visited there once. The same. The arrogance of the people, to stave off the constant numbing fear. In New York it is the fear of black muggers; in Berlin it is the fear of a final Red onslaught that will end our existence."

Sawyer finished his coffee and put down the cup. "Christine Bieler," he reminded Heidegger, letting his voice get edgy.

"Yes . . ." Heidegger dabbed with his napkin at a spot of Bloody Mary on his chin. "It is only information that you want?"

"Information—and then something in East Berlin."

"But, not a body job?"

"No. Just more information. Who contacted you about bringing Christine Bieler out?"

"Her uncle. A quite respectable elderly businessman from—ah, Stuttgart it was. Give me a moment, his name I have forgotten, it wasn't Bieler . . ."

"I know the name," Sawyer told him. "He's dead."

"I'm sorry to hear that. A gentleman. Although, I did have a feeling, I remember, that he was *not* her uncle. Perhaps one of those arrangements. You understand: an elderly man paying to help a young girl escape, so she would be obligated to him. More often than you'd think, that is the case."

Sawyer didn't think this was one of them. "How much did he pay you?"

Heidegger glanced around them at the other tables, and lowered his voice a bit. "Nothing special. The usual. Less than ten thousand dollars. Which is not a high price, when you consider my overhead. First of all I had to give half that amount to the body mover—in this case, Jimmy Gordon. Then there are my running expenses: for rent, up-to-date information, people who see to it I'm not bothered or followed. And I had to make a trip myself to East Berlin—in those days I could still get in and out again—to make the arrangements with the girl."

"Did her mother know about it?"

"No. I had to meet with the daughter while the mother was at her job at the ticket counter in the Bode Museum. It seems her mother is one of the unusual ones: an honestly convinced German Communist."

"And her daughter Christine was anti-Communist?"

Heidegger gave a little shrug. "Maybe, a little. I think she was just bored with her life and wanted a change. That's the real motive, with many of the young ones. At any rate, we made the arrangements. It wasn't complicated. I told her where to be waiting for the pickup, and the exact timing. Her school holiday had just begun, so going was no problem. Especially since she had a relative down in Merseburg she could pretend to be going to visit. She was a bright girl. Understood and later followed everything I told her to do. It went neatly. A trouble-free job."

Nothing he had said lessened Sawyer's certainty about Christine Bieler's real reason for coming to the West, and her part in what had happened to Moira. But it opened no new door, and that was what he needed now.

Heidegger, watching Sawyer's face, asked: "Now, what is it you want in East Berlin?"

Sawyer told him what he wanted.

The body broker considered it. "You understand, *I* can no longer go in there. They know what I do now. I would never get out again."

"But you do have people who can get in."

"It is difficult, right now. As you know, at this point West Berliners are only allowed in there four weeks each year . . ."

"But people from any other part of West Germany can go in whenever they want."

"If they do it too often, East Berlin becomes quite suspicious and detains them for questioning. In some cases arrests them merely on the circumstantial evidence of the frequency of their trips . . ."

Heidegger drummed his fingers on the table, thinking. His round face scowled, then brightened. "However, it happens I do have one young man who would be perfect, if he would care to do it. His official residence is in Kassel, and he's done some body moving across the border down there. But he comes here frequently to see his parents, staying with friends. He knows East Berlin quite well, and hasn't been there too much in the past few years."

"He's here *now?*"

"Yes, you're in luck, Mr. Sawyer." Heidegger leaned back in his chair, cleared his throat. "Now, as to financial arrangements. You must realize, of course, that as the risk continually increases, so does the cost."

"What I want isn't as dangerous as people smuggling," Sawyer pointed out.

"It could be, if they have something against you, over there."

"They don't."

"So you say." Heidegger pushed his chair a bit and picked up his cane. He rolled it between his plump hands and gazed at the twirling silver lion on its handle. "It won't cost you as much as moving a body certainly. But . . ."

"I'll pay two hundred dollars," Sawyer cut in thinly.

"That is not much."

Sawyer told him flatly: "It's enough. If it isn't, I'll phone Meier and get somebody else."

Heidegger shook the silver lion at him with a slight smile. "You're mean, Mr. Sawyer. All right, I'll accept. But you will have to give another two hundred to the man who will go in with you."

"Agreed. Where do I contact him?"

"His friend's place. Let me call, first." Heidegger got up and went inside the restaurant. He took his cane with him, but left his hat where it was, resting on top of a boxed artificial hedge beside their table. A strong breeze had begun to whip along the Kudamm, stirring the hedge.

Sawyer sat there waiting, watching Heidegger's hat tilt with the bend of the hedge, almost fall off, snap back as the hedge straightened, then swing again . . .

Heidegger came out looking annoyed. "He doesn't answer, but I'm sure he won't have gone out this early. He's undoubtedly silenced the phone bell so he can sleep late. I'll go wake him." He saw his hat about to fall off the tilting hedge and grabbed it just in time.

Sawyer signaled to a waiter. "Wait till I pay the bill."

"No, Mr. Sawyer, I have to see him alone. I'll meet you back here later. If he agrees, I'll give you his address."

"I don't want to drag this into tomorrow," Sawyer told him coldly.

"It won't, I promise you. Meet you here in half an hour, at the most." Heidegger hurried to hail a passing cab.

Sawyer paid the bill and went for an impatient stroll.

3

"His name is Himmie Baumeister," Heidegger told Sawyer twenty mintues later. "Use the first name, and he'll call you Peter. He thinks it's good for security. It also gives him the illusion that he does these things out of sentiment, not only for the money."

Sawyer found the building on the edge of the Kreuzberg section Berliners called Istanbul: an area full of Turkish immigrants on whom the country bestowed its highest compliment: "They work even harder than Germans." Sawyer climbed a wide staircase covered with treacherous, torn carpeting, and went down a dim, musty hallway to knock at the last door.

Himmie was in his thirties, with a trim build and warm dark eyes. He was wearing a sloppy bathrobe and slippers, and his good-natured face was sleepy. But he greeted Sawyer cheerfully: "Come in, Peter, make yourself at home."

It was one of those big, old-fashioned apartments you could still find in Berlin, but which most people no longer wanted: huge rooms, high ceilings, large windows, but also expensive to heat, with wiring that didn't take kindly to modern appliances, and noisy plumbing that let you know toilets were flushing at the other end of the building. Most of the furniture was ancient but comfortable. There were a lot of old books in flaking leather bindings in the shelves. And there was a woman asleep under a U. S. Army blanket on an enormous couch.

"You can talk," Himmie told Sawyer when he looked at her, "it won't wake her. Right now you could blow up the apartment and she wouldn't hear it. I stuck the cotton in my phone bell for *me*. Took most of the night to get her to sleep."

Sawyer walked over and looked down at her pale face, listened to her harsh breathing. "What's she on?"

"Pills I got from a neighbor. Heavy stuff. Only way I could knock her out."

The woman twisted in her sleep, moaning. The blanket slipped down, revealing small, beautifully formed breasts. Himmie bent and tucked the blanket back up around her neck. His expression was sad when he stroked her cheek lightly with the back of one hand. But when he straightened and looked at Sawyer he had the smile back in place.

"She needed to be screwed, so I did my best—but it didn't help much. Even half-crazy she knew I wasn't Hans. Her husband. So I fed her the pills."

Himmie's tone stayed cheerful but his eyes were not. "He was shot two nights ago, trying to bring two people out. Now he's in a hospital over there in the DDR, and that is the nicest place he's likely to be in for some years to come."

Sawyer waited patiently for Himmie to get it out of his system. He had a need to talk, like most Berliners. Sawyer didn't blame them. They lived in limbo, enclosed inside a walled city stranded one hundred miles behind the Iron Curtain.

"I warned him," Himmie said, "too many people knew what he was doing. But Hans had this obsession about atoning for his father. A Gestapo man; with a nasty record Hans couldn't forget, once he learned about it."

"Your friend was mixing things that don't belong together," Sawyer told him. "His father was one thing; he's something else. No connection, unless he wants one."

"Think so?" Himmie looked at him for a moment. "When I was sixteen I took a bike trip to Norway. Stopped at a farm to buy a drink of milk. The farmer shook his fist at me and called me a filthy German." Himmie laughed. "I didn't even know what he was angry about, at the time. In school they taught us about your bombing Dresden. They never told us about our bombing London and Coventry first, or our flattening Rotterdam when it was a surrendered open city."

Sawyer shrugged. "You're talking about things that are over and done with."

"I think some things don't change. Tell me how the government they've got now, on the other side of that wall, is any improvement on Hitler's government. Do you know what Brecht said when East Germany crushed a workers' protest by killing two hundred and sixty of them? He said, 'Wouldn't it be simpler if the Government dissolved the People, and elected another?' "

Sawyer counted two hundred dollars' worth of marks into his left hand, and held it. "I know Heidegger told you what I want. I'm going to tell you again." He did, carefully.

Himmie nodded. "Simple enough. I can handle it."

Sawyer gave him the money. "Get dressed and let's go."

"Give me three minutes." Himmie went to a table and picked up a bottle of Steinhäger. "Drink?"

Sawyer shook his head. "You said three minutes."

Himmie poured himself a shot and downed it with a shudder. "Breakfast."

Sawyer was not surprised. Berlin drank big, even for Germany. He watched Himmie stride away down a corridor to another room.

Two minutes later he was back, dressed as Sawyer wanted: cheap business suit, square necktie, hair plastered down with water, and carrying a raincoat. He'd pass for a minor city functionary. Sawyer took a tourist guidebook printed in East Berlin from his jacket pocket, held it in his hand where it would be more conspicuous, and went out first.

He was half a block away when Himmie came out of his building and followed, making no effort to catch up. When they boarded the crowded eastbound S-Bahn train, they stood at opposite ends, ignoring each other. The train rumbled along its elevated track over the Spree, past the high watchtowers along the Wall, and the wide band of raked sand behind it. At Friedrichstrasse Station the train came to a jolting halt. They were inside East Berlin. Everybody got out. A crowd of waiting passengers who had already passed through the control booths got on, and the train moved on its way.

Himmie managed to get near the front of a long line of heavily patient Germans waiting to be checked through. Sawyer took out his passport and joined the much shorter line leading into the visa control for non-German visitors. He did not look up at the heavily armed guards, on their high perches which commanded every part of the station.

Three quarters of an hour later Sawyer had obtained his visa and exchanged dollars for more than the obligatory amount of East German marks. When the next eastbound train came through he boarded it. He didn't look for Himmie, who had gotten through sooner and would have boarded a previous train.

He got off at the Marx-Engels station and quickly

walked the rest of the way. The architecture was no worse than in West Berlin, but there were fewer trees and much fewer people in sight, making Sawyer feel sharply exposed among the featureless façades. The vast open plazas were almost empty, and there was little automobile traffic along the broad avenues. It was working hours, and people were supposed to be inside somewhere doing their jobs. Or staying in their rooms to hide the fact that they were not.

It seemed to Sawyer that among the small number of cars cruising by him, too many were the dark green police Volgas. But he knew that was because he was hyperaware of them. And of the foot-patrol Volkspolizei, walking in twos and threes. There it was mutual. He was an obvious foreigner, and the eyes of each Vopo studied him in passing.

Sawyer swung his guidebook carelessly and looked like a tourist who knew he had a right to be going where he was going. Halfway to the museum he saw Himmie strolling up ahead of him, taking his time. By the time he caught up, Sawyer had made sure Himmie was not being tailed by anyone else.

Sawyer strode on ahead of him without a word, giving Himmie a chance to observe whether *he* was being tailed. Reaching the Bode Museum, Sawyer went in and bought an entrance ticket.

The woman behind the counter was perhaps fifty, with a pleasant, intelligent look. Sawyer turned away from Christine Jonquet's mother and entered the Egyptian collection.

The bust of Akhenaten, Pharaoh of Egypt, was still there; still separated from his wife, Nefertiti, over the Wall in West Berlin's Charlottenburg. Put asunder by the Cold War more than three thousand years after their marriage, their prospects for ever being joined together again were very dim at the moment. Unless some quixotic body mover got a drunken inspiration.

* * *

Himmie entered the Bode Museum and went to the counter to buy his ticket and check his raincoat. As Christine's mother took it from him he stared at her suddenly, then grinned. "But . . . it's Frau Bieler, am I right?"

It was her turn to be startled. "Yes, I am Frau Bieler . . ." She frowned at him, searching her memory.

Himmie looked faintly disappointed. "You've forgotten me, I think. Well, of course you would—it was so long ago. Back in the days when I was studying art. I had some classes with your daughter, and a few times I accompanied her home—since I was living then in Lichtenberg not far from you. She introduced us once, when we happened to meet outside your apartment building."

"Oh yes," Frau Bieler said politely, and unconvincingly. "I remember you now."

His smile was indulgent. "I don't think you do, but no matter. *I* had quite forgotten you worked here." He gestured with one hand to encompass the museum around them. "As you can see, I haven't completely lost my interest in art. Though it's years since I gave it up as a profession. I'm with the government, now. A minor post, of course, but . . ."

Himmie paused suddenly, seeming to remember something. "By the way, how *is* Christine? Do you ever hear from her?"

Frau Bieler's look of pride did not seem to be pretense. "She's still in art—and doing *very* well. As an art historian."

"I had heard . . . Excuse me, Frau Bieler, but one hears all sorts of rumors in government offices . . ." Himmie had lowered his voice, appearing worried and unsure. "I understood that Christine defected to the West."

Frau Bieler stiffened. "That is not true. Who told you such a terrible lie?" Her tone was genuinely indignant, no question about that.

Himmie spread his hands apologetically. "I thought someone had even told me she'd married a Frenchman, and was living in Paris now."

"That is just plain ridiculous. Christine did go to France for some years—to do graduate studies at museums there. But with government permission, *and* financial support."

There was no doubt in Himmie's mind that that was the whole story, as Frau Bieler knew it. He wondered what the real story was, and why Sawyer was so interested in this woman's daughter. "I'm certainly happy to hear that," he told her. "And be sure I'll explain the real situation the next time I hear such a rumor. Christine is still in France?"

"No, as a matter of fact she came back a couple of weeks ago."

"Wonderful! So she's here."

Frau Bieler shook her head, a bit regretful but still proud. "The government liked the work she did in France so well they awarded Christine another grant —to go to Russia for further studies."

"That must be interesting for her. But lonely for you. I imagine she writes to you, though."

Frau Bieler began to look at him strangely. "I got a picture postcard from Moscow . . ." Her voice had become hesitant.

A nervous cramp in Himmie's stomach told him that he couldn't push this interrogation any further, unless he wanted her to stop wondering and become flatly suspicious. "Well, it's certainly pleasant to have met you again, Frau Bieler. I'll say goodbye when I pick up my coat." He forced a rueful laugh. "Which will be shortly, I'm sorry to say. With museum hours coinciding with office hours, I'm lucky when I can manage to visit one for a half hour."

He turned from the counter and walked away feeling a bit dizzy from the strain. And grateful Sawyer had decided he should pose as a government employee. Frau Bieler might be suspicious, but she couldn't be sure of what. In East Germany it was not unknown for the government to question people, for obscure reasons known only to itself. She was unlikely to go ask anyone what was going on—at least, not until he was safely back on the other side of the Wall.

He found Sawyer standing in front of a cabinet of ancient Egyptian coins, studying them with deep concentration. Without making any kind of contact with Sawyer, Himmie wandered around the room. When he was certain that Sawyer was not under any kind of surveillance, Himmie strolled off into the next room—giving Sawyer a chance to check whether *he* was being followed. If either felt the other was being watched, they would not meet again on this side of the Wall.

Sawyer left the museum first. He walked to Unter den Linden, where the number of tourists, from both sides of the Iron Curtain, created a relaxed atmosphere lacking in most areas of East Berlin. Entering a cafe near the opera, Sawyer ordered a coffee. If Himmie came in, and found him waiting, each would know the other considered him free of surveillance.

Four minutes later Himmie entered the cafe, and ordered a small beer at the bar. He gulped it as Sawyer left, and went out a few seconds after him. Sawyer was strolling slowly in the direction of Alexanderplatz. Walking faster, Himmie caught up and started to pass him. They made a show of recognizing and greeting each other, and strolled on together.

Speaking only when no other strollers were too close, Himmie went over his interview with Christine Jonquet's mother—almost word for word, including his estimate of her emotional responses. When he'd finished, Sawyer walked on with him in silence, brooding over it.

"I might have been able to get more from her," Himmie said, "if you'd explained more of what it's about. I asked the questions you wanted me to, but . . ."

"You did fine," Sawyer told him, and continued to brood on the results.

It seemed obvious that Frau Bieler's responses were not those of a woman who thought her daughter dead. As Sawyer had thought, she was still very much alive. But what he'd hoped to get from her was no longer possible. She was now out of his reach.

They'd brought her out of France as soon as her part in kidnaping Moira was done. And they'd taken her to Russia to make sure she wouldn't do any loose talking about it. Sawyer doubted that she was still in Moscow. If she was, they'd have her where no one could get at her.

He could think of only one way left by which he might still be able to extract some information from her. She had written her mother a card on arriving in Moscow. So she did like to correspond with her mother. If Frau Bieler was the kind of person who kept old letters . . .

"Himmie, do you know the Lichtenberg area?"

"Yes, I know it quite well."

"I don't." Sawyer told him what he wanted to do now.

They were crossing a bridge over a bend in the Spree. Himmie stopped dead in the middle of it and stared at him. "Nothing like that was part of our arrangement."

"I'll pay you extra for it."

"No. I won't do it. It's too risky, and right now I'm just too nervous. I'm sorry, Peter. Maybe it's what happened to Hans, or what I went through last night —but I just can't handle anything like that."

Sawyer eyed him calculatingly for a long moment. And saw that if he tried to push it further, Himmie would turn and walk away from him. "All right, I understand. I'll do it myself. But I can't go wandering around the neighborhood like a lost soul, advertising the fact that I don't know it and don't belong there. Just take me there, to the right building. Then you can leave me, without going in, and head for home. I'll take it from there. No further risk for you, no hard feelings from me."

Himmie shut his eyes, opened them. "You must want something in there pretty badly."

"I hope it's there. I won't know until I get in."

"I won't try to talk you out of it," Himmie said angrily. "Your life is your own responsibility, not mine. Let's go."

They took the U-Bahn at Alexanderplatz and got off at the Lichtenberg station. Himmie took Sawyer toward Frau Bieler's address by the most direct walking route, getting there in five minutes. It was in a vast complex of prefabricated apartment developments, of the kind that blighted cities all over the world, from Chicago to Tokyo: block after block of featureless slabs.

They reached a corner building where part of the ground floor had been made into a coffeehouse. Sawyer wondered if it were the same one in which Clarissa Koller had seen Christine Jonquet with the Frenchman who had the birthmark. Down the cross street from it, cranes were raising a new apartment block identical to the others. Closer, there was one almost finished. Himmie led the way across the street and halfway along the next block. He stopped at the entrance of a wide driveway cutting between two buildings.

"You can go through here," he told Sawyer tightly. "It leads to a parking area and children's playground in the center of the buildings on this block. All these blocks are laid out exactly alike. With the building entrances facing in on the center. Walk straight across between the parking and the playground. Judging by the way the numbers run, your address should be directly on the other side."

Sawyer looked at him with a hard smile. "And this is as far as you go."

Himmie nodded. "There's too much bare visibility

around the buildings inside these blocks. And too many old people around them with nothing to do all day but look out their windows. And they spot any strangers, first look."

"Okay, thanks for the help." Sawyer took off his jacket and stuffed the guidebook in a pocket.

"I'll wait for you on the other side of Checkpoint Charlie," Himmie said. His voice was muted and his eyes were miserable. "I'm sorry, Peter."

"I know you are." Carrying his jacket so neither its styling nor the book showed, Sawyer left him and walked through the driveway between the buildings.

The driveway led to a large open space surrounded by the apartment buildings which lined the four sides of the block. It was divided according to usage: the parking space, a community recreation area which included a children's playground, a fenced-in square of trees and grass, wide concrete paths with benches. Sawyer crossed it with the manner of a man engaged in a routine purpose, not hurrying but not dawdling.

As he walked he automatically followed standard procedure for entering potentially dangerous terrain: he noted and analyzed everything around him, estimating escape routes. Lack of prior planning led to confused panic when an emergency situation closed in and there was no time for careful thinking. Survival depended on having the sequence of response tactics prepared ahead of time.

Some of the eyes watching Sawyer were obvious: the woman rocking a baby on one of the benches; two elderly men who halted their Ping-Pong game in the recreation area to look his way; some of the kids in the playground. The eyes he couldn't be sure of were behind some of the hundreds of apartment windows in every direction. Sawyer stopped in the middle, getting out his small note pad and a ballpoint pen. He scribbled on the pad, looked around, and pretended to note down something else. A stranger could be a government building inspector, engaged in doing a routine checkup.

The driveway he'd come through was the only vehicle entrance. But there were narrower pedestrian passageways between buildings. The entrance to each building faced the open community area in the heart of the block. Each building had an exterior fire escape. Sawyer had noticed more on the other sides of the buildings, facing the streets.

Carrying the pad and pen in one hand and his folded jacket in his other, Sawyer strode in the direction of the building which bore the number he was interested in. But he did not enter it immediately, going instead through the passageway between it and the next building. The passage led to a narrow cross street. On the other side was the block of nearly completed buildings, almost ready for their tenants. Beyond that block Sawyer could see the cranes at work, constructing more of the same.

Sawyer went back through the passage and into the building. Frau Bieler's name and apartment number were on one of the mailboxes inside the entrance. He climbed an interior stairway to the third floor. Going along the corridor, he prayed nobody would come out of any of the other doors before he got inside Frau Bieler's apartment.

As he'd hoped, it was not necessary to pick her lock. These low-income apartment projects were the same the world over: constructed quickly, with cheap materials. Her door was out of true, making it a two-second job. Sawyer got a small plastic strip from his pocket, inserted it, and applied pressure to spring the catch. A split second later he was inside, relocking the door.

He was in a tiny entry, with three closed frosted-glass doors. The first one he opened let him into a kitchen with a dining nook. It had a single window, which faced across a passageway to the other side of the next building. There were several windows in the other building from which anyone moving around in Frau Bieler's kitchen could be observed. Sticking close to the wall so he wouldn't be seen, Sawyer got near the window, reached out one hand, and pulled down the shade.

In the building across the passageway, a woman recuperating from a gallstone operation sat propped up against the pillows on her bed, listening to the radio. Her bed faced the bedroom window, which looked across into Frau Bieler's kitchen. She didn't know Frau Bieler well, but she did know certain things *about* her.

She knew that Frau Bieler never pulled down the kitchen shade. She knew that Frau Bieler was never at home at this hour, during a workday; and that her daughter was in the Soviet Union.

Staring at the shade which someone had just pulled down, she thought about something she'd read in a newspaper a few days earlier. It had told about the alarming rise in the number of apartment burglaries in the past few years, and urged everyone to help the authorities to catch the culprits. Otherwise nobody's personal belongings would be safe from theft.

Turning down her radio, the woman picked up the phone beside her bed and called the police.

Sawyer's preliminary survey of the rest of the apartment was accomplished swiftly. There was no need to pull down any of the other shades. The rest of the windows faced across the side street to the nearly completed buildings. Construction there seemed to have been temporarily halted. There were no workers on the site to observe him. The other thing that pleased Sawyer was the lack of clutter in the apartment. Frau Bieler kept each room tidy, which would make it easier to find what he was looking for, if it was there to be found.

Sawyer began his detailed search back in the kitchen, with four picture postcards he'd seen taped neatly to a cabinet over the sink. He took down the one from Moscow first, and concentrated on interpreting what Christine Bieler Jonquet had written on the other side. He could speak German fairly well, but reading it was difficult for him, and took time.

As Sawyer pieced it out, the girl was telling her mother that she was about to leave Moscow for a tour of several months to small museums throughout Russia. She probably would not get a chance to write during the tour, so her mother should not worry about her.

The other three cards were from Paris, over a three-year period. Each wished her mother a happy birthday, said she was doing well in her studies, hoped her mother was well.

Sawyer pressed the cards back into place exactly where he'd found them, and began opening drawers and cabinets. He didn't find any letters from Frau Bieler's daughter, nor an address book that might contain the girl's address when she'd been in France. Nor anything else of any use to him.

Picking his jacket off a dining chair, Sawyer continued his search in the living room, and then Frau Bieler's bedroom. No letters, no address book. Frau Bieler's anticlutter compulsion was working against him. If she'd gotten letters from her daughter she hadn't kept them around to mess up the place. The cards had been kept only because they could be made part of the décor.

Sawyer moved on into the last room. It was a smaller bedroom; and judging by several stuffed dolls, the art books, and the clothes in the closet, it was Christine's. Dropping his jacket on her bed, Sawyer gazed at an object on her bureau which had held his attention the first time through.

It was a slab of delicately painted stone, an Egyptian stele, depicting two beautiful women—or female deities—back to back. Their profiles were almost identical, but the emblems on their heads and in their hands were different.

Sawyer didn't think it was one of those copies museums made for sale to visitors in their entrance shops. The paint was worn and old-looking. And when he picked up the stele, sandy grains of the stone crumbled off in his fingers. If it was a copy, it had been made by a forger to be passed off as the real thing.

Carrying it to the bed, Sawyer stuffed it down inside his jacket pocket with the guidebook, so it was held tightly and could not fall out. Then he continued his search of the room.

Himmie had not been able to bring himself to completely abandon Sawyer. He sat by the window of the corner coffeehouse, soothing his nervous stomach with a glass of milk as he waited for Sawyer to come out. He was raising the glass to his lips when a Vopo car went past carrying three policemen.

It stopped halfway down the next block, in front of the driveway entrance through which Sawyer had gone. Himmie put his glass down, very carefully. The three Vopos climbed out of the car. One remained standing beside it. The other two strode in through the driveway, one carrying a stubby submachine-gun on a sling, the other drawing a pistol from his holster.

Himmie got up and left the coffeehouse—and hesitated. It was just *possible* he could get to Frau Bieler's apartment before the two cops. But getting out again? The Vopo who had stayed by the car turned idly and looked in Himmie's direction. Himmie's stomach knotted. He turned away and walked, forcing himself not to run, back to the U-Bahn station, and took the next train to West Berlin.

The two Vopos entered the building that contained Frau Bieler's apartment, found her number on the mailbox, and climbed to the third floor. They were half skeptical about the hysterical phone call from the female invalid in the next building. They had been involved in a number of these affairs where "burglars" turned out to be tenants, or innocent visitors.

In their experience they'd too often found that the old people in this sort of development were bored with nothing to do, and sometimes imagined things to stir up a little excitement in their lives. Quite possibly, the person inside Frau Bieler's apartment was an invited guest.

So they didn't immediately kick in the door, but first tried what would happen if they merely knocked and demanded that the person inside open up.

Inside Christine's bedroom, Sawyer froze with his jacket in his hand. He'd found nothing that told him about the girl's movements in France, and had been about to leave the way he'd come in. The knock at the door, and the shouted command, ended that possibility. Unfreezing himself, Sawyer snapped into one of the emergency routines he had worked out beforehand. He knotted the sleeves of his jacket around his neck, snatched an imitation-jade necklace from the bureau and stuck it in his belt, and dashed into Frau Bieler's bedroom.

Inside, he threw open her window and looked out. He had already checked the position of the exterior fire escape. It ran down past a hallway window an easy jump from this one. There was no police car in the street below, which meant it was around the other side of the block. One small break.

There was more banging at the apartment door, and the shout this time contained a final warning. Sawyer snatched a small portable radio from the dressing table and stuck it in his belt next to the necklace. If he managed to get out of the immediate area, he'd be helped by their believing they were hunting an ordinary apartment burglar.

The apartment door crashed inward as Sawyer climbed onto the windowsill. He jumped, landed on the fire escape, and scrambled down it. When he reached the pavement, he yanked the necklace and radio from his belt. Dropping them, he angled across the street in a crouched run, heading for a pedestrian passageway between two of the nearly finished buildings on the other side.

A Vopo leaned out of Frau Bieler's bedroom window with a pistol and snapped three fast shots at him. The bullets spanged off the street just behind Sawyer and to his left. He dodged, reached the passageway on the other side, and was twisting into it when a submachine-gun burst tore chunks of concrete from the corner of the building wall on his right, showering him with its dust. The next instant he was inside the passageway, cut off from their angle of fire.

But he didn't have much of a lead on them, he knew. Vopos carried walkie-talkies. They'd have used them before breaking in the door. By now their car would have radioed for reinforcements, and be racing around to cut him off. Sawyer sprinted through the passageway and into the empty open area surrounded by the block's unfinished buildings. Without pause, he ran across it. Not straight across, because in that direction was the new construction site, where there'd be too many people watching which way he went. He angled toward one of the side passageways, across from the driveway entrance.

It was a lot of open space to cover, even at a run. Just as he entered the passageway, a car screamed into the driveway on the other side. Sawyer shot a look behind him and saw it was a police car, with only the driver in it. Sawyer dashed to the end of the passageway, turned the corner, and stopped. Behind him he heard the screeching of tires as the car did a fast swing and went out again, heading around the block to this side.

Sawyer went back into the passageway he'd just come out of. He ran through it, across the big open area, out through the driveway. Without slowing he crossed the street there and went in through the next block of apartment buildings. Heads turned to stare as he raced across the wide-open stretch in the middle of it. Himmie was right, there was too much bare space around here, and he was too exposed in it. But he kept running. There was no hiding place here that would stay secure for long.

His objective was to get out of the immediate area as fast as possible. Right now there were perhaps three Vopos hunting him, and he could outdistance them for a brief period. Soon there would be more coming, from various directions. He had to get out of these development blocks before they had a net around them he couldn't get through.

When he was halfway inside a passageway on the other side of this block, Sawyer slowed to a fast walk, panting, his lungs burning. Without stopping he untied the sleeves of his jacket from around his neck, and draped it over one arm. He strode across the next street, into the next apartment complex. Walking quickly, but not too quickly, he crossed the open area in the heart of it at an angle and entered another passageway. He was almost through it when a Vopo came hurrying into the end of it ahead of him.

The Vopo had a walkie-talkie in his left hand. His other hand went instantly to his holstered pistol when he saw Sawyer coming toward him. Sawyer smiled and wished him a good afternoon in his best German. Without taking his hand from the holstered gun, the Vopo demanded to see his papers. But he did not quite draw the gun. With all the people who lived in these developments, the odds were against Sawyer being the very one the Vopo had been summoned to help search for.

"Of course," Sawyer said, slowing his approach. He raised his jacket with one hand, reached into a pocket with his other.

Then he was close enough. He kicked the Vopo in

the stomach, as hard as he could. The Vopo doubled up with a gasp of agony, and sank to his knees. Sawyer kicked him in the head. The Vopo toppled sideways, rolled over on his back, and sprawled out limply. Sawyer stepped over his unconscious form and walked out the end of the passageway.

There were no more cops in sight yet. On the other side of this street was an older block, with big, stolid Bauhaus apartments. The Thirties version of low-cost housing. Sawyer crossed to one of these buildings, went in the big entrance doorway. He nodded politely to a woman coming down the curved stairway inside, and started up the steps as she crossed the foyer toward the entrance. When she was out of the building, Sawyer doubled back down the stairway and strode through a wide corridor to the back door he'd spotted at the end of it.

He stopped before opening the door, and put on his jacket, buttoning it neatly. Smoothing his hair down and brushing the dust off him, he took the guidebook from his pocket. Then he opened the door and stepped out. There was a lovely garden area with a lot of trees, and thick vines covered the dingy stone of the buildings around it. Gravelled paths divided the garden into separate sections for the different buildings. Sawyer took a path straight across between the gardens, and went out between two houses.

A police car raced around the corner in his direction. Sawyer strolled along the sidewalk, swinging his guidebook. The car kept going, in the direction of the development complex. Sawyer crossed the next street, and hurried through a narrow, high-fenced alley between small gardens behind the row houses on either side.

He changed direction several more times as he worked toward his objective, sticking to older blocks with narrower streets and less visibility, using alleys where he found them, twice entering buildings by one door and leaving by another.

There were no police around the S-Bahn station when he got there. They hadn't gotten to that yet; it was outside the area to which the search was still confined. Sawyer boarded the next westbound train, changed at Alexanderplatz, and got off at Stadtmitte.

He walked the rest of the way to Checkpoint Charlie. They were always faster there than at the elevated train station, and the sooner he was out of East Berlin the better. If the police were buying the idea that it was only a thief they were hunting, there should be no problem getting across. But if they had any suspicion it could be something political, they'd already be making an extremely thorough check of everyone trying to pass through in this direction.

And, they'd be doing personal searches. The little Egyptian stele weighed heavy in the pocket of his jacket. But he had come this far with it, and a perverse stubbornness would not let him get rid of it now. It was the single thing he'd found here which might hold a lead to someone else who'd been involved in kidnaping Moira. Sawyer stuck the guidebook back in his pocket with it, for a little extra concealment, and approached the control point with a tired smile and his American passport and visa.

There wasn't much of a waiting line when he got there, but other weary tourists began piling up behind him while he was being questioned and his passport photo was being compared with his face. An East German customs man looked at the growing crowd and growled at the border guards to hurry it up. Fifteen minutes after arriving at the control point, Sawyer walked through it into West Berlin.

Himmie was standing on the other side staring at him, his face pale and drawn. Sawyer walked over to him and said, "It's all right. Relax."

"You made it," Himmie whispered. He put both arms around Sawyer, pulled him close, and began to weep.

4

Alone in his office in Paris, Alain Gassin sat on a brown leather sofa, listening to a tape recording. From time to time he leaned forward to jot a note on a pad resting on the Tibetan mandala painted on the low ebony table before him. It was a short tape. When it ended he ran it back, and started it again, his mind alert for anything he might have missed the first time. But he had missed nothing.

Gassin's elegant good looks and aristocratic manner sometimes misled people who didn't know him well into underestimating the sensitivity of both his mind and his feelings. Both sensitivities were activated by Sawyer's refusal to tell him what he was up to. It was compounded by the fact that Annique, his own wife, knew but also refused to confide in him.

He could not believe that Sawyer was betraying him, working for a rival firm. And he was quite sure Annique would not tolerate such a betrayal, if she knew about it. ARC was, after all, as much her company as his own. But they were involved in *something* he wasn't privy to. Being left out like that hurt his feelings, and piqued his curiosity.

By yesterday morning he'd had enough of it. He'd assigned two of his specialists to begin mobile electronic surveillance on Annique. What he was listening to now was the first result: a tape of a call Annique had made from a phone booth to Sawyer's young half-brother, Olivier—who was apparently acting as the control center for whatever Sawyer was involved in.

Nothing in the tape recording meant anything of significance to Gassin. When it finished for the second time, he shut off the player and leaned forward to regard the notes he'd made. He crossed out three of them. That left two.

Rising from the sofa, Gassin went to the gilded Louis XV writing desk beside the windows overlooking the Seine. He took two small file cards, wrote one of the notes on the first, the other on the second. Then he crossed to the flat-top oak desk in the middle of his office, pressed the intercom, and told his secretary to get him Laurent Hugonnet from Information Analysis.

When Hugonnet arrived in his office, Gassin impressed upon him that this was a personal inquiry, which he did not want Madame Gassin to know about at the moment. He gave Hugonnet the two cards, and asked him to try to find a coincidence point for the items on them; anything with which both could be associated.

On one card was a not uncommon name: "Martinot." On the other Gassin had written: "Venus figure."

FIFTEEN

1

The day that Sawyer spent in Berlin, Fritz Donhoff and Titine Delisio spent frustratingly in Antwerp. They arrived in the morning. Titine was still driving, but with Donhoff beside her. Inside the city, he directed the way to the address given in the passport of Maurice Ruyter, the man with the gray birthmark.

It was off Falcon Plein, on the edge of a sprawling network of docks and canals in Antwerp's huge harbor along the Scheldt River. Donhoff pointed out Old Man's Street, and Titine turned into it. She parked in front of a tattooing parlor with a huge photograph of its masterwork in the window: a bleeding Jesus vividly incised on a bald head. They were in the core of the port's red-light district, forlornly deserted at this hour, the bar shuttered, and the whores holed up for a day's sleep.

Donhoff gazed from the Citroën with tired gloom. There was no reason to get out. One side of this block of Old Man's Street was lined with seamen's saloons: The Ocean Ferry, American Taxi, Charlie Brown, Irish Glory, Hong Kong Kitty. On the other side was Maurice Ruyter's address—and it no longer existed. The entire block there had been torn down to make room for new building construction. All that was left was a littered lot, with the port's forest of cranes, gantries, and straddle carriers rising beyond it, stretching away toward the North Sea and the Dutch border.

"There may be somebody in the neighborhood who

knows where he moved," Titine said. "Shall I get out and start asking?"

Donhoff shook his head. "Always start with the simplest, most direct approach." He didn't like the exhausted drag of his voice. What little sleep he'd managed to snatch in the moving car had left him worse off than none.

He directed Titine to a small hotel behind Market Square, facing the cathedral. Titine, puzzled, followed Donhoff inside. There was a tiny entrance lobby, with a dining room opening off to one side. Donhoff asked the man at the desk if there was a room available.

The clerk consulted his room chart. "A double, just for this evening?"

"A single," Donhoff told him. "Immediately."

"There is a pleasant room available on the second floor. Would you care to have a look at it?"

"Does it have a bed?" Donhoff asked sourly.

The man stared at him. "But, certainly."

"Then I don't have to look. That's all I'm interested in at the moment. If my associate uses your dining room, put it on my bill." Donhoff gave the clerk his passport, and nodded at a phone on a table next to the lobby sofa. "And I want to make a local call."

"Certainly." The clerk flicked a switch behind his desk, activating the phone.

Donhoff trudged over and sat down heavily on the sofa. He put through a call to Antwerp police headquarters, and asked for Captain Van Orshaegen, a man he'd worked with in the past.

"I'm trying to find a Belgian bargemaster named Maurice Ruyter," Donhoff told him over the phone. He got a slip of paper from his pocket and read off the number of Ruyter's passport. "The address he'd listed here in Antwerp has been demolished."

"I'll run a check on the man," Van Orshaegen said, "here and also through Brussels. But I assume you are in a hurry for this information?"

"I am in a hurry," Donhoff agreed.

"Then I'd say your best bet, while I'm working on it from this end, would be to check with the General Manager's office at Port Administration. They have updated data on everyone connected with harbor operations, and they'll probably come through with what you need faster than I can."

Titine had come over to stand near the sofa, looking down curiously at Donhoff and listening. Donhoff looked up at her as he continued into the phone: "Will you call them and smooth the way for me? I won't be going there myself. I'm sending my assistant, a young woman named Delisio." He spelled it out. "First name, Martine, though she prefers Titine . . . Right. Thank you."

Donhoff hung up, heaved to his feet, and filled Titine in on what Van Orshaegen had said as he got his room key.

"You boasted last night about how good you are," he said. "All right, now is your chance to prove it— while I get some sleep."

After driving all night through most of France and half of Belgium, Titine was feeling pretty tired herself. But she didn't point that out. She asked: "When will you get up?"

"Probably when you wake me. Which you will not do until you have located Maurice Ruyter." Donhoff rubbed a hand against his crumpled face. "If you do find him, don't talk to him. Come back and get me." He turned away and started climbing the stairs.

Titine stopped herself from calling after him to ask where she could find the Port Administration offices. When he was gone, she asked the clerk if he could find out for her.

"Everybody around here knows that," he informed her. "We all make our living off the port, one way or another. The General Management is in the Town Hall, on the square." He pointed, adding: "Twenty seconds' walk, in that direction."

Titine grabbed herself a fast breakfast of coffee and rolls in the hotel restaurant. Then she walked around the corner to Market Square. Morning sunlight struck golden gleams off the ornamental trimmings of the marvelous stone-and-brick guild-house façades on three sides of the square. The Town Hall filled the fourth side. Titine hesitated before the imposing building, looking at the impeccably dressed functionaries going in and out, ties neatly in place, trousers sharply creased.

She was still wearing her motorcycle boots, dungarees, and rainproof imitation-leather jacket. But she had nothing else to change into, and she decided to hell with it, that was one of the few advantages of being young these days: people let you get away with odd dress they wouldn't tolerate in an "adult." So she might as well enjoy it while she could. Titine marched up the steps and into the building, head up, hips swinging.

The secretary who directed her to the room where she was expected was openly startled by her attire. The man waiting for her when she got off the elevator shook her hand and gave her a smile that ignored the way she was dressed. He was a middle-aged man in a very correct gray suit, with a black tie. He might have been an insurance executive, except for the leathery face from years of salty winds, and the old stevedore rope scars on his large hands. Introducing himself as Jacques Glass, an assistant director in Port Management, he led her to a small waiting room. The windows looked down on the River Scheldt, and one wall was entirely covered with a detail map of Antwerp port facilities.

"The police department recommended that we give you maximum co-operation and assistance," Glass told her. "And that is what you're going to get."

"I appreciate that."

"It's the least that Antwerp owes Mr. Donhoff. Captain Van Orshaegen explained about the work he did

What she did tell him was: "There is another man we're looking for. It would help if you could have your files combed for someone of his description. We don't know his name, but he's a stocky man in his mid-thirties, deep voice, pale gray eyes, tough face. And he has a birthmark on one cheek. A gray patch, quite noticeable."

At the other end of the line, there was a sound that might have been a sigh or a groan. "Facial birthmarks—we have thousands in our files. But, of course I'll try."

Titine thanked him, said they'd check with him late that afternoon, and hung up. Then she went to the desk clerk, took a room, told him to wake her at exactly three-thirty, and went up to get some sleep.

The *Leyden Rose* was a narrow old canal barge kept in beautiful condition; the paintwork regularly renewed, all the metalwork gleaming, well-tended flower boxes under the side windows of the wheelhouse. It was tied up near the Royers Sluis just inside the Lefèbvre Dock, next to a wide ore barge with a large modern apartment on its after deck. The living quarters of the *Leyden Rose* were much smaller, but comfortable enough for two people.

"Ruyter was just a poor old man down on his luck," Mrs. Jacobs told Donhoff. She was a heavy whitehaired woman with powerful shoulders and hands, and a soft disposition. "He helped out aboard, as much as he could. And he didn't take up much room. Just a secondhand army cot we put down in the engine room for him."

"Ruyter wasn't even as old as you," her son contradicted sourly, "and he was a drunken bum." He was nothing like his mother: scrawny, hard-faced, looking old before his time. "And the last few months he was nothing but baggage we had to feed. He didn't do any work at all."

"That's true," his mother conceded with a sad

smile, "but what could I do? Throw him off and let him die on the streets somewhere? I couldn't do that."

The room they were in, under the wheelhouse, served as kitchen and living room. Donhoff sat in a battered easy chair questioning mother and son, patiently delving into their memories of Ruyter for some trace of a stocky man with a gray birthmark on one cheek. To no avail.

Titine stood against the old iron stove, not interfering, watching a baby crawl around in a playpen secured to the forward deck of the next barge. She was feeling the letdown as she listened. After coming all the way to Antwerp, they were up against a blank wall.

But Donhoff didn't seem dispirited. He continued to question Mrs. Jacobs and her son, gently persistent. He asked, finally, "Did Ruyter ever have any trouble about his papers, that you know of?"

"Not that I recall." Mrs. Jacobs looked puzzled. "What do you mean?"

"I have reason to believe someone stole his passport, at some time. Or that he lost it, and someone picked it up."

Mrs. Jacobs shook her head. "Not that I know of. If it happened, I'm sure he didn't know, either. He never said anything about it."

Her son laughed unpleasantly. "Ruyter wouldn't have known about it if he'd lost his arm. The condition he was in most of the time."

"*I* wouldn't know if somebody stole my passport," his mother said. "Not for quite some time, anyway. We don't go anywhere except between here and Rotterdam. Everybody knows this barge, and us. Nobody ever asks for our papers. Be silly if they did, every time we went in and out."

"Wait a minute . . ." her son snapped. He frowned, thinking. "Yeah . . . I'm sure. The guy you asked about—with the birthmark. I just remembered, I did see somebody like that once. With Ruyter, in a bar."

Donhoff looked at him with a probing smile. "Here, or in Rotterdam?"

"Here. On Schippers Street. A bar called Capri. I remember, because I was mad at Ruyter. We were scheduled to pull out, and he hadn't come back with some supplies we were waiting for. I found him there in a booth, talking with this other guy—with a funny mark on his cheek."

"Did you get the impression this man was Belgian, or French?"

"I don't know. He didn't say anything while I was there. Not even when I dragged Ruyter out."

"Did Ruyter say anything to you later about this man? To either of you?"

The answer was no. Donhoff left the barge with Titine, and went to Schippers Street. Most of the bars were just opening. In the Capri, the bartender remembered Ruyter; and so did one of the prostitutes beginning their day with coffee at the end of the bar. But none of them remembered a stocky man with a gray birthmark.

It was the same in the other bars along the block; in the Old Sailor, the Copenhagen, and the Istanbul Cafe. "Either everybody else's memory is faulty," Donhoff decided finally, "or the Jacobs boy's is. I'm inclined to think it's him."

Titine nodded. She'd only been working in this line for a couple of years, but she'd already come across that sort of thing before: people who told you what they thought you wanted to hear, often without realizing that was what they were doing.

They went back to the hotel, and Donhoff checked with police headquarters. His friend there had more discouraging news: they'd turned up quite a few facial birthmarks that could be interpreted as grayish in color. But none of the men who had them also fitted all the other particulars of the man Donhoff was interested in.

He put a call through to Olivier in Paris, gave him

Ruyter's passport number, and told him to give it to Annique Gassin the next time she called. To check on whether the man who had used Ruyter's passport twice had used it other times. Paying his bill, and Titine's, Donhoff went out with her to the car.

"We're at a dead end here," he said calmly as they walked toward the Citroën. "This man with the birth-mark found, stole, or bought Ruyter's passport. Either here or in Rotterdam. Or even elsewhere, from the professionals who trade in papers. He had it altered to fit him, and used it twice that we know of. Both times down there in Peille. Perhaps he used it before that, which would help. I doubt that he'd be foolish enough to still be using it."

They reached the car and Titine started to get in behind the wheel. Donhoff stopped her: "*I'll* drive us to Paris. I've had my sleep, and I don't want to get too used to having a chauffeur. This time *you* can curl up in the back."

"I'm not tired," she told him, "just feeling frus-trated. A whole night and day wasted."

Donhoff looked at her. "Better get used to that, if you want to stay in this business. That's what it's all about: all the dead-end inquiries you make, spending hours or days along lines that lead to nothing. All the *time* you spend—waiting, and listening, and watching. That's what you've got to learn to deal with: the time element. If you have the time to keep digging at those dead ends, eventually one of them usually breaks open, somewhere."

They got in the car and headed south toward Paris.

2

The bloodstains and bullet holes in the car were more than six decades old. But the events they had triggered seemed far more remote than that. The car was a Gräf & Stift four-cylinder Doppel-Phaeton-Karosserie, and in 1914 the Archduke Ferdinand had been assassinated in the back seat, beginning the war that finally ended Vienna's glory as capital of the Austro-Hungarian Empire.

The man Lang was tailing was a soldier without uniform in an entirely different kind of war, but the assassination car was the first exhibit he went to after entering Vienna's Military Museum. Having gotten to it, however, he did not seem at all interested. He glanced around the room briefly, and then strolled on, into the hall displaying arms and armor of the Thirty Years' War. He did not appear particularly fascinated with that, either. Nor in the huge room half filled by a gorgeous brocade tent left behind when the Muslims were repulsed at the siege of Vienna in 1683. He strolled past everything disinterestedly, from room to room, floor to floor. But always, he returned to the car in which the First World War had begun.

Lang saw him do it once. The agents who took over from Lang, so the man wouldn't spot the tail job, saw him visit the car three more times.

His name was Gerhard Hubmann, and he was the courier who always carried the code tapes to Tozinski in Budapest. There'd been ample time for the Vienna station to learn his name before Lang resumed the tail there. The previous day had been a total washout. Surveillance agents supplied by station had staked out the airport, with copies made the night before of the photos Lang had taken of the courier. They'd stayed on lookout from first flight to last, to no avail. The courier hadn't shown.

This morning he had. The agent watching the airport's parking area had recognized him as he got out of his Porsche. Lang had gotten there thirty minutes after the courier took off on the first flight to Budapest. He'd taken the license number of the courier's car and phoned it to the Agency station. The desk man there had contacted an officer on the Vienna police force, who lived much more comfortably since he'd started receiving a regular CIA retainer.

It hadn't taken the officer long: the car belonged to Gerhard Hubmann, age thirty-seven, dealer in a small way in tourist souvenirs. Hubmann had no known office. He worked out of his apartment, which he shared with a nineteen-year-old girl who was not his wife. She apparently helped in the business, since she took most of his phone calls, and had no other source of income since she'd quit her job at a Prater hot-dog stand to move in with Hubmann four months before.

Gerhard Hubmann's past was colorless: no criminal record, no annoying political convictions, no previously known contacts to anyone remotely connected with espionage. He did, however, have an interesting bank account: in the past five months his balance had grown larger than at any time in the past. It did not add up to an extraordinary amount, but small regular deposits were building him a comfortable nest egg.

By the time Hubmann returned to Vienna's Schwechat Airport in the early afternoon, Lang had a microtransmitter attached under the chassis of his Porsche. He also had a special surveillance car standing by, with a mobile radar set tuned into the bug. So that when Hubmann drove away from the airport, it was possible to keep a car-to-car tail on him without having to get close enough for him to notice.

Hubmann had driven by the most direct route to his apartment in the city center. He'd stayed inside with his girl friend until late afternoon, and no one had come to visit him. When he'd come out, he'd driven directly to the Military Museum, entering it one hour before it was due to close for the evening.

It was two minutes before closing when he came out. Lang, in the back seat of the radar-equipped car with one of the local agents assigned to him, watched Hubmann stroll away in the direction of his parked Porsche. The agent beside Lang activated a control switch, and the radar screen set into the back of the front seat came to life. The stationary blip that marked the position of Hubmann's Porsche began to glow. Ten seconds later the last agent to take over inside came out of the museum.

"He still didn't make contact with anybody in there," he told Lang as he got in front beside the driver. "And he didn't do a pickup, or leave anything. But sure as hell that's the drop in there. By the old car. That's where he's supposed to wait, in case there's another delivery to take."

"Today it is," Lang agreed quietly. "Tomorrow the rendezvous could be someplace else." The blip began to move on the radar screen's grid. Lang climbed out of the car. "Stay with him and report to control." He shut the door and walked for five minutes before finding a taxi on Prinz Eugen Strasse to take him back into the center of Vienna. Getting out at Singerstrasse, he walked quickly to his control room three short blocks away.

The control setup they'd arranged for Lang was a windowless paper-supply storeroom on the top floor of a building on Spiegelgasse, around the corner from the Graben, the hub of the Old City. The building backed against the rear of the one in which Hubmann had his apartment, which faced Dorotheergasse, around the other side of the block.

A telephone and three radio receivers had been installed between the wide shelves and stacked cartons of paper goods, along with tables, chairs, and two army cots. There were two men on duty when Lang got there. Parker, in charge of communications, sat in front of the radio tuned to the radar car, wearing a headset. The receivers flanking him were for the apartment bugs and phone tap. The other man was Beckel, an Austrian locksmith who'd been getting most of his income from the CIA for some fifteen years. He was stretched on one of the cots, reading a book which he lowered to greet Lang.

"How's it shape up?" Lang asked them.

Parker nodded at the radio in front of him. "Just heard from Bob. Hubmann's settled down in a coffee-house on the Ring, reading the papers and not looking like he's waiting for anybody." He indicated the receivers on either side of him. "We made the outside tap on his phone line. And got on the roof and lowered bugs. One above each of the apartment windows."

"What've you heard so far?"

"Only two calls from shops wanting to know why Hubmann hasn't delivered Hungarian bedspreads he promised weeks ago. Hubmann's girl friend told them he's having unexpected trouble getting the stuff. I got the idea he's been neglecting his customers lately." Parker grinned. "I wonder why."

"Neither of the calls sounded like cover talk?"

"Nope. Not to me."

Lang looked at Beckel. "You haven't been able to get inside yet."

"No opportunity. Hubmann's girl hasn't gone out of the apartment. I went up and had a look at their door. Nothing complicated. I'll be able to open it quickly, when the time comes."

That told Lang it was going to be the same as Tozinski's office. Easy entry meant there was nothing inside worth finding. But it had to be checked anyway.

"Let's hope," Beckel said with a smile, "that they don't decide to stay in for the evening. If they do, we'll have to set fire to the building to get them out."

Lang did not smile. "There are other ways, if it becomes a problem. Let's wait and see."

Beckel consulted his watch. "If the waiting takes more than another hour, I'm on overtime."

Parker told Lang: "You'll need an okay from Keaton for that. And to get men to relieve me and the mobile units, if this is going to go all night."

Roy Keaton was station chief in Vienna. Lang had met him at the American Embassy when he'd arrived:

an officer strong on patriotism, but he reminded Lang of Brusilov's description of General Kornilov, back in the Twenties: a warrior with the heart of a lion and the brain of a sheep.

"He still at the embassy?"

"No, but I've got numbers for him." Parker consulted his time-schedule sheet, dialed a number, and gave the phone to Lang.

Keaton came on and Lang told him the operation would probably continue through the night. Requiring maintenance of all present units, including the surveillance team presently stationed outside Hubmann's apartment building.

There was a sound of extreme displeasure at the other end of the line. "Jesus Christ, Lang, you're using half the people I've got. I do have other operations going, you know. And you're cutting into them."

Lang waited, saying nothing. As station chief, Keaton had the authority over this area. Lang was only a case officer, passing through. But Washington had already notified Keaton that Lang's needs had priority for the moment. It wasn't necessary for Lang to remind him.

"Okay," Keaton said finally. "I know it's important. But how much longer do you expect to be at it?"

"Not long. Then it gets passed to you. I'll fill you in on the details before I leave."

"I'll have time for you tomorrow between noon and one. Now let me get off and arrange for your replacement teams."

"Thank you, sir. And—there's been no message for me concerning Warsaw?"

"Not a thing."

Lang handed the phone back to Parker. If they still couldn't trace the Warsaw number that got the calls from Budapest, it was still his ball game.

A light blinked on the main radio. Parker listened on his earpiece, said: "Hold on," and wrapped his fist around the tiny mike. "It's Bob," he told Lang. "Hubmann has left the coffeehouse and is coming this way."

"Tell them to stay out there with the other team if Hubmann enters his apartment." Lang picked up one of the bug receiver's earphones as Parker passed on the order.

After some fifteen minutes he heard door noises, followed by Hubmann and the girl greeting each other. Lang continued to listen, hoping. It was another twenty minutes before he grinned and put down the earphone. "They're going out to dinner."

Hubmann and his girl friend left the apartment shortly after 8 P.M. They were tailed by both surveillance teams. Three minutes later Beckel and Lang were inside Hubmann's apartment. There were four rooms, and Beckel went through them swiftly. Finding no safe or locked drawers requiring his skills, he went outside to stand lookout while Lang continued his own search.

As Lang had anticipated, he found nothing connected with the espionage work Hubmann was doing, and no encoding machine. Hubmann was just another small link in the communications line, nothing more. The encoder was somewhere further along the line.

Lang left the apartment less than forty minutes after he'd entered it. Beckel relocked the door, and they went down out of the building. Beckel looked at Lang's face as they started back around the block.

"Didn't get anything?"

"No," Lang told him. "You can call it quits for the night. But if you're not going to be home, let me have a number where I can get you in a hurry if I need you."

"I'll be home." They turned into the short, wide shopping street of the Graben, dark and almost empty now. Beckel stopped and stared. "Look at that— they're at it again. The same every night, lately."

He was pointing to the Plague Column, a baroque monument celebrating the end of the Black Death in the seventeenth century. As they walked closer, Lang saw what Beckel meant: the myriad ornate convolutions of the monument were crawling with families of rats.

"It's the subway being extended under Vienna," Beckel said. "That's driving them all up into the open. Have you noticed all the dogs in Vienna wear muzzles?"

Lang shook his head.

"It's not to protect people from dogbite. It's to stop the dogs from eating any of the tons of rat poison the city spreads around."

Lang watched a mother rat carry a baby over a marble head and deposit it out of sight behind an ornate curlicue.

Beckel smiled and shrugged. "Well, we Viennese treasure a constant nostalgia for the glories of our past. If this keeps up we'll have some of that glorious past back with us: the Black Plague."

They parted at Spiegelgasse, and Lang went up to the control room. Parker told him that Hubmann and the girl were having a slow and expensive meal at the Hotel Sacher restaurant. Neither surveillance team had spotted any contacts. Lang went out again, and had dinner in a small garden restaurant behind the looming bulk of St. Stephen's Cathedral. When he returned to control, Parker's night replacement was on duty: a young electronics engineer named Ritchie, recently arrived from Washington.

"Hubmann and his girl are back in the apartment," he informed Lang. "No calls, and it sounds like they're going to make it an early night. And both of the mobile unit night teams are in position."

"Tell them to stay that way." Lang loosened his tie and unbuttoned the collar. "And wake me at six in the morning, unless you hear something of interest before."

"Like if they start screwing?"

Lang formed a smile. You had to be a regular guy, not up-tight, to work well with these men. "No, thanks. Audio without visual is too frustrating."

Ritchie laughed, and Lang took off his shoes and jacket and stretched out on one of the cots. He closed his eyes and thought of Duyen, and their son, and the house where the three of them had lived together so briefly in Da Nang.

3

It was nine in the morning when Hubmann left his apartment. He did not take his Porsche, but walked around the corner to the Graben, through it to St. Stephen's, and went inside. That early there were very few visitors in the cathedral. One of those few was an attractive young woman wearing a Pan Am flight stewardess uniform and carrying a flight bag on a shoulder strap.

She stood near the pulpit, studying the statue of the Servants' Madonna, when Hubmann came in. He strolled past her, and then moved on toward the south door of the cathedral. She followed him. Lang's surveillance man inside the cathedral saw her dip a hand into her flight bag as she entered the south door's atrium, at the same time as Hubmann. The surveillance man watching outside the south side of the cathedral saw that her hand was no longer in the bag when she came out, and she had nothing in either hand.

Hubmann came out immediately behind her. The Pan Am stewardess strolled away up the Karntner-strasse pedestrian mall. Hubmann hurried back through the Graben to his Porsche.

One of Lang's mobile units tailed Hubmann out to the airport, where he took the next plane to Buda-pest. Lang got the word in his control room: there could be no doubt, Hubmann had picked up another code tape. Lang's other mobile unit stayed with the woman who had given it to him.

They followed her to the Hotel Intercontinental. By the time she had changed from her uniform into a dress, and came down to have a drink at the bar with others from her flight crew, they knew her name was Angela Lewis and she regularly worked the New York–Vienna run.

When her 747 took off the next morning for its return flight to New York, one of the people she served breakfast to, in the first-class section, was Lang.

4

The taxi that brought Sawyer back into Paris when he returned from Germany left him off at a building behind the Palais de Chaillot, directly across the Seine from the Eiffel Tower. Sawyer entered and showed his identification, waited until a phone check confirmed his temporary authorization to proceed further, and was passed through to the interior.

The building, constructed just before the First World War, took up all of a huge triangular block. From the outside it looked solid. But it was a shell, wrapped around the sides of the block. Concealed within was another building, the Sogégarde Tower: a massive round structure of reinforced concrete, surrounded by a moat. As impregnable as Fort Knox, it was a maximum-security storage vault for private valuables ranging from gold bars and jewelry to antique furniture and company computer data. Among these valuables was the largest concentration of privately owned art and antiquities in the world.

Sawyer crossed the bridge over the moat, and reached the tower's only entrance door. Like most of the interior doors, it could only be opened from the inside, where security crews were on duty around the clock. The emergency entrance was under the bridge: a water-filled tunnel which could be pumped out to permit guards to crawl through. Sawyer looked directly into a television scanner, gave his name, and said he was expected by Victor Bovis, director of Sogégarde's arts and antiquities section.

A second later the door clicked open. Sawyer stepped inside, between two uniformed guards carrying submachine guns. One shut the door behind him, and it relocked itself. The other escorted him up a short flight of steps past the closed-circuit TV control room. From that point on Sawyer was relayed by guard teams through short corridors, locked doors, and stairways. Television scanners covered him every step of the way. There were no windows.

Victor Bovis' large office was also windowless and under observation by scanners: one angled from each corner. Bovis' own TV screens, a bank of three beside his desk, were focused on locked steel doors in other parts of the building.

Sawyer looked at them. "You've gotten even more gadget crazy around here than the last time I visited."

Bovis smiled. "You ought to know. Alain Gassin helped talk us into updating the system. I imagine he told you."

Sawyer nodded. "Gassin believes in expensive hardware. Especially if somebody else is paying for it." At Sogégarde, he knew, that included sensors which reacted to an intruder's body heat or smell, all linked to a system programmed to seal every door and flood corridors with poison gas.

Taking the seat Bovis indicated, Sawyer glanced at the wall shelves loaded with art books and museum and dealer catalogues from all over the world. "How are you making out with your own catalogue of art works missing since the war?"

Bovis made an unhappy sound. "I found out recently, Siviero down in Rome's Art Recovery Department has been putting together the same thing. I wish I'd heard earlier." He eyed Sawyer shrewdly. "Is this small talk, or are we on the subject you came to see me about?"

Sawyer took out the Egyptian stele he had stolen from Christine Jonquet's room in East Berlin. He opened the tissue paper he'd wrapped around it, and placed the stele face-up on Bovis' desk. "What is this a copy of?"

Bovis picked it up and examined it with interest, but briefly. "Egyptian polychrome stele. I'd say Eighteenth Dynasty, but it could be a bit earlier or later."

"Who are the two beauties on it?"

"Isis and Nephthys." Bovis indicated the symbols on their heads and in their hands. "Sister goddesses, of opposing forces of the universe. Not opposing, actually—but opposite. Reverse sides of the same coin, you might say: daylight and darkness; life and death; fertility and decay; growth and destruction."

Sawyer remembered his talk with Professor Borelli, and felt a small jolt of excitement. He started to ask his next question, but stopped himself when Bovis got up and went over to one wall of bookshelves. Waiting, he watched Bovis search through the shelves, and take down a small book.

Bovis leafed through it, found the page he wanted, and looked mildly pleased with himself. "Here we are." He brought the book back to his desk, and placed it open beside the stele. "This is a catalogue of the works in the Archaeological Museum of Florence. Have a look."

Sawyer was already out of the chair, moving around the desk. The catalogue was open to a full-page picture of the stele.

"Exactly the same," Bovis pointed out, and tapped the picture. "There's your original—in Florence."

Sawyer gave him a quizzical look. "You're quite sure *that's* the original."

Bovis looked at him sharply. "Are you telling me

you think the one in the museum is the copy? And *this* is the original?"

"I don't know, at this point. They could both be copies, for that matter. I'll let you know, when I find out." Sawyer picked up the stele and held it in his palm. "How valuable is it?"

"The real one? If you mean in money, anywhere from seven to nine thousand dollars. Depending on conditions at the time of sale. The antiquities market fluctuates drastically, influenced by changes in fashion, income tax regulations and the effect of inflation on other long-term security items."

So—not worth an enormous amount of money. But, if Sawyer was right, it had meant something special to whoever had given it to Christine Jonquet.

He looked from the stele to Bovis. "These sister goddesses—I know an archaeologist who claims they're a continuation of the opposite natures contained in the paleolithic Venus figure."

The expert in Bovis became cautious: "That is one theory which has some adherents among professionals. I suppose you could interpret it that way . . ."

Sawyer did. Somewhere along the line he was trying to follow, there was someone who had two facets: access to stolen or expertly forged antiquities—and a fixation on the Earth-Mother goddess, in her various guises.

5

Fritz Donhoff knew where everybody was buried, and when he had new visitors he enjoyed using his binoculars to point them all out: Héloïse and Abé-lard, Colette, Oscar Wilde, Sarah Bernhardt and Beaumarchais, Delacroix and Georges Bizet. He was showing them to Titine when Sawyer arrived at Don-hoff's apartment on the top floor of the old building on Avenue Gambetta, overlooking Père-Lachaise Cemetery.

Sawyer was surprised to find Titine there, and Donhoff introduced them, explaining about her. He had another surprise for Sawyer: "I think the time has come for me to take on a regular assistant. She's an eager learner, and a quick one. So we've decided to try how it works out."

Sawyer looked slowly from Titine to Donhoff. "You never had an assistant before."

"Because I never needed one," Donhoff explained simply. "Now, I'm afraid I begin to. My memory stays fairly firm, but I get tired. I can't move around from one point to another as steadily as I used to. If it weren't for Titine, I'd still be in Brussels, one day behind."

"Don't worry," Titine told Sawyer. Her voice had a slight edge to it, in reaction to his expression. "I don't know the purpose of this investigation, and I'm not asking. That's already been explained to me. I understand it, completely. I know how to keep my mouth shut and . . ."

"It's your *mind* you've got to shut. If you're involved, you'll learn certain things. I don't want you trying to put those things together in your head."

"I won't," she promised tightly.

Sawyer still didn't like it. But Donhoff was not a man he could tell what to do, and Donhoff wanted her. He had a simple choice: take Donhoff on his own terms, or drop him. And he needed him.

Donhoff was smiling at him mildly, reading his face. "I've been in touch with Annique, and I've put together what we have—and don't have. Suppose you and I close ourselves in the study, and go down the list."

"I'll go take a bath," Titine said, watching Sawyer with deliberate lack of expression. "You don't have to be nervous about my being in the apartment. I don't listen at doors."

337

"If you don't, you're in the wrong business."

She grinned like an evil child. "All right, I do like to listen at doors, but in this case I'll restrain it."

She went off in the direction of the bathroom, and Sawyer followed Donhoff into his study, closing the door. They sat at the desk and Donhoff got several sheets with neatly written notes from the top drawer, spreading them out neatly. Through Olivier, each had already been filled in by phone on the other's activities—in Berlin and Antwerp. Sawyer showed Donhoff the Egyptian stele he'd brought back, and told him what had been learned from Victor Bovis at Sogégarde.

Donhoff put the stele aside on his desk, and added two short notes on one of his sheets of paper. "Now, let's begin with the reports from Annique. I'm afraid they're all negative. First, your request for known archaeological looters who turn up having worked on digs: Annique found some, but in my opinion none of them fit what we're after. You can check her information on that, perhaps you'll spot something I didn't."

Sawyer shook his head. "We don't have time to waste on duplication of effort. We both know I won't find something where you couldn't. What's next?"

"Maurice Ruyter's passport. Annique has so far found no usage of it in France, except the two times we know of. At Madame Sorel's hotel down in Peille. It hasn't been used anywhere since. Before, you have to go back a long time; to its use in Belgium and Holland, and there obviously by the real Maurice Ruyter. It's possible the man using the passport the times he was in touch with Martinot will use it again, sometime. But I don't believe it. I have a feeling we're dealing with a careful cookie.

"Now: Christine Jonquet's papers. Annique found no usage that gives us anything new on her. After getting her West German papers from Bonn, she apparently went briefly to Stuttgart and then directly to

Paris. Her German papers, and the French ones she got after marrying Jonquet, don't show any movements we don't already know about. She went to America for a few weeks, came back to Paris. Anyplace else she went during the period we're interested in remains a blank.

"We draw another blank on our man with the gray birthmark on his cheek. He doesn't show up on any kind of record, and your Annique really tried—criminal records, birth records, hospital records, insurance records, military records. In France; and elsewhere through Interpol. A number of grayish birthmarks turned up, but not on a man who fits the rest of what we know about the one who interests us. Definitely, no one connected with looting or forging antiquities has such a mark on his face."

Sawyer leaned back in his chair and scowled at the notes. "I think we've assumed something there that we shouldn't. The two people who saw this man—Clarissa Koller in East Berlin, and Madame Sorel in Peille—both described what he had as a birthmark. But, it could be something else."

It was not a new thought for Donhoff: "I agree. It could be a scar, an infection—something he may not have had all his life."

"All we can be certain of is that it's a gray mark of some kind. We know he had it as long as five years ago, in East Berlin—and that he still had it recently, down in Peille."

"Exactly. So where this man is concerned, we can only be sure of what he's looked like for the past five years. Without that gray mark on his cheek, the rest of his description could fit thousands of men. But, whatever that mark is, he *has* had it for five years. Unless he's gotten rid of it somehow, in the last month, we'll know it's him—if we ever find him."

"We will," Sawyer stated firmly. "At this point we've got two main lines of inquiry. The Egyptian stele someone gave to Christine Jonquet—and the

Venus figure *someone* used to snatch Moira. I'm betting both lines lead to our man with the mark."

Donhoff gave him qualified agreement: "It's possible. At any rate, you're right about our two main lines." He pulled two of the sheets closer, and Sawyer hunched forward as they went over the notes on them.

Most of the notes were derived from Annique Gassin's research. Sawyer had trimmed the results considerably, trying to confine them to names with the best chance of turning into leads. Donhoff had narrowed the lists down further, and he explained his reason for each elimination. Sawyer could find no flaw in Donhoff's reasoning on any of them.

"The line on the stele is in Italy," Donhoff pointed out. "At least, it begins there. I'll take that, since my Italian is a good deal better than yours."

"What about the girl?" Sawyer nodded toward the closed door.

"Titine is from Corsica."

"Then her Italian is probably almost as good as her French. Okay, take her along." Sawyer paused, looking at Donhoff somberly. "But, Fritz—please be *very* frugal with what you tell her."

"Don't worry, she's a bright girl."

"You don't have to tell me, it's obvious. *That's* what worries me."

"It needn't. As she told you, I explained the need to limit what she understands, in this case. And, obviously, I trust her. Unless you feel my estimate of people is weak . . . ?"

"It never has been," Sawyer acknowledged, and let it go at that. "Now let's go over our two lines, one last time."

They were in the middle of it when the phone rang. Donhoff answered, and then passed the phone to Sawyer with a troubled glance. "For you. It's Annique. She's calling from ARC."

Sawyer seized the phone from him. Annique was not supposed to make contact from her office, or any-

340

where else at the firm. "What's happened?" he asked her without preamble.

"You'd better get over here," she told him. "Quickly. Alain had me bugged. I just found out. And he's figured out most of what you're doing."

6

"Please contradict me if I've jumped to the wrong conclusions," Gassin told him. "I fervently hope that I have. But unless you can explain where my reasoning is faulty, I have to assume you've gotten yourself dangerously involved in political espionage at the very highest level. That assumption is based on my belief that the wife of an adviser to the President of the United States has been kidnaped, but in such a way that everyone would think her dead."

He stood with his back to the wide desk in the center of his office, looking down at Sawyer. As always when he was genuinely upset, a deep groove had appeared between his eyebrows and his voice had become softly precise. "I admit inferring a great deal from a few fragments of evidence. Starting with the name Martinot and a reference to a Venus figure. But when I added to that . . ."

"I'm not interested in hearing how good a detective you are," Sawyer interrupted in a restrained voice. He sat in a comfortable cane-back chair with his hands gripping the smooth curves of the armrests. His eyes were intent on Gassin's face, searching. "I want to know what you plan to do about it."

Gassin pressed the backs of his legs against the desk top, as though for support. "You know what I have to do," he said uncomfortably. "If I don't, everything I've spent my life building could be destroyed. When it comes out, no one will believe I was unaware of what you were up to."

341

"It won't come out, if you'll keep your mouth shut."

Gassin shook his head. "You can't keep a lid clamped down on something this big; not for long."

"I don't need much longer," Sawyer said with a conviction he was not sure he believed.

"You're not thinking logically, Pierre-Ange. You'll have to admit that French and American intelligence, combined, can bring a great deal more to bear on finding Moira Rhalles quickly than you can."

"Sure. But the way they'll go at it, she'll be dead before anybody finds her."

"Not if we explain the situation to them. I never intended to speak to anyone without first talking to you. I want you to go with me, both to clear yourself of any possible charges—and to outline the circumstances in detail. The men I intend to see are neither stupid nor inhuman. They'll keep the danger to Moira Rhalles in mind, and handle it in ways that won't increase that danger."

"Don't talk like a child," Sawyer said tonelessly. "You know better. There isn't an intelligence or security force in the world that cares about the fate of any single individual."

"You're letting your cynicism run away with you," Gassin told him firmly. "You'll have to trust my judgment, this time."

Sawyer took his hands from the armrests of his chair. He got out a cigarette, lit it, and said tensely: "I want you to keep quiet about this, just a little longer. Give me a chance to do it my way."

Gassin shook his head. "No. I can't risk everything I have—everything I am. The chance of Rhalles' wife coming out of this situation alive is extremely slim, no matter what anyone does or does not do. But I repeat: what I have to do will not hurt what chance she does have. Probably quite the opposite."

Sawyer continued to watch Gassin's face for a moment. His eyes dulled, and his voice became colorless: "You're sure of that."

"I am."

Sawyer dropped his cigarette in an ashtray on the table beside his chair. "I hope you're right. Because if you're wrong, it will have certain consequences for you. If Moira Rhalles dies because of you—first of all, I'll have *you* killed."

Gassin started to smile. "If it comes to killing . . ."

"It doesn't matter what you have done to me," Sawyer told him. "It'll be too late. I'll have already given the contract—to Marcel Alfani."

Gassin lost his smile. Alfani was the Marseilles gangster Sawyer had saved from ruin, at the cost of his own future. And he was a Corsican, for whom such a debt was an affair of personal honor, to be repaid no matter how long it took.

"It's possible he won't be able to do it," Sawyer acknowledged in the same colorless voice. "But there's something else I'm going to do, if Moira Rhalles gets killed because of you. I'm going to wait until your daughter is about twelve, old enough to understand, and then let her know you're not her father. That *I* am. And in case I'm not around by then, for some reason, I'll have left a letter to be delivered to her. She'll ask Annique. We both know Annique is not much for lying, when asked a direct question."

Gassin was staring at him sickly, his face gone pale. "You wouldn't . . . as you say, she *is* yours."

"Not really. I don't even know the kid. *You're* the one who raised her. You're the one who loves her. You couldn't take it—causing her to be hurt like that."

Gassin's right hand came up toward the knot of his necktie, as though to loosen it. But it just hung there, doing nothing. "I don't believe you."

Sawyer's fingers closed again on the smooth arm-rests of his chair. "We know each other—too well. Think again."

Gassin studied him, and slowly lowered his hand. He didn't repeat that he didn't believe Sawyer would do such a thing. When he spoke again, there was more shock than anger in his voice: "You're a vicious animal—I never realized."

"Yes, you did. But it was useful to you, so you liked it. Now it's being used against you. That's the difference." Sawyer pushed his shoulders against the chair back, and drew a slow breath. "All right—you don't want to be killed, or have your daughter hurt. *I* want your word that you won't say anything about what I'm doing, to anybody."

Gassin looked at him in silence for several seconds. Then he walked around his desk to one of the windows. He gazed out through it, his back to Sawyer.

"You have my word on it," he said heavily. "Goodbye, Pierre-Ange."

Sawyer had to force his hands to let go of the armrests as he stood up. "Goodbye."

"I mean—I don't want to see you again."

"I know that, Alain." Sawyer walked out and shut the door quietly behind him.

He went down the steps to the second floor, one hand touching the banister rail all the way, and entered the men's room. An assistant to the director of ARC's special projects was inside, washing his hands. Sawyer greeted him in a normal tone, and began running water in the other basin. When the man left, Sawyer locked the door from the inside, went back to the basin, and became violently sick.

When he came out into the corridor he looked pale but the dizziness was gone from his brain. He took the stairway to the ground floor and went out of the building, walking quickly and steadily.

PART THREE

THE CONVERGING

A hand of smoke ...
A drop of blood in the corner of heaven.
                              —Vasko Popa

SIXTEEN

1

Lang had several minutes of anxiety about being separated from Angela Lewis when he left the Pan Am 747 after its landing at Kennedy. He knew the anxiety to be unjustified. Washington had been notified from Vienna about the stewardess. Well before the plane arrived, the arrangements for total surveillance on her would have been planned and put in operation. Lang was quite sure that some of the maintenance crew, waiting for the plane as it came to a halt at the terminal, where operatives assigned to observe her from the instant she appeared at the open door.

Nevertheless, Lang was relieved when he saw the stringy, dark-faced agent waiting to detour him swiftly past customs and passport control. The man's name was Garcia. Lang had worked with him in the past. He had reason to respect the quickness and thoroughness of his mind.

Garcia began by answering Lang's unspoken question: "The Lewis girl's covered. Has been, since they opened the plane's doors. The first maintenance man aboard was ours. So's one of the ground crew. There're two operatives waiting to pick her up as she comes off. Both female, in Pan Am uniforms; so even if she goes in a ladies' john to make contact, one of them can go in with her. Same from there on—wherever she goes, she's covered like an old maid's ass on a cold night."

He tapped his jacket pocket. "I've got a beeper. It'll signal for a check with communications control if she makes contact, or does anything else interesting." Garcia handed Lang a briefcase. "There's one for you in this."

In addition to the beeper, there were the things Lang had left behind in Washington: his wallet, passport, CIA I.D., a compact .32 pistol with a flat box of ammunition, and his permit to carry. Plus a fat dossier on stewardess Angela Lewis. Garcia continued to fill Lang in as he led him along back passages through the terminal, pausing three times to show an airport security I.D. to guards at doorways.

"She shares an apartment on the East Side with two other stewardesses, has a car parked in a garage around the corner. We've bugged the apartment, tapped the phone, put bugs and a tracer button on her car. And we've got visual and electronic surveillance set up for her roommates. The same with her boy friend—he runs a small travel agency on Third, near Bloomingdale's. We've got him covered, along with his office, apartment, car, and phones."

Lang was impressed. "How big a crew have we got?"

"Including me, you've got nine full-timers assigned to your operation. Plus eight occasionals; and you can get more." Garcia flashed Lang a somewhat envious grin. "And you're the boss. How's it feel to be in the big time?"

It felt good, Lang had to admit. He remembered times he'd been all alone in areas where enemy crews had him boxed in any way he moved. Now the situation was reversed. The Company, he decided, was really worried about this one.

They left the terminal building by a side door. A car was parked at the curb, with an airport security permit stuck under one of the windshield wipers. Garcia removed the card, unlocked the door, and got in behind the wheel. He flicked on a two-way radio tuned to the operation's control center, before starting the engine. Lang slid in front beside him, and got the Angela Lewis dossier out of the briefcase.

"You'll see we haven't missed much," Garcia said with a nod at the dossier. "You've even got transcripts on her shrink sessions in there." He let out the brake and began the drive to Manhattan. "My opinion based on what we've got: this girl doesn't know what she's carrying."

Lang had begun to read the dossier. "You figure she thinks it's business secrets."

"Something like that. Anyway, that's my guess, based on her history and character analyses. Not that it'll save her much grief, when the crunch comes. She knows she's breaking *some* law."

"I'm not interested in getting *her*."

"I know what you're after. But I think you could probably get her co-operation on it, if you scare the shit out of her first."

Lang looked up from the dossier, considering it. But after a moment he shook his head. "No. Chances are, you're right. But I don't want to take *any* risk of being wrong and blowing it. Not when I don't have to, with all the manpower we've got. We do this one slow and sure."

"Okay, no problem. We've got this little girl covered, top, bottom, and sideways. No *way* we can miss. Whoever she gets those code tapes from—the next time one gets delivered to her, we'll be there."

2

Moira enjoyed the sensual warmth of the afternoon sun, soaking into her as she worked on her drawing of the old fortress tower. On each of the last few days, Bruno had allowed her two hours in the open; and from the start she'd asked him for a sketch pad and pencils. This noon, he'd brought them for her. It helped calm her nerves; and so did the warm sunlight.

But getting these short periods outside had so far failed to give her all she'd hoped for.

The most serious failure was that she knew no more than before, about the surroundings of the fortress ruins. Each time, Bruno had brought her directly out of the tower onto the raised inner ward, and chained her there in the middle of it. Always in the same manner: the handcuffs were attached to her left ankle and one end of the chain. The other end of the chain was padlocked to a thick iron ring sunk into the stone flooring, probably once the anchoring piece for a large countersiege weapon such as a balista or mangonel.

The chain was long enough to permit her to walk around a bit. But not far enough to see over a parapet or down through any of the gaps in the broken walls and crumbling fortress buildings. She was confined to a circle which let her see nothing immediately beyond this inner ward. In one direction there was the high wooded hill she knew so well, but she still didn't know what lay between it and the fortress. In all other directions there were only the ruins and the sky.

But she had learned a few things which were useful to her. First of all, she was now certain she'd been wrong in thinking there might be others in the place, whom she hadn't seen. There were only Bruno, who had the room directly under her cell, and Lorenz, whose room was next to a kitchen in the lower part of the tower. And that tower, Moira was almost sure, was the only place inside the ruins which had been kept habitable.

Another thing she got from her times out there in the inner ward was an opportunity to study what she could see attentively, and estimate the possible routes of escape. That was what she was doing now, as she sat cross-legged on a cushion Bruno had placed for her in the center of the inner ward's terrace, with her sketch pad across her thighs.

Beside her was the gaping hole where part of the terrace flooring had collapsed. Moira could see no escape route down there. All the light which showed the wreckage of the fortress stable below came from above. The fallen masonry seemed to have blocked its entrance.

A possibility was one of the gaps in the wall facing the wooded hill. But if she could develop a way to reach a gap, how much of a drop lay waiting on the other side? A few feet, or a hundred?

There was the pointed-arch gateway on the far side of the inner ward, to her left. But it no longer had an opening to the outer ward. Only the interior stairwell leading down under the fortress, to that hole where they'd put her when she'd refused to make the tape. She'd seen other doors and passages on the way down there. But though any one of them might lead to freedom, all of them might only take her to dead ends.

A better possibility was a partly collapsed entrance to the undercroft of the main wall, near the square tower. She didn't know where it led beyond that, but this was the only exit from the inner ward which might lead to the outside, not into another part of the fortress interior.

There was one other possibility: the tower that held her cell. It had only one opening at the bottom, the doorway on the inner ward. But the corkscrew stairway that continued up past her cell must go to an opening onto the roof. And the far wall of the tower, the one she could not see, went down to join the top of a wide outer wall. The tower walls she could see had deteriorated and weathered to the point where they were climbable; with difficulty, but it could be done. If the far wall was in the same condition, and she could get out of her cell, up onto the tower roof . . .

Abruptly, Moira went back to work on her drawing of the tower. Lorenz had appeared in the tower doorway. He stepped out and paused, looking in her direction. Moira glanced toward him, lowered her sketch pad a bit, and motioned to him.

Surprised, Lorenz hesitated. Then he shoved his

hands in his pockets and strolled over, the soles of his shoes crunching tiny fragments of broken stone that littered the inner ward.

Moira braced the pad on her knee and smiled up at him. "What do you think?"

Lorenz looked down at her drawing, then up at the tower, then at the drawing again. "Not bad. That's just what it looks like." He smiled a little. "I didn't know you were an artist."

Moira was aware that he was no longer looking at her sketch of the tower. Earlier, she'd opened the top buttons of her shirt, to get more of the sun. But she appeared not to notice as she held onto her own smile. "I wouldn't call myself an artist." Her tone was relaxed, conversational. "I know my talent's strictly limited, but I do enjoy it. I used to do sketches of my friends, when I was in school. And of course I do a lot of simple drawings at excavation sites, for my work. Sketches of the locations, objects we find—whatever's helpful in supplementing notes."

His attention remained on her opened shirt, and Moira was not sure he heard her words as more than a background sound. She leafed back to the first page of the sketch pad. "Here's something I did earlier. Do you think I caught him?"

It was a three-quarter profile of Bruno, not showing the gray patch on the far cheek. "Of course you've got to bear in mind that I did it from memory. I was afraid if I asked him to sit for me he wouldn't like it."

Lorenz regarded the portrait without pleasure. "That's not how he looks. You're flattering him too much."

Moira frowned at her sketch. "Do you think so?"

"You made the mouth too soft. And the eyes—you missed the meanness. He never looks that relaxed."

"Well, you have to remember, it's only an impression—not a likeness. It's hard to get a person down right unless he poses for you . . ."

Lorenz had stiffened a bit. Moira looked up and saw Bruno coming from behind the ruin of the Romanesque chapel. He was squinting against the sunlight as he walked toward them, but that was not the only reason for his slight scowl.

"If you don't go do the shopping soon," he told Lorenz, "I won't have any meal to cook for us tonight."

He was close enough then for Moira to quickly make a few tiny changes in her sketch of him.

Lorenz shrugged with elaborate carelessness. "She asked me to come have a look at her drawings. I was only being polite." He turned on his heel and walked away across the terrace of the inner ward.

He left it by way of the undercroft entrance at the bottom of the main wall.

Moira was careful not to look too long in that direction. She brought her attention back to Bruno's face, and then quickly erased part of the jawline in her sketch of him, redoing it with two deft pencil movements.

Bruno came closer to look down at what she was doing. He stared at the portrait sketch, startled. After a moment he said: "It's me."

Moira laughed. "Well, at least it's good enough for you to recognize yourself. Like it?"

His answer was slow, and not direct: "You draw quite well." And with no change of tone: "It's time to go in now."

She allowed herself no word or look of reluctance. Obediently, she rose to her feet and waited. Somewhere close, within the ruins or just outside, a car started. Moira listened to the sound of Lorenz driving away, and glanced at the undercroft opening through which he'd left the inner ward. Now she knew the way out.

Bruno took out a ring which held two keys, one for the cuffs and the other for the padlock. He squatted and opened the padlock, detaching it from the ring-bolt in the flooring and snapping it shut again. As always, he faced her as he did this, so no movement she made would escape him. And she already knew the swiftness of his reactions.

Straightening, Bruno nodded at the tower. Moira started toward it, a bit awkward with one end of the chain still attached to her ankle. Bruno followed her, holding the other end. Going up the steps, he held his end of the chain raised, so she wouldn't trip or lose her balance.

When they were inside her cell, he gave her the keys. She sat on the edge of the bed and used one to unlock the cuff from her ankle, while he stood watching her. Taking back the keys, he dropped them in his pocket and looked the chain around his forearm.

He was turning to go when Moira carefully tore his portrait from her sketch pad, and held it out to him. "Here—if you like it."

Bruno frowned at her. "You're giving it to me?"

She nodded and grinned. "A present. Call it a thank-you, for letting me get out in the sun."

He took the sketch from her, not looking at it, still studying her face. "Thank you." He said it slowly. Carrying the sketch and the chain, he went out and closed the door, locking her in.

Moira waited a full five minutes, until she was sure he had gone down the steps. Then she reached into her pockets and took out five small stones she had gathered while sitting out there apparently engrossed in her sketching. The largest was almost as big as the ball of her thumb. The smallest was the size of the fingernail on her little finger. She sat on the bed and slipped the five pebbles out of sight under her pillow, in case Bruno should unexpectedly come to open her door.

Taking off her left boot, Moira placed it on the floor of her cell. She was much more careful about taking off her right boot. The tiny stones she had stuffed down inside it fell to the bottom. Raising her pillow, she turned her boot over and poured them out. Together with the five stones from her pocket, there were now twelve.

In gathering them Moira had left no bare patch out there that Bruno might notice. Each time she'd taken as much of a stroll as the chain allowed, she had managed to kick some of the stone rubble toward the area around her cushion.

Covering all the stones with the pillow, Moira raised the edge of her mattress that rested against the wall. In it she had torn a small hole. Keeping the mattress edge raised with one hand, she used the other to reach under the pillow for a few pebbles at a time, stuffing them inside the hole with the others she'd collected on her previous times out there in the inner ward.

When she was finished she lowered the mattress edge back in place against the wall. Then she stretched out on the bed and waited, staring up at the vaulted ceiling of her cell.

The shadows of dusk were spreading inside the cell when the door was unlocked for her evening meal. Moira swung her legs off the bed and stood up as Bruno came in with her dinner on a tray. Moira smiled and started to say how good it smelled as he put the tray on her bureau. But her smile and words stopped suddenly. There was something else on the tray.

It was a Venus figure. One of the rarest types. With the features of her face still beautifully detailed, in spite of the ravages of age.

"Oh, God . . ." Moira whispered. She reached out to touch it, gently. "She's . . . *Is* she the one Martinot showed us?"

Bruno nodded, watching her reactions. "Yes. The same one."

"Then . . . you must know. Is she genuine? Or a . . ."

"She's real. An authentic Mother goddess." Bruno's

355

deep voice seemed to fondle the words. "You know, she has two natures—good and evil. Lately, I have the feeling she has not been good, for me." He said it lightly, as though half-joking. But there was an undertone that was not light. "Perhaps she'll like being with you better."

Moira tore her gaze from the statuette and looked at Bruno. "You're giving it to me?" She remembered him asking the same, in almost the same tone, when she gave him the sketch.

"Yes, for a time. We'll see, maybe the change will bring both of us luck." Without waiting for her to say more, Bruno left the cell and locked her in.

Moira bent to look more closely into the face of the statuette, and caressed its smooth-worn stone with a fingertip. "Alex," she whispered, "maybe it's a sign . . ."

Her mother, she knew, would have laughed sardonically. But there was a saying Moira was fond of, to stack against her mother's good-natured cynicism: Who knows if it'll help—but it won't hurt.

Half an hour after she'd finished the dinner Bruno came back and took away the tray. Moira waited five minutes after he had gone and relocked her door. Then she removed her right sock and put on both boots. With the boots on it was impossible to see that she wore only one sock. Probing into the hole in her mattress, Moira's finger drew out three of the pebbles. She dropped them into the sock she'd removed. Knowing exactly how many stones she had hidden inside the mattress, Moira counted until the last was inside her sock.

There was a loop string tied to the sock's open end, made from a thread she had unwound from her other sock. Moira slipped the loop around her neck, and let the weighted sock hang down between her breasts. Buttoning her shirt over it, she stood up and looked in the mirror over the bureau.

Her shirt collar hid the loop of thread, and the

bulge of the weighted sock didn't show through the front of her shirt. Moira nodded approvingly and told her mirror image: Thank God you're not flat-chested. Unlooping the weighted sock from around her neck, she closed a hand around the open end and swung it against the palm of her other hand.

It wasn't heavy enough; not yet. But it was going to be. By the time she was finished, what she had here would become a fairly efficient blackjack.

Patting the Earth Mother's small stone head for luck, Moira returned to the bed and began stuffing the stones back inside their hiding place.

3

"To reach Room One, it is necessary to go through Room Two." Donhoff knew Italy well enough not to be confused by the official directions for getting around inside the Archaeological Museum of Florence. It was a matter of ignoring any previous concept about the purpose of a numbering system: "By crossing Room Three one comes to Room Six, from which one enters Room Four."

In Room Four, the Director of the museum was supervising the placement of a new acquisition to the ancient Cypriot vases on display in a glass case. Donhoff introduced himself. "I believe you had a phone call to expect me, from Minister Siviero in Rome."

"Yes, several hours ago. The Minister urged that we give you complete co-operation. But I'm afraid he neglected to explain exactly what it is you wish from us." Behind the Director's polite smile lay a worried mind. With reason. Siviero was in charge of finding stolen works of art for the Italian Government.

Donhoff explained the first part of what he wanted. The Director did not lose his anxiety as he took a last glance at his new display, and led Donhoff down the stairs to the museum's Bas-Reliefs Room. He indicated the right wall. "Is that the one you mean?"

"That's it." Donhoff walked over for a closer examination. Hung on the wall under a glass panel was a painted Egyptian stele depicting the sister goddesses, Isis and Nephthys, back to back.

The Director came up beside Donhoff. "What is wrong with it?"

"Perhaps nothing. See what you think." Donhoff took out the stele that Sawyer had stolen from Christine Jonquet's room in East Berlin, and unwrapped the tissue paper.

The other man scowled at it, reached out tentatively. "With your permission?"

Donhoff gave him the stele. The Director turned it and examined the back and sides, then the face again. He looked several times from it to the identical stele on display, and finally at Donhoff. "It is a remarkably expert copy."

"Which one," Donhoff asked him pointedly. "The one in your hand—or on your wall?"

Half an hour later they had both steles on the desk in the Director's office. The museum's principle authority on Egyptian antiquities stood by the desk, still looking discomfited by his admission that he couldn't determine which was the fake. The Director was on the phone to Rome, explaining the problem to Rodolfo Siviero.

When he hung up, he looked to Donhoff with an expressive shrug. "They will send up a specialist, immediately. He should be here in a few hours. Perhaps a microscopic examination of the stone, and the paint used, will give us our answer."

"I'll check back with you in a few hours, then." Donhoff left the museum, and went to have lunch on the Piazza della Repubblica.

Taking a table outside the Paszkowski Cafe, Donhoff sat with his back to the galleria, so he could keep an eye on the entrance to the Savoy Hotel. He ordered two sandwiches and a half bottle of white wine, and got out the lists he'd been given by Siviero's office in Rome before his flight to Florence.

These lists contained the names of people believed to be involved with the art underworld, with a bit of pertinent information on each. On the plane from Rome, Donhoff had already struck out all the names not involved in the two specialities which interested him: European prehistoric and Egyptian. There were only a few of the former, but a great many of the latter. As he ate, Donhoff devoted himself to eliminating names from his Egyptian list. Since one of the steles had to be a fake, Donhoff was only interested in artists and dealers with a suspicion of forgery attached to their names.

This left him with a much shorter list, but also one he knew to be incomplete. The dealers were probably covered. But there were few artists who did forgeries regularly enough to be in a police record. Many more did such work only occasionally, when the inability to earn a living from their signed paintings drove them to desperation. Some had done it only once. These were going to be the hardest to find.

Donhoff was contemplating this problem over the last of his wine when Titine arrived in front of the Savoy. He called as she got out of the taxi that had brought her from the airport. She strode over carrying her overnight bag, and bent to kiss him on both cheeks before sitting down. Getting a thick manila envelope from her bag, she put it on the table. "Here you are, the new data from Annique Gassin."

By the terms of their partnership contract, Annique could not interfere in her husband's decision to fire any member of their staff. But neither could he interfere in any work she wished to do. The envelope contained data she had worked overnight to compile, on the same subject as the list Donhoff had just been shortening: forgeries of Egyptian antiquities.

"Have you had lunch?" he asked Titine as he opened the envelope.

"On the plane." She nodded at the material he took out. "Half of that's a Xerox, for me. Pierre-Ange made it, when he ran off his own copy."

Donhoff registered her use of the first name, and regarded her thoughtfully. "I'm pleased the two of you have decided to get along. I was a bit worried, at first. I care for him a great deal. But he can be difficult."

"Not for a woman. Whatever else is wrong with your friend, he's a woman lover. It makes the rest worth handling. You'd be surprised, how few men really like women."

"You're very perceptive—but be careful, Titine."

She smiled and patted his hand. "You're not allowed to do that. The Napoleonic Code expressly forbids anyone from interfering with a Frenchwoman's right to get herself into trouble with a man."

Donhoff's slight frown was undermined by amusement. "I hadn't realized you were getting along *that* well."

"We're not. But we probably will, at some point."

Donhoff laughed, shook his head, and dropped the subject. He told her the result of his visit to the archaeological museum. "Whatever they find, we are dealing with art forgery. And we're going to have to split up to cover all the people involved in that line. I'd like you to find a car rental agency and arrange to have two cars waiting for us. Then get over to the museum, and stay there till they have some sort of answer for me."

After she'd gone off, Donhoff went through Annique's lists, comparing the names with those he'd gotten from Rome. He found three that weren't on the Rome list, and added them. Then he restudied what he had. The names that had French addresses would be covered by Sawyer, though he was concentrating on the Venus figure. With Titine, Donhoff would confine his search to Italy, at first. If they failed here, they would have to spread the search to the rest of Europe. He hoped to God it wouldn't have to come to that.

He hoped, too, that nothing they were doing would inadvertently result in the death of Moira Rhalles. He had known investigations which had begun for the best of reasons and caused tragedy. Only a few, but those would never cease to haunt him. He didn't want another like them, at this stage of his life.

Donhoff had finished his work on the lists, and was having coffee with cake, when Titine returned from the museum. The answer she brought was far from conclusive: "That specialist from Rome is a cautious type. He *thinks* the museum's stele is the fake, and the one you brought is authentic."

"But he's not sure."

"Not enough to stand behind it. He's taking them both back with him to Rome, where they'll be put through a complete series of laboratory tests. You're supposed to keep in touch. They'll give you a definite answer when they know."

Donhoff finished his coffee and put it aside. "We already know one thing that's definite enough to go on. The art forger we're looking for is a top professional; good enough so that a miscroscopic examination of his work isn't enough to tell a specialist whether it's a fake. Somebody who made a speciality of Egyptian work, knows how to duplicate the paints used, and how to age them. Bear that in mind."

He gave Titine one copy of Annique Gassin's lists, with more than two thirds of the names crossed out and others added from the Rome lists. "You take the north. I'll start here and work south. We continue to keep in touch through Olivier. And good luck to all of us."

4

In Paris, the sunlight lay heavy against the length of the Louvre, but on the other side of the river the tall, solid buildings along the Quai Voltaire were in deep shadow. Most of the light in the fifth-floor room above the quay came from hidden lamps shining through forty translucent green jade panels in an expanded Chinese screen. It cast a greenish glow over everything in the room, including the old man seated behind the desk, flanked by a prancing bronze horse.

"Marcel Alfani telephoned me from Marseilles this morning, Monsieur Sawyer. I have his assurance that nothing you learn from me will be passed on to the police, or used to harm myself or others I mention."

"You have my assurance, as well," Sawyer told him.

Asadour Bedrozian smiled softly. "Thank you. But I would rather have Alfani's. He makes himself responsible for you. Even at my age, I would not care to betray the trust of such a man."

Bedrozian was ninety, with skin like faded paper. The voice was faded, too. All of his remaining vitality had been sapped from the rest of him, to fill the huge dark eyes. "Tell me, please—who first gave you my name? Marcel Alfani said it was not him."

"There are files on you in three criminal-data banks that I know of," Sawyer told him. "At Interpol in St. Cloud, in Room 265 at Scotland Yard's Art and Antiques Squad, at the Department for Recovery of Missing Art Works in Rome."

"And what do they say about me?" There was no anxiety in the faded voice. The darkness of the vibrant eyes held curiosity, nothing more. "We will call this information the price you pay, for whatever it is you wish to learn from me."

"They say you're prosperous as a legitimate dealer. But you've built a much bigger fortune on looted antiquities. They also believe you have high-level protection, because you've never had trouble with the law in this country." Sawyer smiled briefly. "I'd have to agree with that. There's not a single reference to you in any French police records. I'm assuming you were on file, and had it removed."

"You assume correctly. It was ridiculously expensive." Bedrozian toyed with a Minoan dagger in an ornamented copper sheath. "What else?"

"You financed quite a number of looting excavations at archaeological sites, shortly after their discovery—getting everything of value out before archaeologists could mount authorized digs. But you gave this up some years ago—though Rome and Scotland Yard are both sure you're still buying and selling stolen antiquities."

Bedrozian sighed. "In this field, Monsieur Sawyer, who can say what is stolen—and what is not?" His skeletal hand moved out to stroke the bronze horse beside him. "I believe this was made five hundred years before Christ, by an Athenian sculptor named Calamis. Two centuries later it was in Syracuse. How did it get there? No one knows. But there it was, when Archimedes' ingenious defense engines were finally overcome by the besieging Romans, and they sacked the city. Marcellus took it back to Rome with him. Did he have a right to do so, as the conquering soldier? Or was he no different from a common thief? After his death, it disappears—and reappears fifteen hundred years later, in the estate of a wealthy Italian family outside Parma. There are no family records of how it got there. Thirty years ago what was left of the family knew difficult times, and sold it to me."

The old man patted the bronze horse fondly. "Now, does it belong to me—or is it stolen property? If it is not legally mine, who does it belong to?"

He waved at an exquisite ebony-and-ivory chest. "That is from Constantinople—which no longer exists. One of the noble Crusaders who sacked that city stole it, and brought it back home to France. His descendants still had it, when their estate near Rouen was robbed six years ago. The thieves sold it to me. Does it belong to me, since I bought and paid a reasonable price for it? Or does it belong to the family of the man who stole it from Constantinople? You see how difficult the matter of ownership can be, where genuine antiquities are concerned."

Picking up a silver belt plate he was using as a paperweight, Bedrozian told Sawyer: "This is part of a Celtic treasure which Hungarian workers dredged out of the Danube at the turn of the century. They sold it to an Armenian collector living in Smyrna. He was slaughtered with the rest of his family at the end of the First World War, when the Turks massacred the Armenians and Greeks. A Turkish dealer looted it from his house. I paid a thief to steal it from the dealer's shop in Istanbul. The Turkish Government would say it belongs to Turkey. I find it hard to agree. In fact, I find it hard to agree with most government claims of ownership."

Bedrozian nodded through the single small window at the Louvre on the other side of the Seine. "Does that museum have a right to a mastaba, just because Bonaparte was strong enough to steal it from Egypt? In that case I must think I have a right to it, if I am clever enough to take it from the museum."

Sawyer smiled. "As you say, the problem of ownership in your field is difficult."

"Quite. And now, Monsieur Sawyer, you have indulged me enough. What is it I can do for you?"

Sawyer took out two photographs of Christine Bieler Jonquet. One was the copy of her passport picture, the other from her registration file at the Louvre School. "Have you ever met this girl in your dealings? It would have been in the last four years."

Bedrozian took considerable time studying the photos, before shaking his head. "No. I don't think so."

"What about a man with a grayish mark on his cheek? He's in his thirties, stocky, with pale gray eyes and a deep voice. I don't have a picture of him, and I don't know if the mark on his cheek is a birthmark or a scar of some kind. But it's quite conspicuous; the first thing anyone who's seen him mentions."

The old dealer thought about it for a time. Again he shook his head. "I don't remember a man with such a mark."

Sawyer was getting used to it. He'd been getting the same negative answers over two solid days of talking to people like Bedrozian. Donhoff and Titine, showing the same pictures and asking the same questions in Italy, were being no luckier.

So far the three of them had gotten results only in one area: some new names to check with in the art underworld. By regularly comparing these names, and confining themselves to those that came up most often, they were narrowing the area of their search. But the time left was also narrowing. And they'd found no new lead that went beyond being a possibility, into something solid.

In spite of this, Sawyer was certain they were asking their questions of the right people. His head told him, and so did his instincts. If he was right, there had to be someone in the art underworld who had answers that would open a door for them. As he took out the next picture Sawyer had no special anticipation of finding his breakthrough with Asadour Bedrozian. But at the same time he knew that if it did not come through this man, it would be through the next—or the one after that.

He put the picture on the desk. "Do you know of anything like this being put up for sale secretly, at any time in the past?"

It was a color photograph of the stele depicting Isis and Nephthys back to back. Bedrozian studied it with pleasure. "No, I have never been contacted about this particular piece. But it would be easy to sell, if the price were reasonable. Real or fake?"

"Does it matter?"

"An authentic Egyptian work is always easier. But a really well-made forgery is not too difficult to dispose of, either. *Is* it a forgery?"

Sawyer told him about what Donhoff had learned so far, from the Florence museum. Bedrozian regarded the picture again. "I haven't heard of anyone stealing this piece and replacing it with a copy. This sort of thing is usually the opening gambit of a standard confidence game, you know."

Sawyer nodded. "Steal the real work, replace it with a fake, then notify the authorities anonymously. They check, learn the museum's real piece is gone, and it gets in the newspapers. With that kind of publicity, whoever lifted the real one can make half a dozen more copies—and pass off each one as the authentic stolen work to a different private collector."

"Exactly. But with this one I haven't heard of it being done. And I probably would have. Odd."

"I'd like any idea you might have, on who *could* have been involved in stealing, forging, and fencing this stele."

"Most of them are in Italy." Bedrozian's voice was becoming a bit more faded. He thought for some time before supplying certain names, and where to find the men attached to those names.

Sawyer got out his notebook and marked down the ones he didn't already know. After two days of this, he knew the names on his list by heart. When he had marked down the final name and location, Sawyer had a request: "Monsieur Bedrozian, I'll be seeing some of the people you've mentioned. I'd like your permission to use you as a reference; to tell them you'll vouch for it being safe to talk to me openly."

"That is no problem, since Marcel Alfani remains responsible for you." Bedrozian sighed and leaned back in his chair. "I'm afraid I have not been much help to you with the rest of it."

"There's one thing more." Sawyer held out a composite photograph he'd had made. It was based on Professor Borelli's description of the statuette Martinot had shown him: the stylized hair and individualized features of the Venus figure from Brassempouy, with the body of the one from Gagarino. "Do you know of something like this moving around the under-counter antiquities markets?"

Bedrozian took the photograph from him. "Recently?"

"Or at any time in the past."

The old dealer studied the picture briefly. "No. I have never seen a Venus figure of this kind anywhere —this head, with this figure. Does it really exist?"

"I've reason to think so." Sawyer regarded Bedrozian's expression. "You look skeptical."

"Because I've never seen it before. There are so few of these, you can identify each one immediately."

"Suppose a looter turned one up while rifling a prehistoric excavation. Mightn't he keep it to himself, until he could find a buyer?"

"It's possible. But the demand for such a piece would be so very limited."

"In spite of its rarity?"

"And because of that rarity. Museums are becoming much more timid about purchasing such rarities without proper authenticity and source documents. Newspapers spread stories; governments make difficulties. The only purchaser would be a private collector, content to hide it where no one else could ever admire it."

"But antiquities misers do exist."

"Yes, and a number of them are interested in prehistoric works. But not going as far back as the Paleolithic. What is there from the Stone Age worth collecting? On the one hand you have objects of no beauty and only scientific interest: fragments of pottery and bones, and simple stone tools, which are meaningless except in an over-all museum collection of an entire site. On the other hand, the two things of beauty: The cave paintings, which cannot be removed because they would disintegrate to dust in the process. And the Venus figures, of which there are so few that you could not dispose of one openly without authorization. That leaves private collectors—and none of them, to my knowledge, are building Paleolithic collections."

"And you *would* know."

"I believe so. I am part of a very small shadow world. Word passes through it rather quickly."

"Are you saying that you couldn't get rid of a Venus figure, if you happened to find one?"

Asadour Bedrozian picked up the Minoan dagger again, and leaned back in his chair as he toyed with it. "It would require considerable thought and time, with delicate feelers put out. Even then I might have to resign myself, finally, to keeping it for my own personal pleasure. Which I wouldn't mind, if it were authentic."

Sawyer gestured at the photograph. "And if it's a forgery?"

"In that case it would be of no interest at all to me. And impossible to sell, for a price which would make the effort worthwhile. For the reasons I've already given. But for these same reasons, no one would bother to forge a Venus figure.

"I'm interested in who *could* forge one, whatever the reason for it. Someone skilled enough to fool a specialist in Paleolithic works."

Bedrozian gave that considerable thought. "I know of some sculptors who have done superb copies of later works," he told Sawyer finally. He was beginning to look tired, and the fading in his voice was more pronounced. "Perhaps one of those . . ."

Once more, Sawyer took down the ones that were new to him. When Bedrozian completed his naming of sculpture forgers, Sawyer returned to the other possibility: that the Venus figure was real:

"I accept that there's not enough of a market for a plundering expedition to deliberately go after a Paleolithic site. But let's suppose a crew was excavating for later works—say Bronze Age—and happened to break through into a Stone Age stratum. And one of the looters turned up a Venus figure. And, knowing it was impossible to dispose of, decided to keep it for himself."

Bedrozian's expression was dubious. "Most of the men who make up these site-stripping crews are not that sensitive to such things. But yes, it is a possibility."

"Have you ever heard of professional looters who hit by chance on Stone Age remains, which *might* have contained a Venus figure? It would probably have had to be a cave site."

"Yes, it would . . ." Bedrozian sat frowning to himself for some time, thinking back over the decades. His eyes half closed, as though he were falling asleep. "I seem to recall . . . Wait . . . It was some years ago. Six or eight years . . ."

Sawyer held himself very still, waiting, his narrowed eyes on the old man's face. He watched him struggle with his memories, trying to sort it out.

Bedrozian shook his head unhappily. "You must understand, at my age the memory begins to play nasty tricks. Sometimes I can't remember what I did yesterday. At other times I remember quite vividly things I did as a child. That is why I now come in to work only two hours each day. My daughter and her husband really run the business now. You should talk to them . . ."

"I did," Sawyer reminded him tensely. "Downstairs, before coming up to talk to you."

Bedrozian laughed at himself, and sighed. "Yes . . . true. You see? I forgot." His eyes wandered back to the composite picture of the Venus figure. Suddenly they opened fully, and the sleepiness was gone. "Of course—it was Guy Colpin. He was based in Lyons at the time. Doing what I used to do: financing site-stripping expeditions to newly discovered finds. But on a much smaller scale. And he didn't have my outlets, often had to come to me to act as a middleman for his goods . . ."

Bedrozian paused, frowning, thinking back. Sawyer made no sound. It had finally happened, as he'd known it must.

"As I said," the old dealer resumed, "it was almost ten years ago." He put his clawlike hand on the photograph. "I'm not saying it was this. But it could have been. Colpin told me that he knew of a small stone statuette of a woman that somebody had found with a good many flint and bone artifacts. In a cave somewhere."

"That would fit," Sawyer said tightly. "What else?"

"That was all Colpin knew about it, I think. Whoever had made the find wanted to sell the lot, including the flints and bone points. Colpin wanted to know about the chance of an undercover sale to a museum."

"And?" Sawyer put pressure on himself to hang onto his patience, just a little longer.

Bedrozian shrugged. "I never heard from Colpin about it again. It would not have resulted in a very large sale. So, I forgot about it."

"Where is Guy Colpin now?"

"Unfortunately, I don't know. He's been in hiding from the police for almost a year. A matter of some stolen Picassos. Colpin has a cousin who might know. Jean Dufour—a sculptor who did work for him at one point. But I don't know where you'd find him now. I haven't heard anything of Dufour in years . . ."

Half an hour later Sawyer drove south out of Paris. Jean Dufour had been one of the names in Annique's original listing of antiquities forgers. Sawyer knew how to find him.

5

Jean Dufour was a self-taught sculptor who had never seen the inside of a classroom of any kind. At forty he could speak four languages without thinking about it, though he couldn't read or write in any of them. He was known as the Gargoyle Maker.

In his younger days he had earned his living by repairing and reproducing age-damaged statuary on religious buildings throughout Europe. His specialty had been gargoyles. For some years Dufour had been considered the best man to get when a church needed to replace one of those fantasy monsters out of medieval nightmares. But he'd become unable to curb his own fantasies. Church authorities found themselves getting creatures that had crawled out of his own nightmarish imaginings. When they began refusing to pay for what they hadn't ordered, Dufour had switched to making fakes for the art underworld.

"I don't do much of that these days," he told Sawyer. "I started this shop as a cover for it, but it's gotten to be profitable enough on its own. Last few years, I've only done fakes when the money was *very* good. Or," he added with a dreamy smile, "if it was something amusing, so I just couldn't resist the temptation."

They sat in wicker chairs in front of Dufour's curio shop on the main square of Conques, a medieval town in the heart of the Massif Central. Dufour had phoned Paris, gotten Bedrozian's endorsement of Sawyer, and phoned someone who knew how to get in touch with Guy Colpin. Now they were waiting for Colpin's call.

"You know," Dufour said, "it was because of me that Guy got into his present line. He started by peddling my fakes—and gradually expanded."

Sawyer nodded toward the Romanesque tympanum on the church across the square. It was crammed with sculptured images of heaven and hell, and Sawyer had noted statues similar to the hell images for sale in Dufour's shop. "You have a lot of inspiration over there."

Dufour nodded emphatically. "They're damned exciting, that's sure. But to just copy—a bore. And that's what the government restoration departments always want, naturally. Exact copies. No fun at all. Look how much those old-time sculptors had with the originals." He pointed toward the hell section of the tympanum. "That sinner getting his tongue torn out. And that big rabbit helping a devil cook a poacher who used to steal rabbits from church lands. And how about that girl hung up naked by her ankles, being tortured by two imps."

"Freud would have found some of those pretty interesting."

"I guess you mean they were perverts?" Dufour grinned. "Well, I must be, too. I sure don't want to spend all my time copying *their* perversions, when I can think of enough of my own. That's the nice thing about doing stuff for people like my cousin or Bedrozian. They don't want exact copies. Not of this stuff."

Sawyer nodded. "Everybody knows where the originals of these are. An exact copy wouldn't fool anybody."

"What they need is something different, but that looks *like* the real stuff. Done with the same materials and techniques, and the same kind of gruesome imagination." Dufour giggled. "Like what I do—stuff they can pass off as having just been discovered somewhere, that's *obviously* out of a known period, by a known school of workers."

"But—you don't do it anymore."

Dufour gave Sawyer a sly smile. "Well . . . one of

these days my wife's uncle is going to dig a well on his farm, and come across certain pieces very much like those hell statues over there. Different tortures, but same style and looking just as old. You'll hear about it—museums'll be fighting each other to buy them."

Sawyer glanced impatiently at the shop, then got out his photographs of Christine Jonquet. "Since we're just waiting—have you ever come across this girl?"

He went through the entire routine with the Gargoyle Maker: the pictures and the questions. Dufour, was ready to be helpful, but he had never met Christine, knew no man in his field with a gray mark on one cheek, and had no idea of who had done the stele forgery.

"Egyptian work—and paint—both out of my field."

Sawyer showed him the composite of the Venus figure. "Is this what your cousin mentioned to Bedrozian?"

"I don't know. Guy never showed it to me, if he ever had it to show. Maybe he just knew about somebody else who did."

"Could you copy something like this, well enough to fool an expert?"

"Easy. Any good sculptor could do it, if he spent a little time first studying the technique and kind of stone used."

"Every heard of something like this being faked?"

Dufour shook his head. "No, but that don't mean much. I don't know anything going on outside my own period. Charlemagne to sixteenth century, that's it for me. I stick to the Middle Ages."

Inside his store, the phone began puzzing. Jean Dufour went in and disappeared behind a massive sculpture of a mermaid wrestling a winged serpent with a horned devil's head. Sawyer wasn't sure if it was lust, battle, or a bit of both.

The Gargoyle Maker came out and nodded. "It's

all set. Guy'll see you, if you can be at a house he's using at seven tomorrow morning. Not before that— and he's moving out an hour later."

He gave Sawyer the address. It was south of Arles, on the edge of the Camargue marshes.

6

In New York, stewardess Angela Lewis went out of town with her boy friend, and gave four men Lang had assigned to her two days of fresh air in upper Connecticut. The small converted farmhouse in Litchfield explained where the extra money she'd been depositing into her bank account had gone. From what Lang's tappers got, her lover thought she was paying for the place out of an unexpected inheritance.

They didn't get much else out of the two days. The couple spent their holiday making love, sleeping, eating, taking long walks. No contacts.

Lang stayed in the New York area over the two days, directing surveillance and background investigation on another courier who'd been spotted doing the same job as Angela Lewis. Gerhard Hubmann, still being watched and listened in on by the station agents in Vienna, had picked up another tape for Budapest. This time he'd gotten it beside the Sarajevo car in the Military Museum, from a flight engineer on a New York–Vienna run.

His name was Hendrix. He had an apartment across the river from Manhattan, in Fort Lee, New Jersey. Sharing it with him were a wife and three children. There was no past record on Hendrix, but there was a bank account that had been growing steadily from unknown sources.

Like Angela Lewis, Hendrix did nothing on his return from Vienna that told Lang anything of use. But, again like Angela Lewis, the bank account told Lang what he needed to know: the courier work was not a one-time aberration. Both would do it again. This meant they would have to make contact again with whoever gave them the code tapes. Lang's crews stayed on both of them around the clock. Lang ate and slept in the midtown office from which he controlled both crews, and waited.

On the night after her return from the country, Angela Lewis got out of her lover's bed at 2 A.M., told him she'd like to go to the Litchfield house again when she returned from Vienna, and spent the rest of the night in her own apartment. No contact.

She left in the morning at eight-thirty, carrying her flight bag, and had breakfast in a diner on Lexington Avenue in the Fifties. At 9 A.M. the record-and-tape store across the street opened for business. Two minutes later Angela Lewis came out of the diner, crossed Lexington, and entered the store.

Only the owner was inside at the time. Angela Lewis asked him if he'd gotten the cassette she'd been waiting for. He said it was all ready for her, got a small wrapped package from behind his counter, and gave it to her. Angela Lewis put it in her flight bag and left quickly.

She took a cab eight blocks to the branch of Manufacturers Hanover where she kept her account. One of the tail cars stopped beside the cab at a red light. Angela Lewis was observed to be doing something hurried with what was inside her bag.

At the bank she deposited the regular sum: two hundred dollars. In cash, as always. Then she took another taxi out to Kennedy, and boarded the 747 to which she'd been assigned for that day's flight to Vienna.

By that time Lang was concentrating all his own efforts on the next link in the enemy's communications chain: the owner of the record store on Lexington. He knew it had been too easy so far. When it got hard, he'd know he was close to the source.

7

In Milan, Titine sat in the back office of Roberto Giordano, owner of one of the city's better art galleries. What made him of special value, for Titine's purpose, was that five years ago he had been one of the principal outside advisers for the assembling of a traveling museum exhibition on art forgeries. Giordano was quite willing to use his expertise to help her, but he had to shake his head over the photograph of the Egyptian stele. "I have not heard anything about this work being forged."

"I was hoping you could suggest some artists you feel would be *capable* of doing this one. Or at least any you know who have specialized in Egyptian antiquities."

"I could suggest many names, my dear. But—so very many. Not too helpful for your purpose, I'm afraid. Sometimes it seems that every artist who has ever lived has done forgeries to buy a meal or pay his rent. Look at all the false Michelangelos in circulation. Every year another appears. But in *his* time, even Michelangelo did forgeries, which he passed off as classical antiquities. So you see, it goes with the profession." Giordano frowned again at the photograph Titine had given him. "But artists who understand the composition of paints used in ancient Egypt —I could make a list for you. Far from complete, but . . ."

"I'd appreciate that."

"As I said, far from complete. And at the same time quite long. Perhaps two dozen names . . ." Giordano flicked the picture with a recently manicured fingernail. "You are sure it is the one the museum had which is the forgery?"

"We are now." Titine told Giordano what Donhoff

had learned that morning from Rome: X-rays had revealed, hidden under the supposedly ancient paint on the stele, a quite modern word painted on the stone, "*FALSO*"—fake.

Giordano laughed good-naturedly. "These artists! All with their little egos!"

"I was hoping that narrowed down who the forger might be."

"I'm sorry—for you—but it narrows down the possibilities not at all. So many play these kinds of tricks on us, you see. They are hurt in their pride, because they have to earn money with work that they pretend is not theirs. It is their way of thumbing the nose at the stupidity of the art world. Some have even left their initials, concealed somewhere on a forgery. *That* would help you, but in this case . . ." Giordano shook his head, and got a large address book from the middle drawer of his desk.

"Now I will make you the list I promised. But be forewarned, it will probably . . ."

The phone on his desk rang. Giordano picked it up, listened, and looked to Titine: "It is for you, from Rome."

Titine took the phone. It was Donhoff at the other end: "I'm flying up to Genoa. I've booked rooms for us at the Hotel Bristol. If you leave Milan now, we can meet there by six this evening."

"What's happened?"

"I think I know who it is," Donhoff told her. "The artist who did the stele."

SEVENTEEN

1

"I'm not a crook," Mario Fontanelli told them. "Everybody who buys something from me knows *I* made it. What *they* tell people they sell my work to—that is not my affair."

There was a frayed dignity to the artist as he moved about his workroom in the old warehouse near the Genoa docks, showing his work to Donhoff and Titine. He stopped before two life-size figures in the middle of the cavernous room. "These are pure acts of creation. Born from nothing but a need to express what is in me."

The figures were made of glassy plastic. One was a green dead man hanging by his neck from a blue noose attached to an aluminum tree. The other was a shiny red woman sprawled erotically on her back across a real mattress, her head flung back, legs spread, feet braced apart.

"Unfortunately for me," Fontanelli said bitterly as he turned away from them, "self-expression has so far in my career proved to be the least of my assets. I continue to earn most of my living using my skills to serve the needs of others." He waved a hand at several large purple angels dangling from ceiling wires, and a silvery St. George slaying a gilded dragon. "Also my work—but made on order, to decorate shops on the Via Venti Settembre."

"And over here—a commissioned work of a different kind." He led Donhoff and Titine to a large mosaic tabletop, depicting objects symbolic of the equalizing forces of fate and death, surrounding a grinning skull. It had a look of great age, though it was just in the process of being finished. "This was ordered by a regular customer who never gives his name—but does give me half the fee in advance. It is based on several mosaics found in Pompeii. Though not an exact copy of any one of them, it borrows motifs from all. I can imagine that perhaps the man I make it for will sell it for a great deal more than he pays me, by pretending it is an ancient work he has looted from still-covered parts of Pompeii. But, I am not involved in this. *I* pretend nothing."

Fontanelli looked at Titine, not Donhoff, as he drove his point home: "You understand? Three types of work here: what I do for my own satisfaction; what I do for other reasons that are explained to me; what I do for reasons I can only guess. But all have one thing in common: I made them and I sell them as my own."

Titine nodded solemnly. It seemed to satisfy him. He smiled at her, and motion to Donhoff. Walking back to a long wooden table, he picked up the photograph of the Egyptian stele. "It was the same with this. Even without the phone call from Clarice, I would not be afraid to tell you I made it."

Clarice was the dealer in stolen and forged art who had vouched for Donhoff. She was also the one who had named Fontanelli as the probable creator of the stele. *Probable*—it hadn't been sure until this moment. Titine shot Donhoff a relieved look.

"I asked her to introduce us over the phone," Donhoff explained to Fontanelli, "because I want to talk about someone whose dealings are less open than yours: the person you made this stele for."

"I did it for Archibald Mather," Fontanelli said without hesitation. "I doubt that he would care about anything I tell concerning him. At least, for the next twenty years."

Archie Mather was an English art thief who had

been on one of Annique Gassin's lists. He was doing thirty years in prison for killing a policeman who'd caught him robbing the home of a London collector of early Chinese jades.

"It's nine years since he was sent up." Donhoff spoke half to himself. The timing, and the background of Mather, seemed unrelated to the trail he was trying to follow.

Fontanelli nodded sourly. "Serves him right. If I had known he was so violent, and stupid, I would not have dealt with him. But he seemed perfectly normal at the time. And his request was simple enough."

"He wanted you to copy the stele."

"But with the word 'false' concealed under the paint. And he paid well, considering that it was a fairly easy job. I went to Florence, took pictures of the stele, made my notes, came back. The copy was finished in less than three days. Mather paid me the rest of the fee we'd agreed on, and took it away with him. Three weeks later he decided he wanted five more copies, so he brought back the stele for me to work from."

"Yours—or the museum's?"

"I don't really know," Fontanelli said, with professional pride. "I'm very good, you see. Even *I* couldn't detect any difference between the two. Only an X-ray could answer that."

"You didn't ask Mather?"

Fontanelli's smile was angelic. "I told you—these things are none of my business. I didn't want to know. I do the work—that is all."

"How many more copies did you make?"

"None, as it turned out. You see, I had other work to finish first. Mather went back to England, saying he would return for the new copies in a few weeks. But just when I was ready to begin work on his copies, I heard the idiot had been arrested for murdering a policeman. So there I was, with the stele, and no point in making others."

"Less than a week ago," Donhoff told him, "that stele was found in East Berlin. Any idea of how it got there?"

Fontanelli raised his shoulders and screwed his face into a who-knows grimace. "I kept it for over two years. Then a man who had heard of my work came to see me. An Algerian Arab. He wanted to know if I could do some authentic-looking Etruscan frescoes, and how much they would cost. We discussed these matters, and he said he would probably contact me again after discussing it with someone else. I showed him this stele, as an example of the kind of work I could do. He didn't know what it was, so I explained to him—about Isis and Nephthys as the two faces of the goddess of man's destiny. He was amused."

"Amused?"

"He said it was funny, because he had a young partner in Marseilles who was interested in this subject. He thought it would be an amusing present to give him, if the price was reasonable." Fontanelli shrugged. "A small profit is better than none. I made him a very reasonable price, and he took it. That is the last I know of this stele."

"You told him it was the original?"

"I was quite honest with him. I explained that I could not swear to it, but that it probably was."

"What did he look like?"

"Thin. Short. Dark. An Arab. Typical."

"Do you remember his name?"

"Hamid."

"Half the Arabs in the world are named Hamid, or some variation of it. What is the rest of it?"

"Hamid is all the name he gave."

Titine watched Donhoff exert willpower to remain patient.

"Who sent him to you?"

"Someone in Marseilles, he said. He did not name the person. As I have explained, there is no reason for me to be overly cautious. I cheat no one."

"Did he come back to you, about the Etruscan frescoes he wanted copied?"

"No. I never saw him again."

"Why?"

"I don't know."

Donhoff questioned Fontanelli for twenty minutes longer, without learning anything else.

On their way back to the Hotel Bristol, Titine said tentatively: "It isn't much, is it?"

"It is more than we had before," Donhoff told her. But he was not exactly exuberant about what it was they had: "We know the stele was bought by an Algerian Arab named Hamid. Who is involved in art crime. Who is from Marseilles. Who has a young partner interested in variations of ancient goddesses."

He made a call from the hotel to Olivier in Paris, asking for Sawyer to phone him there. They had dinners sent up to them in Donhoff's room and were having coffee after the dinner when the room phone rang. It was Sawyer, calling from Arles. He explained to Donhoff about his appointment next morning with Guy Colpin, and then asked what was happening in Italy. Donhoff told him.

Sawyer heard him out, and was silent for a long moment after Donhoff finished. Finally he said: "It's too thin, Fritz."

"It's all we have at this point. And it fits what we know. The Arab's partner likes images of ancient goddesses. And he's the last person we know of who had the stele. That's the man we're looking for. And he's in Marseilles."

"*Was.* Seven years ago. *If* Fontanelli's remembering that accurately."

"He is. Trust me—his memory is quite reliable. Frankly, I thought you'd be relieved. Marseilles is one city where you can get all the help you'll need."

"With help or without it, Marseilles is a damned big city. It'll take a lot of time. I don't want to concentrate all that time and effort in one place—and then find out it was the wrong place to invest it."

"It's all we have," Donhoff repeated.

There was another short silence at Sawyer's end. Then: "Stay put where you are, Fritz. I'll call you again tomorrow morning, after I've talked to Colpin."

"Unless you get something better from him," Donhoff told Sawyer, gently but firmly, "Marseilles has to be our next move. You're too emotionally involved. It tires the mind, interferes with the ability to think straight."

"That's possible."

"It's probable. Sleep on it."

2

Under the El at State and Lake the street had a dark-wet sheen in the rainy night. One of Chicago's young patrolmen lay face down in a black puddle. A shotgun blast had struck him in the neck at point-blank range, almost decapitating him. But from the back seat of the car it was impossible to see blood, because the rainwater around the body, rippled by a wind coming off the lake, reflected the red neon sign of a bar nearby.

They'd been driving home from a movie when the first police call on the killing had come over the radio. His grandfather had immediately changed direction and driven to the scene.

"It's not good for Petey to see this," his grandmother said angrily.

"You're wrong," his grandfather told her. "He's old enough to learn what life is like for a cop. How we walk with death every day."

He got out of the car and walked toward the corpse with that slow, steady tread of his. One of the cops spotted him coming and snapped a salute. It all became mixed in the boy's head: the regal stride of his grandfather, the respectful salute, the fallen "soldier" in the puddle at his feet, and the romanticism of his grandfather's phrase.

It was a long time before he realized that the implication in the phrase was not true; cops were not the only ones who walked with death every day. Everyone did. It could come to an impoverished old woman, because the fourteen-year-old kids who mugged her were mad about finding less than a dollar in her pocketbook. To a high-priced call girl because she couldn't get out of her penthouse at the top of a modern building hit by a flash fire from a faulty circuit. To an entire family in a Toyota because a truck driver in another lane had a heart attack from too much driving with lousy food and too little sleep.

And to an archaeologist because her husband left his ivory tower for a while to serve his government.

Sawyer reached out in the darkness and patted his hand on the table beside the bed until he found his watch. The luminous dial showed a few minutes before five in the morning. He hadn't been able to fall asleep until two. And the three hours of sleep had been ragged, nagged by premonitions that he was moving too slowly, that Moira was already dead.

He put down the watch and forced his eyes shut, trying to lull himself back to sleep by concentrating on the sound of the fountain in the square outside the shuttered hotel window. Seconds later the bell in the church tower across the square began to toll the hour. Sawyer's eyes snapped wide open. He was groggy and there was more than an hour left before he had to drive south out of Arles. But his brain was working too fast, going over and over the same ground, to allow him any more sleep.

Sawyer snapped on the bedside lamp and dragged himself out of the bed. It was a large room, with a sink, toilet, and bathtub behind a wicker screen. He filled the tub with tepid water and soaked in it for five minutes, sloshing the water over his head and face repeatedly in an effort to get the rest of his nervous system as awake as his brain. Toweling himself vigorously, he dressed and quietly left the hotel.

He was grateful for the reviving chill in the morning air as he walked briskly past the ruins of the Roman amphitheater, in the direction of the bus terminal on the edge of the old town. The sky was still dark, except for a faint pale blue beginning to stain the horizon in advance of the dawn. The slice of moon was very distinct, in spite of the lights of the bistro and gas station already opening for business along the main road. Sawyer entered the bistro and had a strong coffee with an apple tart for breakfast. His eyes burned with lack of sleep and his body still felt too heavy when he'd finished. He bought another coffee and carried it out to a table on the sidewalk.

Sitting there, he sipped the coffee and sucked cool morning air into his lungs, fighting away the last of the grogginess. Around him night silence still held the town, except for an occasional automobile or bus going past. Sawyer lit a cigarette and smoked it slowly, waiting. Guy Colpin wouldn't like it if he showed up before the scheduled meeting time; and he wanted Colpin in a responsive mood.

The church bells began to toll six o'clock. With the very last of the six clangs, the starlings in the trees on both sides of the main road awoke and began to shrill at each other. Thousands of them. The high-pitched din became enormous, like a roomful of tiny whistles all blasting at the same time. Sawyer got up and walked back to his car, parked behind the hotel. The full light of dawn was pouring through the narrow streets of the town.

It was quarter past six when he drove out of Arles. Fifteen minutes later he was entering the Camargue, a vast expanse of marshes created by the Rhône delta, spreading south all the way to the Mediterranean

Sea. The terrain became dead flat, more water than land, most of it hidden by a heavy fog lifting into the slowly warming air. Sawyer drove between the rice paddies cultivated in the desalinated northern part of the Camargue. The rising sun appeared as a pale disk in the mist.

He came to a fork in the road and took the one to the right. It swung down along the western edge of the Camargue, into the miles of salt marshes and lagoons that were the last refuge in Europe for wild beaver and flamingo. Sawyer slowed a bit, timing himself to arrive at the rendezvous at exactly seven. The mist began to thin out, and quite suddenly the sun materialized in blazing strength, glaring off salt flats and water. There was no other car on the road, and no house in sight; only the dead-flat marshes, stretching in all directions to the horizons.

Four half-wild white horses appeared in the distance, racing across a salt flat. Nearer to the road black cattle waded belly-deep in a marsh, eating clumps of tall grass rising out of the muddy water. Then a ramshackle ranch house appeared, on an artificially raised hump of ground. Sawyer drove past, and glanced at his watch. Two minutes to go. The next house would be the rendezvous.

The ranch house was out of sight behind him when he saw it up ahead: a small clapboard house on the side of the road. It was dilapidated and had the look of being abandoned. But two trucks were parked in front of it. One was a small panel truck. The other was a massive trailer truck. It bore the T.I.R. plate indicating it was licensed for international hauling between Europe and Western Asia. Four men were having trouble lifting a large packing crate out of it, carrying it toward the panel truck. They froze in position, looking at Sawyer's car approaching.

Sawyer slowed and swung to a stop beside the road fifteen feet beyond the two trucks. He took his time turning off the ignition, and placed both hands in plain sight on top of the steering wheel. And waited.

A squat man with a battered face and almost no forehead appeared beside Sawyer's open window. He was wearing an open raincoat. His right hand was out of sight inside the pocket, along with something else. "What do you want here?" he demanded harshly.

Sawyer kept his hands up on the rim of the steering wheel. "My name is Sawyer. Guy Colpin is expecting me."

It took a moment for the squat man to digest it. "Get out of the car. Slowly."

Sawyer did so, careful to do nothing with either hand that might alarm him. The squat man's right hand remained in the pocket as his other patted Sawyer all over, swiftly and expertly. When he was satisfied that Sawyer was not armed, he said, "Wait here." Sawyer nodded and remained beside his car, watching the squat man walk quickly back to the trucks.

The four men with the crate were now loading it into the panel truck. As they finished the squat man got there and spoke to one of them. This man was tall and lean, wearing jeans and a sweater. He looked in Sawyer's direction and motioned for him to stay where he was. Then he turned to two of the men who'd helped with the crate. There was a brief exchange between them. The two men turned and went to the big T.I.R. truck, climbing up into the cab. The tall, thin man shut the rear door of the panel truck and locked it. He came toward Sawyer as the T.I.R. started with a roar and headed north out of the Camargue.

"I'm Colpin," the man said when he reached Sawyer. He had the harried face of an overworked bookkeeper at income-tax time. "That goddamned T.I.R. was late. Had a flat coming out of Italy. It was supposed to be here and gone before you showed up."

"Sorry. Dufour said seven o'clock."

"Not your fault." Colpin got out a pack of cigarettes and offered one to Sawyer, who took it and lighted up for both of them. Colpin blew a perfect smoke ring, admired it, and said: "According to Bedrozian you've got heavy connections with the law. That right?"

Sawyer nodded. "When I need it."

"I might be needing your help with those connections, one of these days."

Sawyer gave him one of his ARC cards. "I'm not with this firm now, but they'll be able to tell you where to reach me."

Colpin looked at the card and pocketed it. "You'll hear from me, if I get caught before I unload that." He jerked a thumb toward the panel truck. "But if I get it sold, I won't be needing any help at all. I'll have enough money to stay out of this damned country and start over someplace else. In style."

"Doesn't look like *that* big a crate."

"Yeah, but it's full of Scythian treasures—little figurines, helmets, shields, buckles, vases, saddle ornaments. All in gold or silver. A German archaeology team located the site a month ago in east Turkey, near Lake Van. They went home to raise money for a dig, and a dealer heard about it and tipped me. I got in there fast with my own crew. Spent ten days digging it all up, and then made a deal with those T.I.R. drivers to bring it out. Now—well you know what Scythian stuff is worth these days."

Sawyer shook his head. "I'm not an expert."

Colpin grinned. "Well, I am, even if I never finished school. You have to become an expert, in this business, or you keep picking up worthless junk."

"Bedrozian told me you once knew of a Venus figure somebody had for sale. Was it authentic?"

Colpin was silent for a few moments, thinking back. "Yeah, I remember. But a long time ago. Eight-nine years. Jean-Pierre Augier had it. I'm pretty sure it was the real thing. He dug it out of a cave in Spain."

Sawyer took out his composite photograph. "Did it look like this?"

Colpin studied the picture of the Venus figure for some time. "Not exactly. But something like it."

"Where can I find this Augier?"

Colpin laughed. "In the cemetery in Dijon. Augier had a stroke. Died about three years ago."

A knot formed in Sawyer's stomach. "What happened to the statuette? You didn't buy it?"

"I couldn't find a dealer who'd pay enough to make it worth the trouble. I guess Bedrozian told you—a Venus figure is too hard to get rid of. But anyway, Augier got lucky. Next time I ran into him, he said he sold it."

Sawyer drew a shallow breath. "Did he mention *who* bought it?"

Colpin shrugged. "Nothing that'll help you, if you're looking for it. Augier didn't tell me the name of the guy. Just that he sold it to some Arab, in Marseilles."

3

Seconds after he entered Prince Georges County, Alexander Rhalles became convinced he was being followed, that this time it was not just his increasingly ragged nerves. The drop for this night was set at exactly 16.3 miles beyond the District of Columbia line, along Central Avenue. Rhalles slowed his car to check the mileage on his panel as he crossed the line. When he had it fixed in his mind, he glanced up into the rearview mirror.

There was a car behind him. The last time he had looked, it had been steadily creeping up on him. He'd been expecting it to swing out to pass him soon. But when he looked this time, it had dropped back a bit. So it had slowed when he had.

His throat swelled and it suddenly became difficult to breathe. Rhalles opened his mouth, but then forced himself to shut it. He'd been doing that too much over the last couple of days: gulping air through his mouth, hyperventilating. He swallowed hard and got his breathing almost normal, at the same time easing his too tight grip on the wheel. Pressing down on the accelerator to abruptly increase speed, Rhalles watched in the rearview mirror. The other car fell further behind, but then began creeping up on him again.

Rhalles slowed abruptly, down to thirty, far below the normal speed for this nearly empty road at this time of night. The other car closed the distance between them swiftly and swung into the other lane to pass him. There were two men in the front seat. Neither looked in Rhalles' direction as they went past.

Rhalles maintained his speed at thirty. The other car swung back into the same lane in front of him, and sped away. Rhalles watched its taillights gradually diminish in the distance without feeling any sense of relief. They could have two cars tailing him, in radio contact with each other.

He couldn't see any other car behind him. But one *could* be there, far back, driving with its lights off.

Rhalles watched for the next turnoff. When it came, he swung into it without signaling the turn. It was a curving suburban lane. Rhalles stopped immediately after entering it, and twisted his head to look back toward Central Avenue. No car turned in after him. But that didn't necessarily mean anything, either. If someone were tailing, they could have stopped back there, lights off, and be waiting for his next move.

Easing his car forward again, Rhalles automatically glanced at the panel, so he could deduct the mileage used up when he returned to Central Avenue. He drove along the lane for exactly a mile, constantly checking his rearview mirror. If a car was following it was staying well back, with no lights. With no prior indication of his move, Rhalles made a tight U-turn and jammed his foot down on the accelerator, racing back toward Central Avenue.

He passed no other car, either coming toward him or parked.

There would have had to be one, if he were being tailed. They had no way to predict that he'd intended to return to Central Avenue. It had been his nerves, after all.

Rhalles stopped in a dark patch under a tree alongside the lane, and set the brake. When he took his hands from the wheel they were shaking. He turned off lights and motor, and then just sat there for a time, getting himself under control.

It had begun two days ago, with a seemingly innocent remark from Masursky, the President's Assistant for National Security Affairs. "I tried to call you last night," Masursky had told him. "A bunch of people dropped by our house, sort of an impromptu party. I figured the diversion might do you some good. Rang your house three times—but no answer."

Rhalles' answer had been unhesitating, and calculated to fit what would have been noticed if he'd been under superficial observation recently: "I was out driving around the country. I've been doing that lately, on nights when I feel too keyed up. It relaxes me."

Masursky had nodded understandingly. But ever since, Rhalles had become increasingly jittery about the possibility that he was under investigation by the government's Ultra Sensitive Positions Program. It was normal routine for anyone in a position like his to be the subject of such a check from time to time. Rhalles had been hoping that before they got around to him Sawyer would have found Moira. If it came before that, he could only hope that the investigation would be sufficiently routine to miss what he was doing, if he stayed vigilant and cautious.

He had increased his precautions over the past two days. For one thing, he no longer recorded the cassettes in the house in Georgetown, because he'd become afraid it might be bugged.

Rhalles reached over on the seat beside him, opened his briefcase, and took out the recorder. Snapping it on, he began telling the pertinent things that had happened that day.

The most important was his discussion with the President of a CIA study confirming that Russia was concentrating its chemical warfare production on nerve gas capable of being delivered by rocket warheads. The President was deeply troubled by the dangers inherent in America responding with a return to its own intensified nerve-gas program. But he was becoming convinced that there was no alternative.

He had quoted Vegetius on the nub of the problem. "I don't suppose I have to remind a Nobel historian what that clear-sighted old Roman had to say on it." His smile had not been a happy one. "It's still an unavoidable truth, Alex: If you wish for peace, prepare to fight for it."

Rhalles recorded this conversation in total, withholding none of it. Maybe it would serve a purpose; and make Jorgen's masters rethink the advisability of their program, in the light of America launching an all-out nerve-gas race against them.

It was possible that he was only trying to find some small justification for his continuing treason. But Rhalles no longer allowed himself to worry very much about what he was doing. There was only one thing left that he cared about: keeping Moira alive.

When he was finished, Rhalles wrapped the cassette in a small plastic bag and drove back onto Central Avenue, checking the mileage indicator. He stayed sharply vigilant all the way, though he saw no indication he was under observation. When he was exactly 16.3 miles from the District of Columbia, he pulled off the road and put the cassette under a rock he found marked with a touch of phosphorescent paint. Then he drove home.

Before going to bed that night he took two strong pills. They were the only way he'd been able to get any sleep, the last two nights. While waiting for them to take effect, he sat in a wing chair in the bedroom and reread Moira's last letter, received two days before her disappearance. It was like pressing a thorn into his flesh to remember the smell of a rose:

"Alex, will you please get your ass over here to France. I miss you, too much. You can just remind our President that the purpose of the government is to serve its people. And right now I need serving, by you. I keep being surprised by how much I'm capable of missing you. After so long together, I should be ready to enjoy a fling on my own.

"And to tell the truth, the first couple weeks apart aren't bad. In fact, they're good, because they remind me how much I need you. Something I tend to forget when I get too used to having you always there. But now it's getting on toward three weeks apart, and that's *too much!* I know chastity is supposed to fill you with lots of energy but it just doesn't work that way for me. I'm getting dragged out. I need energizing, and anything else you can think up.

"It's terrible to be this dependent on someone else, but it's lovely, too. Just as long as you're the same about me. Oh, come on, Alex, get over here, at least for a week . . ."

He had planned to fly to France and join her four days after getting the letter. But by then, it had been too late.

If he'd gone immediately, he knew, nothing would have happened to her.

Rhalles put aside the letter and sat there staring at nothing for a time. Finally, he rose to his feet and snapped off the bedroom lights. In the dark of the house, he went to the bedroom windows and peered out. Below, the street was empty. He went through to the back bedroom, and looked down through the window there, at the small gardens and alley between the houses of the block. He could see no one lurking in the deep shadows there. But that didn't necessarily mean no one was.

The pills were deadening his nerves when he got into their bed, lying now on her side. But sleep was a long time coming. The question wouldn't go away: was it just nerves—or *was* he being checked on? The odds were that this time it was his imagination, but there was scant comfort in that. Eventually it would become a reality.

4

The small record and cassette store on Lexington Avenue, where Angela Lewis had picked up the code tape for delivery to Vienna, was a one-man business. The owner was George Alcazar, a tall, paunchy man of forty-eight, with a fleshy, swarthy face. Having no employee he could leave in charge of the store, Alcazar never went out to lunch. On the day he turned over the tape to the stewardess, he had a hot turkey sandwich and a container of coffee delivered from a nearby diner at noon. By then the telephone company had co-operated in placing cable-strand taps on Alcazar's business and apartment phones, and Lang had been through his apartment.

It was a two-room tenth-floor apartment in the rear of The Century, a venerable, well-maintained building taking up the entire block between Sixty-second and Sixty-third street on Central Park West. Alcazar's rent was $468 per month. Lang didn't find an encoding machine in the apartment, nor anything else pertinent to the investigation. Lang marked Alcazar down as a cutout, whose only purpose in the enemy's communications line was to keep one end from having any contact with the other. When Lang left the apartment his electronics specialist was still at work concealing miniature microphone and transmitter units in each room.

Alcazar closed his store at six that evening. By then Lang had a dossier on him, which Garcia had put together from information in credit bureau, insurance, and divorce court files, in addition to the IRS, the Small Business Administration, and other government records. The dossier added up to a fairly full picture of Alcazar's life, but there was only one item in it that Lang found of interest:

Alcazar had been divorced ten years ago. His wife had been awarded their car and New Jersey home, in addition to stiff alimony payments. Two years ago, when his wife had remarried, the alimony had been ended through a settlement under which Alcazar paid her twenty thousand dollars in a lump sum. The alimony had left him no savings or profit from his store; so the question was: Where had he gotten that lump sum? If it was a loan he'd obtained, there was no record of it. If he was paying off on such a loan, it was not by check and he was not declaring it under expenses.

On leaving his store for the night, Alcazar got his car out of a parking lot on Second Avenue and drove it crosstown through Central Park to a garage on Broadway, one block from the rear of his apartment building. Then he went to his apartment. By the time he came out to go to dinner, a beeper had been attached under his car, so it could tailed from a distance. But Alcazar didn't take his car from the garage. He walked to a restaurant on Central Park South, had an expensive meal, and then walked to a movie house on Fifty-seventh. When he came out he took a cab to his apartment building, watched television for an hour, and went to sleep. No contact had been detected by Lang's teams.

The next morning Alcazar's alarm clock went off at seven. Lang found it strange that Alcazar did not leave his apartment until an hour and fifty minutes later. And this time he didn't use his car to go cross-town to his store, but took a taxi.

"He was waiting for a contact," Lang decided aloud. "This must be when he gets his pickup orders, early in the morning before he opens the store."

Garcia was not so sure: "Maybe he just likes to take a long time getting out of bed."

"He was waiting for contact," Lang repeated flatly. "It didn't come, so he doesn't need his car today."

There was nothing for the rest of that day to make him think he was wrong. Alcazar's first customer that morning was Hendrix, the flight engineer who'd been observed acting as a courier to Vienna. His routine was the same as Angela Lewis', though the result this time was not:

"Have you got that tape I ordered in yet?"

"No," Alcazar told him. "Not today. Maybe next time you come by."

No cassette for Vienna. Hendrix said "Okay," and left Alcazar's store. The team assigned to Hendrix continued to tail him, out to Kennedy Airport. That was the end of it for that day. Alcazar made no further contacts, didn't have a pickup, made no delivery. This time when he closed the store for the night he ate on the East Side, and then took a taxi home. From his apartment he phoned a call girl. She came over and stayed for an hour. Alcazar paid her one hundred dollars for her services. After she left he watched television until eleven-thirty.

It was on this night that Rhalles had his attack of nerves before leaving his cassette under the stone beside Central Avenue, 16.3 miles outside the District of Columbia. By the time Alcazar turned off his TV and went to sleep, Jorgen had picked up the cassette and was at work encoding Rhalles' taped information.

Alcazar's alarm clock went off at seven the next morning, as it did every morning. He forced himself out of bed and opened the blinds to let in daylight. Two dirty pigeons were taking a stroll on the small balcony outside, looking straight ahead and strictly minding their own business like good New Yorkers. Alcazar shuffled into his kitchen to wake himself up with coffee and a packaged doughnut. As he sipped the hot coffee he stared sleepily across narrow Sixty-third at the brown bulk of the West Side YMCA, improbably topped off by a delicate green Moorish minaret. Leaving the kitchen, he went into the bathroom to shower and shave, taking his time. By now he had the timing required to be ready if the call came down to an automatic routine.

The shower brought him fully awake, and he felt pleasantly charged with energy as he got dressed. He always felt especially good the day after using a call girl. He used them on an average of once every three days. Two hundred dollars a week was a hell of a lot cheaper than a wife. He'd never get married again. The screwing you got wasn't worth the screwing you got. Elaine had taught him that lesson, and he'd never forget it.

If it wasn't for Murray, he'd still be paying that killing alimony, and not have enough dough left for a call girl, not even once a month. It was funny, considering how much he owed to Murray, that he didn't even know his last name. But Alcazar was not overly curious about what it was, just as he did not wonder much about where Murray got his investment money. He assumed that Murray was involved in shady business dealings, probably Mafia-connected.

There'd been no papers signed between them. Murray was the kind of guy who'd send leg-breakers, not court summonses, to somebody who didn't pay what he owed. But Murray's terms had been surprisingly lenient, for lending him the money to get Elaine off his back. Alcazar paid him a percentage of the store profits, the amount varying according to how business was that month. It never came to more than half of what he'd been forking out in alimony, and it had enabled him to live again.

So naturally he had not been in a position to say no when Murray had asked for a favor. It had something to do with stealing business secrets from one big corporation, and passing them on to another. But Alcazar was not involved at all in the stealing end. All Murray needed was a go-between in passing the stuff on. It was quite simple, taking little of Alcazar's time and putting him in no danger. And Murray had sweetened it considerably by lowering the percentage he had to pay back each month in which he acted as go-between.

Alcazar glanced at his watch as he strapped it on his wrist. It was fifteen minutes before eight. At least twenty minutes to go. He made himself another cup of coffee and carried it into the living room. Settling down to wait, he sipped the coffee as he looked out the big window at the beautiful golden-red glow of the sunlit smog hanging over New Jersey, on the other side of the Hudson River. Closer, a block behind the Century, the concrete honeycomb of an apartment building under construction was now up to the level of his apartment. Behind it a sliver-painted replica of the Statue of Liberty on the roof of an office building was now hidden up to her waist. Alcazar wondered idly how much of her he'd still be able to see when the new construction was finished—he face, or just her silvery hand holding the torch aloft?

His phone rang. Alcazar looked at it and put down his cup. It rang a second time. He looked at his watch. Seven minutes past eight o'clock. The phone did not ring again. Alcazar waited a few seconds, then picked up the phone and called the garage where he kept his car. Five minutes later, when he got to the garage, the car was waiting for him out front.

He gave the two-dollar tip that ensured this prompt service, and drove across Manhattan to the Queensboro Bridge, taking it over the East River into Queens. Alcazar had no idea where the small packages came from, but the pickup was always someplace in Queens.

The places were prearranged, a different one for each day of the week. He drove to the spot assigned to this day, taking the route that usually proved fastest.

As he came off the Queens end of the bridge, he turned from the long curve of the upper roadway onto Twenty-first Street. He took it up to Astoria Boulevard, and switched over into the Twenty-fifth Avenue. A few blocks from St. Michael's Cemetery he pulled over next to a sidewalk phone booth. Getting out of the car, he walked to the booth and went through the motions of making a call.

Observing through high-power binoculars from a tail car a block away, Lang watched Alcazar reach one hand under the metal ledge below the phone, and then put something in his pocket. Later, after Alcazar had left, an agent from the second tail car found traces of Scotch Tape stuck to the underside of the ledge.

Alcazar drove back into Manhattan, left his car in the parking lot on Second Avenue, and hurried to his store on Lexington. A few minutes after he opened for business, a man entered and asked if Alcazar had the tape he'd ordered. Alcazar told him that he was in luck, and gave him a small, flat package identical to the one he'd given two days before to Angela Lewis.

When the man left the store a surveillance team took over on him. He was tailed to Kennedy. Shortly after getting there the team was able to identify him as the co-pilot on a flight leaving that day for Vienna. By the time the report came in, Lang had left further surveillance on Alcazar to one of his teams and returned to his control center to handle the new problem: how to tag whoever had left the package for Alcazar.

The offices assigned to him while in New York were on East Fifty-first Street between Lexington and Park Avenue. Lang walked there, moving briskly and avoiding windblown papers and piles of plastic-bagged garbage. New York was one of his least favorite cities in all the world: dirty streets, ugly people, oily grit, and exhaust fumes that made deep breathing impossible. On his hate list it was not far behind the worst: Calcutta, the inside of a week-old grave under a midsummer heat.

Reaching his building, Lang took an elevator up to the twentieth floor. At that height the windows gave the only view of Manhattan he liked: the new skyscraper office buildings of the East Side, all hard-edged steel, glass, and aluminum, with sheer sides that in certain light conditions became reflecting pools shimmering with images of other buildings.

The sign on the main door of the suite he entered said: "Kalman Information Services, Inc." Its only permanent installation was a radio-and-telephone communications room, which served the offices temporarily assigned to operations passing through town.

Garcia met Lang as he came in. "Rudofsky's inside waiting for you," he said gravely. "Just got in from Washington."

A special assistant to the deputy chief of the CIA's Soviet Bloc Division, George Rudofsky was responsible for Lang's operation, in addition to others which Lang was not party to. He also acted as the operation's liaison with the Technical Services Division, which was supplying all the electronic expertise Lang was employing, and with Division D, which was responsible for any field operations carried out to help the NSA break codes.

He was a capable expert on Russian affairs, with a few cherished eccentricities. Many years before, Lang had attended the class Rudofsky taught as part of the Soviet Operations Course for CIA officers. He'd had a set routine for seizing the attention of his students on the first day of the course: he'd stroll into the classroom and without a word take a hammer and nail from a pocket of his black raincoat. Turning his back to the class, he'd hammer the nail into the wall. Then he'd take off the raincoat and hang it on the nail, before sitting down, placing the hammer on the desk, and starting his lecture.

Lang entered his office followed by Garcia. Rudofsky's black raincoat was hanging, not on a nail, but in the open closet in one wall. He was slumped comfortably in Lang's black-leather swivel chair, with his feet up on the desk. Socks of fire-engine red glared between the bottoms of his gray flannel slacks and his black shoes. "One has to indulge a certain amount of individualism," he was fond of explaining. He was a handsome man in his fifties, with a deliberately cultivated relaxed manner. Without otherwise moving he raised a hand in greeting. "How's it coming?"

Lang sat down in a chair facing Rudofsky across the desk. "Is somebody worried?"

"A lot of people are, on this one. They've been reading your field information reports. You've already tagged three traitors working for the enemy out of this city alone. There's one school of thinking that it's time to grab them and squeeze."

"That'd be the most stupid move we could make at this stage," Lang said disgustedly.

"I agree. It would be premature. These are non-entities: couriers and cutouts who aren't going to know anything about the code or its source. Squeeze them hard enough, and long enough, and maybe it would lead to the source. But by then chances are he'd have been alerted and be long gone. I'm managing to hold off the idea of taking them, so far. But you're going too slow, Lang. We need a major payoff on this operation, and soon."

When he was pushing a point, Rudofsky's elastic face scowled exaggeratedly. The ends of the long mouth pulled far down, toward the side of his jutting cleft chin, the big lower lip pouting threateningly and the trenches deepening down his fleshy cheeks. Then he relaxed in Lang's swivel chair, the point made, and the rubbery face snapped back to its essential humorous good looks.

401

Lang said, "I take it they're not having any luck cracking the code."

"Not yet, though they're sure they will. Eventually."

Garcia laughed softly. He stood leaning against the closed door, with his hands in his pockets, watching them. "I know some codes they spent ten years trying to crack. And when they did, it was because guys like us found something that solved it for them."

"That's what they're looking for this time," Rudofsky said. "It's one reason we need faster progress. Another problem we're about to have is the FBI. They're beginning to get a smell of this one."

Garcia groaned. "That bunch of fuck-ups."

Lang kept his eyes on Rudofsky. "Are you ready to let them climb all over this operation?"

"We can't keep them out, once they know about it. And they will, before long. We're using a lot of telephone company and local police co-operation, and FBI's connections with both are solid. But I'm pretty sure I can make a deal: they give us some of their people, but strictly under our control. In exchange we give them the headlines: FBI Breaks Spy Ring— With Help of CIA Information."

"That's fine with me," Lang said tightly.

"But the only way they'll go for a deal is if they're pretty sure there'll *be* a payoff doing it your way, and not in the distant future. Brings us right back to home base: How *are* you doing?"

Lang told him about Alcazar picking up the package at the phone-booth drop that morning. Rudofsky brooded over the new information for a moment. "Well, it is a step in the right direction. You'll keep surveillance on that phone booth, to tag the delivery boy if he uses it for the next drop."

"Sure—just in case. But they won't be sticking to a single drop. Odds are they've set up different places."

"But probably limited in number. In which case this one is bound to be used again, sooner or later."

"Later could be a long time coming," Lang pointed

out thinly. "You're the one who was just talking about getting faster progress."

Rudofsky smiled. "What do you have in mind?"

"First of all, I'm assuming the code tapes come here from Washington. If that turns out wrong, we can try other combinations. But until then I'm acting on the assumption, because it fits. Logically, an enemy setup this big would be to milk something out of Washington. And that phone booth is less than ten minutes' easy drive from LaGuardia Airport. The other thing that fits is the flight schedules. I've checked, and the first morning plane from Washington is an Eastern Airlines shuttle that lands at La-Guardia at 8 A.M. Alcazar got the phone signal to make a pickup seven minutes later. The timing's perfect."

Lang went on to explain exactly what he intended to do about it the following morning. And for as many subsequent mornings as proved necessary.

Rudofsky's elastic face went into its exaggerated reflective scowl. "You're planning to invest an awful lot of man-hours in an assumption."

Lang used one of Rudofsky's favorite phrases on him: "The potential payoff justifies the investment."

Rudofsky recognized the phrase and smiled. "Okay, I agree."

5

At seven the next morning, when the first plane from Washington to New York was preparing for takeoff, Lang was positioning his people around the Eastern Airlines shuttle building at LaGuardia. Some were stationed outside near the cab rank, dressed as taxi drivers and porters. Others were spread around the luggage pickup and waiting room, dressed as airline employees or acting like passengers waiting for the next plane out. There were two more assigned to the corridor used by passengers coming off the plane. In addition there were hidden cameras in strategic places, to get a picture of everyone coming off the plane, of any passenger who used one of the terminal phones, and of each cab used by one of these.

The plane landed a few minutes before eight. Lang's small army got ready to go into action. It turned out to be wasted effort.

Alcazar's alarm clock woke him at the usual time that morning. But his phone did not ring the signal for a pickup. Alcazar didn't leave his apartment until shortly before nine, taking a taxi directly to his Lexington Avenue store. No one established contact with him that day.

The following morning Lang and his teams were back at LaGuardia at 7 A.M. When the first plane from Washington landed an hour later, they went through the same motions as on the previous morning. Lang's instructions were to ignore passengers who did not arrive alone, and those who had heavy luggage. Attention was concentrated on those who used the airport phones before leaving the terminal. On this morning five men and one woman coming off the shuttle did use the phones.

In Alcazar's apartment in Manhattan, the phone rang twice. Alcazar waited a few moments after the second ring, and then phoned the garage to have his car ready.

Outside the Eastern shuttle terminal at LaGuardia, the woman who had made a phone call took a bus to midtown Manhattan.

One of the five men who'd used the phones inside boarded a bus headed for Brooklyn.

The other four got into taxis. The number of each of these four taxis was noted down by Lang's observers.

A team assigned to Alcazar tailed his car to Queens. This time the phone booth where Alcazar picked up his package was on the corner of Thirtieth Avenue and Twenty-first Street.

A signal was made to the police department's traffic division, which put out a call to the four taxis used by men who'd made phone calls from the Eastern shuttle terminal. Six minutes later Garcia phoned Lang at LaGuardia and gave him the number of the taxi which had dropped one of these men off at an address in Queens, two blocks from the phone booth at Thirtieth and Twenty-first.

Lang entered an airport toilet which had been sealed off so it could be used as a darkroom. The photographs were all developed, hanging up to dry. Lang took down the damp photo of the passenger who had boarded the taxi that had gone two blocks from the drop where Alcazar had picked up that morning's package.

The picture showed a mild-looking, bald-headed man in his sixties. Lang smiled wolfishly and pocketed it. He told his darkroom man to develop a dozen more prints off the negative. They would be picked up by Garcia after he turned over continuance of this end of the operation to the CIA's New York desk.

Lang left the improvised darkroom and made a call to Rudofsky. He boarded a plane that took off four minutes later—for Washington, to take over the team that would be waiting there to begin tailing the bald-headed courier when he returned from New York.

Through the entire one-hour flight Lang savored the excitement sparking his nerve ends. The thrill of closing in on his quarry was back.

EIGHTEEN

1

The gale had swept across the Mediterranean from North Africa bringing fine grains of sand with the rain slashing Marseilles. Though it was only a few minutes after four in the afternoon the low mass of cloud was imposing early darkness. The wind strummed the rigging of yachts and commercial fishing boats dancing at their moorings in the churned water of the Old Harbor. It swept the surrounding quays, swinging lamps, flapping awnings, overturning sidewalk chairs, skidding torn umbrellas across shiny cobbles and black puddles. Everyone who still had intact umbrellas kept them shut as they hurried between shelters.

One block from the Old Harbor the force of the storm was muted by solid banks of buildings walling the narrow streets. Rainwater soaked Sawyer's corduroy cap and ran off his raincoat as he walked around a deep puddle and turned off the Rue Fortia. He entered a short, wide street partially roofed over by elevated parking ramps.

It was flanked by seafood markets and auto-repair garages. At the other end was one of the few old blocks around the harbor to have survived the war. When the Germans had occupied Marseilles they had dynamited most of these blocks, because each was a miniature casbah of interconnected buildings and mazelike passages in which it had proved impossible to find hiding Resistance fighters and other criminals. Sawyer opened the door in a heavy wooden gate, and stepped inside one of the dead-end drive-in alleys that pierced the innards of this block.

Not much rain fell on the broken cobbles because of the narrow crossover bridges above; two of them at each of the five levels of the buildings on either side. These bridges also kept out the little daylight remaining otuside the block. The deep gloom inside the alley was relieved in places by illumination from some doorways and windows above, and three establishments at ground level: a motorcycle repair garage, a machine shop, and a small printing plant. But as Sawyer walked through the alley toward the deadend, the pools of darkness became larger than the patches of light.

Where the alley ended he could barely make out the sign crudely painted on the blacked-out window: "Club Monte Carlo—Ambience & Hi-Fi." Between that and the "Chinese Friendship Club" was a narrow, murky stairway. Sawyer climbed it to a short corridor with stained plaster walls. It was partly blocked by a table and chairs where four young bruisers sat playing cards under a hanging light bulb, across from a closed door with a sign: "Massilia Karate Club." The players looked at Sawyer thoughtfully as he edged between them and the karate club. When he reached the end of the corridor and turned into another, two of the players got up from their chairs.

The second corridor ended at a locked door with a bronze plaque on which was beautifully inscribed: "Alfani International Transfer." Sawyer knocked at the door and looked back. The two bruisers who'd left the game were standing at the junction of the corridors, watching him.

A lean, dark-faced man with ginger-colored hair opened the door. Sawyer gave his name and said he was looking for Marcel Alfani.

"You got an appointment?"

"No, but he'll see me."

The man looked past Sawyer at the two bruisers

from the card game. They moved in closer, spreading apart. "Wait here a second," the man with the ginger hair told Sawyer, and went back inside the room. The two watchdogs just stood there, eying Sawyer curiously.

Ginger-hair came back out with a battery-operated metal detector, and ran it up and down Sawyer's figure. It squealed when it reached his left pants pocket. Ginger-hair patted the pocket, found it contained some change and keys.

"I'm not carrying a weapon," Sawyer told him patiently.

"Let's have your cap."

Sawyer took it off and gave it to him. Ginger-hair looked inside it and handed it back, motioning for him to come in the office with him. The two bruisers followed as far as the open doorway.

The office was small, with a desk and two comfortable chairs. There was a closed door on the other side of it, and a man seated behind the desk with both hands out of sight on his lap. He watched Sawyer as Ginger-hair picked up a phone and dialed a number. Describing Sawyer and giving his name, he listened for a second before hanging up and nodding at Sawyer. "Okay, come with me."

Sawyer followed him through the other door. One of the bruisers from the card game trailed after Sawyer. They went through another corridor, up a flight of steps, and across one of the walkway bridges over the murky alley. Entering the other building at the third floor, they went up another flight of steps and through a number of other short corridors.

They were taking a different route than on Sawyer's last visit to Alfani, and to a different part of the block. Alfani had good reason for these precautions. For years Marseilles had been sputtering with gang wars that were doing their best to rival the bootleg wars of Prohibition Chicago. Mostly it was between the Corsicans and the Arabs. The last Sawyer had heard, the Pakistani and Indian gangs were lining up with the Arabs, while the Chinese and Vietnamese gangs were with the Corsicans, and the black Africans kept shifting.

Sawyer had an odd feeling as they moved through the labyrinth inside the block; the same one he'd gotten the last time. It was the knowledge that the first time he'd been there, it had been inside his mother's womb. She and Sawyer's father had been hidden inside this block for almost two weeks, until Alfani had been able to slip them over to Spain.

They crossed a bridge over another dark alley, climbed another flight of steps, and entered an unmarked room filled with pinball machines. On the other side of it two of Alfani's bodyguards sat in chairs flanking the open door to an office. Both had guns in belt holsters and looked like men used to taking the guns out of the holsters on short notice. One of them got up and took Sawyer into the office.

He indicated a mirror set into the wall beside a closed door. "Look at yourself in that."

Sawyer looked in the mirror as the bodyguard knocked at the door. A moment later the door opened and Marcel Alfani came out with a warm smile. "Pierre-Ange—it is so good of you to come see me. I'm sorry about all this melodrama. We have a truce here in Marseilles at the moment—but, you never can be sure when trouble will erupt again without notice."

He was a tall, hefty man with short-cropped white hair and a short-trimmed gray-and-black beard he'd grown recently to camouflage his increasing network of wrinkles. Behind the thick lenses of his black-framed glasses his dark eyes looked tiny. He put an arm fondly around Sawyer's shoulders and led him into his inner office. As soon as the door was shut, Sawyer shrugged the arm off.

Alfani looked at him with understanding sadness. "You really must drop this ridiculous attitude toward me, Pierre-Ange. After all, if the Pope could shake the hand of a mass murderer like Dada Amin . . ."

"I'm not the Pope."

"And I am not so unforgivable a sinner as Amin. I'm your godfather, don't forget. Your mother promised that to me, before you were born."

"I've already paid off that debt."

Alfani shook his head as he sat down behind his desk. "That is the sort of debt you can never fully pay off. Just as I can never fully repay you for hurting yourself so much, in order to help me out of my last difficulty. These are the kind of obligations that bind us to each other almost as strongly as blood."

Sawyer glanced at the wall beside the door as he took a chair. As he'd expected, he found himself looking through the back of the mirror at the outer office. He looked across the desk to Alfani. "I'm glad you think so. I need more help."

Alfani spread his hands with a strangely touching expression. "Name it."

Sawyer told him what he needed. He put the photographs of Christine Jonquet on the desk, with those of the Egyptian stele and the composite Venus figure. None of the pictures meant anything to Alfani. And he knew of no man with a gray mark on his cheek who was part of the Marseilles *milieu*, as the underworld called itself.

"As for the Arab—my relationship with the Arabs is not cordial, you know. But with the rest I can help. By asking about your man with the mark, and spreading copies of these pictures, among the many people I do have excellent relations with."

"Good. But I need more: I have two people waiting for me at the Hôtel Nautique. We're going to canvass the town our way, while you're doing it in yours. I need three men to go with us. The kind of men who can vouch for us, and make sure we get straight answers to our questions."

Alfani picked up his phone.

410

Half an hour later Sawyer met Donhoff and Titine at the hotel, and introduced them to the three men Alfani had supplied. Each took one as an escort as they split up to find out if Marseilles really had what they were after.

For three people to search the whole of Marseilles was impossible. It was the largest port in the entire Mediterranean. A hundred investigators would have needed weeks to cover the entire city. But in Marseilles such a widespread search was not necessary, because of the Canebière—a wide boulevard running straight up from the Old Harbor, lined on both sides with bars, cafes, bistros, restaurants, movie theaters, and stores. In Marseilles it was *the* place to go: to see a film, shop, or have an evening out; to meet friends or make new ones; to just sit over a drink and watch the passing parade, or take a stroll and be seen.

Everyone who spent any time in Marseilles visited the Canebière, at least occasionally. Most went there regularly, and many spent part of each day or night there. If Christine Jonquet or the man with the gray mark on his cheek had been in this city, Sawyer knew, someone along the Canebière was going to remember.

He started at the top of it, with his escort from the Marseilles *milieu,* and began working his way down. Donhoff began at the other end, down at the Old Harbor, and worked his way up. Titine worked the side streets on both flanks, starting with the Boulevard d'Athènes, running between the Canebière and main railway station.

But the continuing rainstorm made it a bad night to start. The usually lively, crowded boulevard was virtually deserted. Even the sea serpents glaring from the bases of the old-fashioned green street lamps seemed to be drowning. Other than the barmen and waiters, the only people inside the eating and drinking spots were the diehard lonelies; the ones who couldn't face a return to their empty rooms until they were tired enough or drunk enough to fall immediately to sleep. Some of the bars began closing around midnight, long before their usual time.

Shortly before 1 A.M., Donhoff's underworld escort found Sawyer and informed him that Donhoff had called it quits and gone to the hotel for a night's sleep. It seemed a sensible decision, under the circumstances. Sawyer found Titine, who was soaking wet and more than ready to call it a night after failing to get a single positive response to any of the pictures or questions. They sent the three escorts home after arranging to meet early the next morning, and themselves headed back through the rain to the hotel.

The Nautique was an old, seedy hotel without a trace of elegance. But the location was perfect: on the Quai des Belges, a few steps from the point where the Canebière began on the Old Harbor. As they reached it Sawyer nodded toward the Cintra bar on the corner. "Buy you a nightcap?"

Titine nodded. "Let me get into some dry clothes first."

They went into the hotel, and Sawyer found a message waiting for him to call Olivier in Paris. Telling Titine he'd meet her in the bar, he went to the phone and placed the call.

"I just had a call from Samuel Otto," Olivier told him, giving the code name used by Alexander Rhalles. He put the rest of it as carefully as he could: "He's very worried that he's being . . . observed. I had the feeling he's not sure if it's true, or his imagination. But I thought you should know—he sounded pretty shaky to me."

Sawyer was feeling pretty shaky himself when he hung up the phone and went to his room to change to dry clothes. Whether it was true that Rhalles was being checked on, or it was his nerves, he was obviously getting near to the end of his ability to handle the vise he was caught in. Which meant that whatever was happening at Moira's end, she had to be found very quickly. His insides were churning with the urgency when he left the hotel and strode the ten steps into the Cintra.

Titine wasn't there yet, and all the tables were empty. Not even the usual nighthawk prostitutes were keeping their vigil this night. There were two men drinking morosely at the bar, the barman tallying the day's receipts, and a waiter already stacking chairs on rear tables so he could sweep up and close.

Sawyer sat at one of the tables by the long, rain-spattered front window facing the port, and ordered a double brandy. He downed half of it and moodily contemplated what he was doing there:

An Arab from Marseilles, who had a young partner interested in ancient goddesses, had bought a stolen Egyptian stele depicting Isis and Nephthys.

An Arab from Marseilles—perhaps the same one—had acquired a looted Venus figure.

Were this Arab's partner and the man with the gray patch on his cheek the same?

At any rate, a man with such a mark had been involved with Christine Jonquet—who'd wound up with the Egyptian stele. And a man with the same mark had almost certainly been involved with Gaspard Martinot—who'd wound up with a Venus figure.

Both trails led to Marseilles.

This was the only lead they had, finally, after all the digging, reasoning, data gathering, and hunting. If Marseilles didn't yield some kind of next step, there was nowhere else left to go.

Sawyer finished off his drink as Titine came in shaking drops of water from her hair. She ordered a hot chocolate and Sawyer asked for another brandy. Studying his face, she asked quietly: "Bad news?"

"Not fatal—but not good, either." Sawyer's voice was strained. He took the double the waiter brought him and finished off half of it with a single swallow.

Titine took a sip of her hot chocolate and said lightly: "That's no way to drink brandy."

"It is if you want to get drunk."

Titine put a clamp on her growing curiosity about why this particular investigation meant so much to him. She drank her hot chocolate in silence, watching him stare grimly through the window. Her cup was nearly empty when she spoke again: "If that wind keeps up it'll blow the clouds away by morning. With a clear day, we could get lucky."

"There's a saying in America," Sawyer told her heavily. "From your mouth to God's ear." He finished the second half of the double, looked at his empty glass and at her half-finished cup. "Something stronger?"

She shook her head. "No, I think it's time for bed, if we're going to get an early start tomorrow."

Sawyer nodded. "Go ahead. I'm not ready to sleep yet."

"If you're planning to drink yourself into the mood, I don't think you'll have the time. They're getting ready to close up."

He grinned at her. "There're other bars."

Titine looked down at her cup for a moment, then looked up again and took hold of his left wrist and twisted gently. Sawyer looked at her curiously. She smiled, showing her teeth. "I'm twisting your arm. Come on, let's go to bed."

She gave his wrist a final twist and let go of it, picked up her cup, and finished off the rest of her hot chocolate.

Sawyer looked at his wrist and then at her eyes. He turned his head and looked across the quay at the masts of the fishing boats swinging wildly in the wind-whipped rain. Titine put down her cup and stood up, watching him and waiting. Sawyer left the money for their drinks on the table and left the bar with her. He put his arm around her shoulders as they went through the rain to the hotel.

* * *

It was as Titine had predicted. At dawn the sun rose into a pale-washed sky without a cloud. At eight in the morning they left the hotel to meet their underworld escorts and begin canvassing the Canebière again.

2

Sometime in the night Moira had the dream again. The last time she'd had it she'd been about ten years old. But nothing in it was changed, although this time she knew it was a dream. That made it more disturbing, because even in her sleep she wondered why it had come back to her now, after so long. She couldn't remember thinking about it in years.

A snarling dog was chasing her around and around a long dinner table. A woman sat at the head of the table carving chicken. She looked somewhat like Moira's dead mother, but much older and without the humor. The dog belonged to this woman.

Moira, running, called the woman's attention to the fact that the dog was attacking her. The woman turned with her carving knife and stabbed the dog in the back.

Moira stopped and stared. "I didn't mean you had to *kill* him . . ."

The woman pulled the knife out of her dead dog, wiped it with a napkin, and resumed carving the chicken. Moira, aghast, sat down at the table and the woman served her a slice.

The dream must have occurred somewhere around dawn, because when Moira awoke her cell was full of morning sun and her mind was still disturbed by it. But when she was fully awake the reason for the dream's recurrence was no longer mysterious. It had been dredged from her past by the two days and nights of tightening anxiety: of holding herself in readiness, waiting for the conditions necessary for her escape attempt.

She worked some of the anxiety out of her system with a solid hour of exercises in her cell before Bruno brought her breakfast. But when he returned to take her tray away, and she asked to be allowed out to sketch, her precarious calm disintegrated with his answer.

"Not this morning," he told her. "I have some errands to take care of. Maybe this afternoon, if I come back early enough."

Moira's legs went weak. She stood in the middle of her cell taking a deep, slow breath as Bruno relocked her door from the outside. Two of the conditions she'd been waiting for were about to be presented to her.

The first condition was to have only one of her jailers to deal with; it couldn't be done while both were around. The second was that it be Lorenz who was there when she made the try. She had managed to relax Bruno somewhat, but not enough for her purpose. He remained instinctively too alert when he was near her; and she knew the speed of his reflexes. Only against Lorenz would she have a chance.

Turning, Moira moved to the cell's small window and gripped the rusted bars in tight fists, straining to hear. After about ten minutes it came: the sound of the unseen car being started. She listened to it being driven away. When she could hear it no longer Moira disengaged her hands from the bars. Flakes of rust adhered to her damp palms. She brushed them off against the rough material of her dungarees and began to prepare.

Now it depended on the third condition: timing. On whether Lorenz would bring her lunch before Bruno returned.

Sitting on the edge of the bed, Moira took off her boots, removed her socks, and put the boots back on. Putting aside the sock to which she'd fastened the loop string, Moira began filling the other with the small stones she took from their hiding place inside the mattress. When this sock was full she slipped it down inside the other, and looped the thread over her head and around her neck.

Concealing the loop and the loaded double sock hanging from it under her shirt, she stood and observed herself in the mirror. The bulk of the improvised blackjack didn't show as long as she held perfectly still. But it did when she moved.

She'd worked out what to do about that. Picking up her sketch pad, Moira held it in a natural position with one hand, between her forearm and her breasts. That made the concealment complete. She tried to smile at her image in the mirror and found she could not. The muscles of her face were frozen. It was even becoming difficult to breathe.

But pitted against this paralysis of fear was the excitement coursing through her. There was no need to use her mother's emotion-switching trick now. After being confined so long, her eagerness to seize this chance to break free cut through the terror latent in a possible failure.

Moira opened the sketch pad to a portrait she had begun and deliberately left half finished. She tore the page out neatly and placed it face down on her bed. Turning back to the bureau, she picked up the little stone Venus figure and carried it to her cell window. She placed the statuette on the deep sill, positioned so that the sunlight illuminated it. Turning to a fresh page on her pad and taking up a pencil, Moira began to draw the enigmatic face of the prehistoric mother-goddess.

As the drawing progressed the old disappointment in her lack of talent as an artist returned to plague her. She had no difficulty reproducing the features. But the sketch failed to convey anything of the disturbing balance of warm promise and calm menace emanating from those features.

417

When the drawing was not quite completed, Moira stopped. There was nothing more to be done. Everything necessary for her breakout try was prepared.

Now began the waiting.

The morning grew toward noon with excruciating slowness. As the sun rose higher the changing light on the stone-carved face of the dark goddess gradually altered its expression. Moira continued to stare at it intently, trying to read her fate in the changes. Which aspect of the goddess was being revealed to her now: the life-giving warmth or the dread, consuming calm?

It was around noon that Bruno usually brought Moira her lunch. But noon came and went, and Lorenz did not come to unlock her cell door. Moira waited under increasing tension, listening for the sound of the returning car which would end any possibility of escape.

As closely as she could estimate without a watch, she endured another hour of waiting. Then one of the outside bolts securing her cell door was rasped open. And she had still not heard the car return.

Standing by the window, Moira raised the open sketch pad so that it would shield her chest while she drew. She began adding the finishing touches to her drawing of the goddess as the second lock bolt was drawn free. Lorenz pushed the door open with a foot and came in carrying the tray.

Moira turned from the window, holding the sketch pad in position, and smiled at him. "I *was* getting hungry."

"There's not much," he said brusquely as he set the tray on the bureau. On it were a sandwich and a glass of milk. "I'm not a cook. And anyway, until Bruno gets back with the groceries . . ."

"It's enough for me," Moira assured him. She worked at keeping her tone normal: "After I eat I'd like to do some sketching outside, if you'll let me."

418

Lorenz shook his head. "Can't, until Bruno gets back."

"Oh? Well, of course if you think he'd be angry . . ."

"I don't give a damn if he gets angry or not," Lorenz informed her sourly. "But he's got the keys to that chain, and I'm not taking you outside without it."

Moira nodded understandingly. "That's all right. I can go on working in here as long as this light holds . . ." He was starting to leave, and she had to say the rest of it quickly: "I'd like to finish a portrait of you—if you'll pose for me."

Lorenz stopped and gave her a puzzled frown.

"I started it from memory," she explained, and nodded toward her bed.

He turned slightly to look in that direction.

Moira worked at keeping her voice normal: "So far, it's a pretty good likeness of you, I think . . ."

She had him. Intrigued, Lorenz turned toward the bed. When his back was to her Moira put the sketch pad on the bureau and took a quiet step that brought her closer to him. Lorenz bent to pick up the page lying face-down on the bed. Moira ripped open the front of her shirt with her left hand and her other seized the top of the stone-weighted sock and yanked, breaking the loop thread. She took a long step and swung the improvised blackjack, getting all the strength of her arm and twisting body behind it.

Lorenz heard the movement behind him and started to straighten and turn. He lacked Bruno's instant reflexes, but even so his reaction was almost quick enough. He was flinching from the blow when the weighted sock slammed into his temple and cheekbone with a jarring impact that almost tore it from Moira's hand. It rammed Lorenz chest-down across the bed, his knees sagging to the floor beside it.

But though stunned he had managed to absorb some of the force of the blow with his last-second flinch.

419

Groggily, he braced one hand on the mattress and began trying to shove himself to his feet. His other hand was groping for the pocket where he kept his switchblade knife.

Moira gripped the weighted sock with both hands and clubbed it across the back of Lorenz's head. All her pent-up fury was concentrated into it. The sock split open as it thudded against his skull, spilling stones across the bed and floor. Lorenz rolled off the bed and fell on his side. But he was still not quite unconscious; and his instincts began to take over from his dazed mind. His hands fumbled under him and his head sagged loosely as he tried unsuccessfully to raise himself. Moira leaped over him and out of the cell. She slammed the heavy door shut and shot both bolts into their stone sockets, locking it. Then she was running down the spiral stairway.

She reached the doorway at the bottom of the tower and burst out into the open. With her mouth wide open she breathed in the sun-warmed air avidly, as though she were filling her lungs with fresh oxygen after a long period of near-suffocation. But the heady excitement of having broken free was tempered by a knowledge that it might be too late. She stopped and listened warily for the sound of the car returning.

All she could hear was the twittering of distant birds. But the sense of time running out on her injected decisive urgency into her movements. She sprinted across the broken paving of the inner ward and plunged into the shadowy opening in the undercroft of the main wall. There was only one way to go once she was inside. The crumbling remains of a steep flight of stone steps led straight down into the murky interior of the wall. After the first few steps the daylight filtering in from above grew dimmer and Moira was forced to slow her descent. Soon the darkness was almost total. She had to feel her way, one step at a time, her hands reaching out to touch the wall on either side.

Moira decided that Bruno and Lorenz must have kept a lamp of some kind just inside the undercroft entrance. Without a light the steps were treacherous. Loose fragments of stone turned under her boots. Several times her foot reached down and found no support, forcing her to stop and grope around with her leg until she contacted a portion of the disintegrated step which would bear her weight.

It made for slow progress that tore at her nerves. But finally she reached the bottom. Her foot, questing forward, felt only solid ground under it. Moira drew a quick breath and reached both hands into the darkness in front of her. They touched damp moss growing on the solidity of a rough-surfaced wall. To her left it was the same. But to her right her groping hands reached into emptiness, and in that direction she could see an indistinct wedge of grayness that had to mean a source of light.

Moira moved toward it cautiously, arms outstretched before her. Debris crackled and scraped under the soles of her boots, very loud in the enclosed silence of the darkness under the fortress ruins. A number of times she encountered unseen obstacles and felt her way around them. The gray wedge ahead took on identity: a dusty shaft of dimmed daylight. As she neared it the darkness around her lost its solidity. Moira made out two heavy standing columns, and the shapes of fallen ones, between low squares of raised stone. The vault she was moving through could have been a crypt, but she didn't pause to check it out. The feeling of time running out was increasingly urgent.

When she reached the source of light it turned out to be one end of a short, low tunnel leading away from the vault at a sharp angle. At the other end was an old wooden door, with sunlight spearing through its cracks. Moira hurried through the tunnel, praying that the door would not be locked shut. It wasn't. She pushed it open and stepped out into the

421

sunlight. Squinting against the sudden excess of light, she quickly took in her surroundings.

Immediately to her right was the end of a narrow dirt road, which wound away from the base of the fortress and vanished around a slope of the hill on which it rested. Behind her and to her left loomed the fortress ruins. Directly across from where she stood rose the wooded hill she had been able to see from the window of her cell in the tower. It sloped down into a narrow valley, from which rose the longer, more gradual slope of the hill crowned by the fortress where Moira had been held prisoner. It was when she looked down the near slope that Moira's heart began to thud. Near the bottom was an ancient village; a sprawling jumble of solid, weathered stone houses huddled close together.

Moira began to run down the slope toward it, stifling the urge to shout. The village was too far away for anyone in it to hear her. But as though in echo to her thought, there was a thin cry behind her. Moira stopped and looked back wildly, seeing no one.

The cry was repeated, and a surge of relief went through her. It was Lorenz, shouting through the window of the tower cell for Bruno.

Bruno was not there to hear him, but Moira found herself running faster now, as she continued down the slope toward the old village. She had covered about one third of the distance to it when she heard the car engine behind her.

Moira stumbled to a halt and looked back up the slope again. A blue Renault was churning dust up on the dirt road there, approaching the fortress. Faintly, the sound of Lorenz yelling again reached her. Desperately, Moira looked around for a place to hide. There was none. The few trees on this slope were too stunted, the rocks too small, the wild shrubs and weeds too low.

Terror squirted adrenalin through her veins and she raced on down the slope with the light swiftness of a deer. But she was only halfway to her goal when the sound of the car changed into a whining snarl, which began to grow louder.

Without stopping, Moira looked back over her shoulder and saw what she'd expected: the Renault had left the road. It was bucking and twisting its way down the slope after her. It couldn't go fast, because it had to thread its way in and out between the low rocks. But it was covering the ground a bit faster than Moira could, slowly closing the distance between them.

She stepped into a hole. Even as she lost her footing and fell, she was cursing her stupidity in risking that brief glance behind her. She made herself go into a loose roll as she hit the ground, but there was a hump of rock she couldn't do anything to avoid. The impact as her midsection hit it knocked all the wind out of her and blurred her vision.

She rolled away from the rock in a tightly curled ball of pain, gasping for breath. It took all the will-power she had to get her hands and knees under her and force herself to her feet. She was bent over against the pain, fighting against the dizziness, trying to see through the blurring. And somehow, once more she was heading down the slope toward the village, in a crouched, stumbling run, sobbing with the effort it cost to drag air into her lungs.

Behind her, the noise of the car negotiating its protesting way down the slope became steadily louder. But the village was almost dead ahead of her now, and that gave renewed strength to her legs. She managed to draw her first full breath since falling, and screamed for help. Continuing her run, she watched the village for some reaction.

There was none, though she was now close enough to be clearly heard by its inhabitants. No one appeared among the huddled stone houses. Moira felt a despairing premonition.

She didn't scream again. It took too much out of

her, and she couldn't afford to slow down. The noise of the car was very loud behind her. Without looking back, she sprinted the rest of the way. And reached the village.

There was a narrow gap between two of the squat stone houses. Moira darted into it. Halfway through the gap, the house on her right had a side door: warped, rotted, worm-eaten. Moira yelled and pounded the door with both fists. It broke from the single rusted hinge that had held it, and crashed inward, sending up a cloud of wood dust as it shattered.

Moira stepped inside, and the premonition became a strength-sapping certainty. There was nothing inside except fallen debris from the collapsed roof, through which weeds grew out of the dirt floor. The front door was missing altogether. Panting, drenched with perspiration, Moira moved swiftly through the opening where it had been, out onto the grass that hid most of the cobbles of a narrow street.

There was not even a stray dog in sight. The doors of most of the houses on either side were gone; there was no glass left in any windows, and little was left of the frames. It was a deserted village, abandoned long ago.

The sound of the car had stopped. Swiftly, Moira moved deeper inside the village, her breathing ragged. She entered a roofless room through a gap in the partially collapsed side wall. There were two other ways in and out of the room: a doorway and a large hole where a window had been. The walls provided a momentary sense of security; the openings a choice of exits in three different directions, if she spotted him approaching.

He was on foot now, stalking her through the desolate silence of the empty village. Moira stood still, listening. Wherever he was, he was moving soundlessly. He might be searching through the other end of the village; or closing in on the area where she stood.

Moira stooped and picked up a piece of timber that had been part of the fallen roof. It was almost as thick as her wrist, and almost as long as her arm. An excellent club. Straightening, holding it ready, she moved to the doorway and cautiously peeked out. He was not in the empty street. Moira considered her alternatives as she turned to move through the room toward the hole that had been a window.

One possibility was to hide within the village and hope to stay hidden until dark. But night was a long way off, and any hiding place could become a trap. There was a hole in the floor near one corner of the room, leading down into a dark cellar. Moira glanced at it in passing, before immediately discarding the idea. She had been confined too long. She couldn't stomach burying herself in an underground hole, deliberately resuming a passive waiting role, depending entirely on chance that he would not discover her.

The other alternative was to keep moving: down to the bottom of the village, and out across the narrow valley below it. If she could outdistance Bruno long enough to reach the densely wooded hillslope on the other side, Moira knew she could lose him in there.

She reached the gaping hole in the thick stone wall, where the rear window had been. Carefully, she edged forward and peered out, turning her head quickly to scan both directions. Outside was a tight, twisting alleyway. It was empty, and to her right it twisted down toward the lower part of the village.

Gripping the club tightly, Moira climbed up into the window hole. As she swung down from it into the alley, a small portion of the lower wall gave way under her weight. The dislodged stone fell with a crash that echoed through the silence of the abandoned houses. If Bruno hadn't known where to hunt for her before, he knew now.

Moira darted through the alley and dodged into the next wall opening she came to. Without pause, but placing each step with care to make no further noise, she worked her way downward through the interiors of a series of crumbling buildings, altering her direction drastically several times.

When she stopped she was in another alleyway, just below the center of the village. She looked back listening tensely. There was no sound of pursuit, though she was certain he was back there, somewhere. Moira scanned the broken rooftops, looking for rising dust. There was nothing. No sign or sound of his movements.

For a full minute Moira remained frozen in position, watching and listening. Nothing. Exercising harsh control over her jangling nerves, Moira turned to resume working her way down.

It was then that she heard it: a faint rattle of stones. From somewhere below her, among the lowest houses. Only a small sound, much less than she had made. But in the heavy silence of that dead village it carried distinctly.

He had circled around her position, guessing where she would head, and moving to cut her off. He was down there now, between her and the refuge of that wooded hill.

But—that meant she was between him and the car.

He would have its keys with him. But that presented no obstacle. She'd been fifteen when young Nardy Vizzini, showing off, had taught her how to start a car without a key, by jumping the ignition. A long time ago, but it was one bit of practical lore she hadn't forgotten.

Moira unfroze and turned back the way she'd come. Moving swiftly but quietly, she threaded through the ruined houses toward the upper edge of the village. In a few minutes she was back at the narrow gap between houses, by which she'd come in.

She slowed to a halt as she neared the outer end. Inching forward, she hefted the club to shoulder height, primed to use it on anything that moved near her. There was no one out there to use it on. Nothing but the slope, rising away to the dark ruins of the fortress on its crest. And the blue Renault to her left, its front bumper almost touching a broken house wall.

Its left front fender had been crumpled in its race down the rocky slope after her. But not enough to cut into the tire; and otherwise the car looked sound. The door on the driver's side hung wide open, the way Bruno had left it when he'd jumped out to search for her inside the village.

Moira took a full step out from between the houses, and shot another swift look around her from this new vantage point. There was nothing moving; no one in sight. She moved quickly toward the car.

As she reached it, there was a small scraping sound just to her left. She whirled toward it. Bruno stepped out of a shadowed doorway.

His thick, short-fingered hands were slightly curled, like tensed claws. His face was savage, but his eyes held no more expression than two pieces of dull ice.

The ease with which he'd outthought her made her burn with shame. He'd simply thrown a few small stones toward the lower part of the village, knowing it would lure her in the opposite direction. Out of her shame welled fury, and she did not try to run again. Instead she launched herself at him, swinging the club with all her might.

The burning anger injected unusual speed into her attack. But Bruno's reflex action made it seem slow. He went down on one knee, and the club slashed the air above his bowed head. Before she could recover her balance and swing again, he came up off his knee and his clawed left hand clamped around her wrist, just below the hand that held the club. He jerked her toward him, and his right fist exploded against the underside of her jaw. She was spun out of his grasp, spilling into swirling blackness. She did not feel herself hit the ground.

* * *

427

When she came to, she lay on the bunk in her tower cell. The hinges of her jaws were so sore and swollen she could hardly open her mouth. When she moved, the pain radiated through all of her face and struck needles into the backs of her eyes.

Twilight showed through the cell window. The statuette of the goddess she'd left on the sill was gone. What Moira saw there, instead, was the padlock, attaching one end of her chain to one of the bars.

Moira's slitted eyes followed the length of the chain. The other end was handcuffed securely to her ankle. Bruno's intention was plain: the chain was never going to be removed again. It was long enough to allow her to move anywhere inside the cell. This was the way he intended to keep her from now on.

Nausea rose inside her as she struggled to a sitting position on the bed. She leaned weakly against the rough stone wall of her cell, an old, unpleasant memory returning to plague her.

She'd been extremely awkward as a child, and what her aunt had politely termed "chunky." And at nine she'd fallen from a swing and driven her front teeth back into her gums. That had been the first time she'd had gas at a dentist's, when he'd pulled them out. For three years she'd walked around with no front teeth. And for quite some time afterwards, she'd been unable to shake the complex—of being ugly, clumsy, ridiculous.

That feeling was back with her now, as she leaned against the stone wall fighting the nausea and pain, staring at her chain in the dimming twilight of her cell.

3

The bald, sixtyish courier, who had taken the latest tape using the Budapest Code to New York, returned to Washington late that afternoon. His plane came in over the dark surface of Chesapeake Bay and touched down smoothly at National Airport, braking as it coasted along one of the black runways that angled between strips of patchy grass, and turning in to halt behind the terminal building. The courier was first spotted as he came from the plane into the terminal through Gate 18B.

The spotter was a woman sitting in one of the purple plastic chairs in the shuttle waiting room by the gate. She took a small mirror from the handbag open on her lap and appeared to study herself in it as she rearranged the curl of her mousy hair over her right ear. Pasted to the mirror was a copy of the courier's photograph, which Lang had brought with him from New York. The spotter checked it to make sure the man hurrying past was the one she'd been waiting for. Then she waited until he had gone out of sight into the beige exit corridor. Taking a small radio unit from her handbag, she activated it and gave the two-word alert signal.

The courier came under observation again as he emerged from the top of the stairway leading up from the 18B exit corridor. The spotter this time was in one of the phone booths lined against the wall across from the top of the stairs. The courier paused and took a careful look around him, obviously checking on whether he was being tailed or watched.

The spotter pretended to be engrossed in his telephone conversation. The courier got a coin from his pocket and stepped into one of the other phone booths. The spotter hung up his own phone and counted to ten. Then he stepped out of his booth. When he reached the courier's booth he paused to check his watch, observing as he did so that the courier had just finished dialing. The spotter walked away briskly in the direction of the main waiting room. He was out of sight when the courier came out of the booth.

His phone call had been extremely brief. Again he glanced around warily at the people in his immediate vicinity. All of them seemed to be going purposefully about their own business, with no interest in him. Among them were two new members of the Washington team George Rudofsky had assigned to Lang's operation.

The two agents were converging on the courier from opposite directions when he walked away from the bank of phone booths. The one coming toward him passed him and kept going, turning into the terminal diner. The agent behind the courier followed him out of the building to the taxi stand. The courier got into the line of people waiting for cabs, and the agent did too, directly behind him.

The line moved quickly. In less than two minutes the courier was at the head of it. But when a taxi pulled up in front of him he stood aside and looked at the agent waiting behind him. "Go ahead. I'm waiting for someone." He had a Southern drawl and an assured, slightly aggressive manner.

The agent thanked him, got into the waiting taxi, and gave the driver an address in downtown Washington. His taxi pulled away, another pulled in, and the courier motioned for a woman who was next in line to take it. He got into the next one.

A porter loading a baggage lift nearby bent down behind it and reported the number of the courier's taxi over a small transmitting unit tuned to three waiting surveillance cars.

When the courier's taxi swung out of the airport exit road into the George Washington Memorial Parkway, he turned to glance back through its rear window at the cars behind it. One was an aging Buick sedan: the first surveillance car. The courier took a long look, and then faced forward again. The agent seated next to the driver of the Buick got on the car radio to the other two tail cars, following some distance behind.

The next time the courier looked back, his taxi was crossing the bridge over the Potomac into Washington. The aging Buick was no longer in sight. The car tailing his taxi at that point was a Plymouth station wagon.

Lang's instructions to his Washington team had been strict: play the courier with extreme caution. They were getting close to the source of the Budapest tapes now. In this area the enemy would be nervously alert. If it came to a choice, the members of the team were to lose the courier, rather than run the slightest risk of his detecting their presence. They could always establish contact with him again the following day, or the one after that, now that they knew what he looked like and part of his operational routine.

When the courier's taxi pulled to a stop in front of the Sotuhern Building in the heart of the downtown business area, it was being followed by the third tail car. Lang and one of his team were in the back seat, both wearing hats. The courier climbed out of the taxi and looked at the traffic that had been behind it. The tail car swept past, turned the next corner, and stopped as soon as the buildings cut off his view of it.

Lang took off his hat and dropped it on the seat as he jumped out. His surveillance partner did the same, and strode in the lead back around the corner. Lang followed him as far as the corner, and then diverged, crossing the street and entering a drugstore on the opposite corner.

They had moved too fast. The courier was still getting change from the cabdriver when Lang's man approached him. The taxi pulled away and the courier made another survey of his immediate area. The surveillance man walked past him and kept on going without looking back. The courier glanced after him, and finally turned and hurried into the Southern Building: a solid, white-stone edifice containing ten floors of small commercial offices. Lang left the drugstore, dodged across the street, and walked in after him.

There was a short, wide hallway leading to the elevators. The courier was gone. Lang strode to the elevators and glanced to his left down another hallway that angled from the first. The courier was going out the glass doors at the end of it, into the side street.

It was the same side street where the tail car was parked. Lang hoped the driver was keeping alert enough to spot him. The courier hurried across the street and into an alley on the other side. Reaching the glass doors the courier had used, Lang was about to go out after him when something hit him and he stopped himself.

What had hit him was the fact that the courier had left the building, crossed the street, and disappeared into the alley without once looking back. It was the first time he'd failed to check whether he was being watched or followed. Lang stayed where he was, inside the glass doors, watching the street outside.

A full thirty seconds went by. Lang was about to curse himself for excessive suspicion when a woman appeared from somewhere to the right outside the glass doors and angled across the street toward the alley. She appeared to be in her fifties, a short, solidly built woman wearing a brown cardigan and dark green skirt.

Lang watched her go into the alley. His suspicion had been justified. The courier hadn't looked back because he'd had the woman planted there to make a final check on whether he was being followed.

As soon as she was out of sight, Lang stepped out of the building and looked toward the place where his tail car had been parked. It was gone. Lang activated the compact two-way radio strapped in a shoulder holster under his jacket, and spoke into the lapel-button mike attached to it. The tail car's driver responded quickly: he'd circled the other block and now had the courier in sight, waiting at the other end of the alley.

A moment later the driver reported that the courier had been joined by the woman. They hurried across the street and into a department store. The driver reported that he was going to circle that block in case they came out the other side—and that the other two tail cars were converging on the block.

Lang's surveillance partner appeared at that moment, coming around the corner to Lang's left. He followed as Lang sprinted across the street and through the alley.

They'd been lucky so far, but from that point on their luck abruptly drained out: Lang and his partner combed the inside of the department store's ground floor without spotting the courier and his woman. They'd apparently gone straight through and out the other side of the block. But the nearest tail car had gotten stuck in traffic and failed to circle the block in time to pick them up coming out. Whether they were still on foot, or now using a taxi or private car, they were gone.

All three tail cars immediately spread through the surrounding area, and Lang re-entered the department store with his partner to check out the upper floors. But none of them managed to catch sight of the couple again. Their quarry had vanished, for that day.

4

Garcia arrived in Washington that evening, and he and Lang spent some hours making detailed preparations for the next time the courier would take one of the tapes to New York.

The next time turned out to be the following morning. At 6:30 A.M. the courier arrived by cab at Washington's National Airport and entered the Eastern

Airlines terminal building. The cabdriver who'd brought him told one of Lang's men that he'd picked him up in front of the Hilton Hotel.

When the courier boarded his plane, Garcia had already been aboard for two minutes, dressed in a flight steward's uniform. Shortly after the 7 A.M. take-off, it was Garcia who served the courier a cup of coffee. And when the courier finished it, Garcia was the one who took his empty cup away, handling it with care so as not to disturb the courier's fingerprints on it.

When the plane reached New York's LaGuardia Airport at 7:53 A.M., Garcia did not get off. He remained on board for its return flight to Washington, and personally carried the coffee cup from National Airport to the FBI lab on Pennsylvania Avenue to have the prints lifted and begin processing them.

When the courier returned from New York, his prints had still not been identified, though the computers were working on it. As on the previous day, the courier used one of the phone booths at the top of the stairs in the terminal building to make a call immediately after coming off his plane. Lang had had recording devices installed in each of the phones there during the previous night. The device in the phone the courier used recorded both the number he dialed in Washington, and the short conversation that followed:

A woman answered on the second ring: "Yes?"

Courier: "Sheila, I'm at the airport now."

Woman: "All right."

That was all of it. They both hung up, and the courier went out to take a taxi into the city. Again, three tail cars alternated in following him.

The courier got out of his taxi at the T Street entrance of the Hilton Hotel and went inside. This time the tail car that was on him at that point immediately swung around to cover the hotel's Nineteenth Street entrance, and signaled the other two cars to converge on the hotel via Connecticut Avenue. The courier emerged on Nineteenth Street, and half a minute later the woman came out and joined him. They crossed the street and cut through the adjacent block. The nearest tail car, circling, spotted them driving off in a brand-new red Toyota, and reported the license number over its radio.

Lang got the report over his own car radio. By then he was parked on Columbia Road, across from an expensive, old-fashioned apartment building. The number the courier had phoned from the airport belonged to one of the apartments on the top floor of that building, and to a name which might be real or assumed: Michael Remington.

The building was not far from the Hilton, and very soon after getting the report Lang spotted the red Toyota approaching. It maneuvered into a parking spot down the block. The courier and the woman got out and walked to the apartment building, holding hands. Minutes after they went inside, Garcia came through on Lang's car radio with the news that the name registered for the phone and the top floor apartment was not a phony. The fingerprints on the courier's coffee cup had been matched with prints the U. S. Department of the Army had on file for one of its retired career officers: former Major Michael Remington.

Within the next few hours Lang learned just about everything there was to know about former Major Michael Remington and his wife, Sheila Remington. Except the one vital fact he needed to know most.

Lang began assigning the members of his team to the various tasks necessary for finding out who Remington was getting the tapes from.

NINETEEN

1

Michael and Sheila Remington left their apartment building at six that evening and drove off in the red Toyota. Two of Lang's units followed them to Duke Zeibert's Restaurant on L Street, four blocks from the White House. One of the surveillance men joined the crush of professional lobbyists unwinding at the bar after a hard day's influence-peddling. He watched the Remingtons take a table in the back and spend the next hour over a good dinner, making no contacts.

During that hour Lang entered their apartment with Garcia, an Agency locksmith, and two electronics specialists. The building's large marble entrance lobby, with its fading but still effective air of 1930s luxury, was guarded around the clock by a doorman who doubled as switchboard operator. But there was a rear service door which the locksmith was able to open with relative ease, and a fire-escape stairway by which they climbed to the top floor without being seen.

The Remington apartment consisted of four big, high-ceilinged rooms, comfortably furnished. While the specialists put a tap on the telephone and planted bugs in each room, Lang and Garcia searched the place with practiced precision, missing no possible hiding place but leaving no trace of their work. There was no code machine, and nothing else to indicate that the occupants were part of an enemy espionage line. Lang found only one thing of interest: the alarm clock on the table between the twin beds was set for five o'clock.

The last bug had just been planted when one of Lang's outside men signaled over Garcia's walkie-talkie that the Remingtons were on their way home. They left the apartment and the building the way they'd entered, relocking the doors behind them.

Lang's listening post was inside a van parked half a block from the apartment building. Lang and Garcia joined the two men on duty inside the van. The four of them dined on hamburgers and containers of coffee brought in by one of the team, while they listened to the television programs the Remingtons watched, and to scraps of conversation which revealed no useful information at all.

It was only nine-thirty when Michael and Sheila Remington turned off their TV set and began preparing to go to bed. Lang and Garcia left the van and walked a few blocks to a CIA-owned safehouse for agents in transit, a three-story brown brick building with green trim on Belmont Road. They bought a bottle of Bourbon on the way, and took it up to the room George Rudofsky had reserved for them. It was small and none too clean, with two narrow beds close together. The cream-painted walls were scrawled with graffiti left by previous occupants. Garcia read one choice item aloud as he undressed to go to bed:

> There was a young girl from Catania,
> Who when asked if she had a Vagania,
> Said yes sir I do,
> But I use it to screw,
> And not as an ersatz Lasagna.

"Jesus," Lang groaned, and stretched out on one of the narrow beds. On the wall by his head someone had printed: "God exists, but He's a tease." Whoever had named their profession "intelligence," Lang decided, must have had a fine sense of sarcasm.

They turned off the light and silently passed the

bottle back and forth for some time before managing to force themselves to sleep.

2

The phone on the nightstand between their beds rang in the dark. Lang was fully awake by the time his hand found it and pulled it to him. "Okay . . ."

The voice at the other end belonged to one of the night men assigned to the listening post: "It's four in the morning. I was told to ring you."

"Thanks." Lang hung up the phone and snapped on the light.

Half an hour later he and Garcia were at the listening post inside the parked van.

At 5 A.M. they heard the alarm clock in the Remington bedroom go off.

Fifteen minutes later, when the Remington phone rang, Michael Remington answered it promptly, sounding wide awake: "Good morning."

A man's voice at the other end asked: "How is everything?" There was an accent—Lang pegged it as German.

Remington answered: "Fine. Everything is fine. No problems at all."

"Good," the caller said. "Ontario and Florida." And hung up. It had been much too short to afford any chance of tracing the call.

In less than five minutes Remington and his wife emerged from their apartment building and hurried to the Toyota. By then Lang was on his way with Garcia and two other agents to the juncture of Ontario Road and Florida Avenue. When the Toyota got there, the four men were already hidden at various points around it, watching through binoculars.

There was an open pay phone on one corner. Sheila

Remington, who was driving, pulled the Toyota to a stop beside it. Her husband got out and stepped to the phone. He dropped in a coin and appeared to dial a number. But he failed to dial enough to get through to anything. As he pretended to wait for an answer, Michael Remington reached under the phone box and removed something attached there. He slipped a small, flat package into the left side pocket of his jacket and then, as though the number he had called didn't answer, he hung up and got back into the car.

The entire operation had taken less than fifteen seconds. Sheila Remington drove away. One of Lang's tail units reported shortly that she had dropped her husband at the Ambassador Hotel. From that point he took a taxi, out to National Airport, while his wife drove the Toyota back to their apartment house.

Lang and Garcia got the report over their car radio as they drove to a building in the 1000 block on N.W. Sixteenth Street. It was similar to most of the commercial office buildings on that block: blank-faced and modestly modern. But anyone entering without proof of authorization would find it quite impossible to get above the ground floor.

It had been in this building that Lang had worked in "the pool" while he'd had only provisional clearance, back in his early days with the CIA. The job they'd given him had consisted entirely of punch-taping the names, addresses, and other basic data on every known Yugoslavian college graduate. Nobody doing this and similar jobs had had less than a B.A., and there'd been a number of Masters and even some Fulbright scholars among them. The crushing dullness of their tasks had driven them all crazy, and they'd tried to relieve it each evening by playing roller-chair basketball in the big main offiice, using secretaries' chairs and wastebaskets at each end of the room. Lang had been about at the end of his endurance when relief, in the form of his top security clearance, had finally come through.

The office assigned to him now for his operational headquarters was three floors above the suffering newcomers' pool area. Lang and Garcia settled down in it and talked out the present status of their operation, in preparation for a scheduled nine-o'clock meeting with George Rudofsky.

Rudofsky arrived at 9 A.M. on the dot. Lang and Garcia briefed him on the latest developments in the situation, and then the three of them considered how to get from where they were to their objective: the source of the Budapest Code tapes.

The first problem lay in the enemy's method of operation at this point in its delivery line. The fact that the source had phoned the Remingtons, to tell them where he'd left the tape this morning, meant that he had never left it in the same place. There was no place where they could wait and hope to grab him the next time. The places where he could leave the tapes were limitless; and he'd always be gone from each one before the Remingtons—or anybody else—could respond to his phone call and get there.

So, how were they to make the giant step, from the Remingtons to the man with the German accent who called them?

They *could* seize the Remingtons and rip it out of them—if they knew the answer. There were techniques guaranteed to make them talk, and none of the three men in Lang's office had much compunction about using these techniques under the present circumstances. But the three of them agreed that it was likely to prove counterproductive.

The tapes were encoded before they reached the Remingtons, who probably had no knowledge of what they were about. Their position in the enemy's delivery system, operating between the source and New York, served only one purpose: helping the source to maintain his invisibility. If this was their function, they almost certainly would not know the true identity of the man who phoned them, nor how to find him.

Under those circumstances, seizing the Remingtons would achieve nothing except to alert their source—and blow the whole thing. That brought the three of them back, after an hour's discussion, to the point at which they'd started: how to get from the Remingtons to the man who left the tapes for them?

In the ensuing silence, Rudofsky dropped a quiet bomb: "FBI's asked to take over the operation. It's a formal demand through channels this time. My guess is they'll get what they want—unless we can produce the source of those tapes first. Which means—*mighty fast.*"

Garcia cursed, softly and viciously.

Lang drew a slow breath. "There's one way that might work." He explained what he had in mind, in a deliberately matter-of-fact tone.

Rudofsky stared at him. After a moment he said: "That's an extremely nasty way . . ."

"I know it is," Lang told him soberly. "But it's the only way I can think of, if we need the results that fast."

Garcia was frowning at Rudofsky. "You're pretty finicky all of a sudden," he said with guarded anger, "considering they're both traitors."

The anger with which Rudofsky lashed back was not at all guarded: "I don't give a *fuck* what happens to Remington and his wife. It's our outfit I'm concerned about." He looked again to Lang, scowling. "You'd have to be damned *careful,*" he said slowly, "that it could never be traced back to us."

Lang nodded. "That I know."

Rudofsky continued to worry it in his mind, pulling at his rubbery cheek with the fingers of one hand. Finally he got to his feet and looked down at Lang, still worrying. "All right," he told Lang. "Go ahead and do it."

3

Jorgen woke up that afternoon with a constriction in his chest. His first thought was that it was his old heart trouble starting again. But he was experiencing none of the other symptoms associated with this, and he finally concluded that the constriction was the result of anxiety. That disturbed him more than if it had been his heart, because he couldn't identify the source of the anxiety feeling.

He had long ago learned not to allow the normal, constantly present hazard of operating behind enemy lines to wear at his nerves. And he was aware of nothing unusual that had occurred to trigger the anxiety.

For some time, Jorgen continued to lie in bed, breathing the faintly musty odor of the old house, searching for what it was that bothered him. The alarm clock beside his bed told him that it was a few minutes past two in the afternoon. As always when he'd spent the night encoding one of Alexander Rhalles' tapes, he had gone to sleep shortly after his post-5 A.M. phone call to Remington. So he'd had more than the eight hours of sleep he required. As he was accustomed to night work, his sleep was never disturbed, even subconsciously, by the amount of daylight and street noises filtering through the closed window and shade of his bedroom. And if he'd had a bad dream, he could not recall it.

Scowling, Jorgen stretched himself. That made him conscious of the fact that he was alone in the bed, and suddenly it came to him that this must be what was bothering him: the lack of a woman. There was one among the women he sometimes talked with, in the bar he frequented around the block, whom he fancied: a good-looking Puerto Rican widow in her forties. But the peculiar timing of his daily routine, and the presence of the coding machine in the living room of his apartment, made it virtually impossible for him to establish a relationship with her. And prostitutes did not appeal to him. It was not only the physical sex act that he required, but the emotional content of shared pleasure, however brief.

That was a basic part of his nature. He needed a woman in his life. Not having one, he began to feel old, and this feeling provoked anxiety.

Having identified its source to his satisfaction, Jorgen felt the constriction in his chest slowly ease. Smiling at his human frailty, he left the bed and went into the kitchen to make his breakfast: tea and buttered toast with honey. That his frailty could assert itself, when he was involved in such a demanding and dangerous profressional life, did not annoy him. On the contrary, his need of a woman was satisfying proof of the life surge still very active in him. And it never interfered with his professionalism. Once, back in 1943 in Brussels, it had even saved his skin.

Jorgen ate his breakfast seated at the kitchen table, facing an opened window. It looked out across an open lot littered with garbage, to a high brick wall on which neighborhood artists had garishly painted a huge yellow anl red devil, brandishing a black hypodermic needle in one hand and spilling white powder from the other. Under the devil were painted words: "The Evils of Drugs." Scattered around the words were dead black children, and black muggers knifing black victims. Jorgen gazed at it absently as he remembered that time in '43.

He had been one of the few who'd escaped when the Red Orchestra's spy circuit in Berlin had been wiped out by the "hounds"—Soviet espionage terminology for enemy counterespionage agents. In that case the hounds had been officers of German military intelligence, working in unusual co-operation with Branch IV of the Reich Central Security Department. While they'd made their final roll-up of the circuit, dragging the last of its members to the Gestapo head-quarters at 8 Prinz-Albrecht-Strasse, Jorgen had managed to slip through the dragnet and reach Belgium.

He had made contact with the Red Orchestra's Brussels circuit, and joined it. Two months later the German "hounds" had closed down that one, too. In one night, Abwehr and Gestapo flying squads had struck almost simultaneously at the sleeping quarters of every member of the Brussels circuit.

But they'd missed Jorgen, because he hadn't been in his room that night. He'd spent that night in the apartment of an uninvolved woman he'd met a few days before. Because of her he'd survived, to learn the next morning that he was the last member of the circuit left. He'd slipped through the enemy dragnet into France, and from there back into Germany, where he'd spent the rest of the war hidden in the farmhouse of a widow who later became his wife.

Jorgen put the morose memories out of his mind as he washed up his breakfast dishes. He showered, shaved, and got dressed to go out for some of the fresh air and mild exercise Dr. Brauer had prescribed for his heart condition. Before leaving, Jorgen shut and locked the kitchen window. He attached a tiny bit of Scotch Tape between it and its frame, so that he would know if anyone opened the window from outside while he was away.

All the windows of his apartment were rigged with this simple warning device. And after stepping out of the apartment and locking the door, he fixed another bit of tape between the top of it and the frame. It was invisible there, but a touch of his finger would reveal if the door had been opened in his absence. Jorgen left the house and walked to his car.

One of the pleasures of Washington, for Jorgen, was the ease of getting out of it into the surrounding country. Fifteen minutes after getting into his car, he was across the District of Columbia line driving out River Road through the dwindling suburban communities and increasingly wild wooded areas of Montgomery County. Exactly sixteen miles beyond the line, he pulled to a stop on the shoulder of the road by a densely timbered stretch with not a house in sight.

Locking his car, Jorgen entered a dirt path that wound through the woods and began his almost daily hour of jogging. On rainy days he did an hour of setting-up exercises in his apartment, instead. But this was far less boring. He had the timing down to an instinct, and no longer had to glance at his wristwatch: alternating one minute of jogging with half a minute's fast walking, filling his lungs and refreshing his blood with the clean country air. When he returned to the car he had a pleasurable awareness of every nerve ending and muscle in his body, and a delicious sense of lightness.

Before getting into his car he picked up a flat stone a bit larger than his spread-fingered hand. This was the spot for that night's drop, if Rhalles had another tape for him.

Jorgen took a tube of luminescent paint from his glove compartment and smeared some of it on the stone. As the paint dried it virtually disappeared. But it would be visible in the dark, just enough to be spotted by someone who knew where to look closely for it. Waiting until there were no cars on the road, Jorgen leaned out his open door and placed the stone on the ground. Then he shut the door, started the car, and drove back into Washington.

He had lunch in the Columbia Station, an informal neighborhood bar-restaurant around the corner from the house in which he lived. It was late for lunch; some of the others at the tables in the two long rooms were already ordering dinner. Jorgen had a tuna salad with a glass of draft beer. The woman he liked wasn't there, but as Jorgen finished eating an elderly Cuban exile came in carrying a folded chessboard and a box of pieces. He raised his eyebrows at Jorgen, who nodded and pushed his plate aside.

445

The Cuban sat down without a word of greeting, opened his board, and they began setting out the pieces. Jorgen didn't know if the man was a refugee from Batista's Cuba or from the subsequent Castro regime; and the Cuban had never expressed any interest in Jorgen's background. That was the peculiar nature of chess intimacy: the only thing about you that anyone cared about was the strength of your game.

Jorgen and the Cuban fought to a draw, and Jorgen declined the offer of a rematch. It was 6:30 P.M., according to the Ballantine beer clock over the entrance door. Time to go home and begin waiting.

He bought lamb chops in a supermarket on the way, for his supper later that night in his apartment. Reaching the old house, he went in and up the steps to his floor. Before opening his door he reached up and ran one finger along the edge. The bit of Scotch Tape was still in place.

Inside the apartment Jorgen checked the tapes on all the windows. None of them had been disturbed. He didn't bother to check the coding machine on the table. If anyone had tampered with that he'd have known it the instant he'd opened the apartment door; or even before.

Putting the chops in the refrigerator, he got a book from the table beside his bed. It was a copy of Alexander Rhalles' study of the Haitian slave revolution. Carrying it into the living room, Jorgen settled into a battered armchair, opened it to the page he'd marked with a scrap of paper, and resumed reading where he'd left off.

At nine-thirty his phone rang.

Jorgen put aside the book and picked up the phone. He listened, saying nothing. At the other end of the line, Alexander Rhalles said: "I have a delivery for you." And hung up without waiting for a response.

Jorgen put on his jacket and went out, after seeing to the usual precautions. He took a brisk half-hour walk before going to his car. Habit kept him alert for possible tails. Driving out River Road, he reached the point where he'd left the marked stone, and kept going, watching his rear view mirror. One mile further he pulled off the road and stopped, watching two cars that had been behind him speed past.

When there were no other cars in sight coming from either direction, Jorgen executed a U-turn and drove back one mile. He pulled over onto the shoulder of the road by the densely wooded stretch, and switched off his headlights. Opening the glove compartment, he drew out a small pair of binoculars equipped with powerful night lenses.

Remaining seated behind the wheel, Jorgen spent five minutes methodically inspecting the surrounding darkness. When he was satisfied he put the binoculars away, waited again until there were no other cars coming, and opened his side door. There was a faint glow on the ground beside his car. It wasn't even necessary to get out. Leaning sideways he reached down wth one hand. turned over the marked stone, and picked up the plasti-wrapped tape cassette Rhalles had left for him.

Slipping it in his jacket pocket, Jorgen shut the door, snapped on his headlights, and drove back to Washington, regularly checking on whether he was being followed.

Back inside his apartment, he put Rhalles' cassette on his tape player and settled down at the coding machine to begin his night of work. At midnight he took a break and broiled the lamb chops. He ate them with a tomato and two slices of heavily buttered Italian bread, finished with a cup of instant coffee, and went back to work.

At a few minutes before 4 A.M. he was finished. He wrapped the code cassette he took from the machine, together with payment for whichever member of a flight crew picked it up in New York for transport to

Vienna, in a paper that he sealed with tape. Putting this in his jacket pocket, Jorgen unwound Rhalles' clear-text tape from its cassette and burned it in the bathroom, flushing the ashes down the toilet. Then he did ten miniutes of calisthenics to loosen up after the hours of sitting hunched over the code machine. Washing his hands and face, Jorgen put on his jacket and went out to the car.

He drove in the direction of Union Station, through dark, deserted streets. It was ten minutes after 5 A.M. when he stopped beside a pay phone at the corner of Parker and Congress Streets. Getting out of the car, he made certain nobody else was in sight before taking the flat package from his pocket and taping it under the telephone. When his watch showed exactly 5:15 A.M., he dropped a coin in the phone and dialed the Remingtons' apartment.

It rang five times without being picked up.

Jorgen hung up the phone, staring at it. Retrieving the coin, he reinserted it and dialed the Remington number again, carefully.

Again there was no answer.

This time Jorgen hung up after the fourth ring. He forced himself to take a deep breath, and let it out slow. Once more he used the coin, this time dialing the switchboard number in the lobby of the Remingtons' building.

The night doorman came on sounding drugged with sleep. Jorgen spoke slowly to make his accent less noticeable: "I'm sorry to bother you at this time of the morning, but I've been trying to reach Mr. and Mrs. Michael Remington. I'm Mrs. Remington's uncle, and I've just arrived in town. They were expecting me, but I've tried calling their apartment and they don't answer. Could you possibly check to see if they're there?"

There was a short silence at the other end. Then the nightman said uneasily: "Jesus, I'm sorry to be the one to tell you . . . Mr. and Mrs. Remington were in a bad accident yesterday afternoon, with their car. Got smashed into by a truck. Drunk driver, from what I heard. They're both in George Washington Hospital . . . in pretty bad shape, I'm afraid. If you want . . ."

Jorgen hung up on him. The call had already taken too long, if there was a trace being put through on it. He snatched the package from under the phone and shoved it back in his pocket as he wrenched open his car door. He drove out of the area quickly, waiting until he was on the other side of the city before allowing himself to begin thinking out what had happened—and what it might mean.

The constriction in his chest had returned.

4

The dawn light spreading through the deserted streets made it easy for Jorgen to watch for any car that might be trying to tail him. He saw nothing to indicate that he was being followed at this point. Of course, the enemy could be trailing out of sight, by means of a homing device planted in his car. If so, once he left the car they would have to fall back on old-fashioned person-to-person surveillance.

Jorgen chose the solidly black area north of Thomas Circle, because it would be easy to spot anyone who didn't belong there. He parked in a block where many of the brick row houses were abandoned and partially gutted, with smashed windows and signs of squatter occupancy. This was the heart of the street-level drug traffic, a violent-crime area unsafe to wander in by night or day. But at dawn even the heroin-starved muggers were holed up trying to sleep. Jorgen left his car, crossed the street, and entered an alley.

Reaching the other end of it, he paused and looked out, taking his time to do it thoroughly. There were no pedestrians in sight, anywhere. No car came around the corner in his direction, though he waited two minutes, and none cruised past either end of the street. Jorgen stepped out of the alley and circled the block. When he was back to the street where he'd left his car, he did a check in both directions. There were no moving cars in sight, and none of the parked cars were new ones.

So he was not being followed. This did not make Jorgen feel much easier. It only meant that if the operation had been blown, it had not happened at his end. If the Remingtons had been taken, they didn't know enough to lead the enemy's hounds to him.

But if they had been taken, everything else was finished. Irina Frejenko had made that plain: if the network was breached, at any point, the operation was to be immediately terminated.

The first order of business was to find out if the Remingtons had actually been in a car accident, and, if they had, whether the accident had been a planned one. Until Jorgen knew the answers, the code tape in his pocket would have to wait. If the accident turned out to be genuine, with no sinister planning behind it, the tape could be delivered the following morning.

The simplest way to begin finding out would be to contact George Washington Hospital. But if it were a trap, the enemy's hounds would be waiting there to grab him. And they'd be set up for a trace on any phone inquiry about the condition of the Remingtons. Even routine handling of such an inquiry would take enough time for them to finish the trace, and they'd be on top of him by the time the call was completed.

Jorgen drove to within a block of the Hilton Hotel, and walked the rest of the way. It was one place where, even at that hour of the morning, there was enough activity so his presence in the big lobby area would not draw curious stares. He closed himself in

450

one of the lobby phone booths on the lower level, and dialed a number.

He had been given this number, and a code name —John Harmon—to use in case of emergency. He knew nothing about "John Harmon" except that the man also had his number—in case the emergency developed in some other part of the operation.

A voice fighting its way out of sleep answered: "Hello?"

Jorgen said: "Good morning, John."

"I'm afraid you have the wrong number," the man at the other end told him.

That was the response he was supposed to give. Jorgen said, "Mr. Harmon, this is Jorgen."

There was no trace of sleepiness left in the voice at the other end of the line: "Yes, what's the problem?"

Jorgen explained the problem. The other man listened, and then said, "I've got a contact who can probably find the answer for you without too much difficulty. But I can't call him this early in the morning. I'll get in touch with you in . . . say about three hours."

"Make it at exactly nine-thirty," Jorgen told him, and gave the number of the phone he was using.

He did not return to his apartment after leaving the hotel. Instead he drove to an all-night diner on Fifteenth Street, and forced himself to eat a full breakfast. He ordered tea, buttered toast, eggs, and bacon. It was more than he usually had for breakfast, but he'd learned long ago that when there was a chance of suddenly finding yourself on the run it was a good idea to nourish yourself while you could.

Jorgen ate slowly, remembering that other morning so long ago in Brussels: when he'd wakened to discover that the rest of his circuit had been rolled up during the night, and he was the only one left—with the entire enemy dragnet concentrating now on him.

When he left the diner, Jorgen walked to Lafayette Square. People were beginning to populate the streets, hurrying to early-starting jobs, and he was not conspicuous. As he strolled through the square, squirrels recognized him and approached for a handout. Jorgen shook his head and continued his stroll, across Pennsylvania Avenue, around the White House and the Ellipse. An ordinary tourist, out early to take in the sights before the crowds showed up: the Washington Monument and along the Mall to the Lincoln Memorial, and up to Kennedy Center.

Walking helped him to keep his thinking coolly logical. If what had happened to Michael and Sheila Remington *was* an accident, it was only an inconvenience, not a disaster. If the accident had been faked, the worst response was panic.

At nine-thirty Jorgen was back in the Hilton, waiting in the lobby phone booth. He picked up the phone on the first ring, and recognized the voice of the caller: "Hello, this is John."

"I'm afraid you have the wrong number," Jorgen said, "this is the Jorgen phone."

"John Harmon" then quickly told him what he'd found out, through a contact on the city's police force: the accident was undoubtedly real; Michael Remington had died in the hospital four hours earlier, and Sheila Remington was on the critical list, with an outside chance of pulling through.

It had happened a few blocks from the Remingtons' apartment building. The timing indicated that it had occurred when they were driving home, after Michael Remington's return from New York yesterday. A heavy truck loaded with refrigerators had gone through a stop sign and crashed into the side of the Toyota, demolishing it. The driver of the truck had fled the scene, but he'd been caught half an hour later. Medical tests had proved he had a very high alcohol content in his blood. He was presently in jail, being held without bail, and his wife was hysterically demanding that the Teamsters Union come up with enough money to hire a good criminal lawyer.

Jorgen was finally convinced: it had been a freak accident. He was relieved, but that still left him with a practical problem. Jorgen explained it to his contact, who promised to pass it on through his own emergency channels.

Leaving the hotel, Jorgen drove back to his own neighborhood to have a solid lunch and spend the rest of the day sleeping. He was going to need it, if Rhalles had another tape for him to encode that night, because in the morning he would have to fly to New York.

A replacement would be sent, eventually, to take over the Remingtons' place in the communications chain. But it would take time. Until the replacement arrived, Jorgen would have to do the Remingtons' job, as well as his own.

5

As Jorgen had anticipated, Alexander Rhalles phoned him that night to signal that he was leaving another tape. It was almost five in the morning when Jorgen finished encoding it. Half an hour later he drove out to Washington's National Airport carrying that night's code tape and the previous one. He left his car in the airport's public parking lot, and crossed to the Eastern Airlines terminal building to line up for the first flight on the shuttle to New York.

By this point Lang had considerably refined the operations of his people. That early in the morning there was a relatively small number of people arriving at the terminal. Each was photographed from concealment, and the method of arrival noted.

When the flight landed at LaGuardia Airport, Jorgen entered the shuttle building and used one of its pay phones to call the New York pickup man: George Alcazar.

Jorgen was one of four people who used the terminal phones after getting off that first flight from Washington. Each was observed doing so. And every pay phone in the building had been rigged with a recording device. The one in the phone Jorgen used recorded the fact that it was Alcazar's number he dialed, and that he hung up after letting it ring exactly two times.

Jorgen went outside and took a cab into Queens, to leave the two code tapes for Alcazar to pick up. The agent who had watched Jorgen make the call got on the next plane to Washington. When he reached National Airport, Lang showed him the pictures that had been taken of every man who'd boarded the first flight to New York.

The agent tapped the photograph of Jorgen.

When Jorgen returned from New York, he studied everyone around him attentively before going to his car. And did it again before driving away from the airport.

Lang's alternating surveillance units, keeping well out of Jorgen's range of vision, began the job of tailing him, using receivers tuned in on the oscillator that had been fastened to the underside of his car.

TWENTY

1

In Marseilles, Sawyer, Donhoff, and Titine had can-
vassed the area on both sides of the Canebière for two
frustrating days with the underworld escorts provided
by Marcel Alfani. Endlessly showing the same photographs and asking the same questions. It was on the
morning of the third day that Sawyer entered the
ground-floor bistro of the dilapidated Hotel Tunis,
one block from the Canebière, and got the first affirmative response.

It was raining again that morning: the sky soggy
with a low, milky overhang from which infinitely
tiny drops drifted without quite merging into mist.
On the sidewalk in front of the bistro, two blond teen-
age girls stood under the green and white awning of
a hot-seafood stand watching their boy friends tin-
kering with a motorcycle, one doing the work while
the other held an orange umbrella over him. Inside
the bistro the only customers were three shrunken old
women in plastic raincoats and black shawls, huddled
around one of the tables having a postbreakfast *pastis*.

The room had art-deco woodwork, fading murals
of frolicking mermaids, and harsh neon lighting. The
woman behind the bar was a plump, middle-aged
Arab, her crisp hair dyed red and a bright spot of
rouge on each prominent cheekbone. Sawyer's escort
introduced her as "Zu-Zu," and explained that she and
her husband owned both the bistro and hotel. To
Zu-Zu he explained that Marcel Alfani would appre-

ciate her answering truthfully, and would not appreciate it at all if she held anything back.

She shook Sawyer's hand with a warm, relaxed smile. He began by asking her about the man with the gray birthmark or scar on one cheek. Zu-Zu thought about it before shaking her head and saying she couldn't remember such a man. Her voice was soft and soothing.

He next spread the three photographs on the bar. The pictures of the Egyptian stele and the prehistoric goddess didn't mean anything to Zu-Zu. But she hesitated over the one of Christine Jonquet, frowning. Finally she nodded to herself. "Yes . . . she's the one. I don't know her name, but she stayed here in the hotel for a few days, about two months ago. With Jean-Marc."

"Who is Jean-Marc?"

She shrugged. "Just a guy. He used to stay here in the hotel a lot." She glanced toward the three old women at the table and lowered her voice. "I never knew exactly what he did, except he's something in the *milieu*. At least he used to be, in the old days. I hadn't seen him in . . . oh, six or seven years. I almost didn't recognize him when he showed up with this girl. He's got a beard now."

Sawyer thought about that. This Jean-Marc obviously hadn't had a gray mark on his cheek when Zu-Zu had known him in the past. But it could have been acquired since. The beard—either a fake or one grown before returning to Marseilles two months ago, and shaved off after leaving—could have hidden it.

He asked Zu-Zu: "What did he look like? Before the beard."

"Not very tall, but strong. Pretty good-looking, in a tough way . . ."

"Pale gray eyes?" Sawyer prompted, and she nodded. "Deep voice?"

She nodded again, and grinned. "Tough and sexy, like his face."

"What's his last name?"

"I don't know. I don't remember, if I ever knew it. It's that way with a lot of these guys in the *milieu,* you know."

"If he stayed in your hotel," Sawyer reminded her, "you'll have his name in your register."

Zu-Zu looked uncomfortably at his escort. The smile he gave her was encouraging but held a potential menace. She looked back at Sawyer and lowered her voice again: "We don't always register people who stay here. Some of them don't want to be registered, you understand?"

Sawyer understood. It was a place where criminals could hole up and not have their presence passed on to the police. In return, the hotel didn't bother to report income from them and pay taxes on it.

"Jean-Marc didn't want to be registered when he came with this girl," Zu-Zu went on, "just like he never did in the old days, when him and Hamid used to stay here."

Sawyer beamed at her. Hamid was the name of the Arab who had bought the Egyptian stele from Mario Fontanelli in Genoa—for a partner who liked ancient goddesses. And an Algerian Arab, name unknown, had bought the Venus figure—for someone. "You don't happen to remember this Hamid's last name?"

She laughed softly and shook her head. "No, I'm sorry. He was something in the *milieu,* like Jean-Marc, and I know he was from Algeria, but that's all. Come to think of it, I haven't seen *him* around Marseilles in about seven years either."

"Perhaps your husband has a better memory for names?"

"That's an idea—he just might know . . ." Zu-Zu turned to a button on the wall beside the cash register and pressed it three times. "That'll bring him down."

"Were Jean-Marc and Hamid partners," Sawyer asked her, "in whatever it was they did?"

"I don't know. They were pretty good friends. I think they were working for the same man, but I don't know who."

Sawyer glanced at his escort. "Do the two names together mean anything to you?"

"No, but seven years ago was before my time. I'm only in Marseilles a couple of years. Alfani might know, or be able to find out."

Zu-Zu's husband came down the stairs at the end of the bar. He was a scrawny, tired-looking man with a lean, aristocratic face and sparse yellow hair. Zu-Zu showed him the picture of Christine Jonquet. "Remember when this girl was staying here with Jean-Marc for a few days, a couple of months back?"

Her husband scowled at the photograph, uncertain. "I remember he was here with some girl—I'm not sure this is the same one. Looks *something* like her . . . could be."

Sawyer's escort asked him: "Do you know this Jean-Marc's last name?"

Zu-Zu's husband nodded, without having to search his mind for the answer. "Bruno," he said. "His name's Jean-Marc Bruno."

2

It took half an hour for Sawyer's escort to find Donhoff. By the time Donhoff got to the hotel, Sawyer had made two phone calls and sent Titine to the airport to take the next plane to Paris. Charged with new excitement, he told Donhoff what had happened, and filled him in on what he'd done about it so far.

"I've called Annique in Paris. She's running a check on Jean-Marc Bruno. It shouldn't take her long to at least come up with his I.D. or passport application picture. Titine's going to pick it up from her and take it to the two women who've seen our man with

458

the marked cheek: the one who saw him with Christine Jonquet in East Berlin, and the woman in the hotel he used in Peille.

"I also called Alfani. He'll call us back as soon as he finds out who this Jean-Marc Bruno used to work for here in Marseilles.

"Now you can phone your contacts in Barcelonnette. See if anyone there knows what's become of the Bruno whose daughter was raped and killed in that cave by Gaspard Martinot at the end of the war. And find out if that child she had by her SS lover was named Jean-Marc."

Sawyer's excitement was compelling. Donhoff tried to keep a rein on his own. "That's not an uncommon last name in the South of France," he pointed out. "It doesn't have to be the same Bruno."

"No," Sawyer agreed, "but it would fit. The murdered girl's father would be too old, now. But her son wouldn't. He'd be about the age of our man with the marked cheek. And that would certainly explain certain things, wouldn't it."

Donhoff nodded slowly. "Such as why it was Martinot who was picked to die. And why it was done in that particular cave."

3

When Titine phoned Marseilles from Paris, Sawyer and Donhoff were no longer there. Sawyer had left for a meeting with an underworld fence whom Jean-Marc Bruno had once worked for. And Donhoff was on his way to see Roger Bruno, the father of the girl Martinot had killed in the cave.

Titine left a message for them with Sawyer's brother, Olivier: she had gotten a passport photo of Jean-Marc Bruno from Annique Gassin, and showed it to Clarissa Koller, the art gallery owner who knew Christine Jonquet from East Berlin. There was no mark of any kind on the face of Jean-Marc Bruno in the photo. But Clarissa Koller was able to make a positive identification: it was the same man she'd seen with Christine Jonquet.

4

When the Catholic Church launched its crusade against the rival Christian sect known as the Cathars, in the thirteenth century, refugees fleeing before the Pope's army in southwestern France crowded into the walled town of Béziers, not far from the Pyrenees. The advancing army took the town, but once inside its general found himself with a difficult problem. All Cathars were under sentence of death, but the population of Béziers also contained a large number of Catholics. Most of the Cathars refused to come forward and identify themselves as such; and the Catholics of the town refused to give them away.

The General consulted the Pope's legate about this problem. The Legate cut it with the sword of religious logic: "Kill everybody. God will know his own." On the twenty-second of July, 1209, that order was carried out to the full, though most of the population had crowded into the town's churches seeking the protection of God.

Donhoff found Roger Bruno in the market square, facing the spot where seven thousand men, women, and children were executed inside the Church of the Madeleine. There were few clouds in the sky over Béziers when Donhoff got there that afternoon. The old man was seated outside on a cafe terrace, his seamed face tilted to catch the last of the sunlight's warmth. He was in his eighties, a small, bony man in a shabby black suit that hung loosely, a souvenir from a time when he'd had a good deal more flesh on him.

When Donhoff stopped before him, he frowned slightly. But it was a reaction to the sudden shadow across his face, not to Donhoff. After some years of diminishing eyesight, the man who'd pointed him out to Donhoff had explained, he had become blind for the last two.

"Monsieur Bruno?"

"Yes?" The frown was puzzled by the unknown voice.

Donhoff introduced himself and explained that he worked for an organization doing a psychological study of the nature and affects of wartime atrocities. "May I sit and talk with you for a bit?"

"Of course . . . But I don't quite understand . . ."

Donhoff took the empty chair at Roger Bruno's table. "Do you know a man from Barcelonnette named Gaspard Martinot?"

The dead eyes turned to Donhoff. The bitterness had been dimmed by the years, but it was still there. "Yes. That pig murdered my daughter. But God will make him pay for it, someday. And then he'll continue to pay, forever, in the pit of hell."

So he didn't know about Martinot's death. "This is the type of atrocity that interests us even more than those committed by the Nazis," Donhoff said. "Because they were so much rarer, and the causes and results so much more complex. How did it happen, exactly?" Donhoff was prepared to explain the motives for his probing with further lies, but it proved unnecessary:

"How did it happen?" Roger Bruno repeated. "Do you know how many times I asked myself that same question? It *shouldn't* have happened. I'm a loyal Frenchman—more than most of those cowardly swine who boast about their patriotism. Part of the money I live on is from the pension the government of France pays me for the way I proved it in the war of '14–'18. I was gassed in the Battle of the Marne. My lungs and eyes were never the same after that; and my sight has

461

finally deteriorated to—what you see now. So when the Germans occupied Barcelonnette in the Second War, I was as strong as everyone else against them."

He paused, face turning toward the warmth of the sun, head cocked slightly, listening to an old, unforgotten sorrow. "But my daughter, she was young and willful. I suppose I had spoiled her, raising her without a woman to help. Her mother, you see, died a few years after she was born. The girl, she was so pretty, so full of life . . . Yes, I spoiled her . . .

"When the Germans came—as conquerors—she began seeing one of them. On the sly, at first. But then openly. The others in our town began calling her names. But she was defiant, and in love. The German was a very good-looking boy. And, I think he loved her, too. I ordered him to stop seeing my daughter. I even struck him, not caring about the consequences. But there were none. He didn't report what I had done; and my daughter continued to go with him.

"I finally beat her. She left my house, and moved into a room. The German paid for it. And for her food, better food than any of the rest of us had at that time; and he brought her pretty clothes . . . And she had his child. Everybody of our town hated her. I hated her too—God forgive me."

Roger Bruno fell into a brooding silence. Donhoff resisted the impulse to prompt the old man, waiting patiently until he resumed of his own accord:

"When the Americans landed on the south coast below us, and the Germans left our town to join the retreat, I knew the time of my daughter's punishment had come. I only did not know how terrible it would be.

"Her German was killed on the road just outside Barcelonnette, by one of the *maquis* Resistance groups striking at the retreating troops. The next day the *maquis* poured into our town to celebrate the Liberation. My daughter was dragged from her room. My

462

grandson—her child—tried to fight the men taking her. One of them hit him and locked him in the room. It's strange, he has never been able to remember any of it. Shock, I suppose . . .

"They were shaving my daughter's head in the middle of the Place Manuel when I got there. I tried to stop them, but some of the men held me. When her head was bare a number of the younger *maquisards* led her away through the town, with everybody jeering and laughing at her. After they let me go, I searched for her. I met some of the men who had taken her, coming back, and begged them to tell me where she was. They said they didn't know; that they'd let her go and told her never to return.

"It was days before I learned the truth: that they had left her with Martinot—and he had murdered her. I tried to have him arrested. But none of the swine who knew the truth would tell it."

He fell silent again, and Donhoff said gently: "They were probably too ashamed, once the passions cooled down."

"They deserve their shame." Roger Bruno's voice was quiet, but trembling with remembered rage. "I took my grandson and left there. My sister had married a winegrower here. We came to live with them. I never went back."

But his grandson *had* gone back, Donhoff knew, and recently. Only Roger Bruno didn't know about that. Donhoff said: "I believe your daughter's child is named Jean-Marc?"

"Yes. My grandson. Jean-Marc."

Donhoff hesitated, and then began to probe for what he had really come to find out. It was not pleasant, tricking this blind old man into betraying his own. But the life of Moira Rhalles depended on his doing it. This was not the first time that Donhoff's profession had forced him into doing something he knew to be evil, in order to achieve something good. He was aware, however, that this was precisely what

463

the Pope's army and legate had thought they were doing, on that day of mass slaughter here in Béziers, back in 1209.

"I'd like to talk to your grandson," he told Roger Bruno, "to find out how what happened to his mother has affected his life."

The response was not what Donhoff had hoped for: "I can tell you about that. After all, I raised him. As I told you, he couldn't remember afterwards, about what had happened. But I told him. All of it. When he was old enough to understand. Maybe I shouldn't have. It only caused him trouble. The other children in school were naturally curious about where his mother and father were. Once he knew, he told them—the truth. He was a straightforward, honest boy, not given to lying.

"But he soon learned that was a mistake. The other boys began taunting him—calling him 'The Hun,' and 'the German bastard.' He began to have fights with them, every day . . ."

Roger Bruno's smile held a stiff pride: "But he won every fight, Jean-Marc did. He was strong, and he became fierce. The others soon learned to stop tormenting him. But he was never friends with any of them again, after that. He came to hate the French. They'd called him a German, and that's what he decided he really was: his father's son. He even started to learn German, as he grew older, and he'd talk about someday going to Germany to find his dead father's family. And he never played with any of the other boys around here. Never again.

"There *was* one boy he did spend time with, part of every summer for a number of years. A German boy. Child of a rich banking family from Frankfurt. They used to own a large estate just outside the town here, where they'd come to spend part of each summer. Naegele, the family's name was. Apparently they had property all over the world. Jean-Marc used to spend all his time with their boy when they were here. He insisted on always talking German with him, to improve his grasp of the language."

Donhoff tried again: "Does your grandson still live here in Béziers with you?"

"Oh no. Jean-Marc left long ago. When he was seventeen." According to Roger Bruno, his grandson had intended to go to Paris, find a small job that would pay for a room and food, and try to get into the university. Instead he'd wound up in Marseilles, working full-time for an import-export firm of some kind. His grandfather didn't know which one, but Jean-Marc had apparently been doing well enough to give him money whenever he visited Béziers. But about seven years ago there'd been some trouble, and he'd been forced to leave Marseilles.

"What kind of trouble?" Donhoff asked.

"I don't know. An argument; somebody threw acid at him. There was a terrible acid burn on one side of his face when he came to see me. But he didn't want to talk about it. He'd just come to say goodbye. He said he'd had his stomach full of France. He was going to Germany, to try to find his father's family. I didn't see him again for a long time after that. Years. Not till a few months ago, when he suddenly showed up here for a few hours, to see how I was getting along."

"Had he found any of his father's family?"

Roger Bruno nodded. "Both of the parents. They live in East Germany. They didn't have any other children, and when Jean-Marc explained who he was they were happy to take him in to live with them. Jean-Marc told me they're both staunch Communists now. And he's become one, too."

"Do you mind that?"

The old man shrugged. "Why should I—if it makes Jean-Marc happy? God knows, he's had little enough of that in his life."

"It would still be very interesting," Donhoff persisted, "for me to talk with him personally, for the purpose of our study. Where can I get in touch with him?"

"I don't know. I think he's gone back to Germany."

"East Germany?"

"Maybe. Or maybe West Germany. Jean-Marc told me he spent a lot of time there, too. He even met Gunther again, and they've renewed their old friendship."

"Gunther?"

"The German boy Jean-Marc used to play with here. Gunther Naegele. Only he's not a boy anymore, of course. He runs his family's banking business now, in Frankfurt. That's where Jean-Marc said he ran into him again. And he's visited with him a number of times since. Gunther might be able to tell you where Jean-Marc is at the moment, if it's that important for you to talk to him."

When Donhoff left Béziers he drove back in the direction of Marseilles. But he didn't go all the way, stopping when he reached Marignane Airport. He booked a flight to Frankfurt by way of Paris. While he waited for his plane, he phoned Olivier in Paris. He told him everything he'd learned from Roger Bruno—to be passed on to Sawyer when he returned to Marseilles from Franco Vesperini's place.

5

Franco Vesperini had been born in Sicily, the only son of a wealthy, respected Mafia *capo*. When he was eighteen he went hunting with a group of friends, and accidentally shot one of them. The boy he'd killed was the son of a Mafia figure as powerful in his own area as Franco Vesperini's father was in his own. Although the two boys had been close friends, and it had been a tragic accident, the grief of the dead boy's father was almost certain to drive him to seek revenge, sooner

466

or later. If that happened, Franco Vesperini's father would retaliate with his considerable army.

The war that would have ensued could have torn the Mafia apart. To avert this, the leading figures of the Sicilian Mafia met in conference in Palermo, with the fathers of both boys, the killer and the slain. They finally worked out a solution that both sides agreed to abide by:

Franco Vesperini was to be exiled from society, so that his presence in it would not be a constant incitement to the dead boy's father. His place of exile was to be a prison, as punishment for having caused the boy's death. But to placate Vesperini's father, the prison had to be a comfortable one; even luxurious. Franco Vesperini was sentenced to spend the rest of his life in a suite of rooms taking up most of the top floor of one of the best hotels in Palermo, with a view of the harbor.

There were guards to make sure he never left that floor; and to ensure that the dead boy's father could not get to it, if in a wild moment he found himself unable to contain his vengeful grief. The arrangement simultaneously took cognizance of one father's obligation to avenge his own, and the other father's obligation to protect his own.

Within the rooms of his large suite Vesperini was entitled to anything he desired and his father could pay for: the best of food, wine, and women, interesting visitors, the latest films to be shown on his own projector. As the years wore on he became completely adjusted to life in this expensive prison. But he soon came to realize that he had no desire to fatten himself with overeating, did not care to become a lush, and had a sexual appetite that was satisfied by an occasional visit from some lovely and accomplished young lady.

The life of a comfortable prisoner taught him, in fact, what he would never otherwise have learned: that his tastes were almost monkish, and that he had a leaning toward a scholarly existence. Books were brought in to him; and then teachers, from the best universities in Europe and America. After several years of this, his interests finally centered around art and antiquities.

Dealers and gallery owners began bringing their wares to him. His purchases became increasingly knowledgeable. By the time his exile in the hotel ended, Vesperini had quite a valuable collection in the rooms of his top-floor suite.

The end came when Mussolini's police declared war on the Mafia, and wiped out both Vesperini's father and the father of the boy he'd shot. After that it would have been only a matter of time before the Fascist police got around to arresting Vesperini and confiscating his property. After over a decade of confinement to a single hotel floor, going outside was something of a trauma. But he did it, bribing the necessary people to get himself and his collection transferred to a ship sailing from Palermo to Marseilles.

Vesperini arrived in Marseilles with very little money left. And he had no intention of breaking up his collection for sale. What he did have were his extensive knowledge as a connoisseur of the arts and contacts with certain of his late father's friends. One of these friends was Marcel Alfani.

It was Alfani who introduced him into the Marseilles underworld. Vesperini began as an appraiser of stolen art and looted antiquities. He became in time an independent buyer and seller: a fence. Unlike most of the people in this line, Vesperini had a passion for the objects with which he dealt. Occasionally, when one of the items was especially to his taste, he added it to his collection instead of selling it for a profit.

His place was east of Marseilles, along the coast. Sawyer was driven there by Alfani's niece and chief bookkeeper, a large, sharp-eyed woman in her forties named Joëlle Matana. They cut through the outer edge of Marseilles—the factories, freight sheds, railroad sidings, and drab gray-plaster houses—and out past small level farm plots and fenced marshy squares piled with the city's refuse: wrecked cars, worn-out bathtubs, rusted oil drums, cracked sewer pipes. As they left the last vestiges of the city behind, Sawyer reflected grimly on the days that had been lost in canvassing the Canebière.

It wouldn't have been necessary, as it had developed, if Vesperini hadn't been out of the country for the past few weeks. He had returned only today, to find the questions and photographs that Alfani had sent waiting for him. Among them were the question about a man with a peculiar birthmark or scar on one cheek and the composite photograph of a rare Venus figure.

Vesperini had some years ago been the employer of Jean-Marc Bruno. And, until quite recently, he'd been the owner of the Venus figure.

Joëlle Matana turned the car into a narrow road that twisted its way through rugged hills above the sea. Here the rocks, cliffs, and exposed earth took on a strong orange to brick-red color, gorgeous against the varied greens of trees and bushes. At the bottom of the hills to the right the red color of the earth continued beyond the shore, spreading out across the surface of the sea. Only in the distance was it finally absorbed into the gray-blue of the surging waters.

Alfani's niece pulled off the road and stopped the car. On one side a narrow stream ran red-brown between banks of gnarled evergreens. On the other the ground sloped down to a double railroad track. She led the way on foot down the slope and across the tracks. They came to a small abandoned quarry with a sign warning trespassers to keep out.

They entered the quarry. There was a narrow opening in the base of one wall of red rock. Just inside it was a locked steel door. Hanging beside it was a small electronic speaker unit. Joëlle Matana spoke into it, identifying herself and Sawyer. A moment later there was a clicking sound in the door's lock. She pushed the door open and they stepped through, closing it behind them.

They were in a floodlit tunnel burrowing underneath a hill. It inclined gradually downward. Following it, they came out into the daylight at the other end. The tunnel exit was high on the right slope of a densely wooded gully that widened as it descended below them to the sea. At the bottom Sawyer could see the surf creaming over the red stones of a narrow beach, and smashing against the red cliffs on either side.

His guide led him down a dirt path that worked its way between the close-set trees and wild bushes clothing the right slope of the gully. Halfway down to the beach the path ended at a long, narrow steel footbridge which spanned the gully. On the other side of the gully, at the far end of the bridge, a modern white and blue villa could be glimpsed behind well-tended trees, perched at the top of a cliff.

Their end of the bridge was barred by a locked steel-mesh gate. There was more steel mesh along the sides of the bridge and curving over it, forming a tunnel-cage of its entire length. The reason for the cage was immediately obvious: on the other side of the gate at Sawyer's end were two Doberman guard dogs, snarling and trembling with kill lust.

"We just stand here and wait," Joëlle Matana told Sawyer, "while Vesperini has a look at us through his binoculars."

She shrugged. "It amuses him, I think. But also, he does have an extremely valuable personal museum over there, in addition to quite a great deal of merchandise for sale."

"His house doesn't look that big."

"Most of it is underground. He built the house over an old bunker. Fortifications the French Army dug inside the cliff before the war. That gives him a lot of storage room. *And* a passage that leads down to the beach. That's where he takes delivery of goods smuggled in from other countries."

A fat man in dungarees and a checked work shirt appeared at the other end of the bridge and hurried over it to the dogs. The kill-trained Dobermans transformed themselves into playful puppies when he reached them, fawning on him and nipping at his boots. He snapped a chain leash to the collar of each, and led them back across the footbridge. At the other end he closed them inside a small cage of steel bars, and pressed something on a post beside it. The gate at Sawyer's end of the bridge clicked open.

Joëlle Matana led him through it, and across the bridge, up a flight of brick steps at the other end leading to the house. Franco Vesperini was waiting for them in an open doorway, smiling.

He was a distinguished-looking man, lean of face and figure, with alert eyes and a long, sharp nose. His thick black hair was tinged with white, and neatly brushed. He kissed Alfani's niece on both cheeks and held out a pale hand to Sawyer. The foyer he led them through was flanked by a Byzantine icon and an ornate Louis XIV bracket clock. They entered a hallway crowded with Islamic bronzes, swords, helmets, and ceramics.

"A bit cluttered," Vesperini apologized, "but it's all part of a recent shipment I haven't had time to appraise as yet."

Joëlle Matana said she had a few business calls make while the two men had their talk. Vesperini told her to use his study, and took Sawyer through the hallway, gesturing at the objects cluttering it. "All from Lebanon. It's the same after every war, you know. Art flees from lost battles, and redistributes itself."

They entered a small sitting room with a short bar. Behind the bar was a window-wall looking out on a tiled terrace wrapped around a curved swimming pool on the edge of the cliff. Sawyer couldn't identify most of the paintings on the other three walls, but he recognized a Bonnard and a Monet.

Vesperini, opening a bottle of wine at the bar for them, noticed his interest. "My best pieces are in my storage vault, under the house. I'd enjoy showing you, but I believe you are in rather a hurry today."

Sawyer nodded and put his copy of the Venus figure photograph on the bar. "I was told you used to own this."

"Not quite the same, but very similar. I'm surprised to learn there's another so much like it."

"There probably isn't," Sawyer explained, "this is a composite picture I had made up."

"Ah—now I understand. I did believe mine was unique."

"How long did you have it?"

"Many years. I found it too interesting to sell, for the small amount it would bring. It was bought for me by Hamid Azzed, a man who worked for me over a considerable period." Vesperini poured wine into two glasses and gave one to Sawyer. "Hamid was the one who brought me Jean-Marc Bruno, in whom Alfani tells me you are most interested."

They sat on a couch facing the terrace window, between tables on which stood two exquisitely worked silver candlesticks. Vesperini's smile held remembered amusement. "The friendship of Hamid and Jean-Marc seemed to be based on their shared hatred of France and the French. Since I am a Sicilian, they had no objection to working for me. Good men, both of them."

Sawyer plunged into the basic question: "Can you tell me where to find Bruno?"

"I have no idea. Sorry. And I can't think of anyone who might know. I gave this considerable thought before you arrived."

"What about this man Hamid?"

"Hamid is dead. He was killed almost seven years ago, in Naples."

Containing his disappointment, Sawyer began probing for the background information, seeking a lead there: "What did Bruno do for you?"

"He worked always with Hamid. They made an excellent team. Generally I used them to collect merchandise for me from abroad. In my line there is always a danger of goods being hijacked in transit. But they were a pair who could deal with such a problem. And other problems. There was a Turk on Cyprus, for example, who after agreeing to sell me a group of icons he had stolen, claimed they had been stolen from him before he could deliver. I sent Hamid and Jean-Marc to investigate. They learned the Turk had had a better offer, but persuaded him it would be more sensible to honor his prior agreement with me. You may have noticed one of those icons in my foyer when you came in. Their methods of persuasion were rather harsh, I fear, but they got results. Good men, I sorely miss them."

"Why did Bruno quit you?"

Vesperini took a sip of wine. "It was immediately after Hamid was killed. I had sent them both to Italy. A Roman villa had just been discovered buried under a hill south of Naples. They supervised a secret dig for me, and extracted everything that was small enough to be transported, and valuable enough to be worth the trouble and cost. In Naples, they had all of it crated and put aboard a cargo ship due to leave for Marseilles. But shortly before sailing, three Italian hijackers disguised as sailors boarded the ship.

"One of them threw acid at Hamid and Jean-Marc, to distract them long enough for the other two to draw guns. Hamid was killed in the exchange of gunfire, but Jean-Marc managed to kill two of the hijackers and drive the third away. His cheek had been badly burned by the acid, but he stayed with the shipment and delivered it here to me.

"By then I already had heard something of the affair in Naples. One of the dead hijackers belonged to a large and formidable family. As you may know, I have some understanding of the long arms of Italian family vengeance. I advised Jean-Marc to disappear from Marseilles before they came for him."

"Where did he go?"

"I don't know. He had enough money to go anywhere. My men know that in case of trouble I will always be generous to them, and their families. I gave Jean-Marc a large bonus, as severance pay."

Sawyer asked: "Is that when you gave him the Venus figure?"

"No, not then. Much later, when he came back for it a few months ago. He had always wanted it, when he worked for me. I remember when he first saw it here, in my private collection, and was curious about what it was. I explained to him about the mysterious multiple significances of the prehistoric mother-goddess, and he was quite fascinated. He did a good deal of reading about it, and several times offered to buy it. But he didn't have enough money, in those days, to make an offer large enough to induce me to part with it."

"But when he came back, he did have enough."

Vesperini nodded. "He offered far more than I could reasonably resist."

"I understand," Sawyer said, "that he had a beard when he showed up here a few months ago."

"A false one. Too many people in this area know him from the past, and he didn't want his presence widely advertised."

Sawyer took out his picture of the Egyptian stele. "Do you know this?"

"Oh yes—I recognized it from the photograph Alfani sent me. Jean-Marc showed it to me when he returned from Naples. Hamid had bought it from an artist I asked him to see while he was in Italy—as a birthday present for Jean-Marc."

Sawyer talked with Vesperini for another hour. By the time he left, he knew a great deal about Jean-Marc Bruno's past. But nothing that told him where Bruno was now.

Unless Fritz Donhoff came up with something better, Sawyer reflected as he was driven back to Marseilles, they could have a difficult hunt ahead of them.

6

In his Washington apartment, Jorgen woke that evening at 6 P.M. His head was heavy and groggy, and there were little pains in his joints. He'd had only four hours sleep after his return from New York, and it had not been sound sleep. The anxiety and extra demands on him caused by the Remingtons' accident had left a residue of jitteriness. He hoped that this would turn out to be one of the nights when there'd be no phone call from Rhalles, and no new tape to encode.

Getting out of bed, his eyes burning, Jorgen made himself a cup of tea. His stomach wasn't ready for anything more. The tea helped, soothing his nerves and bringing him more awake. Ten minutes of mild exercises, and a hot and cold shower, cleared his head. After shaving and dressing he felt ready for another cup of tea, this time with buttered toast and honey. It was 7 P.M. when he went out for a walk.

Five minutes after he'd gone, Lang went up to Jorgen's apartment with his locksmith and electronics team. Garcia remained outside the building, in radio contact with both Lang and the units tailing Jorgen. On reaching the door to Jorgen's apartment, Lang and the locksmith were careful not to touch it until they had examined it thoroughly. The lock was studied with a magnifier and flashlight. Lang, running fingertips around the edge of the door, found the invisible bit of adhesive attached between it and the frame at the top. His locksmith got a razor blade from his kit, and delicately peeled the tape away from the frame, leaving it stuck to the door itself.

After that it was a matter of six minutes' work to get the door unlocked without leaving any giveaway scratches. The first thing Lang saw when they entered the living room was the encoding machine.

Lang gazed upon it with a small smile. His feeling of achievement could not have been greater if he had suddenly found himself confronted with the Holy Grail. He was quite sure what the machine was, and he did not touch it. This was out of his field of expertise. What he needed now were some specialists.

Coming quickly to a decision, Lang warned his electronics team to stay where they were. The phone line from this apartment had already been tapped, several blocks from the house. That was enough, for the moment. The tape on the door was a warning. There might be other devices inside the apartment that would be activated to warn the occupant of implanted room bugs. It was a risk not worth chancing, at this point. They were too close.

Moving cautiously, taking care to leave no sign of his presence behind, Lang began to go through the apartment searching for anything that would give him a lead to the source of the information that was encoded here. He had found nothing when the signal came over his radio unit from Garcia outside: Jorgen was on his way back.

They left the apartment quickly. The door was re-locked, and the tape at its top was pressed back into place against the frame, leaving no evidence that it had been opened in Jorgen's absence. They were out of the building, and out of sight, when Jorgen re-entered it.

Lang spread the word to all members of his team: surveillance on Jorgen was to be tightened. Under no circumstance were they to lose him, from that point on. All units were to hold themselves in readiness to seize him, instantly, whenever Lang gave the signal.

But he wasn't ready to seize Jorgen, not yet. That could alert the source of the information, and give him time to get away before Jorgen could be made to spill his guts. If possible, Lang wanted to seize both the encoder and the source at the same time. There was a chance that the code could be broken by an examination of the encoding machine. That would enable the NSA experts to decode past tapes, and the nature of the information in them might reveal their source.

Lang phoned George Rudofsky. An hour later two men arrived to join Lang in waiting for the next opportunity to enter Jorgen's apartment. One was an NSA code-machine specialist. The other was the chief of the team that had been trying to break the Budapest Code: Benjamin Scovil.

Jorgen had picked up groceries during his walk. At 8:30 P.M. he made himself a dinner of eggs, bacon, and potatoes. He finished off with strong coffee, to keep himself sharply awake in case Alexander Rhalles called. Picking up Rhalles' book, Jorgen settled down beside his phone to read while he waited.

He waited until eleven, well past the time Rhalles usually called, before gratefully accepting the fact that there would be no tape to encode this night; and no flight to be made to New York the following morning. The relief of knowing he could get as much sleep as he needed, that night and the next morning, immediately left him feeling less tired. And his nerves were still too keyed up to allow him to sleep.

Jorgen made himself a cup of tea. But after he'd finished it he was still not ready to go to bed. Taking the book with him, Jorgen left the apartment and went around the corner to the bar. The woman he fancied wasn't there; and neither was the man he sometimes played chess with. Jorgen ordered a beer, and settled at a table in the back, sipping his beer as he reopened Rhalles' book.

A young woman in tight jeans and leather jacket, who had come in shortly after Jorgen, sat on a bar-stool having a rum-and-cola. She couldn't make out the title of the book Jorgen was reading from there, but she wasn't particularly interested in doing so. Her only interest was to signal Garcia, over the radio trans-mitter in the car she'd parked outside, whenever Jorgen left the bar.

Getting into Jorgen's apartment was quicker this time, because they didn't have to search for booby traps. The tape was neatly peeled away at the top of the door, and the lock picked. The locksmith re-mained outside as Lang went in with the two men from NSA.

Lang went immediately to the living-room window and looked down through the fire escape to the shadowy entrance of an alley across the street. Garcia was there, with the radio unit to which the one in Lang's hand was tuned. Staying close to the window, Lang turned to watch the two men from NSA.

Scovil had carried in a code machine the size of a suitcase, NSA's newest small unit in that line. It was hoped that, if they could figure out the workings of the enemy machine, the NSA unit could be keyed to the same sequence. Scovil put it down carefully on the table next to Jorgen's machine. The code-machine expert set a large equipment case on the floor, opened it, and examined the exterior of Jorgen's machine for booby traps. He found no indication of one, and began a prolonged detailed study of the machine's exposed working parts: the keyboard and the tape reels on which the machine's coded messages were recorded.

Finally he announced: "We're going to have to open her up for a look inside."

Scovil smiled. "Well, we're not going to learn much

just standing here and staring at the damned thing."

The other man squinted at the small bolt heads in the back of the machine, and selected a screwdriver from his case. The first bolt came out with no trouble at all. He had the second one partly unscrewed when the code machine exploded.

The force effects of any explosion are notoriously haphazard. This one tore the code-machine expert apart, killing him instantly. It picked Scovil up, spun him across the room, and slammed him against the wall, knocking him unconscious. But when he came to later he found that other than a slight concussion and having most of his clothes torn off, he had nothing the matter with him except a large number of bruises and scratches. The locksmith, who had been standing in the open doorway, found himself sprawled on the corridor floor, and it was some moments before he realized that both of his legs had been broken.

The code machine itself disintegrated into tiny fragments. The main force of the explosion shot most of these fragments in the direction of the living-room window. Lang was hurled backwards crashing through the window and falling on the fire-escape landing outside. Though stunned he did not lose consciousness, and his nervous system had already gone into shock, cutting off pain. But he couldn't see. When he put a hand to his face, fingers groping for the place where his eyes should have been, they could find only blood and shredded flesh.

The sound of the explosion, though muted by the distance, was heard distinctly in the bar around the corner. Everyone looked up, wondering. Jorgen sat frozen for a moment. Then he snapped shut the book he'd been reading and hurried out of the bar, striding toward the corner.

He didn't have to go any further. From the corner he could see smoke issuing from the smashed window of his apartment, and the man sprawled on the fire-escape landing outside it. The band that seemed to be constricting his chest increased its pressure. Jorgen turned abruptly and walked swiftly toward his parked car. Two men walked after him, less than half a block behind, but Jorgen didn't look back and see them. He didn't have to; he knew he was being shadowed.

He didn't remember he was still carrying the book until he got into his car. Dropping it on the seat beside him, he stabbed the key into the ignition lock. It was at that moment that Garcia issued the radio call to pick Jorgen up. The two men who'd been walking after him began to run.

Jorgen saw them coming, in his rearview mirror. He gunned the motor and his car shot away from the curb, speeding off down the street and screeching out of sight around the next corner. One of the men running after his car stumbled to a halt. The other had stopped several yards behind him, and was shouting into the radio transmitter in his hand.

Seconds later Garcia was issuing a general alert to all vehicle units, to spread out through the area until they picked up the signal from the bug on Jorgen's car, and then home in on it. With another of Lang's men sprinting after him, Garcia headed for his own car to join the hunt.

Changing streets frequently, Jorgen drove in a southeasterly direction through the city, glancing constantly at his rearview mirror. There were no cars chasing him. But there would be soon. He didn't need to know about the homing device attached to his car to realize that he should ditch it as soon as he had a bit more distance from the area of his apartment. They had the car's description and license number. By now the hounds were combing the city for it.

But attempting to get away was only his third obligation. His first was to get rid of the last item that might give away the purpose of the operation. His second was to alert his organization, so the termination signal could be passed on immediately to those responsible for carrying out the prepared responses.

480

Jorgen stopped once, to dump Rhalles' book in a trash can, and drove on. The next time he stopped it was beside a phone booth near the Congressional Cemetery on Kentucky Avenue. His breathing was labored as he climbed out of the car. He dropped in a coin and dialed the number of his unknown Washington contact.

The voice he recognized came on the other end: "Hello?"

Jorgen forced himself to hold to the routine opening: "Hello, John."

"I'm afraid you have the wrong number."

"Mr. Harmon, this is Jorgen."

"Yes, what's the problem?"

Jorgen told him all that he had to at this point: "The operation is finished, blown. Pass it on, immediately. The signal is: *Terminate*. Understand?"

"Understood. What is your personal situation, Jorgen?"

A car with several men in it came cruising into sight at the end of the block. It stopped for a split second, then made a tight turn and came in toward Jorgen and his car, accelerating.

Jorgen hung up the phone, breaking the connection, and looked around frantically. Another car swung in toward him, from the other end of the block. There were two men in it. Jorgen's side of the block was lined with old apartment buildings. He dashed into the entrance of the nearest one, ran through it toward the rear.

The constriction in his chest was hurting now, and there were painful cramps developing in the muscles of his thighs and calves. He knew the symptoms, and what they meant. But he kept running, through the building.

The back door was metal, and securely locked. There was a back stairway beside it. Jorgen started up the stairs, as fast as he could push himself. If he could reach the roof, there might be another way down.

His legs buckled when he was halfway up. He fell, dragged himself up again, and kept going. On the top landing there was a ladder, leading to a trapdoor in the roof. He climbed the ladder. The trapdoor had a simple hook lock. He opened it and shoved the trapdoor up. It fell with a crash on the roof beside the opening.

Jorgen climbed out onto the roof, panting. The pain was expanding through his chest and legs, and there were worse pains in his forearms, twisting them against his stomach. He spotted another trapdoor, on the roof of the adjoining building, and staggered toward it.

He fell before reaching it. Rolling on his side, he tried to get up. He couldn't make it all the way. The pain was terrible, riveting him in a sitting position on the roof.

There was the thick mast of a television antenna beside him. Resting his weight on one hip, Jorgen leaned until one shoulder and the side of his head were against it. He watched Garcia and another agent climb out of the opened trapdoor, their guns drawn. They advanced across the roof to him and stopped on either side, looking down.

Jorgen smiled bleakly. "Bad luck for you," he whispered. "You're too late . . . Far too late."

The ambulance that came for him sped to D.C.-General, the nearest hospital. His heart stopped working before he got there. He was pronounced dead on arrival.

7

It was two o'clock in the morning, in Washington, when "John Harmon" got through on the phone to the number he'd been given to call in Paris, and passed on Jorgen's message. The time in Paris was six hours later: eight o'clock. Irina Frejenko took the call in her apartment. She lowered herself slowly into a straight-back chair as she listened to the man at the other end repeating the code word: "Terminate."

Irina Frejenko hung up her phone and sat there for a time beside it, staring at the wall. Then her mind began to function again, reluctantly, along the regulation channels.

She picked up the phone again, dialed a Paris number she had never used before, and asked for "Patrick." The woman who answered said he wasn't there but would be in a couple hours. Irina Frejenko left a message that Patrick should call her number immediately on his arrival. Then she hung up and began waiting.

Part of her mind began methodically working on the arrangements that would have to be taken care of before that day was finished, while the rest of her mind continued to stare at an empty future.

She would have to arrange to be on that night's flight to Moscow. Even if her husband were not there, it would never have occurred to her not to go back to face the consequences of her plan's failure. She was incapable of considering any alternative.

She would have to arrange for two seats. One for herself, the other for Lorenz. There was no phone down there in the ruined fortress which she could call. And this was the day on which Lorenz was scheduled to drive up to Paris with the latest taped message from Moira Rhalles, to be delivered to her husband through Jorgen. If Lorenz arrived in Paris at his usual hour there would be no problem. It would leave just enough time, if they hurried, to reach the plane before takeoff.

She would make these arrangements after she got the call from Patrick.

Irina Prejenko did not know who Patrick was, or

what his other duties in Paris might be. She knew only one of his duties, which he had been instructed to carry out whenever she gave him the order: to drive down to the ruin and dispose of Moira Rhalles.

It was sixteen minutes after eight that morning when Sawyer got the call in his Marseilles hotel room, from Fritz Donhoff in Frankfurt.

"I've just spoken with Gunther Naegele," Donhoff told Sawyer. "He *has* seen our Jean-Marc Bruno a number of times in the past few years. But unfortunately, he knows nothing about where Bruno might be now."

"When was the last time he saw Bruno?"

"Four months ago, here in Frankfurt. There was a property Naegele owned in France, down in the Ardèche, close to the Rhône River. An old fortress, pretty much in ruins. He took Bruno along with him once, when he went down there to look it over. Four months ago Bruno showed up here with a German named Lorenz, who was interested in buying that property. He offered a good price, so Naegele sold. He hasn't seen Bruno or heard from him since."

"Have you tried to contact this man Lorenz? He might have some idea on Bruno's whereabouts."

"I've already tried to reach him at the address in Hamburg he gave when he bought the Ardèche property. But apparently he no longer lives there. I'm about to put a trace on him. He *might* be at this place Naegele sold him, but there's no phone down there— and it's a long way from here."

"It's a lot nearer to me," Sawyer said. "I'll drive up and have a look. Exactly *where* in the Ardèche?"

TWENTY-ONE

1

After Moira had recorded the message to her husband that morning in her tower cell, Bruno tossed her the key. She used it to unlock the cuff which secured her ankle to the chain. He watched her stonily as she washed her feet at the sink. When she had dried them he tossed her a fresh pair of socks. He no longer spoke to her unless it was absolutely necessary. After a few attempts to talk with him she had given up.

She sat on the edge of the bed and drew on the socks. Her movements had become lethargic, her expression dulled and sullen. This did not cause him to relax his attention. She would get no further chance to betray him. He only hoped that despair would not make her sick. Not because of any personal concern for her. It would be inconvenient, that was all.

Bruno wondered if she understood how grateful she should be to him, for not allowing Lorenz to come near her anymore. That had not been easy to enforce. Lorenz was still seething with hatred for the ease with which she'd made a fool of him. Bruno had been able to prevent Lorenz from taking revenge only by using against him some of his own pent-up fury toward her.

He watched now as she pulled on her boots and closed the metal cuff at the end of the chain around her ankle. Making sure it was well locked, Bruno took the key from her and picked up the cassette recorder. She was staring numbly at the wall of her cell when he went out. He shut the door of her cell and pushed the locking bolts into their wall sockets.

Going down the winding tower steps to his room, Bruno removed the cassette from the machine and put it in a small plastic bag. He took it to Lorenz, who was waiting in the courtyard outside, ready for his drive to Paris. When he got there, Bruno told him, he wanted Irina Frejenko informed that he wanted her to send a replacement to take over his job here. He was getting too restless to continue with it much longer; he needed something more demanding than being a jailer.

Lorenz nodded curtly and took the cassette without speaking. Bruno watched him head for the car. He wondered how Moira Rhalles would fare, when he was no longer there to protect her. But he really didn't care. He had allowed her to cynically trick him into treating her with consideration. Her betrayal of him reinforced his lifelong conviction that his fellow man could not be trusted.

Bruno thought of the only people in his life he had cared about: he couldn't remember his father and could hardly remember his mother. Hamid was dead and his grandfather soon would be. And Gunther Naegele he could no longer be honest with.

There was only Christine; she was the only one with whom he could be open about himself, the only one left in whom he could trust. He found himself wondering where she was now; and when he would ever see her again.

As for his prisoner, once he left here his responsibility for her would be finished.

2

The man Irina Frejenko knew only as "Patrick" was about forty years old. His dark brown suit fitted him loosely, but his dark striped necktie was knotted with exacting neatness. He was of average height, solid and capable-looking, with a melancholy, intelligent face. There was a calm, efficient ruthlessness in his eyes, without a trace of malice.

"This man Bruno who is guarding her now," Irina Frejenko told him, "is quite capable of disposing of her himself. But there is no phone down there, and besides . . ."

"And besides," he interrupted her, "it is my job."

"You must be certain, afterwards, that her body will never be found."

"I have my instructions. You don't have to explain further." If he was irritated, it showed only in the slight swinging of the brown hat hanging from the finger and thumb of his left hand.

"Yes. Well . . ." Irina Frejenko glanced at her watch. "You had better get started. It's a long way."

Patrick nodded and shook her hand. He put on his hat as he left her apartment. His car was parked in front of her building. He got into it and drove south out of Paris.

3

It was shortly before one o'clock that afternoon when Jean-Marc Bruno took Moira Rhalles' lunch up to her on a tray. He left it with her and climbed the rest of the steps to the tower roof.

From there he could see a great deal of the hilly country spreading away around the ruins below him: for miles in every direction, except the one blocked by the wooded hill on the other side of the narrow valley. In all other directions the limiting of his view occurred much further off: At the end of a long, wide valley, a forest concealed behind it the river winding between marshy banks. In the distance to the east, a mountain range showed in pale outline through a curtain of haze. Much nearer, but still far from the ruins of the fortress, loomed massive hills, dark purple below and mossy green above, out of which serrated teeth of bare granite leaped upward into the pale blue sky.

Between these limits and his tower, Bruno could see no vehicle on any of the few country roads, no inhabited house, no person, no movement. From far away came the brief, faint sound of an unseen truck. The sound was gone an instant later, and the soft, sun-warmed air was silent again, except for the twittering of birds. Everything was as it should be.

A flock of birds rose suddenly out of the wooded top of the nearby hill on the other side of the narrow valley from the fortress. Bruno squinted at it, shading his eyes from the sun with one hand. He studied the forested slope there for some time, until he was satisfied that there was nothing there to be alarmed about. Everything was as it should be. . . .

Just under the crest of the wooded hill, Sawyer sat in the wild grass with his back against the trunk of the fig tree whose shadow gave him concealment. He was watching Jean-Marc Bruno through the powerful lenses of his binoculars. There was no question that this was who the man on top of the tower was. The grayish burn scar on one cheek was quite distinct.

Studying him, Sawyer had the uncanny feeling he was looking at a distorted mirror image of himself. They had been born at about the same time, under much the same circumstances. Both of them had had French mothers and foreign fathers. They were both souvenirs of the war. And their fathers had died at the end of that war, not far from each other.

There was only the one vital difference, ordaining the difference of their subsequent lives: Sawyer's father had died fighting for the winning side; Bruno's had died for the side which had lost. In France, the mother of one had been able to draw added pride from the nationality of her man; while the mother of the other had been killed because of her man's nation.

Sawyer remembered the cave explorer from Barcelonnette talking about the tricks destiny played with people's lives. If Germany had won the war, and America had lost it—would he be Bruno now, and Bruno him?

The man Sawyer was watching left the roof of the tower, going down out of sight inside it. Sawyer focused his binoculars on the doorway at the base of the tower, waiting. Bruno did not come out. After a time, Sawyer lowered the binoculars and studied the fortress ruins without them.

All he knew at this point, for certain, was that Jean-Marc Bruno was in there. That didn't necessarily mean that Moira was, too. She might be, but it was just as possible that she wasn't. Bruno's only function could have been to capture her, and turn her over to someone else. If so, it was even money that Bruno wouldn't be able to reveal where Moira was now, no matter how much pressure was put on him.

Grabbing Bruno would have to wait. First Sawyer had to find out if, in finding Bruno, he had also found Moira. From his inspection of the ruined fortress, that tower seemed to be the only place left that was still habitable. Sawyer brought the binoculars back to his eyes, and studied the tower again through them.

This time, he noted that one of the tower windows was barred. Only the one. Sawyer focused on the barred window. But the room behind it was too shadowed for him to make out anything in it. Raising his knees until he could brace his elbows on them, Sawyer kept the binoculars focused on the barred window in the tower, waiting.

He waited a long time. Nothing moved behind the barred window. There was the start of a cramp across the back of his neck and down his right shoulder blade. Sawyer continued to peer through the lenses at the barred window.

His eyes tired and finally began to burn, fogging his vision. Sawyer lowered the binoculars and put them in the crushed grass beside him, wiping a hand across his eyes. He stretched his arms and legs, looking around to give his eyes and brain a chance to recover.

Gradually, he became aware again of the tangy-sweet smell of pine needles and wild flowers in the warm afternoon air, and of the sounds of thousands of birds among the trees of the slope on which he sat. Close to him, bees and little butterflies were going patiently from flower to flower. He looked down at the deserted stone village at the bottom of the other slope, and up to the ruins atop the other hill.

The pale sky above was cut by a high jetliner, sunlight striking a silver glint from its underbelly, leaving four sharp exhaust trails behind it. Far back, the four merged into one fat one, spreading in a high wind. A bird suddenly blotted out the plane, and much of the sky, as it flitted past close to Sawyer's face. A spider climbed over his ankle and circled the binoculars. Sawyer picked them up, raised his knees in position, leaned forward to rest his elbows on them, and focused on the barred tower window again.

The afternoon wore on. There was still nothing to be seen in the room inside the barred window. Sawyer lowered the binoculars and gave his eyes another rest.

The sun was lowering behind the hillcrest at his back. Sawyer watched the shadow of his hill move out into the narrow valley below. The movement was very slow; almost imperceptible. He could detect it only by concentrating for a long moment on a single house in the abandoned village at the foot of the other slope. It was in strong sunlight just at the edge of the shadow. Sawyer watched it gradually become engulfed, as the shadow of his hill moved up the other slope.

The shadow was like a coastline, with long sweeping curves and deep inlets. The fortress ruins were inside a sunny inlet now. When the edge of the shadow line touched the base of the outer wall, Sawyer raised the binoculars to his eyes and resumed his vigil.

The advancing shadow was reaching for the lower part of the tower when something moved in the room behind the barred window. Sawyer held himself perfectly still, watching. He had another impression of movement in there; and then a head materialized briefly, before disappearing.

It appeared again, moving past inside the window. Someone was pacing in there; Sawyer couldn't see if it was a man or a woman. His lips moved, silently: Closer, dammit . . .

The head stopped moving. It seemed to turn. Two hands reached out through the window, grasping the bars. Moira's face leaped into sharp focus in the lenses, staring straight at him.

Sawyer put down the binoculars. He wiped his palms across his knees. His hands were trembling, but he didn't look at them. He was still looking at the barred tower window. Without the binoculars the face was only a small palish blur. That didn't matter, he knew who it belonged to.

A moment later the face vanished. That didn't matter, either. He knew she was there, now; and exactly where.

He also knew that there was a way to get down inside that tower, from the roof. And he had studied the tower wall enough to decide it was climbable.

What he didn't know was how many men were inside there guarding her. He'd seen only one: Bruno. But he hadn't seen Bruno again since that one time; there could be others.

Another thing he didn't know was where they were, in relation to Moira. It might be necessary to go through them to reach her. One or more of them might be with her, all the time, assigned to the job of killing her the instant there was any sign of an attack.

Sawyer made himself think it out one step at a time: he had found her. Now the job was to find out exactly what her situation was in there; then to get to her without alerting her guards; and finally to pry her out of there alive.

But these steps could not be dealt with that neatly, in order, separated from each other. Each had problems related to another.

He couldn't learn her exact situation, in relation to her guards, until it was dark enough for him to slip inside the fortress.

He was going to need help in getting her out. But the more men who went in with him, the greater the chance of a slipup that would result in her being dead by the time they got to her. So he was going to have to be alone, the first time he went in to study the situation.

But he did need to have help standing by, especially if he found there was more than one guard on her. One trouble there was that he couldn't afford to spend much time summoning that help, now, nor in waiting for it to arrive. Moira was being kept in there, and probably that was where she was going to stay. The possibility remained, however, that at any time from here on, they *could* intend to move her somewhere else.

Once he got back to his car, it would be a twenty-minute drive to the nearest village where he could use a phone. He couldn't call the police. First of all, he couldn't depend on them to do exactly what he told them. Secondly, even if they did manage to get to Moira while she was still alive, their doing so could not be kept a secret. The result would be the ruin of Moira's husband. That was a secondary consideration, but it did have to be considered, as long as it didn't endanger Moira further.

There was another kind of help he could summon. It would take them a lot longer to get here than the police, but he could depend on them to follow his orders.

Picking up the binoculars, Sawyer got to his feet

and took a final look at the fortress on the other hill. Then he went up his hill and over the crest, keeping to cover all the way until he was on the other side. His car was some distance from the bottom of the other side of the hill. He'd left it that far so the sound of its approach wouldn't carry to the fortress, and it took him time to get back to it. After that, eighteen minutes' driving brought him into the square of a small village above the Rhône River.

He parked in front of the old church and crossed the square to the only bistro. It was a small room. Five men were playing cards at a table and they glanced up at him curiously as he went past to the bar. He ordered a brandy and asked the owner if he could use the phone to call Marseilles. The man put the phone on his bar, dialed the operator, and told her to let him know the cost when the call was finished. Then he pushed the phone to Sawyer, who gave the operator Marcel Alfani's business number in Marseilles.

As he listened to it ring, he prayed that Alfani wouldn't have just left for his home. On the third ring it was picked up by one of Alfani's men. Sawyer gave his name. While waiting, he framed what he was going to say. The bistro owner was observing him with open interest; and the card players had ears, too.

When Alfani came on, Sawyer explained where he was and said: "It's the only bistro in town. A lot of customers here, for this time of evening."

He stopped at that, and after a moment Alfani said: "I understand. People are around you and you have to watch what you say. Go ahead."

Sawyer told him: "I wish I'd brought some of your family along. I could use the company."

"How many men do you need?"

"Five, if you can manage it on short notice."

"I can. You know it will be at least three hours before they can get there."

"Yes. I may not be here when they arrive. Tell

493

them to wait for me. The bistro across from the church."

When he hung up the phone he took his brandy and drank it down. It burned its way into his stomach. He hadn't eaten since breakfast, and he should have been hungry but wasn't. After the operator called back he paid for the call and the drink, and went outside.

The sun had set and darkness was spreading when Sawyer crossed the square. He got into his car and unlocked the glove compartment. The hard-leather belt holster he took out held a shortened version of the standard American police revolver he'd learned to use when he was a cop: a Model 10 Smith & Wesson .38, with a two-inch barrel. He checked the loads and clipped it to his belt. Then he drove back toward the fortress.

4

It was dark when he climbed the crest of the wooded hill. On the other hilltop across the narrow valley, lamplight showed in the windows of the fortress tower. All of them, including the one with bars across it. In the ruins around the tower, and the surrounding country, there was no other light to be seen.

Sawyer went down through the trees to the bottom of the valley. He crossed it and worked his way up through the black passages of the deserted village. From there, he swung to his left around the side of the hill under the fortress ruins. He had studied them long enough to remember the positioning of everything he'd seen, and the route he'd chosen to reach the tower. Moving quietly, he merged with the darkness of the slope as he climbed. A number of times he paused and listened, scanning the looming sections of the broken outer wall above him.

494

He halted when he reached the base of a high, jagged wall section. The high-pitched croaking of frogs was the only sound. It was magnified in the night silence, and he could hear nothing else. Sawyer tugged the gun from its stiff holster and brought it up in ready position. Trailing the fingers of his left hand across the cold, bulging stones of the wall, he led the way with the gun held in his other. He reached an opening where part of the wall had collapsed, and stopped again, peering inside.

In the increasing starlight he studied the disordered shadows between the darker solid shapes of shattered buildings and fallen battlements. Nothing was moving in any of the shadows. Sawyer started in. The rubble of the collapsed section of wall formed an overgrown pile in the opening. He climbed over the pile cautiously, testing with each step to make sure his weight wouldn't start some of the rubble sliding.

As he came down inside the pile, there was a faint flash of light to his left. Sawyer whirled in that direction, finger sliding across the trigger of the gun in his right fist. There were more flashes, all around him, close to the ground. Fireflies, their pulsing glow very bright in the blackness near the base of the wall. Sawyer relaxed a notch, his finger leaving the trigger, resting against the hard edge of its guard. Near the inside of the outer wall only a few building remnants were left. There were wide areas between them, but these areas did have cover points: shadow-creating mounds of earth, trees and bushes, fallen masonry. Sawyer moved away from the wall, advancing deeper into the fortress.

He was conscious always that at any moment during his advance someone he wasn't aware of could be looking in his direction. Though he kept to the general direction he had calculated earlier, there were frequent short detours. Each stage of his advance was determined by the available cover; and where there was no solid cover he followed the darkest stretches of shadow.

Sawyer slowed when he judged that he was nearing a section of moat he knew lay across his path: a wide, shallow ditch choked with brush and small trees, with a gradual, lumpy rise on the other side. Crouching, squinting across the terrain ahead, he spotted it. Closer than he'd expected. A few more steps brought him to the edge.

Going to the ground, Sawyer braced his forearms on the edge and lowered himself into the ditch. His arms were over his head when his feet touched bottom. Turning, he moved through the darkness under the trees, feeling his way around tangles of brush. The faint rustling of bushes caused in his passage across the ditch was covered by the frog chorus, louder here. When he got to the other side he reached up and hauled himself out. For a time he remained stretched flat on the ground there, listening and looking for signs of enemy presence.

There was nothing that he could detect. Getting his feet under him, he raised his head, turning it slowly to reckon his exact position by the upper shapes of ruins outlined against the night sky. To his left was one side of a stone house; all that was left. It contained a square filled with stars, a single window opening. Dead ahead of him was a long, low wall, much older than the outer wall. At an angle to the right was the crumbling base of a stone gatehouse, where the wall ended. Sawyer started up the rise on his side of the ditch, angling to the right.

There was an alien sound. Sawyer halted his advance and went low, peering ahead at the length of low wall. A dim figure was moving along the top.

Sawyer controlled his breathing, keeping it shallow and slow. Other than that, no part of him moved. But his nerves quivered as he watched the figure. Bruno, or another guard, just out for a night stroll along the parapet? Or a routine security check? Or had his presence been detected, drawing that figure out to determine his exact position? The figure stopped moving, and looked down through an embrasure between two uneven merlons, head and shoulders sharply defined against the night sky.

Frozen in place, Sawyer waited. He was in an exposed position. Absolute stillness and his closeness to the ground were his only form of cover. As long as he didn't move he was one of a confusing myriad of night shadows there. Unless the man on the parapet suspected his presence, had gotten to know all the shadows that *should* be there, and was making a detailed survey.

It felt like minutes, but Sawyer knew it was only seconds, before the figure up there moved again. It turned, and headed slowly back the way it had come. Strolling, Sawyer decided.

But when the figure was gone, he still did not move. For three minutes he remained in exactly the same position. And when he did finally move, there were parts of him where small muscles remained tightly bunched, waiting for the impact of a bullet.

Nothing happened. Sawyer reached the truncated, gatehouse at the end of the wall, and entered through a gap at its base. There was no roofing left. From the crest of the other hill, in daylight, the gatehouse had appeared simple to get through. But inside, at night, it was not so simple. The broken upper structure kept out most of the starlight, and the interior was a labyrinth of shadows within shadows. Sawyer had to work his way through by touch alone, feeling his way over and around mounds of rubble, angles of fallen timber, and networks of thick vines.

When he emerged into the starlight again, he was in a passage between two lines of brick rubble that had once been inner defense walls. From this point Sawyer could see, through the ruins ahead, the upper part of the tower where Moira was kept. But he could not see her window, nor any others. His angle of approach was taking him to a side where there were none. On this side there was an inner fortress wall that was joined to the tower, halfway from the top.

Sawyer followed the passage between the lines of rubble and went through a wide opening, into a small courtyard. The wide, open well he had seen from the other hill was in the center of it. Sticking close to the wall, Sawyer circled the courtyard and reached another opening. He stepped through it and stopped, holding himself ready to swing the gun in his hand in either direction. But no one was there, waiting for him. He was still alone.

He was inside what had been the fortress great hall. It was wide and long, and now roofless. The long wall to his right contained a mammoth fireplace. The one along the left side had caved in at one point. Through the break, he knew, lay the area where the dirt road winding up the hill ended. But the wall that interested Sawyer was the one at the far end of the hall.

It was about twenty feet high, and it angled against a higher wall at a point where its upper structure had collapsed. It was this other wall which stretched away for a short distance, rising, to join the tower which was Sawyer's goal.

When he reached the other end of the great hall, he found the surface of the wall there as it had seemed through his binoculars: between each of the large blocks of stone that formed it were deep cracks. They provided secure toeholds and grips for the fingers. It was like climbing a solid ladder. When he was on the top, he moved along it in a low crouch to the other wall. There it was only a matter of reaching just above his head and hauling himself up.

He had holstered the .38 before climbing out of the great hall. The instant he was on top of the other wall he drew it and went flat. Eyes narrowed, he surveyed all the danger points in sight around him from his new position. He studied each in turn, taking the time to do it thoroughly. Only when he was certain there was no enemy presence close enough to observe him did he commence his crawl along the top of this wall.

Where it joined the tower, he rose to his feet. With his left hand he examined the surface of the tower wall. Again, the cracks between the heavy stones were quite deep. It would be slow but not difficult. Sawyer stuck the revolver back in its belt holster, securely.

He had begun the climb when he heard the sound of an automobile. He paused, made the decision, and continued his climb.

He was halfway to the roof of the tower when car headlights appeared, coming around the bend below and approaching the outer wall of the fortress.

When the car reached the end of the dirt road, Patrick stopped and set the hand brake. He dropped his right hand to his lap and used his left to cut the ignition and switch off the headlights.

Bruno's figure materialized out of the shadows beside the car. His hands held a leveled carbine, its muzzle aimed through the open window at Patrick's head.

"This property is private," he said harshly.

The man in the car told him: "My name is Patrick."

For a moment Bruno seemed not to react, though he understood what the name meant. Then he lowered the barrel of the carbine. "Mine is Bruno."

"The word," Patrick told him, "is *terminate*."

"What's happened?"

"I haven't the faintest idea. All I know are my orders." Patrick opened the car door, and Bruno saw that he was holding a Luger pistol on one thigh. Patrick climbed out and put the gun away, inside a shoulder holster hidden under the left side of his jacket.

"Where is the girl?"

Well, Bruno thought, at least it's over. If he felt anything else, he didn't let himself know about it. He had his orders, too; and he intended to carry them out. Turning from the car, he led Patrick into the ruins of the fortress.

On reaching the top of the tower, Sawyer found a trapdoor covering the way down through the roof. It was of wood, with a sheet of tin nailed to the top. One side was hinged. He went to one knee by the other side. His finger was across the trigger as he held the gun pointed downward. The fingers of his left hand hooked under the edge of the trapdoor, and pulled it up with a single, steady movement. The hinges creaked before he got it all the way open.

He had the .38 aimed down through the opening. But there was no one in sight down there. Only the worn stone steps, spiraling into the interior of the tower. Dim light filtered up the steps from somewhere below its first tight turn. Easing himself through the opening, Sawyer soundlessly descended the steps. He pointed the way with the gun, looking down its stubby barrel, ready to fire. If the creaking of the trapdoor hinges had been heard, someone would be coming up the steps.

No one did. The first landing he came to was, he judged, at the level where he'd seen Moira's face behind the barred window. There was an electric bulb hanging from a small hook set in the stone ceiling. And there was a heavy locked door. When Sawyer saw that it was locked only by the two outside bolts he experienced a tight surge of relief. No lock that required picking. And no guard inside with her; they wouldn't have locked their own man in. He hadn't expected this part to be that easy.

Sawyer edged sideways to the door. After that one quick glance at it he kept his eyes on the same point his gun was aimed at: the spot where the steps below disappeared around the next tight bend. With his left hand he felt for the top bolt. He drew it slowly, making hardly any sound. Feeling for the other bolt, he drew it from its wall socket just as carefully. Keeping his attention on the steps below, he put his left hand against the door and pushed it open.

There was a thin rattling noise inside. A voice whispered tensely: "I *knew* Alex would do it!"

That provoked a swift, angry glance inside from Sawyer. He saw her standing there in the middle of the cell, staring at him, grinning exultantly. "Look again," he whispered back sourly, "it's not Alex."

"But he's the one who sent you."

Sawyer's attention snapped back to the spot where his revolver was pointed. He had seen the chain running from her ankle to the window bar. It wasn't going to be so easy, after all.

There was another thin sound from the chain as Moira moved through the cell to him, as far as the chain would allow. That brought her to the doorway, beside him.

Without looking away from the area down the steps, he asked her softly: "How many of them are there in here?"

"Two." Her voice was shaky, but as low as his. "One went away this morning, but I just heard a car, so I guess he's back."

"Somebody is. How often do they check on you?"

"They shouldn't, for the rest of the night. I've already had dinner. Unless there's a special reason, nobody should come up again until morning."

Sawyer prayed it was so. He told Moira, "I'm going to . . ." and abruptly stopped himself and pushed her back inside the cell.

There was the sound of footsteps below.

Patrick came into sight around the bend of the stairway there, looking up. Bruno was close behind him, but jumped back out of sight when Patrick saw Sawyer and reacted.

Patrick's reaction involved three co-ordinated move-

501

ments at the same instant. He twisted his torso side-wise, dropped to one knee, and snatched under his jacket for the holstered Luger. His reaction time was a good deal faster than Sawyer's, but Sawyer didn't have to draw his gun. It was already aimed in the right direction. All he had to do was turn it a fraction of an inch and squeeze the trigger.

In the confines of the stairwell the gunshot was deafening. The recoil of the stubby .38 jerked its muzzle upward and rammed the grip into the pad of Sawyer's thumb. The bullet thudded into the side of Patrick's chest, beraking bone and burrowing through flesh. It twisted him off his knee and threw him against the curved wall. He bounced off it and fell forward across the stone steps.

But the Luger was in his hand, and it came up as his head did.

Sawyer steadied the .38 down and fired again. The shot hammered into the front of Patrick's head and kicked it backward. His neck went loose and his head rolled forward, smashing face-down on a stone step. No part of him moved again.

Sawyer went to both knees aiming the .38 at the point above the sprawled body where Bruno would appear if he tried coming up the steps. He was breathing with his mouth open, and his eyes were shiny with concentrated fear and viciousness.

Bruno did not reappear. He could be about to, at any moment; or he could be doing one of two other things. Sawyer knew he couldn't go on waiting. There was something that had to be done now, and a risk that had to be taken in doing it. He motioned to Moira with his free hand.

She came as far as the chain allowed to the door-way. "Lie down," he hissed. "Toward me."

Moira got it. When she lay down on the stone floor-ing her cuffed ankle was still inside the doorway, but the rest of her was stretched out on the landing, her head close to Sawyer's. "I've handled guns before," she told him. "I can do it."

"Hold it with both hands. If he shows, keep shooting as long as you can see him." He let her take the .38 from him, watched the way she gripped it between her hands, aiming at a point two feet above the body of the man in the brown suit. Satisfied, he got an envelope from his pocket and took two short wires out of it.

One was very thin, and flexible. The other was a bit thicker, and rigid. Sawyer crawled to the cell doorway. He sat on the floor by Moira's booted feet, and went to work on the lock of the metal cuff around her left ankle.

It took him two and a half minutes to get it open. That was a lot of time, under the circumstances. And there was still no sign of Bruno. He could be still waiting for them on the steps, just below the bend down there. Or he could be outside the door at the bottom of the tower, where he could both watch that exit and have a clear shot at the top of the tower. Or, he could be circling to cover the other side of the tower, the route Sawyer had used to get in.

Sawyer and Moira had two choices: go up or go down. Bruno knew that. Which would he choose?

Sawyer went inside the cell and picked up the pillow from the bed. Carrying it with his left hand, he went back out to the landing and took the gun from Moira. Holding it ready, he tossed the pillow. It sailed down over the body on the stairs, struck against the bend of the wall, and fell out of sight.

That got absolutely nothing. No shot, no sound. Either Bruno was not down there, or his reactions were very sharp.

Motioning Moira to come with him, Sawyer began backing up the steps of the tower. When they were just under the open trapdoor, Sawyer raised his head enough to see out. The roof was empty. Returning his attention to the steps below them, he motioned for Moira to stay flat as she climbed out. When she was flat down on the roof he swung up beside her.

Stretching out on his belly, Sawyer snaked to one edge of the roof. He paused, and then slowly moved his head until he could just see over. From this vantage point he was looking down into the courtyard of the inner ward, the place where the door at the bottom of the tower led. He scanned the shadows there, and then did it again, more slowly, studying each one.

He was about to give up when one of the shadows moved slightly, over near an opening to the undercroft of the main wall.

It had to be Bruno. There was no wind, and there was nothing else down there capable of moving itself.

Sawyer did not consider trying for a shot. At that range it would be difficult with a handgun, even in good light. With the confusion of night shadows down there, it was impossible. But it was not an impossible shot for Bruno. The top of the tower was illuminated sharply in the light of the moon. And Bruno had a rifle. Sawyer had glimpsed it, in the split-second Bruno had shown himself on the steps inside. For a rifle, this range was just fine—if Bruno could see them. From the courtyard, he wouldn't be able to see the other side of the tower.

Sawyer snaked back across the roof past Moira. When he reached the opposite edge he motioned her to come up beside him. Softly, he told her exactly what to do. She nodded and he stuck the .38 securely in its holster before carefully going over the edge.

He felt for toeholds and found them in the deep cracks between the stones of the tower wall. He lowered himself until he found gripping places for his fingers in the wall descended a short way, and waited. Moira came down over the edge of the tower roof just as carefully, but with more agility. Sawyer watched her quickly find grips for her hands and feet as she came down to him, and stopped worrying about her. She was a better climber than he was. He resumed his descent, and was more than halfway down when a chunk of stone broke loose under his right foot.

He managed to quickly find another hold for his foot. But the loosened stone fell and struck the top of the wall below, bounced off, and clattered to the broken paving below. It was the kind of noise that carried a long way.

"*Move* it," Sawyer hissed, and went down the rest of the tower as fast as he could. The instant his feet were on top of the wall below, he snatched the gun from his belt holster and turned to scan the darkness below both sides of it.

Moira was down with him a second later. She stayed right behind him as he walked quickly along the top of the wall. When he reached the end of it, he sat down and lowered himself to the top of the other wall, at one end of the great hall.

There was a flash of movement inside the shadowy depths of the hall below. Muscles spasmed in Sawyer's midsection and he swung toward it. In the same moment a rifle blasted.

Sawyer's turn saved him from the full impact of the bullet. But it slashed the left side of his chest, skidding across a rib and taking flesh with it. The burning force of it twisted him and his legs tangled. He lost his footing and fell, inside the great hall.

He wrenched himself around as he went down, turning to land on his spread feet, knees ready to bend and absorb the shock. But he landed on loose brick rubble that rolled under the impact of his feet, and struck the ground with the flat of his back. The force of it jolted the gun out of his hand and sent it skittering across the ground. Sawyer did a fast roll to his hands and knees and scrambled after it. He was halfway to it when Bruno stepped from the shadows, lowering his carbine for the killing shot.

Moira launched herself from the top of the wall

above them, plummeting down at Bruno. He dodged in the last instant, and most of her falling weight failed to strike him squarely. Her hip glanced off his shoulder, knocking him backward. The rest of her struck across his arms, ripping the carbine from his grasp and taking it to the ground with her.

She law sprawled across its barrel, conscious but too stunned by the impact to move. Bruno recovered his balance and leaped forward, bending to yank the carbine out from under her. His hand was a few inches from it when he froze in position, staring over her sprawled figure.

Sawyer was on one knee, the .38 in his hand aimed at Bruno's face. Bruno remained bent over with one hand stretched toward the carbine, looking into the dark mouth of the gun in Sawyer's hand, and waiting.

Sawyer looked back at him, his breathing shaky, lips thinned back, showing his teeth. His finger was on the trigger, but he did not squeeze it.

After a long moment, he said, "Right now I have no special reason to kill you. Unless you force it . . ." His voice was savage. But there was an edge inside it that was almost pleading.

Bruno continued to stare at him for what seemed a long time, as though puzzled. Finally, slowly, he drew back his outstretched hand, and straightened up. He was still watching Sawyer, not quite believing.

Sawyer stayed down on one knee. He became aware for the first time of the burning pain high across the left side of his chest, and the warm wetness spreading from there to his waist. "Moira?" he growled, without looking in her direction. His eyes, and his gun, stayed on Bruno.

Still groggy, Moira slowly and with difficulty shoved herself to a sitting position on the ground. "Yes . . ." Her voice was unsteady. "Give me a minute . . ."

Sawyer and Bruno waited, looking at each other. Finally, Moira felt for the carbine and picked it up with one hand. Bracing the other hand against the ground, she got her feet under her and stood up. She swayed, steadied herself, waited for the last of the dizziness to pass. When it did, she took a grip on the carbine with both hands, turning it to cover Bruno. "All right," she told Sawyer. "I'm okay now."

Sawyer stood up slowly and tried to take a deep breath. Instantly, scalding pain laced through his rib cage. One of his ribs, he decided, was definitely cracked. At least one. Keeping his breathing light, he gestured at Bruno with the .38. "Out that way," he told him, motioning at the break in the side wall of the great hall. "Turn and walk. Slow."

Bruno turned his head slowly to look toward the break. As he did, moonlight fell across the bad side of his face. In that light the burn mark on his cheek looked black. He looked again to Sawyer, studying him. Then he turned and began walking toward the break in the wall, his shoulders slightly hunched, as though waiting for the bullet to strike between them.

Sawyer and Moira followed him, keeping pace, one with the carbine, the other with the revolver. Bruno went through the opening, continued for several steps, and halted.

"Keep going," Sawyer said behind him, stepping through the break in the wall. "Straight ahead."

Bruno glanced back over his shoulder at them, then faced forward and resumed his slow walk. When he reached the side of the dirt road Sawyer snapped, "That's it. Stop there."

Bruno stopped. He didn't look behind him this time. His gaze was in the direction of the wooded hill on the other side of the narrow valley. His shoulders were still hunched.

Sawyer took the carbine from Moira, and holstered the revolver. There was sticky wetness on the holster. He was losing more blood than he cared to think about. "You once told me," he said to Moira, "that you can start cars without a key. *Can* you?"

"Sure."

507

He nodded toward the car parked at the end of the road off to their left. "Do it."

Moira hurried away to the car. Sawyer trained the carbine on Bruno. "Stay here. Don't move until we're gone." He began backing after Moira, watching Bruno and holding the carbine ready. He heard the car's engine start before he reached it. Bruno remained standing beside the road, head turned slightly now, watching him.

When Sawyer got to the car Moira was behind the wheel, leaning over to open the other door for him. "You'll never know," she told him. "The key was in the ignition." She grinned, but it was forced.

He drew the .38 from its sticky holster, and put the carbine on the floor behind the front seat. Sliding in next to Moira, he shut the door. The movement ripped a groan from him, and he clenched his teeth to keep from groaning again. "Just follow this road until we hit the paved road," he told her. "There you turn right."

Moira switched on the lights, let out the brake, and drove away from the fortress. Sawyer brought up the gun, aiming it through the open window as the car neared the man standing beside the dirt road. Bruno didn't move, other than the turning of his head as he watched them go past.

Just before the car rounded the hill, Sawyer looked back. Bruno was still standing there under the fortress walls, looking after them.

EPILOGUE

On the morning following the explosion of the code machine in Jorgen's apartment, arrests were made, in New York and Vienna, of members of a spy ring involved in spiriting secrets out of the United States. It was also known that three members of this ring had operated in Washington, but these three had died, two as a result of a car accident and the other from a heart attack suffered shortly after capture.

The nature of the secrets the spy ring dealt with has never been determined, nor what foreign power it was operating for.

The NSA failed to break the Budapest Code. Benjamin Scovil, his team, and the cipher-solving computers of the Puzzle Palace have long since been assigned to other code work.

Several days later there was a report from Paris that archaeologist Moira Rhalles, believed dead in a cave accident, had turned up alive but suffering from amnesia. She had obviously survived the fall which killed her two companions, and somehow left the cave and wandered off without being seen. But the shock had left her with no memory of this, nor of where she had been since—until she came out of her amnesia to find herself walking along a road near Paris.

Since someone must have given her shelter and food, an appeal was issued for information from anyone who had seen her during this considerable period. That appeal has never received a response.

It was further reported that her husband, Nobel historian Alexander Rhalles, had resigned his position as adviser to the American President, to fly to Paris and join his wife. Newsmen there who tried to locate them for more information learned they had left France. It was believed they had gone to Denmark, to vacation in strictest privacy and give Mrs. Rhalles time to recover from her experience. But Danish reporters were unable to trace their whereabouts.

There were those who regarded the reported version of what had happened to Moira Rhalles with a certain amount of puzzlement, or downright suspicion. But since no one—to this date—has been able to come up with hard proof to the contrary, her amnesia explanation has never been openly challenged.

Alexander and Moira Rhalles spent two months on an island off the coast of Sweden before returning to the farm in Pennsylvania. By then their news value had considerably dwindled. The few reporters who sought them out at the farm learned that Moira Rhalles still suffered amnesia concerning the period in her life following the accident in the cave. That was the only thing new they did learn, and it was not worth more than a small item on an inside page of any newspaper.

Her memory blank concerning that one period remained when Moira Rhalles resumed her career, but otherwise she has fully recovered, mentally and physically. She is presently in charge of a dig in Sicily. Her husband is with her, working to complete his latest historical study.

Irina Frejenko and her husband are at this time engaged in work for the Soviet Government at a camp for political criminals and intellectual undesirables, in a remote area of subarctic eastern Siberia. She is the camp's doctor, and he is in charge of planning new housing. Their frequent letters to the authorities, asking for transfer back to Moscow, have so far gone unanswered.

Irina Frejenko's former superior in Subdirectorate T of the KGB, Vasily Pokryshkin, has been placed in charge of a similar camp.

Lorenz is a guard in still another.

Christine Bieler Jonquet is teaching art to the school children of an isolated farming community in southeastern Russia.

Lang was retired from the service on full pay, plus injury benefits for the blindness incurred in carrying out hazardous duty. His sister was flown to Washington at government expense to take him back to his beach house in California.

One morning several days later, she took him out on the beach in front of the house to sit in the sun. He sat there for a time, listening to the Pacific and remembering the house on the other side of it, where he had lived with his wife, Duyen.

When his sister came out to get him for lunch, he was gone. A beach stroller, who hadn't known Lang was blind, later reported having seen him get up and walk into the ocean. Lang's body has never been found.

The following year a group of hunters in the Ardèche wandered into a deserted fortress ruin, and found the corpse of a man lying on a tower stairway, with an unfired Luger pistol beside him. The man had been shot twice, in the chest and head. There were no papers on him, and his identity has not been discovered.

Sawyer and Fritz Donhoff have become partners in a new firm, based in Paris. At present they have a staff of two: Titine Delisio and Sawyer's half-brother, Olivier.

The present whereabouts of Jean-Marc Bruno is not known.

What happened to the ancient statuette of the dark mother-goddess is also unknown.